THE BURDEN OF LIES

Also by Richard Beasley

Cyanide Games
Me and Rory MacBeath
The Ambulance Chaser
Hell Has Harbour Views

RICHARD BEASLEY

THE BURDEN OF LIES

SIMON & SCHUSTER

London · New York · Sydney · Toronto · New Delhi

A CBS COMPANY

THE BURDEN OF LIES
First published in Australia in 2017 by
Simon & Schuster (Australia) Pty Limited
Suite 19A, Level 1, Building C, 450 Miller Street, Cammeray, NSW 2062

10 9 8 7 6 5 4 3 2 1

A CBS Company
Sydney New York London Toronto New Delhi
Visit our website at www.simonandschuster.com.au

© Richard Beasley 2017

All rights reserved. No part of this publication may be reproduced, stored in a retrieval system, or transmitted in any form or by any means, electronic, mechanical, photocopying, recording or otherwise, without prior permission of the publisher.

National Library of Australia Cataloguing-in-Publication entry
Creator: Beasley, Richard, author.
Title: The Burden of Lies/Richard Beasley.
ISBN: 9781925368154 (paperback)
         9781925368161 (ebook)
Subjects: Truthfulness and falsehood—Fiction.
          Lawyers—Fiction.

Cover design: Lewis Csizmazia
Cover image: wx-bradwang/Getty Images
Typeset by Midland Typesetters, Australia
Printed and bound in Australia by Griffin Press

The paper this book is printed on is certified against the Forest Stewardship Council® Standards. Griffin Press holds FSC chain of custody certification SGS-COC-005088. FSC promotes environmentally responsible, socially beneficial and economically viable management of the world's forests.

THE BURDEN OF LIES

PRELUDE

2012

Oliver Randall told his driver to park in a side street and said he'd be twenty minutes.

The bar he was going to was familiar territory. It was where exchanges were made, contracts settled.

He ordered a drink and found a stool in the beer garden. It was nearly six on a Friday, and the place was beginning to hum with the after-work crowd. He was looking at a table around which four women were laughing when a man sat opposite him. He hadn't noticed him approach.

'You're Garry, I assume?' the man said.

In the moment it took Randall to process a series of observations – mid-thirties, well groomed, expensive suit – the man spoke again.

'Brad sent me,' he said.

It was 'Brad' he was due to meet. Randall kept a small and exclusive list. Selling to too many people increased the risk. Brad and the other regulars supplied Oliver Randall with large amounts of cash. He, in turn, provided them with precise quantities of high-quality cocaine that he acquired frequently, but which he never had to pay for himself.

'He's busy,' the man said, unprompted by Randall.

Randall picked his drink up and took another sip. 'Who are you?'

The man smiled. He had his own drink, a beer, which he placed next to Randall's. 'A colleague of Brad's,' he said.

'He hasn't mentioned you.' Randall had always dealt directly with his customers, never with a middleman. *He* was the middleman.

'We're business partners.'

'How do I know that – ?'

'I've got the cash in my car,' the man said. 'Do you have what Brad ordered?' He took a sip of his beer, and smiled at Randall again.

Randall drained his glass, nodded, then followed the man out.

Randall did two lines of coke in the back of the bank's Mercedes on the way to the casino. He was now up to three grams a day, every day of the week. For consumption, he'd turned semi-pro. He was sure he could control it. Work remained unaffected. Profits had never been higher.

The South-East Banking Corporation had had a few nervous weeks at the peak of the GFC – mainly in that brief period when it seemed like the world's lines of credit might freeze up, and who knew for how long. That was a lifetime ago. SEBC's balance-sheet stability soon presented once-in-a-lifetime opportunities. They'd swallowed some competitors at rock-bottom prices in the bloodbath. Some of the deals were blackmail.

Tonight, Randall was entertaining four clients. Each was in the construction and development game. Infrastructure, resorts, high-density apartments. A radio 'personality' had been invited, someone from a reality TV show, and a retired football star. Those three would go through more coke than the profit-creating clients combined. And it wouldn't surprise him if they wanted more than one girl. They had before, and it always created a problem. The coke and the girls were provided by the same supplier. You could get them individually, but for 'client entertainment', Randall had authority to take the package deal.

Randall had booked a penthouse as their HQ. Several suites and premium rooms had also been reserved and allocated according to the amount of business each of the guests did with SEBC, or the amount the bank hoped to attract.

Friday night traffic across the city pushed his timing out, and he was nearly half an hour late. The bank's guests were sitting on a long, crescent shaped couch in front of the big television when he arrived, drinking vintage champagne and watching a game of rugby. What a combination, he thought.

Finger food had been set up on the marble benches and the dining table. Mezes of all kinds; Sydney rock oysters on trays of ice. In the background, through the wraparound windows, the lights of the west side of the city had lit up for them.

Randall was about to greet the clients on the couch when he felt a hand on his shoulder.

'Here he is,' the man said loudly. 'Scandal Randall.'

It was Jeff Maxwell. The more repugnant half of a detestable radio duo. Still, he somehow added 'reach' for the bank's advertising.

'Maxy,' Randall said loudly, giving his best smile. 'What can I get you? Another drink?'

'The agenda, mate,' Maxwell said, winking and smiling.

The agenda meant the running sheet of the night's activities. They had a wine merchant coming for dinner, who was going to take them through his latest fancies of Nebbiolo and Barolo from northern Piedmont. Then they'd hit the tables for high rollers in the inner sanctum or sovereign room. Randall had two grands' worth of chips to give each client. It frequently only took an hour or two for most of them to either blow that amount, cut their loses, or decide to keep their winnings. After the eye and nose candy arrived, there was usually about an hour of 'partying' before the clients wanted to retreat to the privacy of their rooms.

Randall touched Maxwell near the elbow, a conspiratorial gesture he seemed to like. 'Come with me,' he said, looking in the direction of the bedrooms.

Randall gave Maxwell the remaining line of coke he had on him. 'You'll find it's up to the usual standard,' he said as he arranged it on one of the tables next to the king bed, before handing Maxwell a small straw. He'd joked with another executive at the bank about getting the SEBC logo printed on some straws, just for nights like this.

Maxwell smiled weakly, and looked at him. 'I take it – later there'll be . . . ?'

'A lot more,' Randall said. 'And they'll be bringing it with them.'

Maxwell's smile broadened. A child in a cocaine and hookers store.

Hours later, after tables of chance were played to varying degrees of success, Randall had the bank's guests rounded up in the gambling salons and assembled back in the Penthouse like kids on a school excursion. The girls were waiting.

There were seven guests, and two bankers as well as Randall. There were ten girls, and a dozen eight balls of cocaine. It was rare for a girl to be untaken, but there was always coke left over. What Randall didn't use personally, he sold to trusted customers. He had a big salary, but he paid a lot of tax. The coke was a kind of refund.

A new girl caught his eye when they arrived, and he asked her name after he'd settled with the representative of the goods and services provider who'd made delivery. 'Angie' had long brown hair and legs, and eyes so startling he thought they had to be contacts. If Randall knew how to describe colours with more precision he would have said they were jade. In his own mind he settled for green. She had green eyes, and she was beautiful. So beautiful she looked like an android created in the future for men who wanted perfection beyond the usual specifications of our species. He stared at her, and she nearly melted what coke and commercial banking had left of his heart. He didn't care what any client had in mind. She was his.

Oliver Randall's daughter looked up when he walked into their kitchen the next morning. She glared at him for long enough to register something – contempt, disgust, perhaps both? – before looking back down at her single slice of toast. He put his house keys on the end of the kitchen island where she was eating, and said hi. No response. She was in her school hockey gear. She had a game at noon, he remembered now. He hoped his wife was preparing to take her. He was in no state to drive.

As he considered the options for Saturday school sport transportation, his wife appeared in the kitchen. She looked at him for no longer than his daughter. The exact same look, one that unambiguously suggested a serious monologue was brewing on the horizon.

'I couldn't leave before the clients,' he said.

His wife didn't reply. She'd wait until their daughter was gone before starting. He'd be up for it by then. The house in Bellevue Hill hadn't materialised out of thin air. He'd earned it. He was about to ask her when she was taking their daughter to sport when the front gate intercom sounded. He walked to the far wall of the kitchen and pushed a button.

'Yes.' A long pause. 'Yes.'

'Mr Randall? Umm . . . it's Jess. Jess Bailey. I'm – I'm here . . .'

'Oh,' he said. The Baileys had come to take his daughter to sport with their own. 'I'll buzz you in.'

'Mr Randall?' the girl said, sounding anxious.

'Yes?'

'There are some men here.'

'What men?'

'They want to see you. It's – they're police.'

He could feel a strong pulse in his wrist. His chest tightened. For a moment he didn't breathe.

There were eight of them. They had a search warrant. One of them explained what it said. Another had a video camera. The one who spoke to him – a senior detective, early fifties, sounding almost bored – told him he could have a witness for the search, that he could call a lawyer.

He had coke in his jacket. Two eight balls. It was the first thing they found. That was all though. He did not have the packages one of them said they'd found in his study. He started to tell the cop who was in charge that he'd never seen whatever was in those packages before. The man next to him took off his glasses. He gave a wry smile. He was a good-looking guy.

He was 'Brad's' colleague from the pub last night.

6 years later

The flat in Redfern smelt of cooking fat. He'd cleaned the kitchen three times now with bleach, even used drain cleaner. It had to be in the walls. Still, it was what he could afford. People on parole, looking for work, rarely moved straight back to somewhere like Bellevue Hill.

He heard the knock on the door as he was about to turn the TV off. The screen was tiny. It ran against the circle of life. Your televisions were supposed to get bigger.

He walked to the door. If it was that girl again, he'd be firmer this time, tell her to piss off.

'Hello?'

'Oliver? It's me, mate.'

The voice sounded vaguely familiar. When he opened the door, the face was not.

The man pushed him backwards. He held a gun. 'Go down there,' the man said.

Once in the kitchen, Oliver Randall no longer smelt fat. In his panic, he'd started to disassociate. 'I'm not saying anything,' he said.

The man pointed the gun at Randall's right knee, pulled the trigger. The bullet hit the patella in the middle, blowing it into half-a-dozen pieces.

Randall made a primordial noise, grabbed at his leg. The next bullet missed the other knee, hit the bottom of the left femur.

Randall didn't feel the heat from the nozzle near his forehead. His pain response had pushed his system to overload. He heard the man, though. An apology.

'Sorry, mate,' he said. 'They told me to do it this way.'

1

Defending a racist wasn't the lowest point of Tanner's career. He'd helped worse people than Corey Wilson walk free. Wilson wouldn't make the most-heinous top twenty. Still, acting for him hadn't put a spring in Tanner's step.

Wilson was loosely affiliated with a new political group called Take Back Australia.

'Who are you taking it back from?' Tanner asked his client in the short conference the day before the trial.

'What?'

'Australia. Who are you taking it off?'

There was a long pause, and Brendan Wilson, Corey's father, answered for him. 'You know who,' he said.

It was important, in Tanner's game, to reserve as many judgements as he could. 'Are you giving it back to anyone in particular?'

Brendan Wilson had a more specific answer for this. 'Us.'

Tanner laughed, but mainly in despair. 'Don't include me.'

Brendan Wilson shrugged. 'Suit yourself.'

Racial vilification wasn't Tanner's bread and butter. He preferred not to get out of bed unless blood had been spilt. But the lawyer instructing him had lost the counsel she'd briefed two days before the hearing to a trial running over schedule. Jennifer Singh – and more importantly her boss – had thrown a lot of crime Tanner's way over the years. She called in a favour he couldn't refuse.

Wilson's case began as scheduled at ten am in Court 5A of the Local Criminal Court in the Downing Centre in the south of the CBD.

'Mr Wilson will be pleading guilty to the graffiti charge, your Honour,' Tanner told the presiding magistrate. 'It's the vilification charge where there's a contest.'

The magistrate looked at the file he'd been given, sucked in a deep breath, then slowly let it out. 'Do I fine him extra for the typo?' he said, looking up at Tanner.

Corey Wilson had been charged with spray-painting graffiti on the front wall of an Islamic primary school in the west of Sydney. While Wilson was occupied, the other three defendants – who were all wearing balaclavas to hide their faces – tied a human effigy they'd made to the locked grille fence at the entrance to the school. It had a tea towel wrapped around its head. In front of the security camera directed on the gate, they had then 'beheaded' the effigy with a knife. Wilson and his friends were hoping they'd be filmed, but the cameras had motion sensors, which emailed stills of the film to a company that regularly checked for such things and ran night-time patrols. Two armed guards were rounding Wilson and his mates up before his paint was dry.

Wilson was sprung for the graffiti, and they were all charged with aggravated racial vilification. At the time of their apprehension, Wilson had gotten no further with his political message than *'Fuck off, where full – Your not fucking welcome –'*. Probably most kids from Year 3 up at the school they defaced would have spotted the mistakes.

'I'd be the first to concede my client needs some lessons beyond improving his grammar,' Tanner said.

The magistrate looked at him, and then at the accused. 'Let's hear your defence.'

Wilson was charged with one count of racial vilification and one of aggravated racial vilification. He was willing to plead guilty to being a racist, but not to being a serious racist. That carried the likelihood of a larger fine and, although unlikely for a first offender, the possibility of jail. The more serious charge was based on the beheading of the effigy, on the back of Wilson's message to the five- to twelve-year-olds that attended the school – the vast majority of whom were born in Australia. Wilson's defence to the aggravated charge was that he knew nothing about the effigy, or of any plan to 'behead' it. When his co-accused – who had already pleaded guilty – picked him up that night, they had failed to tell him what they had in the boot of the car, and Wilson played no part in the 'execution'.

The magistrate bought Wilson's version of events – or at least he didn't feel enough doubt had been thrown on it to warrant a conviction. Tanner called the three other participants, who backed up Wilson's plea of ignorance. The prosecutor didn't shake their story, and in fairness, the others appeared to have more rat cunning than the accused, who was able to stick to his script, and otherwise give a good impression of being someone who was flat out distinguishing 'we're' from 'where'.

When the magistrate found Wilson not guilty of the more serious charge, Tanner glanced at his client and recognised an expression he'd seen many times before: mild surprise and relief, quickly supplanted by the smugness of a punk who's just caught a break.

The magistrate told Wilson his behaviour was contemptible, and that he needed re-educating, which he ordered by way of some community service. He then fined him $550 for the graffiti offence and $550 for racial vilification, before formally finding him not guilty of the aggravated racial vilification charge. A smile spread over Wilson's face, and over the faces of the three other racists who'd just lied for him.

'Is that all?' Tanner said, looking at the magistrate.

The magistrate looked confused. 'I'm sorry, Mr Tanner?'

'That's it? Eleven hundred? For what he did?'

'You want me to fine your client more, Mr Tanner?'

Tanner felt a tug on the sleeve of his jacket. It was his instructing solicitor, Jenny Singh. 'Pete, what the hell are you – ?'

'I'd like you to add a couple of zeros to the five hundred and fifty, your Honour.'

'Mr Tanner . . .'

Behind Tanner, in the gallery of the court, Brendan Wilson was shouting, then someone else shouted, 'Fucking bastard!'

Jenny Singh grabbed his arm more tightly. 'Pete,' she said loudly near his ear.

'I'm disposing of this case in the manner I've ordered,' the magistrate said. He glared at Tanner for a moment, then adjourned the court.

Tanner ignored the abuse from the Wilson family and support crew. He gathered his papers and prepared to leave. Jenny Singh grabbed him by the arm again.

'Pete, that was totally unacceptable,' she said. She looked close to tears.

Tanner took a deep breath, then said to her, 'Five hundred and fifty bucks? For doing that on a primary school wall? That, Jen, is totally unacceptable.'

'It's my reputation, not just yours,' she said. She was a brown-skinned lawyer, and her boss, Kit Gallagher, had allocated her a white racist to defend.

He paused before saying the first stupid thing that came to him. 'I'm not sure you'll make your reputation acting for people like Wilson,' he said.

He walked up the aisle of the courtroom towards the Wilsons and their friends. Brendan Wilson blocked his path. His face was puce, his right fist clenched. Tanner could see, and sense, every defect in the Anglo gene pool. When he reached Wilson, he said, 'Brendan, I know at least three people who aren't in jail because of me who would peel your face off if I asked them to. If you want to make a complaint, complain about me, not Jenny.' Wilson showed no sign of moving. 'I mean it, mate,' Tanner said. 'They'd *enjoy* doing it. I reckon all I'd have to do is pay them, say, five hundred and fifty bucks. That sounds fair, don't you think?'

2

Tanner walked back to his chambers under the shade of the Moreton Bay figs that lined the central avenue of Hyde Park. His jacket was slung over one shoulder, while his other arm hung behind him, dragging a wheelie bag. It was a degree or two cooler in the park than taking the walk from court down Elizabeth Street, but the humidity could not be escaped. His shirt clung to his back. He wanted to go home; drink a cold beer. He wanted to punch Corey and Brendan Wilson in the face.

He was fifteen minutes late for the conference, and both the client – who was being handed a mineral water by his clerk – and his solicitor, gave him an irritated glare when they saw him.

'Don't look at me like you've been waiting all day, Sam,' Tanner said as he walked past them without breaking stride. He sensed that the solicitor had started to follow him. 'Pam will tell you when I'm ready,' he said, not bothering to turn around.

He threw his jacket over the lounge chair in the corner of his room. He dropped his bag in the centre of the floor, then shoved it with his foot firmly towards the joinery that housed his briefs, both current and ancient. He sat behind his desk, slumped in his chair, and let out a long sigh. He had hoped it would calm him. It didn't. He picked up the papers that had been sent to him by Sam Nassim about the client waiting for him out in reception.

Sam Nassim had three offices: one in the western suburbs, one south of the city, and the latest in the CBD. He still did his own court appearances for minor matters. He'd laid the foundations of his empire by charging up to fifteen thousand a plea to members of his local community who found themselves before the courts for the kind of drug cases he was confident would receive a non-custodial sentence. He occasionally told his most naïve customers that five thousand was for him, five was for the police prosecutor, and five for the presiding magistrate or judge. The whole fifteen was always for Nassim. He was somewhere in middle management of one of the larger drug syndicates in town.

'Pete, this is Jordan Symonds,' Nassim said as he sat in front of Tanner's desk after he'd been sent around by the receptionist.

Symonds was in Tanner's chambers because he'd been charged by police with assault and intentionally causing damage to property following a road-rage incident a few weeks before. During that rage he got out of his Bentley Continental when it was stopped at a red light, took one of his golf clubs from the boot, and smashed it across the back window and boot of the car in front. He'd soon left the scene for work, but someone had taken his licence plate details.

Symonds sat with his legs crossed, elbow on the armrest of the chair, cheek on his fist like he was bored. Tanner guessed the dark charcoal suit he had on was made to measure, and upwards of five thousand. His hair had been black, based on his brows, but his head was now shaved. As Tanner was about to speak, Symonds' phone sounded. He looked at the caller ID and, without saying a word, left the room to talk in the corridor.

'Why are you bringing this to me?' Tanner said to Nassim.

Nassim shrugged. 'What do you mean?'

'He beat up a woman's car with a golf club. I'd only expect to be briefed if he'd killed her with it.'

Nassim smiled. 'It's – what do you call it again? A "no-budget" defence.'

'There's a defence for what he did?'

'I'm sure you'll think of something, Pete.'

'This is a plea, Sam.'

'No, no,' Nassim said quickly, sitting forward. 'This guy can't get a conviction. Something to do with his licence, or the company's licence. We've got to sort a deal with this woman. He only gave her a scare.'

Nassim was interrupted by Symonds coming back in the room. He sat, and put his elaborately sized smartphone on Tanner's desk.

'Would you mind shutting the door, Mr Symonds?' Tanner said.

'What?'

Nassim was quickly on his feet. 'I'll do it.'

Symonds' phone rang again. He looked at it, but this time declined the call.

'Maybe you'd like to turn that off while we're in conference?' Tanner said.

Symonds shook his head. 'I'm waiting on an urgent call from an investment manager. I'll have to take it if he rings.'

Tanner let out a deep breath. 'What do you do for a living, Mr Symonds?' he asked.

A moment passed before Symonds answered, as though he was considering the relevance of the question. 'I run a hedge fund,' he said.

'What kind?'

Symonds paused again. 'Does that matter?'

'Who knows? What type?'

Symonds shifted in his seat. 'We're equity focused,' he said. 'We manage mainly long/short funds.'

'Good for you.'

Symonds shook his head. 'Sam says you're good at what you do. Can we get to the point?'

'I'm glad Sam thinks I'm good at my job,' Tanner said. 'That's a ringing endorsement given the number of mutual clients we currently have in prison. What point is it you want me to get to?'

'The point where you make this go away?'

Tanner narrowed his eyes. 'Go away?'

'Yeah,' Symonds said. 'I need this to go away.'

Tanner nodded and smiled. 'You were in a hurry that day, on the morning of this – this incident.'

Symonds sighed. 'Yes, I was in a hurry.'

'Why?'

Symonds uncrossed his legs and leant forward. 'Look, I know this is in the materials Sam has sent you. I want to know how you can get me out of this, not to discuss –'

'Indulge me.'

Tanner and Symonds glared at each other. Tanner guessed that his client wasn't regularly interrupted.

'Like I explained to Sam,' Symonds began, 'I had a meeting with some people representing some institutional investors that morning, and I was running late.'

'What was the urgency?'

'They – they weren't happy about a particular fund. They said our stock picking was – it doesn't matter, they were threatening to take their money from us.'

'Sounds like I'm better at my job than you are at yours.'

'What the fuck does that mean?' Symonds said.

'It means I'm never late for court, Mr Symonds. So that means when I'm driving to court, and I'm stuck behind a car that doesn't make a right turn at an intersection of a busy road as quickly as I'd like, I might use my horn, but that's it. I don't get a golf club from the back of my car and run amok.'

There was a long silence before Symonds responded. He turned from Tanner and looked at Nassim. Nassim looked like he might speak, but then Symonds beat him to it. 'I've paid for the damage I did to that woman's car. I've apologised. I've offered her more money.' He gazed at Tanner, appearing to look for acknowledgement of these good deeds. 'Now I'm paying you money to make this go away.'

Tanner shook his head and let out a laugh.

'This is funny to you?' Symonds asked.

'Are you familiar with the judicial system, Mr Symonds? Do hedge fund managers need any kind of understanding of it?'

'I've suffered enough embarrassment from the media over this. I can't be convicted for assault. I'll pay her — whatever. She just needs to say it was a misunderstanding. That she wasn't afraid I'd —'

'A misunderstanding? You expect me to tell a judge you mistook her Hyundai i30 for a golf ball?'

'Look —'

'You put a woman in fear of her life, Mr Symonds. Paying her money won't decrease the state's interest in prosecuting you.'

'I'm willing to —'

'She might happily take more money. The Director of Prosecutions will still expect her to come to court and tell a magistrate what you did.'

Symonds leant forward again and let out a deep breath. 'There must be some reasonable figure this woman will accept to agree not to go to court.'

Tanner laughed again. 'That's called attempting to pervert the course of justice, Mr Symonds. That's not part of my MO. Not unless you're a close friend.'

'Sam told me —'

'You've got one option. Plead guilty.'

This time Symonds let out an irritated laugh. 'I'm not pleading —'

'Six witnesses saw you pop the boot of your car and take a 4 iron to the rear of the car in front of you. You gave — Mrs Cornwall — a really big fright. She reasonably thought you might belt her. That's assault. There's no defence.'

'I've explained everything to Sam,' Symonds said, anger rising in his voice. 'I was stressed. I was running late because one of my kids — I couldn't afford to be late for this meeting. We are talking a lot of money. More money than I think you can . . . She sat at that fucking light like she was dead. I sounded my horn. I blasted her. She started to move, then the moment the light turns orange, she stops. I lost it. I admit it, I lost it.

I shouldn't have done it. I shouldn't have taken a piece out of her car. I paid for that. I didn't get close to her personally with the club. Now what I want to hear from you, and I'm fucking leaving if you tell me –'

'Being stressed isn't a defence to assault, Mr Symonds. Nor to malicious damage to property. Running late isn't a defence. It's not even an excuse. Being a hedge fund manager isn't a defence either, although it may be an explanation.'

Symonds slowly nodded, then stood. He looked at Nassim. 'Sam, you told me this guy –'

'You need to plead guilty, Mr Symonds. At the first opportunity. You're also going to have to show how sorry you are to the court, or at least pretend to. You're not looking very sorry, and you should be.'

Now Nassim stood. 'Peter, I'm very unhappy about the way you've conducted this conference. It's been –'

'How unhappy, Sam?'

Nassim paused for a moment. 'What?'

'Got a golf club on you? Want to smash my desk? Are you that unhappy?'

'We're leaving,' Nassim said. He looked at his client. 'Sorry about this.'

Tanner stood, walked past Symonds to the door, and locked it. 'You're not going until Mr Symonds shows some remorse,' he said, looking at Nassim.

'What?'

'Some remorse. I want to see it, Mr Symonds. I want you to tell me you're sorry.'

Symonds looked at Nassim, then back to Tanner. 'Open the fucking door,' he said.

In the corner of Tanner's room was a brand-new cricket bat. One of the junior clerks had picked it up for him that morning from a sports store. It was for his son, Daniel. Tanner picked the bat up, walked over towards Symonds, then lifted it over his head like he was a Saudi executioner. Symonds ducked and raised his hands.

The bat snapped at the handle when it hit Tanner's desk. The desk itself, which was made from reclaimed hardwood, appeared unscathed. Bits of Symonds's smartphone flew around the room like shrapnel.

After taking a moment to work out what had happened, Symonds spoke first. 'What the fuck do – ?'

'Get out,' Tanner said loudly.

'You are –'

'Get out before I hit you with what's left of this bat.'

Symonds moved backwards towards the door. Nassim remained mute, still in shock. Symonds looked at Tanner. 'I'm going to . . . mate, I am fucking reporting you to . . . whoever. You are going to pay more for that –'

'The Bar Association,' Tanner said. 'That's the organisation you're looking for. Or you can ring the police. I just assaulted you, and committed an act of malicious damage on your phone.'

Symonds shook his head. 'You are fucking crazy –'

'Get out.'

Nassim and Symonds exchanged a glance. 'I don't know what's wrong with you, Peter,' Nassim said, 'I suggest –'

'I suggest you empty that safe in your Newtown office of all the ice and coke you keep in it for some of your clients, Sam. Because if this prick makes any kind of complaint against me, you'll have cops from the Drug Squad paying your premises a visit soon.'

Tanner stood in the corridor and watched Symonds and Nassim leave. He was still holding the bat. He tapped it into the palm of his hand. The bat gave a little where it had cracked at the handle.

He went back into his room and sat for a minute or two, staring at his door. He looked down at the desk, and saw the main body of Symonds's phone, its face splintered. Tanner threw the phone in the bin. He then picked up his own phone, found a number in his contacts list, and placed a call.

'Linda Greig's practice.'

'Jane? It's Pete Tanner. I need to see Linda.'

'Hi Pete,' the receptionist said. 'It's been a while, hasn't it? Let me have a look. I don't think she's got anything until next –'

'It's an emergency.'

There was a short pause before the receptionist spoke. 'Has something happ–'

'A few minutes ago I nearly killed a client with a cricket bat,' Tanner said, sounding calm, or so he thought.

'Let me see if I can interrupt her,' Jane said.

She came back on the line within a minute. 'Can you come at seven?'

3

It was right on seven when he walked up the steps to the bungalow Linda Greig shared with two other shrinks. Her consulting rooms were at the back of Bronte Park, not far from the beach and around the corner from the private hospital where Tanner had met her seven years earlier.

A cool breeze had now begun to blow, dark clouds starting to roll up the coast from the south. The six o'clock patient was leaving when he arrived, a young woman who rushed past him on the front porch, head down, skirt blown up as the wind took hold, her heels tapping on the concrete path like she was running from trouble.

Greig was in the reception area when he opened the door, fiddling with the air-conditioning control on the wall.

'Awful, isn't it?' she said. 'This humidity?'

Tanner shrugged. He turned to close the door, and looked at the clouds over the ocean. 'Storm's coming. Temperature's dropping.'

'Not in here it isn't. I'll get some water. Go in.'

Her room had changed since his last visit. She had a new glass-top desk, and a new chair to sit in behind it. A familiar black leather chair was positioned in front of a new white leather sofa that she motioned for him to sit on.

'You're means testing your patients these days?' Tanner said as he sat.

She smiled. 'The wealthy are as depressed and anxiety ridden as the poor.'

'But they pay better to tell you their afflictions.'

She shook her head. 'We're both in business, Pete, aren't we?' She considered him for a moment. 'Yours must be keeping you busy. It's been nearly six months.'

He nodded.

'What happened?'

'I broke a cricket bat,' he said.

She gave him a tight-lipped smile. 'I said I'd be home by seven thirty tonight, Pete. We've got guests.'

'I smashed a man's phone with the same swing.'

'Are you serious?'

'I middled it, so my hand–eye is still good. Not a stroke Bradman would have played. More a 20/20 shot.'

'A client's phone?'

He nodded, and picked up the glass of water that was on the coffee table. 'Safe to say ex-client.'

'Was the phone a substitute for him?'

'Clocking him would have been more community minded of me.'

She made a note in the black book she kept on her lap. 'What prompted this?'

He put the glass back on the coffee table. 'I think it started with the racist I appeared for in court this morning.'

'We both know it started before that, but tell me anyway.'

'Being his lawyer tested my will to live. Then I get back to chambers, and my next client runs a hedge fund.'

'Was that sufficient incentive to smash his phone?'

'This man took a golf club to a woman's car.'

Greig tilted her head back. 'Oh,' she said. 'That hedge fund guy. I saw something about it in the paper.'

'He wanted me to . . . "make it go away" were his words.'

'"Make it go away"?'

'The details don't matter. He had no remorse.'

She gazed at him for a few moments. 'Was it deliberate, Pete?'

'Deliberate?'

She raised her eyebrows and looked at him over the rims of her glasses. 'Yes,' she said. 'Are you deliberately getting angry? Are you indulging yourself?'

'The anger was real, Linda.'

'You're not stopping yourself. You could, but you don't want to.'

'The word in my game would be "premeditated".'

'You had a choice. Pick the bat up, or not pick it up. You could have resisted. We've been here many times. We've discussed the techniques. You could have said no to that impulse. You chose not to.'

'I chose his phone, not his head,' Tanner said. 'That was the choice I had.'

'Do *you* feel remorse, Pete?' Greig said quickly. 'Sitting here?'

He looked down at the coffee table and took a deep breath. 'Not really.'

'Do you still feel angry?'

He shook his head.

'Have you been depressed?'

He picked up his glass again. 'I haven't had time.'

Linda Greig put her notebook on the coffee table and leant forward. 'There's always time for that,' she said. 'You had that trial late last year, your friend in China. Then I assume you've had a break in January when it was all over? You haven't felt down at all since then?'

He'd taken Dan and one of his school friends down the south coast for a week after New Year. They surfed every day, swam, ate like a herd of horses. In the quiet moments, lying on the beach, in his bed late at night, he felt like something heavy was covering him, that he might suffocate. When he walked towards the ocean to swim, he moved in slow motion, the rest of the world and its people passing in a blur. And at breakfast or at dinner with the boys, they might be talking and laughing, and he would leave them, drift away.

'Do you think we should think about medication again?'

He shook his head. 'I'd rather talk.'

Greig looked at him for a moment, made a note in her book. 'Regardless of this man's behaviour with a golf club, this isn't something you want to be doing, is it? It's one step from disaster.'

'I don't want to argue with you about that, Linda, because you're right. I will point out though that the criminal law does draw a reasonably large distinction between belting a smart-phone with a cricket bat, and belting a human with one.'

She shook her head, smiled. 'You'd started seeing someone last time we talked. A lawyer. You were –'

'That's over. Something to do with my friend in China I can't tell you about.'

'Can't you – ?'

'She's got a tattoo on her shoulder that reminds her what an arsehole I am every day.'

'When did you last speak to her?'

'I don't need an AVO against me, Linda.'

'Has this made you depressed? Angrier than usual?'

'I don't know.'

'You're here for a reason, Pete. You're feeling remorseful about your conduct. You're frightened by it.'

'I'm not feeling remorse, Linda,' Tanner said. 'I'm feeling regret. I should have hit him, not his phone.'

'And the woman you were seeing? How are you feeling about not seeing her any more?'

He paused, then said, 'Regret about that too.'

'Pete,' she said more firmly this time, 'how are you feeling about it?'

'Worse than I thought I would.'

This time Greig paused before speaking. 'Maybe that's a good thing, in one way. Obviously you cared about her?'

He shrugged, didn't have to answer with words.

'I think I should see you regularly for a while,' she said, standing to finish. 'Call and make some appointments tomorrow.'

They left her rooms together. A gale had arrived, heavy rain with it. She walked him from the porch to his car under an umbrella. A wild gust caught the brolly, blew it inside out as they reached his car, leaving them both laughing, getting drenched. When he got in his car he had a flashback to when he'd first seen her years ago.

He thought there'd been a storm like a tempest that day. He drove off for home, wondered the whole way if it was just his memory playing tricks.

4

Tanner called Jenny Singh on Monday to apologise.

'You took your time,' she said.

'It only happened Friday.'

'Friday morning.'

'If it makes you feel better, I smashed a client's phone with a cricket bat that afternoon.'

There was a pause, then Jenny Singh said, 'That doesn't make me feel better. You need help.'

'Corey Wilson needs help.'

'His father's making a complaint to the Bar Association.'

'I hope my punishment's not life membership.'

She laughed.

'Are we okay, Jen?'

There was a pause before she spoke. 'You'll have to call Kit. She's pissed off.' Kit was Kathleen Gallagher, the head partner and principal owner of Gallagher Criminal Lawyers, for whom Jenny worked.

'Does she think I've jeopardised your growing practice in representing racists?'

'You need to call her, Pete. Grovel. I can make it worth your while. We need someone else for the Leonard case.'

'Leonard?'

'Tina Leonard. The woman charged with having her former banker killed last year.'

'That's a crime?'

'You don't –'

'I know what you're talking about. Some property developer, right?'

'Ex-property developer.'

'You said you need someone else. What's – ?'

'Take me to lunch, Pete. I'll tell you all about it. Then see Kit tomorrow. If you're sorry enough about Wilson, maybe you'll get the gig.'

Jenny Singh was Indian-Fijian bred, Australian born and educated. She'd been engaged when Tanner first met her, to a medical graduate her parents highly favoured. His ambition was to be a cardiologist. She'd dissected his heart into a thousand leaking ventricles. Tanner suspected she'd do the same to many untruthful witnesses in a courtroom one day.

He'd made a reservation at a restaurant that distinguished between pinot- and chardonnay-dominant champagnes. It was intimate and expensive. No further apology required.

She arrived twenty-five minutes late. Her dress, heels and lipstick, which oscillated between lilac and violet depending on the light, indicated she'd not been in the arraignment list that morning.

'What wealthy miscreant did you counsel this morning?'

'I asked Kit for a loan. I needed to feel strong.'

Tanner ordered two glasses of champagne, then said, 'You look like you should be lending her money.'

'Crime doesn't pay at my level.'

'What's the loan for?'

'The balance of a deposit.'

'For a house?'

She tilted her head like she was deciding what level of idiot she was dealing with. 'In Sydney? No, an apartment.'

'Where?'

'Paddington. Near Woollahra. You approve?'

'I haven't seen it.'

'Of the area?'

'The only clients you're likely to run into are the guys shifting coke and pingers. The white-collar crims are more Vaucluse and Darling Point.'

'That's how you rate a place to live? The kind of criminals it has?'

'It's a good system. How much did she lend you, can I ask?'

'No.'

'Is this something she does frequently? Does she lend to other staff?'

'She lends money to anyone if they can repay or provide security. Even criminal clients.'

'I didn't know that.'

'Kit's very entrepreneurial. She's just hired a class-action specialist from Corcorans.'

'Male or female?'

'Male. Why?'

'I know someone there. It doesn't matter.'

'She break your heart, Pete?'

'I'm still working that out. I'm worried that she may have.'

'Is that the reason for your outburst on Friday?'

'Maybe,' he said. 'Other injustices are probably at play.'

'Are we having two courses, or three?'

He smiled. 'You don't want to dwell on my broken wings?'

She smiled back. 'I think of you as bruised and brooding, but not broken.'

'You should have asked me for the loan.'

'It's better asking Kit,' she said, holding up her glass to clink his. 'Now she has an incentive to see me succeed.'

'Your father's done well, hasn't he? Why didn't you – ?' he said, but she was already shaking her head.

'He charges higher interest.'

'Seriously?'

'Not interest on money. A different kind of interest.'

'Meaning?'

'It's complicated.' She looked down at the menu. 'I'm having three courses.'

She ordered raw fish preserved with watermelon peel, followed by coral trout with clams and black vinegar.

Tanner's father loved wild salmon, pickled herrings and smorgasbords. Perhaps because of this, Tanner was big on red meat, and never liked a buffet. He ordered lamb, but it was from New England. He also ordered a French burgundy, in the expectation that he would get the Leonard brief, and it would not be for legal-aid rates.

'What's the client like?' Tanner asked when the wine arrived and Singh had approved it.

'Tina?'

He nodded. 'I googled her after I rang you. I've seen stuff about her over the years. Quite a high flyer till her fall. Not many women in that world. So she's killed the banker that pulled the pin on her company?'

'You've always said to me that the most important word in the English language is "alleged".'

'The most important sentence is "The money's in trust". She's out of bankruptcy?'

'For a while now. Leonard Developments went into liquidation about five years ago. She'd just commenced construction on a development on the harbour when she ran out of cash to finish it.'

'Near Blackwattle Bay. It's nearly complete now; I think I've seen it. Massive project. I bet someone got a paper bag of money for approving that.'

'Tina has all kinds of wild theories about what brought her down. She sounds credible face to face. Best you hear it all from her. Assuming you get the brief.'

'I read the victim was just out of prison? Five years for some drug bust?'

'Oliver Randall. Shot in the kitchen of his flat six months ago. He'd only been out about five weeks.'

Tanner took a sip of wine and watched Jenny Singh eat her raw fish. 'And the sole connection between your client and this

Randall guy is that he was once her banker and — there was some kind of civil case she lost?'

Singh put her fork down, finished chewing, picked up her wine glass and sat back. She was very deliberate and unhurried. She passed on client instructions carefully and thoroughly. You couldn't rush her. When he worked with her, Tanner found he ended up adopting her pace.

'The cops arrested a guy within an hour. The idiot was trying to get away from an RBT. Some ice addict called Jayden Webb. Still had the freshly discharged gun under his seat. He kept his mouth shut at first, then about a week later said Tina paid him to have Randall killed. Anyway, they looked into Tina, found she'd been bankrupted by SEBC — the bank Randall once worked for — came up with motive.'

'Which is?'

'Revenge. You need to read the judgement. Tina said Randall promised some extension of her loans when her cash flow tightened. Next thing, he's sending in receivers and selling her land — all her projects, including the one on the harbour you mentioned. It's called Limani Views. In the end she lost the company and all her assets. The family home. Her kids ended up with her ex.'

'Sounds like motive.' Tanner leant back while the sommelier, whom he knew well, poured more wine.

'How is it?' the sommelier asked.

'Fantastic body, a full, herbal set of breasts. Complex mineralogy. Does that sound right?'

'Good to me. I'll open another bottle?'

When the sommelier left, Tanner said, 'So, what's the defence?'

'Tina says she didn't have him killed.'

'Why is the shooter fingering her?'

'You mean the shooter our client agrees she gave fifty thousand in cash a few days before he killed Randall?'

'Ouch. This isn't a plea?'

'He was shot in both knees first, did you read that in your internet trawl? Then the head.'

'What's the theory on that?'

She shrugged. 'The Crown has another witness too. Some guy called Bitar. A construction industry heavy. He said that Tina asked him to do the job, and he refused.'

'Did the previous barrister quit this as a lost cause?'

She shook her head. 'Scanlon. Appointed to the bench not long after the committal.'

'And she's on bail? How did that happen?'

'Luck. The right judge. She has to live with her sister. The bond was a million, cash.'

'Wow,' he said. 'How does a recent bankrupt have that hanging around?'

'Plenty more for the defence costs. Kit can tell you.'

Tanner nodded. 'How pissed is she about my outburst over Corey Wilson?'

Singh raised her eyebrows and smiled. 'Not happy. I can fix it, though. I'll remind her of your glorious history. For a favour.'

'You want to instruct on the case?'

She shook her head. 'I want the junior brief.'

'You want to appear with me at the trial?'

She smiled. 'I'm going to the bar. That's part of the reason for the loan from Kit. We won't tell her that yet. I want the junior brief, and a small room in your chambers. I've looked at the work I've sent you over the last five years. You owe me.'

Her boldness almost shocked him. Her generation was something else. 'That's a very direct pitch, Jen.'

'I'm not allowed to be ambitious?'

'Sure you are. When do you want me to drop your name with Kit?'

'When I tell you. Just make sure you apologise properly tomorrow. Wear your best suit. The one you had on in court the other day, what was that?'

He smiled. 'What I wear to court is always bespoke. Only the arguments I make are off the rack.'

She smiled, shook her head.

'Tina Leonard –' he said. 'Is her defence more intriguing than "It wasn't me"? Because that's the ultimate off the rack defence.'

Jenny Singh lifted her glass. 'I'm counting on us both finding out.'

5

The glass door to Kit Gallagher's office was closed, but Tanner went in anyway. He put a bottle of wine on her desk.

'How was your holiday?' he said.

Gallagher typed something, stopped, leant back in her chair. 'Asked any judges to increase your client's sentence lately, Pete?'

'I was making a point that the sentencing options were a joke.'

'Our client didn't see the humour in it.'

'He thinks writing racist slogans on primary school walls is funny. It's safe to say we don't laugh at the same things.'

Kit Gallagher shook her head slowly. Her hair was now dyed black. Expensive salon, Tanner guessed, but there were days when he thought the colourist was overdoing it. Liquorice so dense that gravity couldn't escape.

'You're looking relaxed,' Tanner said. 'I love that suit. Is it new?' Gallagher was tall and slim. Favoured suits, not dresses. She was in black with a very fine white thread, white silk shirt under the jacket.

'What do you want?'

'What I've always wanted from you, Kit. Your unconditional love, and parts of your wardrobe.'

Five years ago, Kit Gallagher and her partner Victoria had exchanged vows in a civil ceremony. Gallagher's sister was best woman. Tanner was best man. Ten years before that, Gallagher had divorced her husband, who was a political lobbyist. These events had occupied as much space in the local papers as some of her more prominent cases.

'Make an appointment if you want to see me, Pete.'

Kathleen Gallagher was a girl from Kogarah when it was working class. She'd gone to a tough high school. Now she had celebrity clients. It's a universal rule of the legal profession that criminal counsel, even the best, receive only begrudging respect. The Australian legal profession has always regarded its stars as those that serve capital, not justice. Gallagher's clients, though – they gave her respect.

'I'm saving you the cost of a courier for the papers on Tina Leonard,' Tanner said.

Gallagher smiled crookedly. 'You think you're in a position to ask me for work right now?'

'Your client wants the best, doesn't she?'

'There are others as good as you, mate.'

Tanner laughed. 'When you've had a few drinks, Kit, I've heard what you really think of my competitors.'

Gallagher had been sending work Tanner's way for fifteen years, from not long after she'd set up her own firm. Most of it had come after his wife had died. *When you're ready to work again, Peter,* she'd told him at the time, *I'll keep you as busy as you want to be.* He'd be her best man in ten weddings after that.

She took a deep breath, let it out slowly. She'd turned fifty a few years back, and she looked – well, she looked fifty-ish, he thought. Good bones, sharp angles. A person you avoided saying stupid things to.

'I don't respect what you did in court the other day,' she said. 'In fact, I'd condemn it. It's someone else's job to punish him. You mocked him. If you can't handle his crime without comment like that, don't take the brief. You don't get to act like a child in a courtroom. Then you threaten the father? If you want to do that, it won't be with my firm behind you.'

Tanner nodded, took his own deep breath. She was right. He looked to the corner of the desk and saw a new photo: Gallagher and Vic in a gondola in a canal in Venice. One of the usual spots for legal conferences.

'You were quick getting that into a frame,' Tanner said. 'Very old school of you. What was Venice like at Christmas? Did you give a paper on the difficulty some people in this country have reconciling racial vilification laws and freedom to be a bigot?'

Gallagher let her eyes stray to the photo, then looked back. 'We were in New York for Christmas. Venice was New Year.'

'Wow,' Tanner said. 'The year you first briefed me you had your summer holiday . . . up the coast somewhere? Was it Hawks Nest?'

'Having to spend several summers there was one reason for divorcing Malcolm. As soon as he bought the place in Palm Beach, I knew I had to marry a woman.'

Tanner laughed. 'I'm sorry, Kit. I was having a bad day. I — shit, I'm glad the next client wasn't one of yours.'

'Why?'

'Doesn't matter. It won't happen again.'

She glared at him, then swivelled around in her chair, picked up a folder from the bench behind her desk, slid it across the table. 'If she gets convicted,' she said, 'don't ask for the death penalty.'

Tanner looked down at the folder, which was labelled *Athina Ireni Leonard*. 'Will she get convicted?'

Gallagher shrugged. 'Two people say she set it up. The shooter, who's getting a reduced sentence for ratting on her, and some muscle-for-hire called Mick Bitar. Construction site thug. Beats up union officials, bribes or threatens councillors. He says she went to him first.'

'Did she?'

'How would I know?' she said, turning her palms up like Christ. 'Probably. She gave fifty thousand to Webb, the guy who shot the victim. She's got a great conspiracy theory though. You'll love it. It's in her statement. Read it, then I'll set up a conference. We haven't had much time to follow up a lot of what she's saying. We picked this up from another firm.'

'This is a paying brief, right?'

Gallagher looked at Tanner over the top of the reading glasses she never wore in public. 'There's a substantial defence fund,' she said. 'Even factoring in your rates.'

'How is that?'

'The firm that acted for Leonard that we got this off did a Family Provision matter for her a year or so ago after her father died. She did pretty well. Not as well as her brothers, but she got a slice of a big pie.'

'She was left out of her father's will? Did she kill him too?'

'Tina Leonard was born Athina Ioannidis. Old man Achilles was the founder of Ioannidis & Sons. You must have heard of them? Pretty big construction company now. He started as a small-scale builder. The two sons run it. Tina worked for the family business for a while, didn't like how she was treated, set up on her own. She's an architect by profession. Anyway, Achilles and the family didn't like that move. Something to do with women should know their place, I suspect, and that place isn't in business and certainly not in construction and development. Then she did well, which made things worse. At some stage she got cut from the estate. Tina says that was after her father got dementia. She didn't prove that, but she got four mil out of a seventy-mil cash estate. No shares in the family business, though.'

'That seems fair,' Tanner said. 'Thirty-plus mil for the boys plus the company, four for the daughter.'

'I know. It was divided four ways in the end. There's a younger sister. The boys got about twenty-five each, plus most of the company. Anastasia is the youngest. She got fifteen, I think, plus some shares.'

'Jesus.'

'Four million's a lot if you're just coming out of bankruptcy.'

Tanner nodded. 'So you've now got four mil to play with for defence costs?'

Gallagher pretended to be offended. 'We won't get through that.'

Kathleen Gallagher had earned the right to charge a high fee. She'd started her business running pleas in court, and minor trials as well. As the practice grew, she had less time for court appearances, and now most court work was done by her staff, or the independent criminal bar on their instructions for the more serious matters. Gallagher restricted herself to rainmaking, public commentary on criminal law, mentoring and supervision. She still made appearances in court from time to time, but only for the more minor criminal infractions of the celebrity set, or the very wealthy. Her stature and suits, her intelligent looks, lent a veil of dignity to those occasions that her clients utterly lacked for themselves.

No matter what her high-profile clients had done – it could be drink driving, drug possession, an 'altercation' with a spouse, or assaulting some poor member of the public – Gallagher made it sound as though the offence was really someone else's fault. A conspiracy against them had led her clients to the wise justice of the court. The conspiracy might involve other people, a poor background, unreliable parents and friends, a range of illnesses, or any of the normal vicissitudes of life that had mutated so unfairly that the defendant had no control over their actions or the events. Gallagher was good in front of a camera as well as a magistrate. She had a strong voice that was hard to resist. An advocate's best friend, Tanner called a voice like that.

'When do I meet her?' Tanner said.

'When you've read that folder and the other two I'll give you. How's tomorrow sound?'

'How's next week?'

Gallagher shook her head. 'Trial's in twelve weeks. There's a few things to do. Tomorrow.'

'Three folders? Can you at least have them couriered to me rather than make me carry them?'

She shook her head. 'I'm cracking down on overheads. If you're here, you can carry them.'

Tanner looked at the photo of Gallagher in a gondola again. 'Cracking down on overheads? Where'd you stay in Venice, Kit? The Cipriani? The Metropol?'

She paused for a moment. 'The Gritti Palace,' she said, almost softly.

'That sounds like a place we could start a revolution from.'

'I've earned my money.'

'Is there a junior in this?' Tanner asked.

'Who do you want?'

'I'll think about it. Let you know.'

Gallagher nodded. 'Send me an email.'

'I'll write the name on a piece of paper, Kit,' he said, picking up the folder and two others she'd pushed his way, 'and I'll have it couriered to you.'

6

The following morning, before meeting Tina Leonard later that day, Tanner read most of the documents in his brief, including the judgement of his Honour Justice David Kerr in the case of *South-East Banking Corporation v Leonard Developments*.

Tina Leonard had hit the big league of property developers before she turned forty. Her company, Leonard Developments, built a reputation that was an abstraction in a city noted for repetitious, poorly constructed apartment buildings. Leonard's mantra was that if she wouldn't live in it, she wouldn't build it. Her competitors, she said, had made billions constructing the slums of the future.

Limani Views was her biggest sole venture. The final development consent for the project was for a thirty-level tower of one hundred and forty apartments, with fifty 'luxury villas' spread around it. Finishes were to be high end. The apartments and villas would have views of the bay and the harbour to the north, the city to the east. Low-level two-bedroom apartments were marketed at $1.5 mil. Higher up, you were looking at more than double that, more again for four bedrooms or a villa.

The development consent went to court three times. A local residents' action group tried to stop the project for several years. The litigation and the aftermath of the GFC took its toll. Construction had barely commenced when the company missed a payment to its primary banker, SEBC. With other, smaller projects on the go, Leonard Developments had more than two hundred million dollars' worth of debt it couldn't pay back without winding up the show.

Meetings took place between Leonard, her executive team and SEBC about restructuring the company's loans. There was one key meeting between Leonard, her ex-husband Adrian Leonard, her company's CFO, and Oliver Randall for SEBC. At the trial, Leonard's evidence was that Randall agreed on behalf of SEBC to alter the company's loan repayments to provide a flexible structure during the two years it would take for Limani to be completed. Randall's version, supported by bank documents, was that SEBC told Leonard it was time to cut her losses. Whatever was said at the meeting, less than a fortnight later SEBC called in all of its loans on the basis of a default, and appointed receivers to the Limani Views development.

When SEBC sued Leonard Developments for the shortfall on their loans after the sale of all its assets, the company and Leonard brought counterclaims in reply. First, they alleged that Oliver Randall was a liar, and that he had agreed on the bank's behalf to new loan terms, which the company would have been able to honour. Secondly, they claimed damages on the basis that the site was sold for a clear undervalue to Lovro Constructions, one of the biggest developers in the country. In Tina's words, one of the nation's most prominent slum builders.

Leonard's witnesses were to be her ex-husband, and her company's former CFO. Neither showed up at the trial. SEBC did a deal with Adrian Leonard. The CFO disappeared. Randall's evidence was supported by contemporaneous documents and bank files, by logic, and the terms of the loan contracts. He was believed. The judge found Lovro Constructions got a bargain, but gave a probity tick to the tender process for the sale of the site. A year later an appellate court found no error in his reasoning. Leonard Developments was put into liquidation. Tina Leonard, who had guaranteed its debts, eventually joined the ranks of the bankrupt.

Five months after the trial, Oliver Randall was paid a visit by the police, and soon after commenced his five-and-a-half-year stint in prison.

The crime scene shots of the aftermath of the head wound weren't pretty. Nor were the close-ups of Randall's knees.

The woman said to have ordered this execution sat with her hands clasped together on one side of Kit Gallagher's conference room table. She stood to greet Tanner. She was in an ivory suit, one button on the jacket, tightly tailored at the waist. She was short, but the heels gave her enough height. Long straight black hair, deep black eyes that could have looked over the Nile from a palace five thousand years ago. The rest was the Golden Age of Athens.

Gallagher ran through Tanner's CV. If Tina Leonard was impressed, she didn't show it. She looked like she made her own mind up about people. She had a pink rock on a finger you weren't meant to miss, smaller stones of the same kind on each ear. Her ring finger was clear. Her marriage, like her business, had crumbled post the GFC.

'Do you know the prosecution's witnesses?' Tanner said once his career highlights had been covered.

'Not as friends,' Tina Leonard said. 'I'm sure you've gathered that.' Contralto voice, which lesser men would run from. Those who didn't would do what they were told.

'Let's start with Mick Bitar. How long have you known him?'

An eyebrow arched, her black eyes went back in time. 'Twenty years. Twenty-five.'

'How?'

'He performed services for my father,' she said. 'He did the same for my brothers. For some of that time I was working for the family company.' She said the last words like they were the ugliest in the English language.

'Services?'

A faint smile appeared. 'He's a facilitator. He calls himself a fixer.'

'What does he fix, Tina?'

'He often makes arrangements for the smooth running of construction sites.'

'What does that mean?'

Her smile broadened. 'Usually no more than mediation between people who are failing to communicate.'

'What people?'

'Everyone. Builders. Trades people. Union officials. Local government.'

'Are his mediation techniques legal?'

The smile faded away. 'Not every detail of my father's business was made known to me.'

'Anything else?'

She shrugged. 'I've heard he's quite convincing when it comes to marginal development applications. He's been known to persuade members of local government to see things from a developer's point of view.'

'One of those acts of persuasion got him a criminal record.'

'My brothers say Mick leads people to water,' she said, 'and then he makes them drink.'

'Sounds like the sort of person to introduce to an ex-banker you've got bad memories of.'

There was a flash from her dark eyes, almost like a camera at night. 'I didn't ask him to kill Oliver Randall. If I'd wanted that done, I would have done it myself.'

Tanner smiled. 'If I call you to give evidence at your trial, Tina, don't answer that way. It sounded too close to having the ring of truth.'

She looked at him, nodded slowly.

'Jayden Webb. He did kill Randall. How does he have fifty thousand of your dollars at his flat?'

'I know you've read the brief, Peter,' she said. 'Kit told me you were thorough.'

'Reading the brief isn't being thorough, Tina. It isn't even first base. You read the brief in the dugout. I'm going to hear your whole story in your words. Then I'll listen to it again. We might go over it ten, fifteen times. There are only two rules: you tell me the truth, and you tell me everything. Why did Webb have your money at his home when he killed Randall?'

Tina Leonard told them that the money was for Bitar. She wanted a meeting with her brothers. She wanted back into the family empire. He was their associate. When they wouldn't meet or even talk to her, she contacted Bitar, had lunch with him. He said he could make it happen. Fifty thousand was his fee. Webb was a labourer on building sites. Bitar sent him to pick up the cash.

'Why would you want back in?' Tanner asked. 'Didn't you want out years ago? Wasn't that what setting up your own company was all about? Freedom from the tyranny of the men? That's my take on it from your statement. Am I wrong?'

She picked up the glass in front of her almost in slow motion, took a sip, put it down. 'I'd been bankrupted, Peter. Obliterated. I was ready to get back to work, to what I'm good at. I wasn't ready to start on my own again. That I'd do later.'

'Even with four million of your father's money?'

'That was my money,' she said sharply. 'That and more. My brothers have contacts. They're in the building game. I needed to reacquaint myself with it before I ran on my own again.'

Tanner nodded, made a note to get Gallagher to make attempts to talk to Leonard's brothers, confirming their resistance to meeting with her. 'Why the animosity with your brothers, Tina? Where's that come from?'

She looked at him blankly, then at Gallagher. 'We're going to cover my whole family history today? Don't you want to hear about who actually killed Oliver?'

'We'll get to that. What happened?'

Leonard took them back more than twenty years, to when she was Athina Ioannidis. She was spoilt, she admitted. 'My father had become wealthy by the time I was a little girl. I got treated to things my brothers hadn't. From toys to travel to the homeland. My sister and I did well at school, the boys – they didn't really apply themselves. We got into university, they went to work for Dad.'

She loved buildings, design, studied hard, got into architecture. 'I worked for my father when I finished uni,' she said. 'He had his architects let me help them. I was good with numbers, I did budgets, drafted development and project applications – he let me have a finger in everything. I did an MBA. My brothers hated how involved I was. They hated me more once I left and became successful on my own without our father's company behind us. They've built nothing on their own. I have.'

'Simple as that? Sibling rivalry?'

'Sibling envy, Peter,' she said. 'But as simple as that. My brothers inherited my father's views about women. They inherited what I can guarantee are high levels of testosterone. They didn't want me in the family business. I wasn't a man. Then they liked me less when I stood on my own two feet.'

'And they didn't like you any more when your business failed?'

Her eyes flashed that light again. She had fire in her, he could see that.

'Jesus, Pete,' Gallagher muttered, not quite under her breath.

Tina Leonard's mouth opened slightly, but she waited a moment before she spoke. 'You should read your brief, Peter,' she said calmly. 'My business didn't fail. Things got tight. Then Oliver Randall lied to me. He and his bank stole Limani from me, and sold it to one of the big boys. Lovro Constructions.' She pointed to one of the folders Tanner had in front of him. 'It's all in there. If you're interested?'

Tanner nodded. 'You're paying me to be interested, Tina, so I will be.'

She tilted her head upwards. The pharaoh's queen looking at some commoner. A clever slave, perhaps. 'You wouldn't be otherwise?'

'I don't wish to upset you, Tina, but no, not particularly. You have my full attention because you're my client. I like to make that clear to people from the get-go. I have a professional interest in helping you beat this charge. Otherwise, I really don't care who shot Oliver Randall.'

'I'm glad you've made that clear,' she said, leaning towards him, elbows now on the desk, hands clasped together under her chin. 'Can I be clear too? I don't need a knight on a white charger. I never have. Right now, I want the best lawyer. I hope that's you.'

'The prosecutors say you had Randall shot because he ruined you. They're right about the last bit at least, aren't they? You had cause?'

She smiled faintly again. 'Oliver did over five years in prison. What do I need with revenge?'

'How does a bank executive end up doing five and a half years for supplying commercial amounts of coke?'

Tina Leonard put her arms down on the table. 'He used to feed it to his clients,' she said. 'The bank's clients. Coke. Girls. The budget was substantial for both.'

'Girls and coke?' Tanner said. 'My client development practices are behind the times. What's the name of this bank again?'

'South-East Banking Corporation,' she said.

'How do you know this – about Randall? Were you invited to any of these parties?'

She laughed, spontaneity mixed with bitters. 'They're not used to women clients. Not as property developers. This was male-structured entertainment. Oliver made that clear.'

'He told you himself?'

She took a deep breath, shook her head. 'Not about the girls. I heard that from – well, it doesn't matter, it was true. He told me about the drugs once, not in – just in an unguarded moment.'

'An unguarded moment?'

'My first lender was Nipori Bank. Its Australian business went bust in the GFC. They were bought by SEBC. I had a close relationship with the banker I originally had at Nipori before SEBC bought it out. He was a bit of a surrogate father – at least in the lending world. He introduced Oliver to me when SEBC took over, did things he didn't have to do given the – well, given the circumstances. Oliver took a real interest in Leonard Developments. We had a good rapport.'

'That's quite a betrayal then? Randall was the main witness in the proceedings when the bank sued you.'

She paused again, he saw her reaching back for what she felt at the time, stopping herself. 'He was a puppet,' she said. 'Other people pulled the strings.'

'Tell me what went wrong first.'

Leonard sighed, but then said, 'They were funding my biggest development. Something I'd worked on for years. When I was still with my father. Something he started.'

'Your father started?'

She nodded, smiled. 'The bay where Limani Views is situated was where my father built his first big home. Nothing like Hunters Hill, where we ended up, but . . . Anyway, he bought up land in the area. Houses. Flats. He had a grand plan, got distracted by other grand plans. I bought some apartment blocks in the area when I started to make money with the business, then with my ex-husband. Then an old warehouse went up for sale right on the river foreshore. I was the only person who could develop the site properly, because we owned so much of the surrounding land.'

'You did Limani with your father?'

She shook her head, gave a sad smile. 'We weren't talking by then. He never forgave me for going off on my own. He –' Leonard paused, and Gallagher took the time to pour her some water. There was the barest moment when Leonard's top lip quivered, but Tanner could see that tears weren't a common part of her game. She knew how to bury grief, even if whatever she felt remained unresolved. 'He sold the land to me. He did a business deal with me. He let Leonard Developments buy out Ioannidis & Sons' properties in the area. My brothers –' She tipped her head back and smiled, and the effort nearly pushed a tear from an eye. 'My elder brother Theo prides himself on maintaining control, but Jimmy – he rang me and called me names you don't call women.'

Construction work at Limani Views was held up by court challenges to the development approvals. Leonard had other projects on the go, other debts to pay. Pre-sales were slow. A monthly loan payment was only partially met, then the same happened the following month. There was a meeting she had with her estranged husband, who still had a stake in the business, their CFO and Randall. They put a plan to Randall to manage their loans, a long-term prognosis and strategy. 'He promised us a twenty-four-month loan extension, and a repayment restructure. They called in our loans eight days later.'

'What happened then?'

Tina Leonard looked at her glass of water in disgust. 'They sued for the entire debt. Over two hundred million. They put in receivers to Limani, sold it at a public tender for a pittance. Just before the tender, the bank released a report saying the land and the sediments in the river where the marina was to be built were highly polluted. Lovro Constructions bought my project for a quarter of its worth. And guess what – it turned out that the land wasn't that polluted after all. Now Lovro has a project worth a couple of billion. How fortunate for one of SEBC's biggest global clients.'

'You obviously think this is the result of a conspiracy between SEBC and Lovro Constructions?'

'I know it is,' she said, raising her voice. 'Oliver told me.'

Tanner added to some notes he'd already made of things he was going to ask Kit Gallagher to do, things that needed following up. 'He wrote to you right before his release?'

She nodded.

'I read the letter. It does say he wanted to apologise in person for something. The things he wished he hadn't done to you? You say he spilt the beans when you met him?'

'He told me the whole story. How SEBC managed not to lose money, how Luka Ravic from Lovro and –'

'Hold up,' Tanner said. 'I don't want to get to that yet. People saw you arguing with Randall in a café about a week before he was killed. What was that about?'

She let out a kind of ironic laugh. 'Timing.'

'Timing?'

'I asked him to help me. To tell his story. To a court if I sued, to my lawyer, to a journalist – I hadn't worked it out. He wasn't ready. He said he would, but he had things he had to straighten out first.'

'Like what?'

'Something to do with his family. He was scared of these people. They had the drugs planted in his house. He did nearly six years in prison because of them. He wanted to make some sort of peace with his daughter. She was thirteen, I think, when he went to prison. She – well, he wanted to do that. I was anxious to move forward. I lost my temper. It was momentary.'

'You're saying the coke was planted at Randall's house?'

'Yes. That's what he told me.'

'Meaning your conspiracy theory involves the police?'

'Certain police.'

'Why – why would they do that?'

'Because SEBC saw him as a liability – I've spelt this all out in my statement.'

Tanner blew out a long breath. 'So, Tina,' he said, 'our case theory for your defence? SEBC or Lovro Constructions find out Oliver Randall might spill the beans on the wicked game they played on you, and they had him killed?'

She glared at him before answering. 'You don't believe me, Peter?'

He laughed. Some kind of reflex. 'Not yet, no. But I don't disbelieve you yet, either.'

'I was hoping for better than that.'

'This man Webb – he didn't name you at first as having hired him to kill Randall. That was a few days later. You say he was got at?'

'There is something interesting there,' Gallagher said. 'Webb's solicitor – Tom Clayton – he's been known to act for Mick Bitar.'

'So?'

'So, he wasn't Webb's first lawyer. He had someone else for a few days, then Clayton steps in. Then Webb does a deal, and fingers Tina.'

'What's our theory about that? That Bitar sent his lawyer to Webb to get him to cut a deal and blame Tina, when really someone else paid him to kill Randall?'

'It's not a theory, Peter,' Leonard said sharply.

'Why does Mick Bitar hate you so much? Why would he lie and say you asked him to kill Randall?'

'He knows Luka Ravic, the head of Lovro Constructions. He does business with them. They would either have used him, or Mick has seen a way to make money by setting me up as their scapegoat for killing Randall.'

'That's an interesting case theory, Tina,' Tanner said. He closed the folder in front of him. He'd had enough for now. He had in his brief the story she'd laid out in the statement, so the main thing was to check that she didn't seem crazy. She'd passed that test, even if he wasn't sure her story did. 'You said you have a younger sister?'

'Anastasia. Taz.'

'You're living with her now you're on bail?'

She nodded. 'Much to the delight of her husband.'

'How does Taz get along with your brothers?'

'Better than me.'

'I like specific answers to my questions, Tina. You'll need to follow that protocol.'

'Taz wasn't interested in the family business. She's married to a guy who's got his own money. She raised a family. They ... they don't disapprove of Taz like they disapprove of me.'

'You have your own children?'

She smiled. 'Two boys. Alex and Chris.'

'How old are they?'

'Nineteen and sixteen.'

'And they're –'

'They're with my ex-husband,' she said. The smile faded. It was a topic to drop.

'We'll talk many times, Tina,' Tanner said. 'In the meantime, do you have any questions for me?'

'You haven't asked me if I had Oliver Randall killed, Peter.'

'Should I ask? Sounds like a trap for beginners to be so direct.' He stood to leave. 'Did you keep your papers from your case with SEBC? Affidavits, pleadings, that kind of thing?'

'I can find them somewhere.'

'Send them to Kit.'

'Oliver Randall was worth a lot more to me alive than dead, Peter,' she said as he shook her hand in farewell. 'I didn't have him killed.'

7

On Friday afternoon, Tanner threw a bag of clothes in the car, and drove to the Hunter Valley with his son Daniel. From the moment he'd left Linda Greig's rooms the Friday before he'd wanted to get out of the city, leave the racists and the hedge fund sociopaths behind.

It was the last weekend before the new school year. He'd booked a villa at a golf resort. The irony that golf clubs and resorts might be hot spots for hedge fund sociopaths wasn't lost on him. Still, he hadn't played with Dan for maybe a year, and had a new-found desire for it. He silently thanked Mr Symonds for the urge to hit something with a stick.

He'd played golf with his father in his early teens. Karl Tanner had taken up the game in Australia soon after he'd emigrated from Sweden, just as his homeland was becoming obsessed with tennis and Bjorn Borg. A work colleague had managed to fast track Karl's membership into a golf club. The membership was cancelled within weeks of its confirmation after he was charged with fraud.

They played Saturday afternoon and mid-morning Sunday. Dan was good for someone who'd rarely played. He had an athletic swing, good balance, didn't mind if he hit a good shot or a complete hack, kept a sense of humour. Tanner could never do that. The perfectionism he demanded from himself in his work slid its tentacles into other parts of his life. Even into a game where you hit a small stationary ball into a not much bigger hole. Especially that. That, and a hundred other things.

'Is something wrong?' Dan asked Tanner after they'd ordered dinner in the resort restaurant on the Saturday night.

The question caught him off guard. The first time he'd asked either of his parents if they were 'okay' was when he was older than Dan. Seventeen, eighteen? A prison visit to his father. 'What do you mean wrong?'

Dan shrugged. 'It's like you're going to tell me something's up. Kind of a rushed thing, coming here. You seem – I don't know –'

'I just wanted to get away for the weekend before school starts.'

'We've just been away.'

'I needed to relax this weekend. It's easier to do that out of town.'

'Weren't you meant to be relaxing on the holiday?'

Tanner picked up his glass of wine, took a sip. 'The holiday may not have worked the way it should have.'

'Something happen?' Dan had a thoughtful expression. Pensive, heading towards concern. It burned Tanner. His son shouldn't have to worry about him.

'I got angry recently when I shouldn't have. Or I should have controlled it better.'

Dan nodded. 'At work?'

'Yeah.'

'What about?'

'I got angry at some clients.'

'Why?'

'Because . . .' Tanner thought about it, smiled, '. . . because they're criminals.'

Dan looked confused for a moment, then smiled too. 'Isn't that – that's why they're seeing you, right?'

'It's not compulsory for them to be guilty. It's just – relatively frequent. And they're sometimes not as contrite as I think they should be. I find that . . . disheartening.'

'You've told me it's your job to defend guilty people. Don't you like it any more?'

Interesting question. 'There are degrees of guilt.'

'I don't – what's that mean?'

'The world isn't fair. It's rigged. Advantages and privilege aren't handed out equally.' Tanner paused, smiled. 'This is a very big topic.'

'I get it, Dad. Rich and poor.'

'Succinctly put,' Tanner said. 'Don't confuse me with the lawyers helping to rig the game. I'm more of a cleaner.'

Dan looked confused again, nearly laughed. 'Dad, I have no idea what you're talking about.'

'I clean up messes, Dan. The mess people make. Sometimes I get tired of that.'

Tanner took another sip of wine, and wondered if this was the kind of territory he should get into with his son. He was fourteen now, metamorphosed daily it seemed. Sometimes more than once a day. He was a man, he was a child, he was a teenager. He saw things as an adult and others as a boy. He said something acutely insightful, then grunted like a Neanderthal. 'I need to control my disappointment in people,' Tanner said.

Dan nodded. 'Do you talk to Karl about this?'

Tanner nodded, smiled. His system flooded with warmth. There was something reassuring that his son considered it a good idea for Tanner to discuss his struggles with anger and disappointment with his septuagenarian, ex-con father. Dan was now one year younger than Tanner had been when Karl started his seven-year stretch. Fortunately, Tanner had put himself on the right side of the legal system. His clients paid him, but they were the ones who went to prison. The boy wasn't going to lose him.

'Are you angry about Lisa?' Dan said after their steaks had arrived. The question came right out of nowhere. And, he guessed, had been brewing for weeks.

Tanner paused before answering. Mainly because he didn't know what to say. 'Why do you say that?'

'She just disappeared, Dad, and you haven't said anything. Did you think I wouldn't notice?'

It was Tanner who felt fourteen. 'I lied to her about something. I had to. She – it wasn't the sort of thing she's going to forgive me for.'

'What was it?'

'I – I'll have to tell you about it later. It's – I think we should do this in full later. I promised I'd do something for her, and I did something to help Joe instead. To get him out of China. I didn't see a way of doing both. I couldn't.'

Dan glared at him, then nodded slowly. 'I liked her,' he said. 'She was cool.'

Tanner wondered if Dan would ever blame him for not having a mother. He'd been six when Karen died. Eight years. They'd never talked about another woman. At least not in the role of a parent. That was his fault, he knew that. He found love elusive. He said that to Linda Greig one day. He'd had long discussions with her about his failure to love but his enduring capacity for lust. She'd told him that was a lie. It wasn't eluding him. You can't find something if you're not prepared to look.

He might have been half in love with Lisa Ilves. He could – honourably he thought, almost honourably, and with only a hint of hyperbole – say that he put a man's freedom above that.

He'd told Linda Greig he'd deprived Dan of a mother. Greig told him cancer had done that. She'd told him that blaming himself for his son not having a mother was an example of his cognitive dissonance. He'd told her holding two, three, four contrary beliefs at the one time was a prerequisite for survival at the criminal defence bar.

He told his clients he never judged people. That was a lie. He was always worried, delusionally and rationally, conveniently and inconveniently, that the women he dated were wrong for Dan. It didn't take much to set that in motion. Greig told him that was not a real barometer. It was an excuse.

Karen had been a calm person. He'd been afraid that her death would make Dan an anxious kid, but it hadn't. He had her DNA for staying cool, not sweating small stuff. Before his first surfing lesson, Tanner had asked him if he was nervous. 'How hard can it be?' was the reply. Pretty hard, Tanner thought. And there are sharks. Big bastards in this part of the world. Dan had a clear sense of what he could do. He wasn't afraid. Jesus, he admired that in the kid.

Tanner was a nervous wreck before trials. He was only okay once the game began. Then he became a shark. A big bastard; a Great White.

'You were on TV a few days ago,' Dan said. 'Maybe Thursday? They were talking about you, anyway. Some news show.'

'What?'

'They mentioned you. You asked for a client to get a higher penalty. They had someone criticising you. Other people thought it was cool.'

Tanner shook his head. He was never going to live that down.

'Not usually part of your job, is it?' Dan said.

'What?'

'Asking for a tougher penalty?' The boy was smiling.

Tanner shrugged. 'I shouldn't have said it.'

'What did he get?'

'Two five-hundred-and-fifty-dollar fines. For writing a revolting message on the wall of a primary school.'

'Not enough?'

'What do you think? Philosophically?'

Dan paused. 'What do you mean, exactly?'

'Apply your values and your sense of justice. What penalty do you think is fair?'

'What did he do again?'

Tanner told him.

'A hundred thousand?'

Bloody hell. Hanging judge. 'What if he can't pay? What if he doesn't have a hundred grand? Or what if he said he was just exercising his right to free speech, that he shouldn't be guilty of anything?'

Dan paused. 'If he can't pay the fine, I'd jail him,' he said.

Jesus. That escalated quickly from a fine. 'For how long?'

'A year?'

Tanner looked at the boy, said nothing.

'Two?'

Prosecutor in the making. The default position of most adolescents, except when it came to themselves, where they showed expertise in a wide range of defences, partial and absolute.

'What would jail teach my client?'

'I don't know,' Dan said. 'Don't do it again?'

'Would it teach him not to be a racist?'

'More than a five-hundred-buck fine, I reckon.'

'I doubt it.'

'What then?'

'My client wasn't the most privileged person. It's complicated. I'm probably out of my depth.'

'Your job is to get him off.'

'Yeah.'

'And that's not enough for you.'

Tanner looked at his son for a moment. 'That really is a good question.'

Dan laughed, like he was recognising something. A close friend being both reassuringly and sadly predictable. 'It wasn't a question, Dad,' he said. 'And you're kind of old not to know that.'

8

It was a ten-minute walk from the wharf to the apartment complex on the ocean side of Manly. The apartment was owned by Max Rourke. Six years ago, not long before he retired, he'd acted for Oliver Randall on his drug charge.

The victim in the Tina Leonard case was as important to get to know as the accused. Leonard said Randall had been framed for his drug charges, and she had a theory about why. Max Rourke QC was the first port of call for investigating Oliver Randall.

'Beautiful building,' Jenny Singh said to Tanner when they reached the outside gate of the complex. It was a development of six, the top four with balconies overlooking the ocean. Max Rourke had owned a huge house in Mosman when Tanner had first met him nearly twenty years earlier, when he was fresh out of law school. He and his wife had now downsized, and Max had packed life in at the courts. Or had it packed in for him.

'Money's not Max's problem,' Tanner said as he pushed one of the buzzers next to the front gate.

Mary Rourke greeted them at the door. Wearing black slacks, flats, a white blouse, and a pink cardigan over the top, even though it was thirty degrees outside. She had a long strand of white pearls around her neck. She kissed Tanner on the cheek, grabbed him by the elbows, leant back to take him in.

He introduced her to Jenny Singh. She offered them tea, and asked about Dan.

'Fourteen?' she said, after he told her. 'I can remember when – God it only seems such a short time since he was born.' She asked for a photo. He showed her on his phone.

'Looks like you,' she said. Dan looked like Karen, but he suspected Mary Rourke hadn't wanted to say that. 'How's he going at school?'

Tanner shrugged. 'There's a "yes" grunt and a "no" grunt. He likes sport. He smelt bad last year unless I made him shower. This year he's never out of the shower, and his room smells like a Rexona factory. I think that's because he meets up with a girl after school at Bondi Junction a few times a week. He and his friends play electronic games that involve a high level of violence. The kind of stuff I've built my career on.'

Mary laughed. 'Let me take you to Max.' She turned and started to walk off, but stopped. 'It's not a bad day,' she said. 'If he wants to talk about some old case . . . you'll just let him? It can take a while.'

Tanner smiled. 'Our client has four million to play with on her defence,' he said. 'Max can take all day.'

He was sitting in a brown leather chair when they walked in. The room was part study, part library. There was an old wooden desk, out of context with the modern apartment. Rourke's chair was side-on to the window, which was floor to ceiling and looked over the beach. There was a two-seater couch against the far wall for Tanner and Singh to sit on.

Rourke was wearing tan corduroy pants, a thick shirt and a heavy button-up sweater. Dressed for winter, not summer. He took his glasses off when Tanner walked into the room, and started trying to get up.

'Sit, Max,' Tanner said, sounding like he was talking to a dog. Rourke gave up standing, until he saw Jenny Singh, who provoked a second effort. He was uncertain on his feet, though, and nearly fell sideways. Singh reacted first, grabbed him under the arm to steady him. When she had, she took his hand, introduced herself, helped him back in his seat. Only then did Tanner shake Rourke's hand. The older man's hair was combed, but inexpertly. His eyes looked cloudy. For an awful moment, Tanner wondered if Rourke recognised who he was. Then Rourke almost shouted out 'Peter!', as though the name had suddenly come to him.

Fifteen years before, Tanner had been junior counsel to Rourke in a murder trial that provided a hundred headlines. He was not yet thirty, had been spared evil until then. He came face to face with it in the form of Matko Juric. Matko killed eight women. At least eight. Hitchhikers, runaways, street kids. Anyone alone and vulnerable, and who somehow fell for whatever charms Matko had. He charmed them in dingy bars, cheap clubs, by the side of the road. They were strangled, buried. Not even Max Rourke's legendary control of a jury could stave off a guilty verdict after only four hours' deliberation following a ten-week trial. It wasn't so much the forensic evidence, which was enough anyway – Juric radiated evil. You could feel it, smell it. It left an actual taste in Tanner's mouth, bitter and dry. He remembered starting to sweat the first time he was in an interview room with Juric. He'd felt his pulse quickening, had wanted to get out.

'Keeping busy?' Tanner asked when they'd sat down. It was a stupid thing to say. Rourke looked confused. 'You're not missing running trials?' he then said, and wondered if that was worse.

Max Rourke didn't say anything, but lifted a hand and lowered it quickly to pretend that the answer was no. Next to him, on a small side table, was a leather-bound notebook, the kind he'd used his whole career. That was why they were there.

'We should do a case again soon,' Rourke said, sounding uncertain, looking at Tanner.

'Sure,' Tanner said softly.

'So he was killed, Randall?' Max Rourke then said.

'Yes,' Tanner said quickly, wanting to grab him before he lost him. 'I'm acting for –'

'Didn't know he was out.'

'He was released six months ago,' Singh said. Rourke looked at her. A look of wonder. *Who the hell is this?*

'Tina Leonard is my client,' Tanner said. 'The alleged killer.'

Rourke nodded. 'Shot him?'

'They say she arranged it. The prosecution's got two witnesses who finger her. The killer and someone they say she approached first.'

Rourke shifted in his seat, smiled, shook his head. 'Tough case, Peter,' he said. 'What do you think? She's guilty?'

Tanner smiled. 'Max, c'mon. You taught me not to worry about that. Jury's job.'

Rourke nodded his head. His mistake.

'You remember Oliver Randall?' Tanner asked.

Rourke frowned. 'Guilty plea,' he said. 'I thought it was a trial.' He picked up the notebook that was on the side table. 'Pleaded. Should've been a trial.'

Mary Rourke walked in carrying a tray of tea and biscuits, and there was an agonising moment when Max tried to take the tea cup from her instead of letting her put it on his table. He lost control, the cup tipped over. Tea filled the saucer, then spilt over his pants. He shouted out, blamed her. She fetched a cloth. Arcing silence filled the room.

'Can't have a real drink any more,' Rourke said to no one when his wife had gone for the cloth.

There had been many, many drinks in the career of Max Rourke QC. Whisky after court. Wine with dinner. 'This bottle is for you, this one for me,' he'd said to Tanner before ordering food at the first lunch he'd taken him to. He drank wine until he was glassy-eyed and numb, was barred by several restaurants, but never barked at judges or the moon. There was whisky in his study at night. Then the drinks were taken in the mornings before court, and at lunch. Then one day, not long before he 'retired', he forgot the name of the client he was appearing for. He was sixty-six. He was now seventy-one, and was rapidly heading towards a future of permanent care. 'ARBI, the specialist called it,' Mary Rourke had told Tanner on the phone when it had started to happen. Alcohol-related brain injury.

'It was going to be a long case,' Rourke said when Mary had finished and some dignity had been restored. 'He worked for a bank. Six kilos of cocaine. Denied it was his at first.'

'What happened? Why'd he plead?' Tanner asked.

Rourke picked up a sweet biscuit, found his mouth, took half of it inside, lost the rest under his shirt. He looked at his notebook. 'Can't work it out,' he said. 'It was going to be a long trial.'

'I read the judgement,' Tanner said. 'The sentencing judgement.' He waited for Rourke to acknowledge this, but he just glared at him. 'Alan was your junior. Alan Murdoch.'

Rourke shook his head vehemently. 'No, the junior was Jack,' he said. Tanner didn't know who Jack was. Rourke would have read his notebook before they arrived. The book would have told him Alan Murdoch was his junior counsel. Part of what he'd read he would have already forgotten. Perhaps 'Jack' was the solicitor. Perhaps he was a junior from a quarter-century ago.

'The arresting officer was Brian Crawford,' Tanner said, moving on. 'Do you – ?'

'Corrupt bastard,' Rourke interrupted, almost chuckling. Not all memory was lost. 'Corrupt Crawfy. Still around?'

Tanner shook his head. 'He retired early,' he said.

Rourke nodded. 'Can't live in Sydney on a copper's wage,' he said. 'Not an honest cop, anyway. He was undercover.'

Singh started to correct him, and said, 'No, that was –'

'He was Drug Squad,' Tanner said over the top.

Rourke looked at him, confused again. 'It was going to be a trial.'

'Do you know what happened, Max? Why did Randall change to a plea?'

Rourke looked at him, said nothing. Tanner wasn't sure if he'd understood. He doubted that even Max Rourke at his best had an answer to his question. If he did, it was in his notes.

He'd kept the notebooks for over forty years. Briefs were always returned to the solicitors who sent them. Rourke's books were for him. 'He would never let me throw them away,' Mary Rourke had told Tanner when he'd first rung her about needing to see Rourke. 'Those notes are his memories. What's in his head is –' A day later she'd rung and said she'd found the book he needed.

'It's okay if we take this, Max?' Tanner said, looking at the notebook.

'Not sure what good it'll do,' Rourke said. 'Bring it back. Always something that helps with a new case in an old book.'

Tanner smiled, stood and picked up the book. He opened it. The handwriting was a fluent cursive he recognised immediately. It was almost beautiful.

When they were about to leave, Rourke said once more, 'Must do a case together again soon.'

Tanner nodded, tried to smile.

'Have a morale-boosting lunch too. And a bloody drink.'

After walking back towards the wharf in silence for a few minutes, Tanner said, 'Think I'll end up like that one day?'

Jenny Singh looked at him closely. 'How much do you drink?'

'Never when a trial is on,' Tanner said. 'Too much when one isn't.'

Singh paused for a long moment before answering. 'Keep busy,' she finally said.

'Glorious hand,' Jenny Singh said. They were sitting on the bench of a ferry headed back to Circular Quay. It was hot, the only breeze created by the movement of the ferry, which was nearly empty, the gulls following it outnumbering the passengers by at least five to one. Tanner had Max Rourke's notebook for the Oliver Randall defence open on his lap. 'Never work off scraps of paper,' Rourke had told him when he'd first started at the criminal bar. 'It's for cheapskates.'

The notes were brief, but in the main complete sentences. Some were easy to follow because they married up with the facts recorded by the sentencing judge in his written judgement, which Tanner had read online from a case-base website. Six kilos of cocaine found in wrapped one-kilo packets in Randall's home following the execution of a police warrant. The packets were in a gym bag that had been shoved to the back of the top cabinet in Randall's home office. He'd denied the drugs were his, but admitted to possession of thirty or so grams found in the jacket of his suit pocket, and to selling the same amount to an undercover police officer late on the afternoon before the warrant was obtained on the back of that sale. He'd told Rourke and his solicitor that the drugs had been planted.

'What's that mean?' Singh asked, pointing to the words *SEBC. Don't mention.* They were in a section of notes that had clearly been prepared for a bail application.

Tanner shrugged and kept reading. Shortly after he came across a sentence in capitals which read: *GAVE CLIENT THREE DAYS TO COOL OFF RE PLEA. INSISTENT. SIGNED DOCUMENT RE ACKNOWLEDGEMENT OF GUILT + CHANGE OF INSTRUCTIONS + RECEIVING ADVICE RE LIKELY SENTENCE.* What followed was easy enough to follow as the notes Rourke had made for his submissions on mitigation and sentence at the hearing of Randall's guilty plea before a judge in the District Court. Rourke had predicted a sentence of eight to eleven years. Randall got seven and half, with five and a half non-parole.

'Light sentence for six kilos of coke,' Tanner said.

'I can't see anything about why he changed his instructions,' Singh said when they'd reached the end. 'You're going to speak to the solicitor? Stockman?'

'At some stage,' he said. 'Someone else first.'

9

Dunks had been Max Rourke's preferred city drinking hole. It was owned by Billy Dunk, a now near seventy-year-old grog artist with pores in his nose deep enough to drown your sorrows in. His wine list did not reflect the avant-garde in modern vinification. Dunks, or 'Drunks' as it was unimaginatively referred to, had a crew of Chinese men in the kitchen who cooked steak and chips, and chicken schnitzels. Billy was more often than not able to negotiate the extraction of a cork from a wine bottle, although the conversion to screw caps had been a godsend. Rourke had once purchased a bottle of Hill of Grace after a satisfying win, only to find that Billy had left several pieces of desiccated cork in the wine following his eccentric attempts to extract it from the bottle. Rourke had looked at the wine and floating pieces of cork in his glass, and said, 'This is a centre of excellence, from which the corks from fine bottles of wine are removed with world's best practice.' From then on the lawyers who took second chair to Rourke in his criminal trials referred to Dunks as the Centre of Excellence, or, if they attended frequently, simply as 'the Centre'.

That night, Tanner found the Centre unchanged from the last time he'd been there. It was six pm, it held a licence for a hundred and twenty, and was currently occupied by eight patrons. Tanner guessed all were mid-level public servants about to cash in their superannuation and who drank for New South Wales, and perhaps even for Australia. It was the kind of place that he felt lost its *je ne sais quoi* without the presence of Max Rourke. Blond wood tables and wooden benches. A few bar stools. Brown tiles on the floor. Advertisements for P&O cruises from the sixties and seventies on the wall. Toilets that had the third-world ambiance of those of an all-boys private school. The upside was that Tanner was always the best-looking man in the bar when he went to the Centre. The downside was that not many women tended to go there, and those who did had complexions as florid as the owner's.

Alan Murdoch walked in after Billy Dunk had finished catching up with Tanner and handed him two glasses and a bottle of red. The men shook hands and retreated to a table in a far, dark corner. No matter how fine the weather, the ambiance in Dunks was such that you felt certain that a hard, bleak rain was falling outside. Murdoch was now a federal prosecutor. His targets could be drug mules, the syndicates that ran them, or tax crooks.

'How's life acting for the Commonwealth?' Tanner said.

'A life without guilt.'

Tanner lifted his gaze from the glass he was pouring wine into. 'Sounds boring,' he said.

'How's Max?'

Tanner gave him the run down. Failed memory. Lost coordination. Mood swings. 'The whole dipso catastrophe.'

'Been years since I saw him,' Murdoch said, picking up his wine glass, studying the contents. 'He didn't approve of me changing sides at the bar table.'

'He said defence was the side of the angels.'

'Do you?'

Tanner took a long sip of wine. 'I don't drink enough to fool myself that way.'

Murdoch smiled, and clinked his glass with Tanner's. 'Good to see you, Pete, it's been too long.'

'Yeah.'

'Sounds to me like you want to join my side. What happened with that redneck the other day?'

Tanner sighed. 'That news has reached you?'

Murdoch laughed, and nodded.

'I had one of those moments where I thought I was having a private thought but I was talking out loud. It happens when I act for racists or see men in lycra.'

'We'd be happy to have you.'

Tanner nodded. 'Do you remember much about Oliver Randall?'

Murdoch shrugged, leant back against the wall of the booth. 'Max was no help?'

'He gave me his notebook.'

Murdoch narrowed his eyes. 'Should you have that?'

Tanner shook his head. 'The client's dead, Alan. He ceased to care about privilege after the third bullet wound.'

'He was going to plead not guilty.'

'How long did that last?'

'I saw him first, with the solicitor. Without Max, I mean. Before we got him bail. He was adamant the six kilos had been planted. Wouldn't say why, but I kept thinking he wanted to. He was happy to admit to having a few grams in his jacket, but said he'd never had more than ten or so eight balls at home, which he kept locked away. He had a thirteen-year-old daughter at private school. He said he'd never leave six bricks in an unlocked gym bag.'

'Did you believe him?'

Murdoch nodded. 'I did.'

'Where was he sourcing what he had?'

'Wouldn't say at first,' Murdoch said. He laughed at a memory. 'Then Max got hold of him.'

'And?'

'The bank. South-East.'

'What?'

'His employer. He got the coke through them.'

Tanner drew in a deep breath and gave his colleague a hard look. 'I don't like banks much,' he said, 'but they're making coke?'

'Buying it.'

'Why?'

'Client entertainment.'

'The Commonwealth Bank gave me a piggy bank when I was a kid. They had a nice man come out to our school to help us set up a savings account. Banking's really changed. Who do they get the coke from? Their Colombian branch?'

'Hookers,' Murdoch said. 'A package deal with girls from some up-market brothel that rents out girls and sells coke.'

'He told you this?'

'He said they did it regularly. Select people at their biggest clients who they'd sussed out liked to be entertained in – a particular way.'

'And Randall was in charge of – what? This level of corporate entertainment?'

'Often, he told us. He confessed to over-ordering on the coke – some scratch-each-other's-back deal he had going with the pimp who ran the girls. What wasn't used at the bank's parties, he kept. Some for personal use – and he admitted having a problem – the rest to sell. Ultimately to an undercover cop from the Drug Squad. It all sounded out there, but I believed him. And I believed him when he said the six kilos wasn't his.'

'What private school did the thirteen-year-old go to? Maybe it was hers?'

'Jesus, Pete,' Murdoch said, laughing. 'Anyway, Randall didn't want us to say a word about the bank. They still hadn't fired him when we got him bail. I think he hoped he could talk to someone there and –'

'To get him out of it?'

'No, no,' Murdoch said. 'I think more along the lines of maybe paying his defence costs, not terminating him. I don't know for sure – maybe paying him out.'

'Sounds naïve.'

'He was desperate. He was on big money and bonuses, but had a huge pile in Bellevue Hill, they'd just renovated, school fees for his kid. He said you couldn't move in their bedroom because of his wife's empty shoe boxes. A sports car each, a massive Range Rover for his wife for the school sports runs, holidays in Europe, skiing in Colorado. The whole Eastern Suburbs extravaganza.'

Tanner raised his eyebrows, refilled the glasses. 'Anyway,' Murdoch continued, 'he wouldn't let us say anything about the bank in the bail hearing. Only that he was not guilty. It looked bad for him, but we got him bail on a hundred grand because he still had a job, and had ties like his family, clean record, all of that. Two weeks after he gets bail, he tells us he wants to plead. Or at least his solicitor rang me and said that was what was happening, could I call the DPP and tell them.'

'And the reason for this?'

'Never told us,' Murdoch said. 'He told us he had a big problem, the coke was his, he sold in small but frequent amounts to the social set, he was very sorry he'd misled us, and sorrier he'd fucked up his life. He then had us rat out two of his clients to try to shave some time off his sentence. Some cokehead cosmetic surgeon, and some poor bastard who was a finance broker. The cops only had his word about it, though, so neither got charged.'

'Who'd Randall say he got six kilos of coke from? Did the bank buy in bulk?'

'Wouldn't tell us,' Murdoch said, 'even after Max went off his nut. Max handed the brief back for a while after Randall said he was changing his plea. I think he wanted to go after the cop. Crawford?'

'What calmed Max down?'

'I think the solicitor – Greg Stockman was his name, some big-firm show-pony – promised him some white-collar crime he said they had.'

'Was that true?'

'Don't know. Probably not.' He finished what was left in his wine glass, then said, 'to tell you the truth, Max may have been starting to lose it then. He kept calling the solicitor Graham instead of Greg.'

'You said he was a show-pony?'

Murdoch nodded. 'Up himself, anyway.'

'That would have been deliberate. Max always made mistakes on purpose with the names of people he didn't like. Especially judges. Remember Justice Gant? Max actually got a formal Bar Association reprimand for the way he used to pronounce it.'

Murdoch laughed. 'Why is this important to you, anyway? How does it fit in with your case?'

'You know me. I'm a details kind of guy. I never know what might be important at the beginning,' Tanner said. He told Murdoch what he knew about the South-East Banking Corporation case against Tina Leonard, and the evidence Oliver Randall had given that Leonard said was a lie, but held back the other details she had given him. Then he said, 'My client told me some things she said Randall confessed to when he got out that it's best we not discuss. She says she met with him, though, and he told her the six kilos weren't his.'

Murdoch paused before responding, twirling the stem of his empty wine glass in his fingers. 'I don't know what more I can tell you, Pete. I believed him more when he said the drugs were planted than when he told us they were his.'

'Why?'

'He seemed like a guy who used coke – a lot – but what he told us about the bank seemed like the truth. He was working deals around the clock, entertaining himself and the clients. I'm sure he sold to rich people to big note himself, but I can't see him having a gym bag full of it. It was a hobby, not a business. I could be wrong, but that's what my gut told me.'

'Where's Crawford now? He left the Drug Squad a while ago, didn't he?'

Murdoch shrugged. 'I can probably find out for you, if you like.'

'Thanks,' Tanner said. 'I'll get my own guy on it too.'

Murdoch laughed. 'You still using that old bank robber?'

'He robbed homes,' Tanner said. 'No record of violence.'
'Noble of you to keep him in employment.'
'He does well without me.'
'By honest means?'
'Not for me,' Tanner said.

Murdoch picked the wine bottle up to fill Tanner's glass, but it was empty. Tanner asked him how his wife and family were. Murdoch had a partner to go home to. Tanner didn't.

'You'll say hi to Max for me, next time you see him?' Murdoch said.

Tanner nodded.

'Sad what's happened. He was razor sharp. It was electric when he went after a witness. Makes you wonder about this stuff.' Murdoch held up his glass.

Tanner stood. 'I'll get another bottle.'

10

Rachel Roth came close to asking someone to walk her back to her car. The whole day she'd had an uneasy feeling that she couldn't shake.

She'd been at a meeting late Friday afternoon in the city with the company's accountants. The meeting ended at five thirty, and she took the chance to have a drink in the CBD with friends. She was back in the office in Surry Hills by quarter to eight for the staff dinner at the pub bistro that was walking distance away in Crown Street. In the pub, she caught the eye of some guy at the bar who kept looking at her. She told herself not to be paranoid. Maybe he thought she was looking at him.

Roth owned a third of the shares in the company that published *The Daily Informant*. Her father owned another third. The rest were owned by a charitable trust set up in honour of her late brother. Her father owned a lot of things. Commercial and rural property. A macadamia nut farm. Two wineries. Many, many old cars he'd restored himself. And art. Serious, expensive art. Her father's money had got the publication off the ground. It was one of the adventures he wanted to do with her. He did all he could to make them feel like partners, but she hadn't fully bought into that concept yet.

Roth had spent her primary years in Sydney, but her teens in Manhattan. Her father had started in an investment bank in

Sydney, moved to the US, MBA at Harvard, then Wall Street. He was smart, charming. He made a *lot* of money. Then there was the accident. After her brother's funeral, he and her mother had what they called a 'life reassessment'. Her mother had been a lawyer who didn't work. She wrote a novel about the sudden loss of a child. It was well received. They moved back to Sydney. Her father seeded start-ups, sat on boards, took up surfing again. He'd grown up on Cronulla Beach, been in the water most of his childhood. She took it up with him.

The magazine and online paper was a joint idea. Roth had a degree in media and comms, but the business model for hard copy journalism seemed fatally wounded, and TV had no appeal. She had no attraction for compromise, and didn't like the idea of wearing an inch of make-up. Being an owner, making the decisions – the opportunity her father's money gave her was too good to turn down.

The media company they'd started employed a big crew by their competitors' standards: a political, finance and arts editor, four other journos on the payroll, a subscription manager, and sundry support staff. Beyond that, they used freelancers, and writers on commission. Her father spent most of his time, when he wasn't analysing who to give money to for ventures of various sorts, sitting on the boards of public companies or charity organisations. He put some sharp people on the DI board – people who understood journalism and communication in the digital age. Rachel was the managing editor, although she wrote articles too. The hard-copy magazine came out monthly – a financial indulgence of her father's that occasionally she saw as a vanity project, more often though as his rage against the slow death of something important. He'd insisted that it print long articles and essays; he'd tired of the old press well before the internet tsunami struck it, when money from advertising and classifieds still rolled in. He thought the financial press was lazy. Not quite as sheep-like as the analysts most investment banks started to employ by the late nineties, but mediocre by his standards. They were great at analysis *after* something had happened. So he wanted to make sure that, courtesy of his money, his staff were given time to produce a better kind of product, at least for the magazine. It and its daily online little sister had been running for nearly three years now. Advertising was picking up slowly, as were subscriptions. They were on target to break even in about twenty years.

Because the magazine only came out once a month, each edition was special. Hence the staff dinner in the pub. A night of beer, comfort food, moderately priced wine bought in large quantities, loud voices, laughter. People liked working for *The Daily Informant*.

'Ray' Roth gave up on the idea of asking Scott Marchand to walk her back to her car once closing time came around. He might get the wrong idea. They'd been engaged. They ended it with what appeared to be mutual consent. Third parties were involved on both sides in an ephemeral but telling way. At least none of them involved anyone else in the office. She wasn't sure why he'd cheated. Her motivation had been not wanting to join the list of media couples. There was something incestuous about it. If anyone was going to change her position on that, it wasn't going to be Scott Marchand. He was tall and bordering on beautiful, but he had more ambition than substance. He wrote slick copy; 'smooth as a gravy sandwich' was how her father described the style. She always thought, 'This is good,' when she read Scott. And within a short period of time she'd completely forgotten what it was about. A kind of metaphor of their relationship.

After initial acceptance, he'd started to take the break-up hard. She wasn't sure if it was the idea of her money he was in love with, or her. He wasn't shallow that way, she didn't think, but then again ... He'd suggested counselling. She'd laughed out loud, not meaning to be cruel. If you need counselling to save an engagement, the coming marriage hardly seemed founded on rock. What was she thinking, saying yes? He'd caught her by surprise, and her answer shocked her. Then she was stuck with it for a while. He was still hoping for a reconciliation, she knew that. Which meant he'd have to go at some stage. That was going to be a fucker of a conversation, but it was coming.

She didn't feel watched in the back lane of their building in Riley Street where her car was parked. She still had an uneasy feeling, though. She wasn't driving – too much red wine for that – but she'd left the keys to her flat in the car, and had to get them before going back to Riley or Crown to hail a cab, or get an Uber if the Friday night closing competition was too great.

Calling it a flat was underselling it. She had the whole top floor of an Art Deco building in Bondi, a few streets back from Campbell Parade. A penthouse. Her father had wanted to buy her a house. This was the compromise. Houses were for families. She had a dog. She was always looking for ways to make trade-offs for having wealthy parents. She might have made more adjustments and pacts against reliance on privilege if her brother hadn't died. She told herself that anyway, and intermittently believed it. So she let her parents buy her the luxury pad, but the dog was from a kennel. He was a mix of a few things, but silky terrier had won out. Her dog walker would have walked him that evening. The lady she used had a key to her flat to come and go with the dog, the alarm passcode, an e-tag needed to send the lift to the top. The dog was called Ziggy. Her mother had grown up listening to Bowie.

When the lift door opened, she saw that her front door was too. Not busted open, just open. She looked at it for what felt like a long time. Her stomach dropped, churned, her throat tightened. She dropped her bag and rushed in.

She called the dog's name before she was inside. He slept in the bathroom. She ran there first, calling him again, slapped at the wall for the light switch, but his basket was empty.

The only light was from her bedroom. A soft light, the bedside lamp. She ran in. Ziggy was stretched out on her bed. He'd been laid out. She screamed his name, knew the dog was dead before she touched him, hoped from way down deep inside that she was wrong. She dived for the bed, scooped her hands under the dog and lifted. His head hung like it was partly severed.

A small blob of blood was congealing in the corner of his mouth. She screamed his name again, and started crying.

She wasn't sure how long she had lain with the dog when she became aware of her buzzer sounding. She left the dog on the bed, almost in a trance, and answered. It was Tim, the guy who lived downstairs with his boyfriend. He'd heard her screaming. Was she okay? Should he call the police? She buzzed him up, let him in, walked back into her bedroom without speaking.

Tim was wearing a kimono. He looked at her, saw she was okay, looked at the dog, saw it was not, and put his hand to his mouth. By now she was crying again, cradling the dead dog.

Tim took a step forward, took his hand away from his mouth. 'Do we – do we call the police now?' he said.

11

"Knew, Lawyers" advertised their legal services as a 'new way of doing things'.

It was cute, he supposed, as he looked around the reception area, primary colours bursting everywhere, casually dressed staff walking around chatting and smiling. He wondered if he was old-fashioned. Tanner wasn't a fan of cute when it came to the law.

Terrance Faulkner didn't come out to meet him. A girl in a short red dress and knee-high boots took Tanner to him. Faulkner was sitting at a white table among several that made the room look like a café. There was a coffee machine on a stand near a wall, behind which was a man who appeared to have the skills of a barista. The chair Faulkner was sitting on was moulded plastic and shaped like a 5 with the top missing. The chair was white. Each of the six tables had a white, a red, a clear and a black chair.

Faulkner rose and shook hands. Tanner looked at the chairs warily and took the red.

'Thanks for agreeing to see me,' he said.

'Of course.' He was in a navy shirt with a large blue pokadot, sleeves rolled to just below the elbows. The pants were pastel like the walls, probably officially described as salmon. Tan loafers, no socks, a reasonable amount of ankle being shown. Round glasses; very closely cropped receding dark hair. Tanner wondered if the staff called Terrance 'Terry'. He'd stick with Terrance unless invited to shorten. Terrance took Tanner's coffee order and sang out to the barista for a latte and a long black.

'This looks like a fun place to work,' Tanner said.

'We're aiming for a different work environment from traditional firms.'

'Does it help?'

'It helps with our lawyers' mental states.'

'The mental state of lawyers is one of my main fields of expertise. I could write a novel about mine. I haven't seen a big firm appear so relaxed.'

Faulkner shook his head. 'We're not a big firm. I used to work for a big firm, I know the difference.'

'My apologies. That was an unthinking slur. So, what's the secret to your success here?'

'We don't just put our clients first, but our staff too. We don't want unhappy lawyers.'

'Unhappy lawyers are a burden the world should be rid of.'

'We're goal orientated, not fee orientated, so we don't time cost. We want our clients and our lawyers to enjoy working with each other. We want them to have time for adventures outside of work.'

Tanner didn't like the sound of any of it. Somewhere in the building there was a pastel-coloured dungeon. 'Are you pitching a job to me?'

Faulkner smiled. 'I'm sure our litigation team could use you.'

'How many clients do you have that are drug peddlers or violent sociopaths?'

Faulkner paused for perhaps longer than he should have. 'None,' he said.

'Then you can't use me.'

'I'm sure not all your clients are like that.'

'I was talking about my colleagues and some members of the judiciary.'

The barista brought over their coffees. When he left, Tanner said, 'He doesn't have a law degree, does he? I know times are tough in some parts of our game.'

Faulkner shifted in his seat. 'We move in very different legal worlds, I guess.'

'We should swap for a day. I'll swap with the barista.'

'You called about Tina Leonard.'

'Sorry,' Tanner said, 'I felt we could chat all day, given you're not time costing.'

Faulkner looked at his Tag Heuer. 'I have a meeting in half an hour.'

'I've read the judgement,' Tanner said. 'Did you believe her?'

'Tina?' Faulkner said, tilting his head slightly, looking up for a moment. 'I did.'

'She said the bank hoodwinked her. That Oliver Randall said it would all be sweet with her loans for a couple of years, then they pulled the pin the following week. You thought she was telling the truth? He was lying?'

Faulkner sipped his latte then said, 'It didn't stack up with the bank's documents. Her version of events didn't. But – look, she seemed sincere, despite the bank being able to cross the i's and dot the t's of calling in its loans.'

'When you say "documents", what do you mean?'

'All the documents were consistently against her. The company did default on two loan payments – not full defaults, part payments were made. The bank's terms allowed it to call in all loans then. They wrote saying they were doing that. Tina said that Randall told her that was just a formal letter the bank had to send to protect its position, that they were happy to restructure the loans if her company could put a sensible long-term proposal to them. The development – Limani – still looked a winner. She says they met, it was all agreed, but she got nothing in writing. Then a week later she gets letters of demand. There was no documentary support for her version – but I believed her, if that's what you want to know.'

'Can we try it the other way around?' Tanner said. 'Did you feel Randall came across as a liar?'

'I wouldn't go that far, no, not from memory. I don't think I felt he was obviously lying. But –' Faulkner clasped his hands together and looked at the ceiling like he was searching for the words he wanted up there.

'But?'

He looked down and gave Tanner a soft smile. 'People hear what they want to hear sometimes, don't they?'

'My clients always want to hear "not guilty".'

'There was nothing in writing from Tina, either. The judge put some weight on that. No letter from her company saying, you know, "Thanks for the meeting, Oliver, just confirming that the bank will be extending our loan period for another two years, restructuring payments, etc.", that kind of thing.'

Tanner shrugged. 'She's a property developer, not a lawyer. That's the sort of letter we'd write. Normal people don't act the way lawyers or some judges think they should.'

'Maybe. It was a pretty big development and a pretty big loan, though.'

'Tina's told me that she and Randall were kind of close at first. She had a tight relationship with her banker at Nipori, and the same with Randall. Did she say that?'

Faulkner shook his head. 'By the time Tina instructed us on this case, she hated him. Sorry – I know that's probably not what you want to hear in the current circumstances. It was – I'm not sure how to describe it. A very bad marriage break-up.'

'Their relationship. It wasn't more than professional, was it?'

Faulkner shrugged. 'Tina certainly never said anything like that. All I can tell you is that – well, sorry, but it was hatred.'

'Long time to keep hating someone, Terrance. Nearly six years. Especially given he got sent to the can.'

'It was visceral.'

'Tina's ex-husband,' Tanner said, 'he swore an affidavit supporting her version, which I assume you or one of your team would have drafted with him, then he doesn't turn up for court. What happened?'

Faulkner put his elbows on the desk, his hands together and chin resting on them, and leant forward conspiratorially. 'He did a deal with the bank.'

'A deal?'

Faulkner nodded.

'That sounds illegal.'

'Nothing we'd ever be able to prove.'

'What do you mean?'

'Part of the bank's security portfolio for the company loans included the family home and personal guarantees. Tina and Adrian had a lovely place at Lurline Bay. A huge pile on the edge of the cliff overlooking the ocean. The bank sold it up, but he kept quite a lot of the equity.'

'How?'

'He had his own lawyers by then. He alleged SEBC and Tina had misled him about the extent of the company's loans, that he would have taken steps to have his guarantee cancelled or his share in the house quarantined if he'd known the true position. It was the exact mirror of the stay-at-home-wife defence, who's signed a mortgage for her husband's business. Adrian walked away with over four million. I think the house sold for eight-point-five.'

'How did he pull that off?'

'You'd have to ask him.'

'Would he talk to me?'

'I really doubt it, Peter. Why are you asking me all this, anyway? Are you trying to prove Tina wouldn't have had a motive to kill Randall? I don't –'

Tanner laughed. 'She had motive,' he said. 'I'm just trying to find out if she's a liar by craft. That'll help me provide her with the best possible defence. I also like to know everything. I am time costing for my fees, so it suits me to take a meditational, detailed and painstaking approach to my client's not guilty plea.'

Faulkner half smiled, nodded, looked at his watch.

'You don't have any documents?' Tanner asked.

Faulkner shook his head.

'None you might have kept on your computer system?'

Faulkner sighed. 'I could look for you. This file was closed several years ago. We may have something still on the claim of bad faith sale – an opinion on prospects, maybe.'

'Do you recall what the nub of the opinion was?'

'Guarded,' Faulkner said quickly. 'Proving sale at undervalue is very hard – we had to show lack of good faith. We had expert valuers who said the bank sold the development for a fraction of what it was really worth, but the sale was public tender, so that made winning the case hard.'

'What was his name – the valuer?'

Faulkner turned up his hands, not quite in exasperation, but heading there. 'I can't remember that. I can find out. Perhaps your client remembers? Tina might also have some documents you might be interested in?'

'I don't like the client necessarily knowing everything I'm doing, Terrance.'

'The pollution report was the killer,' Faulkner said. 'When SEBC took over the Limani site, they commissioned a firm to test soils and the water – the sediments of the harbour – where the marina was going. They said they had to disclose that report to the tender market. It indicated a big clean-up bill would be required. That really depressed the sale price.'

'Tina says that turned out to be bullshit.'

'Well, if it was, it was too late for our case.'

'This crowd Lovro that bought the land – Tina says they're a huge client of SEBC. Did that strike you as strange?'

Faulkner shook his head. 'Banks have relationships with a lot of big companies, and vice versa. We couldn't make anything of that.'

Tanner nodded, closed the notebook he had with him. 'Any papers you can find – I'd appreciate seeing them.'

'I'm getting regular calls about this, you know?'

'About Tina?'

'Absolutely about her – every court and crime reporter in town has put in a call to me since she was charged, to try to get a quote about the litigation she was involved in with SEBC. The police served a warrant for the papers – but I think they were able to get them all from the bank and the court archives anyway. Someone rang me before all this, though. She came here to interview me.'

'Before Tina was charged?'

Faulkner nodded. 'I'm not even sure Randall was out of prison. I think she mentioned she was going to talk to him.'

'Who are you talking about?'

'Someone from an online thing – *The Daily Informant*? It's got a magazine that comes out from time to time as well.'

Tanner nodded. He'd heard of it, and had occasionally bought the magazine if the cover took him. 'What was her name?'

'Roth,' Faulkner said. 'I've just got a mental blank on her first name.'

'And she was asking you what?'

'What you are – was Tina telling the truth? Were Randall and the bank lying? – that kind of thing. It was a very different conversation from the one we're having, though, from my end.'

'How so?'

Faulkner looked at him like he was stupid. 'Peter, you're acting for Tina on a murder charge. I've made the assumption, which I think would be more than reasonable, that she's happy for me to talk frankly about all aspects of the work we did for her that I can recall. I didn't make that assumption with a member of the press. I confirmed what was on the public record, no more.'

Tanner nodded slowly. 'Why was she asking you this, though? What was she investigating?'

'She said her magazine was doing a piece on banking practices. She said she thought the downfall of Leonard Developments was an interesting case.'

'Did you see the article?'

'If what she was working on has been published, I missed it.'

Tanner scribbled in the small notebook he'd bought with him, and underlined 'Roth' and 'Daily Informant' as things to follow up. 'You had other things you needed to prove,' he said. 'Part of the case was also showing that she could have saved the company if the bank had let her know they were going to pull the pin?'

Faulkner shook his head. 'Part of our damages case. We scrambled around for evidence on that. Foreign lenders, second and third tier. Tried to get some of the bigger developers to say they might have gone into a joint venture with her. No one really wanted to give evidence against SEBC.'

'You could have asked Randall about his coke habit.'

'Well,' Faulkner said, smiling, standing, 'it would have been nice to have known that at the time. We didn't.'

'Was Tina able to pay all your legal fees?'

'Not all at first. We acted for her on her claim for her father's will. She paid us what was still owing then.'

'Honourable.'

'She came to us first when she was charged. I told her she needed criminal specialists.'

'I like commercial lawyers who know their place.'

'I think she knew we weren't right for the job. Like most of our clients, she's very loyal.'

Tanner stood to leave. 'At last we've found one thing your clients and mine have in common.'

12

A woman opened the door to let Tanner in. He knew she wasn't family, and she wore the bored disposition of domestic staff who've been inconvenienced by having to get the door for a guest. She gestured with her hand for him to head down the hallway. It was long enough to host the Olympic sprint final. Somewhere at its end, through the glass, was Sydney Harbour. Mosaic-tiled swimming pool out the back metres from the water. A jetty, substantial boat moored next to it. A large number of salons, bedrooms, bathrooms. Chef's kitchen, the German economy boosted by its various machines, and the eight-car garage underneath them.

Alejandro Alvares was in a 'media' room with his two youngest children. A technician was setting up a new TV. It was curved, sleek, and the size of a cinema screen. The woman failed to announce Tanner's appearance, and Alvares failed to acknowledge it. He had his eyes on the television, listening to the instructions of the man showing him the range of remote control options.

'Hello, Alejandro,' Tanner said.

One of the children, a pretty, plump, dark-haired boy, maybe twelve or thirteen, with rings under his eyes, gave Tanner a desultory look, but his father didn't move. 'I'll be with you in a moment, Peter,' he said.

A few minutes later, Alvares stood and approached Tanner. Tanner was about to hold out his hand, but Alvares walked past him, saying, 'Let's go out on the patio, it's a lovely day.' He continued towards some French doors that lead to a back verandah. He stopped in the doorway, and looked in the direction of the woman, who was about ten metres away in the kitchen, putting something on one side of the fridge. He said only one word to her: 'Coffee.'

They sat at a small table at one end of the patio, overlooking the pool, the city sparkling under the sun in the far distance. Alvares knew what this city had to offer, and he'd taken it. It'd always been generous to the biggest kind of crook. His seat was partly in the sun, and it caught his hair. If Tanner had had a fourteen-year-old daughter, he guessed she would crave for such a sheen, such a rich brown. If anything it was longer than before. As gorgeous as it was, Alvares had now breached the boundary of what a man of middle age could get away with. As Alvares looked over his domain, the wind picked up, and the branches and leaves of the trees suddenly shook, as if sensing their master's presence.

Tanner had twice before sat on the same back patio, in the same chair, discussing legal matters. His client was a property developer. He was also the head of a drug syndicate, but more removed from day-to-day operations than in his other business.

'How's Tomas?' Tanner asked when the trees froze back into place.

Alvares continued looking ahead for a few moments. Tomas was his nephew, in jail for two more years on a four-year stint that Tanner felt would have been double, but for him. 'You're not really interested in how he is, are you, Peter?' Alvares said.

'Not really,' Tanner replied. There were times when it paid to be honest with Alvares, times when it didn't. It was an art to judge. 'I thought it polite to ask.'

'Will your client be paying for us to chat about my nephew's well-being?'

'I'm not on the clock, Alejandro. It's a lovely Saturday afternoon. Who works on such a day?'

There was a kind of vague smile on Alvares's face, but he said nothing.

'Do you know anything about someone called Oliver Randall?' Tanner said, getting to the point.

Alvares's expression didn't change, and he said nothing.

'He did five and a half years for possessing six kilos of coke. He made a sale to an undercover cop, they got a warrant afterwards.'

'How negligent,' Alvares said.

'He got parole last year, which was bad luck for him, because someone shot him in the head at close range not long after. They shot him in the knees too. Have you heard of him?'

'Why would I know of this man, Peter?'

'I didn't mean personally, Alejandro. You read the papers, don't you? I know you watch TV.'

'I am certain I didn't know him.'

'He was some big-shot banker. Large commercial loans – building and construction, infrastructure, that kind of scale. How does a guy like that end up with six kilos of coke?'

'I'm not very interested in this conversation.'

'Could you find out?'

Alvares turned his head quickly from the harbour to Tanner. 'How would I know where someone gets that amount of cocaine from, Peter?'

Tanner wanted to laugh out loud. The trees rustled in the warm breeze again, in on the joke. 'He claimed he was innocent at first. Agreed he sold a social amount to the cop, said the six k's were planted. A little bit guilty, a lot innocent. Just like the story Tomas sold me. Maybe he knows about Randall. Perhaps I'll ask him?'

'Whatever debt you thought I owed you, Peter, I more than made it up to you last year.'

'You were generous,' Tanner said. 'We're all square. I'm just looking for some help. I'm acting for Tina Leonard. She's the woman who's meant to have arranged the hit on Randall. You must know of her. Probably her father too when he was alive.

Ioannidis & Sons? I'm sure you've been following her problems with interest.'

The woman came out with the coffees. Both black, a small jug of milk and sugar on the tray, two glasses of water with ice. Alvares said nothing until she'd left.

'Is she an undercover Fed, Alejandro?' Tanner said.

Alvares glared at Tanner for a moment, dropped a sugar cube in his black coffee, stirred slowly. 'I knew Achilles Ioannidis,' Alvares said. 'Big Al. His English was –' He searched for the right word. 'Our conversations were brief. I don't care for his sons. They are –' Once again Alvares searched for the right words, again gave up. 'Tina has charm, style. She's a good architect. It showed in some of her developments. But she bit off more than she could chew.'

'You mean Limani Views?'

Alvares shook his head. 'Not just that,' he said. 'She had too many projects at once.'

'She wasn't the only person who didn't see the GFC coming.'

Alvares laughed lightly, almost to himself. 'The GFC didn't finish her, Peter. Debt did. Over extension. Flying too high, too soon. Limani Views was a project only a much bigger company could manage and carry through.'

'Tina says her bank screwed her.'

Alvares raised his eyebrows, a grand gesture for him. 'She wasn't the only one,' he said.

'No?'

'They did the same thing to a friend of mine.'

'What thing?'

'I had a friend in Melbourne who was told he'd be given time to refinance a residential project after SEBC took over his loans. They gave him a month. This is nearly a year before they cut off Tina's head.'

'Did he sue them?'

Alvares shook his head. 'I bought the development from him myself. I saved his company personally.'

'I always took you for a knight in shining armour, Alejandro.

A real conquistador. How did you come through the GFC so well? Diversification?'

Alvares sighed slowly. 'By living within my means.'

Tanner laughed, gestured to the house and its surrounds. 'Of course,' he said. 'Can I talk to your friend?'

'No,' Alvares said.

'I only want to ask him about SEBC, nothing more.'

'He's dead. Bowel cancer. I'm sure it was the stress. They should be charged with something.'

Tanner shook his head, made a note to follow the matter up later with Alvares. 'I'm a socialist, Alejandro. I'd nationalise the banks if I was running the place.'

'It's a good thing you're not,' Alvares said. 'It's strange, you telling me of your aversion to private enterprise and the market. I don't recall you charging me like a socialist.'

'The spirit is willing but the flesh is weak. Brian Crawford, Alejandro. Does that name mean anything to you?'

Alvares shook his head almost imperceptibly.

'Top echelon of the Drug Squad when Randall was fixed up. Made the arrest in Randall's home. You don't know of any person or any group that had a cosier relationship than they should have with someone in such a position?'

Alvares looked at his watch. Patek Philippe told him it was nearly noon. 'Good luck with your trial, Peter. I wish Tina well. I'm sure the case against her is some hideous misunderstanding.'

'Oliver Randall, Alejandro,' Tanner said, standing. 'If you were to hear where that six kilos came from – if, for example, it was sourced by a certain cop, and paid for by a certain bank, or who knows? – could you let me know if information like that came your way?'

Alvares stood, looked at the water. 'Do I look like your investigator?'

'You're a much more attractive man than him.'

'Do you think I know where every illegal substance in this town comes from?'

'Six kilos? If it went to a cop? I think someone must know.'

'I lack your curiosity for such things.'

'Tina might be innocent, Alejandro. You want to see justice done, don't you? The innocent acquitted, the guilty punished?'

'Perhaps you should look in other places,' Alvares said as he stretched.

'You're offering me strategic advice for the defence?'

Alvares shrugged. 'Lovro Constructions got an amazing bargain for Tina's land.'

'So she says. What are you telling me?'

'Nothing but that. I assume you've researched about the company? Luka Ravic?'

'I'm getting there. He's the owner, right? You have a view about him?'

'Do your homework, Peter.'

'Is Ravic friend or foe to you?'

Alvares smiled. 'Do you like nice things, Peter? Nice buildings?'

'What's that mean?'

'Have a look around town at Lovro's buildings. The residential projects. The man is – no prison sentence is long enough.'

'Is this professional jealousy, or something personal?'

Alvares glared at him as he stood. 'Good luck with your trial,' he said finally, walking off. 'I know you can see yourself out.'

13

Rachel Roth dumped her bag at the foot of the barstool next to Tanner and sat down. She'd agreed to meet him at a pub in Surry Hills near her office. The description he'd given of himself was obviously accurate enough.

She shook his hand. Not much of a smile. She had deep auburn hair, skin made for a cold climate. Australia had sprinkled freckles across her nose. Jeans, a shamrock blouse that went with the eyes. She was slight enough that he immediately wanted to suggest food. He suggested beer instead.

'I subscribed,' he said.

She nodded, nearly smiled, nearly didn't.

'To the magazine as well as online.' When he'd rung to talk to her, she said she was busy. When he pushed, she told him he'd have to buy a subscription to *The Daily Informant*. 'If tonight goes well I'll buy one of your coffee mugs too,' he said.

Roth glared, said nothing. Some people just don't like lawyers. They don't know what they're missing.

'You don't look pleased to meet me.'

She dropped her guard for a moment. 'Long day,' she said. 'My dog just died. I've – yeah, I missed him today.'

'I'm sorry to hear that. I'm a dog person. What kind was it?'

'A small mix of many things. Some kind of terrier won out.'

'We've got a Cairn Terrier at home. She looks like Toto.

From *The Wizard of Oz*? She's the love of my life. What happened?'

'Natural causes,' she said softly. 'We covered the trial you did last year,' she then said as her beer was put in front of her. 'Justin Matheson?'

He nodded. Tanner had won Matheson an acquittal on a murder charge. He was innocent of that crime, guilty of others more moral than statutory.

'We also tried to speak to your friend who had those problems in China.'

'Did he speak to you?'

'It was a short and unilluminating conversation.'

'Joe values his life and mine.' Joe Cheung was a lawyer who'd been 'detained' in China for most of the previous year on a corruption charge. That turned out to be a huge misunderstanding when Tanner both threatened and preserved the interests of some powerful people in a mining giant, and parlayed that into Joe's early return home.

She sipped her ale, looked at the board behind the bar listing the various beers. 'We would love to know why the Chinese released him.'

'You can ask them,' he said. 'Be prepared for it to take a few decades to get hold of the right person.'

'Maybe you can tell me?'

'Joe was innocent. The Chinese worked that out. They're very clever.'

'Perhaps you could tell me more than that?'

'I think I was appointed a special advisor to the Chinese Government at some stage. I don't think I can ethically say any more. You could try his Chinese lawyer.'

'We did.'

'How is Yinshi?'

'He can say the words "no comment" in fluent English.'

'Investigative journalism might die in the West before it catches on in China. He was probably confused about your function. You like this beer?'

'It's okay,' she said. 'You had a meeting with people from Citadel Mining while you were in China?'

Tanner glared at her, took a long draw of his beer. 'Is this a quid pro quo exercise? I get something if I give you a gift first?'

She tilted her head, glared back.

'I'm meant to be asking you questions.'

'I ask questions for a living.'

'So do I.'

'My job is to expose things,' she said, 'not conceal them.'

'That's a cynical view of the role of defence counsel in the criminal justice system.'

She smiled faintly, perhaps smugly. 'You're out to expose the truth, are you?'

'That depends what the truth is.'

'What's the truth about Tina Leonard?' she said. 'It doesn't look that good for her, from what I've read in the papers.'

'Journalists tend to focus on the prosecution's strengths. Like the evidence, for example.'

'You don't focus on the evidence?'

'I focus on the defence.'

'Which is?'

'A work in progress.'

'And you think I can help you?'

'Can you?'

'No.'

'That sounds prematurely definitive,' he said.

She shrugged, and downed a third of her beer in one swig.

'You seem interested in my client,' he said. 'You paid a visit to the lawyer who acted for her against SEBC in the case that involved the deceased.'

'That's got nothing to do with your case,' she said flatly.

'Of course it has.'

She paused. 'There was no deceased at the time.'

'Why were you interested in Leonard's case from six years ago?'

She shook her head like the answer didn't matter. 'I was doing an article on banks,' she said.

'What kind of article?'

'On how some of them operate.'

'They lend money. They expect to get it back with interest. They ruin lives, communities and civilisation in between. How else do they operate?'

She looked at him and smiled, no friendliness in it. 'Do you breach your clients' confidences?'

'All the time. Who's your client?'

'I was making a more general point about confidentiality. The confidence belongs to *The Daily Informant*, our company.'

'Did it publish this article?'

She took another long sip of beer, sighed, turned her head to look at him squarely. 'Why would I talk to you? What's in it for us?'

'You might end up helping an innocent woman who's been wrongly charged with murder.'

She smiled, like he'd amused her slightly. 'Is she innocent?'

'Until she's proven guilty beyond reasonable doubt.'

'That's not really good enough for me. You must have an opinion?'

'I'm a defence counsel, not a juror.'

'You don't have an opinion about whether your clients are guilty or innocent?'

'None that matters.'

She shook her head, drank more beer. He ordered another two. 'Nothing I've been working on is going to help your client.'

'I'd like to be the judge of that,' he said. 'What's so interesting about SEBC?'

'It's interesting because it's a bank,' she said.

'And Tina Leonard?'

'She said they'd deceived her. She wasn't the only one.'

'Who else?'

She smiled at him, not opening her mouth. 'Do your own homework.'

'Would any of them want to kill Oliver Randall?'

She laughed lightly. 'None more so than your client.'

'That's not helpful.'

'What do you expect for two beers?'

'You want more? I'm hungry. I could buy you dinner.'

'No,' she said firmly. 'I've been working on something for a long time. I'm not blowing my research on you.'

'Someone's life is at stake.'

She burst out laughing, this time a girl's laugh. 'Are you going to get down on your knees, clasp your hands and beg? You're good at melodrama.'

'I was being serious,' he said.

She smiled, leant in close to his ear. 'I don't care,' she whispered. Her voice was gravel, coated with molasses, tinged with craft beer, finished with chilli. She leant away from him, still with a smile on her face.

'Maybe we can reach a deal?' he said. 'Tell me what you know, I'll stay quiet until trial, or until your article's published. You must be going to print soon?'

She laughed again. 'Do you want to draw up a contract now? You do it, you're the lawyer. Let's use a napkin.'

'Does your amusement imply you don't trust me?'

'Yes. I don't trust you.'

'You're quick to judge. I'm a person of good character. A wide range of villains and psychopaths can vouch for me.'

'Lisa Ilves told me not to trust you,' she said. She raised an eyebrow at him like it was a weapon being armed.

The mention of Lisa Ilves set him back. He took a long sip of beer to recover. Lisa Ilves had helped him secure Joe Cheung's release the year before. Her reward was betrayal.

'How is she?' he said.

'Good. She's met a great guy. He's a TV producer at the ABC.'

It could have been worse, Tanner thought. He could have been a producer at one of the commercial networks. He nodded, and Ray Roth smiled at him. She was enjoying this.

'How do you know her?' he asked.

Roth shrugged like it was obvious. 'She's a class-action specialist. We've used her to help us understand a few of the cases she's had, or other firms have had, that are newsworthy. At least worthy of us. She's great for off-the-record comments about cases and other legal stuff.'

'What were her off-the-record comments about me?'

She laughed. '"Ray, don't trust him."'

'How did I come up?'

She looked at him like he was an idiot. 'We know about you and Lisa.'

'What do you know?'

She smiled, something approaching evil, and drained the last of her second beer. He wondered how much Lisa would have said. Not enough to put him or Joe in danger, he thought, but probably enough to ensure Rachel Roth's strong disapproval.

'Got to go,' she said. 'Thanks for the beers.'

'If I find out something,' he said as she picked up her bag, 'can I run it by you? Confidentially. Maybe we can share stuff?'

She shook her head, and turned to leave.

'I've got a good network of people who can find things out. Some of them are even out of prison.'

She turned back, swinging her hair around. 'I'll take my chances,' she said.

14

Tanner saw Linda Greig the following evening. Even without any particular new trauma, he knew there were ancient mechanisms of his male brain that benefited from regular examination, and had decided to follow her advice to see her at least fortnightly for the foreseeable future.

'Hit anyone with a cricket bat since we last talked, Pete?' she asked when they'd taken their seats.

'No.'

'Any thoughts about hitting anyone?'

'Not every day.'

'Any remorse for your actions?'

'For a thousand of them. Not that one.'

He'd discussed remorse many times with Linda Greig. He had a desire to go back in time, repeat his life without the screw-ups. He'd stop his father from committing a crime. Stop his mother drinking. Get Karen to have a brain scan when her tumour was two cells into it. Greig explained that this kind of thinking was common in people who'd suffered loss, but self-defeating. It was avoidance. He didn't care. He wanted to find a way to go back. Some of his clients suffered from the same hopeless yearning. For others, a biological and environmental conspiracy laid out its red carpet to their crimes.

'How's Dan?' she asked.

'Clever. Personality both dulled and electrified by hormones. He's got a girlfriend now. I haven't met her. They text and snapchat with some frequency. He "likes" her Instagram posts.'

'Do you want to talk about that today?'

When they weren't talking about grief and anger management, or avoidance, they spent a lot of time talking about cognitive dissonance mixed with single parenting . He wasn't showing the boy leadership. He hadn't shown him what a loving relationship looks like with a partner. And his job provided unique complexities – adolescents find defending people charged with heinous crime a hard thing to wrap their heads around.

'Still the same things setting you off, or anything new?'

He shook his head. The same stuff made him angry. The things his clients did. The things that had been done to them. The dystopian nature of many of his clients' lives, brought to them courtesy of – who? Well, that depended on how you viewed the world, and from which side.

'Have you felt in more control since I last saw you?' Greig said. 'Since the incident with the bat?'

He shrugged. 'I'm busy. That makes me take control. Perhaps it's an illusion.'

'Busy with what?'

'Murder. Not one I committed.'

'Busy might keep you from spiralling down to the bottom, Pete. It's not the answer.'

Tanner wasn't sure he'd ever spiralled to the bottom. What does the bottom look like? How does it feel? Like when his father went to prison? When he could no longer pretend that his mother wasn't drinking herself into the grave? When Karen died? He'd felt disconnected from the world at those times, but found a way to function. He wondered if he was too selfish to be completely overwhelmed by something. If Dan had died, not Karen, would that have been worse? What a question that was. Still, he'd asked it. That awful question had run through his head like news ticker. He declined to answer.

The anger was in his bones. He put on a mask to hide it, put on a wig and gown. He walked into courtrooms, and the competition started, and he forgot about the anger for a while.

The answer, according to Linda Greig, was to let the anger go, but not by venting it. 'You can control it, Pete,' she'd said a hundred times. 'Do you want to?' Sometimes with Greig he felt they travelled in circles; returned to the same spot.

'Your murder case,' she asked him, 'who's it involve?'

'No one you know personally, I'm sure.'

'You never know.'

'Your clients have that much anger, do they?'

'I can't discuss my other clients.'

'My client is a property developer who is charged with killing her banker.'

She smiled. 'Something tells me you'll find a way of suggesting those facts alone should amount to a defence.'

'That might be all I have.'

'I hope you win,' she said. 'I know the case you're talking about, by the way. You'll be a media star again, like last year.'

'I'm going to give my final address via a series of tweets. It'll become the post-modern approach to litigation.'

She'd told him many times to take a year off work. There was always one more important case getting in the way of that, though. She'd told him that he carried his anger around in his bag; the barrister's bag that he took to court containing his robes and books.

'No,' he'd told her. 'I carry my sins in that bag. It's already full.'

15

Legal contests can slide, if the players let them. For a criminal trial, last moment is a place founded on desperation; where rash decisions are made; errors compounded. Last moment in murder trials usually ends after thirty years. Tina Leonard had been committed for trial the previous October. It was now only eight weeks away. Some people might think that a long time to prepare. Tanner knew how fast the clock was ticking.

When Tom Cable walked into Tanner's room, he went straight to the bar fridge and took out a Coke. 'Okay?' he said, holding the bottle up.

'I only stock them for you,' Tanner said.

Cable took a sip and sat down. He looked around the room. 'You ever going to renovate, Pete? It's not the image I'd expect if I was one of your clients.'

Most of the other barristers in his chambers had modernised their rooms, filled them with expensive joinery, glass, modern art, vases of flowers, computer nooks separate from the main desk, high-tech lighting. The décor in Tanner's room eschewed such excesses. Agents from the KGB would have felt at home there.

'You were one of my clients.'

'This room doesn't signal "success".'

'Three years for a lifetime of thieving is a success in my book.'

'I wasn't charged with a lifetime's worth.'

'Most of my clients don't care about the appointments of my room. They're not necessarily the sort of people I'd listen to on issues concerning the philosophy of design.'

'It's too dark in here,' Cable said. 'Speaking of clients, this case is obviously not legal aid?'

Tanner shook his head. 'The aim is to secure an acquittal, while ensuring the client can look forward to a life of poverty. It's a close relative of all litigators' business plans.'

Kit Gallagher and Jenny Singh arrived not long after four. The purpose of the meeting was to discuss the defence case theory for the trial. Based on the committal transcript, it had been limited to attacking the prosecution witnesses. Jayden Webb, the hitman, was, after all, a murderer. Mick Bitar had so far stopped short of that crime, at least as far as anyone had been able to prove. The trial would have to involve more than an attack on their credibility, though. Any lawyer would be able to point out to a jury the records of the State's witnesses.

'We know from Alan Murdoch that Randall told him that the drugs he admitted to having were bought by him with the authority of SEBC. He didn't want that out there though.'

'You think they threatened him?' Singh asked.

Tanner shrugged. 'I'm sure the people more senior to him who knew about the bank's style of entertaining clients didn't want that advertised.'

'How high up do these things go?'

'We'll have to find out.'

'Did Alan know why he changed his plea?' Singh asked.

Tanner shook his head.

'Tina's theory – that the cops planted the six kilos – nothing Alan said makes that less likely?'

'I'm saying it's what Randall first told his lawyer, and his lawyer believed him. I'm saying I know this lawyer, and his judgement is good,' Tanner said.

'And it's not a theory, Jenny,' Gallagher said sharply. 'Our client's instructions are that Randall told her that the bank set him up to teach him a lesson.'

Singh had clearly told Gallagher she was leaving for the bar. Tanner wondered if he had a junior now or not.

'What do you want me to do?' Cable asked.

'Look for someone called Brian Crawford.'

'Who is?'

'The head detective involved in Randall's arrest. He's left the Drug Squad. Find him. I'll make my own inquiries too.'

'How does this fit into a case theory?' Gallagher asked. 'What's it got to do with Bitar and Webb?'

'If it's got to do with the victim, it's got to do with them.'

'So what are we running with? Bitar had Randall killed by Webb, not on Tina's orders, but for some reason to do with drugs? Or the bank had him killed? Or the new owner of Limani had him whacked?'

'All of the above for now,' Tanner said. 'And let's not leave out the cops who set him up for his drug bust. Or whoever was supplying him with drugs, or anyone else who was wound up or bankrupted by Randall after the GFC. Randall's wife divorced him. I'll talk to her. If I like her for it, we'll throw her into the mix. Maybe it was Tina's ex-husband. Let's just get all the facts first, then worry about narrowing our focus.'

'There are times with you, Pete, when I can't work out what's serious and what's not,' Singh said.

'Then are you sure you're ready to go to the criminal bar?'

She didn't look like she took kindly to what he said.

'Everything I ask you to do for a criminal case will be serious. A murder trial particularly. Tina's told us there was a conspiracy to ruin her. Randall was part of it, then got stung by it as well. She says because he was greedy. She says he told her all about it. I don't know what the truth is. We run with everything for the time being.'

Attacking a prosecution case was one way of winning a criminal trial. Tanner had succeeded with that kind of approach. He also had former clients doing ten to twenty because that's all the defence had. Telling a jury an alternative story gave you a better chance. It had to be a consistent story, and it had to be plausible. 'Someone else did it' was a kind of alternative story. 'This other guy did it' was a better one if you could make some of the mud stick. Making a case look as complicated as possible sometimes helped too.

Maybe the case was simple. Tina Leonard, who had a motive and wanted revenge, asked Mick Bitar to use the skill she knew he had for violence on Oliver Randall, the man who had ruined her life. When Bitar said no, she found someone else. Webb's services cost her fifty thousand. Tanner's job was to see it didn't cost her thirty years.

'Speaking of truth,' Gallagher said, 'how did the meeting with the journalist go? The one from *The Daily Informant*?'

'I think she knows a lot about SEBC.'

'And?'

'She's not talking.'

'She didn't tell you anything useful?'

'Only that to get something from her we'll have to give something. I'll work on it.'

'Where did you meet?'

'A pub in Surry Hills. Her suggestion, near her office.'

'And you're going to meet with her again?'

'I'll try.'

Singh looked at him and raised one of her eyebrows. 'Are you going to bill us for this?'

'For what?'

'Drinks at the pub with Rachel Roth.'

'Of course,' Tanner said. 'Did Kit make you a partner, Jenny? I thought you were coming to the bar? Doesn't sound like you want this junior brief.'

'That's beneath you, Pete.'

'You don't know me well enough.'

'Can I say something?' Gallagher said. 'Tina's conspiracy sounds out there, but I'm not sure I buy the prosecution's theory on motive. Maybe if Tina had Randall killed straight after she lost the trial with the bank I might, but why all these years later? Randall got more than five years' jail. Isn't that enough revenge for Tina?'

Tanner shrugged. 'I've acted for people who exacted violent revenge decades after a slight. Jail for Randall wasn't personal revenge for Tina.'

'Can I ask something?' Tom Cable said. 'My only job for now is to find out where this Brian Crawford is? The ex-drug cop?'

'I'll send you a note with a few more things I want checked on Mick Bitar. Tina's brothers gave statements to the police. That makes me instantly not trust them. I'm going to need some proper mud to throw if Tina's theories are going to make it into a courtroom.'

16

'I don't want to be seen with you, Tanner.'

'Can't colleagues share a friendly drink?'

There was a short pause before Detective Sergeant Mark Woods replied. 'We're not colleagues. What do you want?'

'A few minutes of your time.'

'I'm busy.'

'How about I pay you a short visit at home? Where do you live?'

'I live outside your jurisdiction.'

'I've done trials everywhere, Mark. There's no such place. Where do you live?'

Another pause. 'Woolooware.'

'Where's that?'

A snort of derision. 'South. Honest cops can't afford the Eastern Suburbs or Mosman.'

'Neither can criminal lawyers,' Tanner said. 'Woolooware's not south of the Sutherland Local Court, I hope?'

'It is.'

'Further south than the Sutherland Courthouse is Antarctica.'

'Fuck you.'

They met a few hours later in the sports bar of a pub near North Cronulla Beach. It was twilight, still warm, wispy clouds hanging lazily in the eastern sky, pale orange but thinking about grey. Friday evening, crowded beach, good surf. Kids wading with parents, plenty of boards further out.

The bar was packed, but Tanner saw Woods as soon as he walked in. He was sitting on a stool by a small table, watching a replay of a game of rugby league from the previous season on a big TV screen, no drink yet. Tanner ordered two schooners from a young woman who had a tattoo running down her left forearm and a lot of metal in her face. When he put one of the beers on the table in front of him, Woods glanced at him and then the drink, before turning his gaze back to the TV without saying a word.

'Primitive game,' Tanner said.

Woods picked up the beer, sipped.

'I always feel like I'm watching prospective clients. Is that elitist of me?'

Woods shook his head, looked at him. He was in casuals, blue jeans, white T-shirt, solid biceps on display, thick athlete's veins in his forearms. 'What's your game, Tanner? Croquet?'

'Cross-examining liars. I have a low handicap.'

'I'd hate to be your kid.'

'He's taken up Australian Rules football. I enjoy it. In some matches the rules seem to apply, in others they don't. As a lawyer, I find that interesting.'

Woods drank more beer, turned back to the screen.

'How was the wine?' Tanner asked. Late the previous year he'd sent Woods a box of wine for assistance he'd provided in a murder trial and a misunderstanding in China.

'You shouldn't have sent it to work.'

'I couldn't afford a courier to Woolooware.'

Woods shook his head. 'What do you want?'

'Brian Crawford. Ex-Drug Squad. Left about five years ago. You know him?'

Woods sipped his beer, right bicep bulging under its weight, looked at the men on the TV. 'Why?' he said.

'Don't be like that, detective.'

Woods shrugged. 'More know of him.'

'Is he a crook?'

Woods furrowed his brow, almost smiled. 'Are you wearing a wire?'

Tanner laughed. 'Not common attire for defence counsel, mate.'

'I'd put nothing past you,' Woods said. 'I'd only been in Drugs for a year or so when he left.'

'He was one of the head guys?'

'Senior Sergeant, if that's what you mean. He wasn't the Super.' Woods picked his glass up, drew on the beer slowly. 'Why are you asking me?'

'You remember Oliver Randall? A banker at SEBC? Six one-kilo packages found in his home in Bellevue Hill. Long way north of here, Bellevue Hill. Full of corporate crooks. I pay private school kids to letterbox my business cards there and the surrounding suburbs. I think a couple of the cocaine cartels do the same thing.'

'I don't know anything that can help you.'

'Randall did five years in Long Bay because someone fixed him up, then got shot as soon as he made parole.'

'Shot on the orders of your client. And who said he was fixed up?'

'He did.'

'Don't all your guilty clients tell you they're innocent?'

'I've learnt not to believe everything I hear.'

'You really think Tina Leonard's not guilty?'

Tanner picked up his beer, and put on a look of mock outrage. 'Detective, what kind of question is that?'

'One between colleagues.'

'But we're friends, Mark. Not colleagues.'

'What do you want?'

'Do you know anything about Randall's arrest? Was Crawford involved in a way he shouldn't have been?'

Woods shook his head. 'I'd only just come across from the Gang Squad when Randall was arrested. Nothing to do with me.'

'That's not an answer. Do you have something you want to confess, detective? You look like you do.'

'You're not my priest.'

'I charge more. Do you go to church?'

'Yes.'

'And you pray?'

'Yes.'

'What for?'

'For the souls of people like you.'

Tanner laughed. 'My client says Oliver Randall found Jesus in prison. It's why he was thinking on past sins and spilling the beans, then ending up dead.'

Woods rolled his eyes. 'Why are two witnesses saying your client arranged for him to be offed?'

'My client probably wanted him dead. That doesn't mean she arranged to have it happen.' Tanner moved the empty beer glasses to the side of the table, leant closer to Woods. 'Were the drugs planted, Mark?'

'No idea,' he said. 'No one's ever told me that.'

'Randall also told his lawyer that before he changed his plea.'

'You guys are told lies all the time. What's that like?'

'I only care if it's to do with when my bill will be paid.'

Woods stopped himself laughing. 'What's it like to live in a moral vacuum?'

'Not as quiet as you think. Randall sold some coke to an undercover cop. He always admitted that. You know his name?'

Woods smiled ruefully, shook his head. 'Another beer,' he said.

When Tanner came back, Woods said, 'Matt Rajovic.'

'The undercover cop?'

'Loved undercover work.'

'Serb or Croatian?'

Woods shrugged. 'Don't know. Never asked. Why's that matter?'

'It doesn't to me. To them, there's quite a distinction. He was young?'

'My age.'

'But not in your squad now?'

Woods shook his head. 'Left about a year after Crawford.'

'Where?'

'Who knows.'

'What about Crawford?'

Woods paused before answering. 'We weren't friends,' he eventually said. 'He moved into security somewhere. I could tell you for another case of that wine.'

'That information's worth a six pack of beer, detective.'

'Find out yourself, then.'

Tanner shook his head, glared at Woods.

'Where did Randall work?'

'His bank? South-East. SEBC. My client says they stole her land.'

'Where's their HQ?'

Tanner shrugged.

'You might want to look that up if you want to find Brian Crawford.'

'What?' Tanner was silent for several seconds, staring at Woods.

Woods sipped his beer, nodded his head slowly.

'Do you think that's as odd as I do, detective?'

'What is?'

'He busts a senior banker at SEBC, then ends up working for that bank? In – security?'

'It's a strange town we live in, Tanner.'

'What kind of security work? Making sure the other bankers aren't on coke, or making sure they get it?'

'I wouldn't know.'

'How long's he been there?'

Woods shrugged. They sat in silence for a minute, Tanner wondering how far the cop would be willing to go.

'Mark,' he said, 'did – did Crawford ever ask you to do anything – anything that made you feel uncomfortable? Because that was his reputation. Did he do that to any of your colleagues?'

'What would that be?'

'I don't know. I've only known you to commit crimes when innocent people's lives were at stake. Did he have a different way of doing things?'

Woods took a long sip of his beer, and turned back to the rugby league. Tanner waited. 'I dropped some things to Crawford at his home once,' Woods said.

'What things?'

'Doesn't matter.'

'And?'

Woods smiled a sour kind of smile. 'He lived a lot closer to town than I do,' he said. 'In a much bigger house.'

17

Taz Bennett – once Anastasia Ioannidis, younger sister of Tina Leonard – had told Kit Gallagher that it would be more convenient to meet Tanner at her home rather than at his chambers in town. The Bennett house was also the current residence of Tina Leonard as part of her bail agreement. They fixed a time and Leonard was asked to make herself scarce for the hour or so the meeting might take.

Tanner pulled his old Jag up to the kerb in front of a house that matched the address he'd been given. The house was built into the steep hill that rose above Balmoral Beach. It was three storeys high, relatively young, and looked pleased with itself. He buzzed the intercom at the front gate, and was let in by a Filipino woman in her forties. Tanner assumed she was the cleaner. She had a Dyson cordless vacuum in her hand, so he didn't feel he was profiling.

The woman smiled, and showed him into a large foyer, before leading him down a long hallway lined with paintings. He passed a few nudes, too moody to be figurative, before they reached a proud, white, curving staircase. He was politely directed to the lounge room that was opposite it. The room had an L-shaped couch that could sit ten comfortably, over which a light fixture hung that Tanner guessed would have cost upwards of $50K. Outside the windows, at the base of the property, was a long, thin pool, tiled to match the colour of the harbour water below on a sunny day. On one wall facing the TV was a huge photograph of a young girl's face, and on the wall next to the TV was a landscape, mustard with swirling greens and blues.

'Are you a fan?'

He knew the voice belonged to Taz Bennett. She sounded like her sister. He turned and looked. She was taller. She was in sports gear, like she was coming or going to the gym. Grey leggings, powder blue tank top. She had medium-length dark hair, a southern Med tan, dimples when she flashed the smile.

He smiled back, nodded. 'Are the nudes Garry Shead? In the hallway?'

'I love them,' she said, walking into the room, directing him to the couch. 'Sorry about the attire. I've been on the treadmill.'

She shook his hand, and they exchanged first names. There were no signs of perspiration, no flushing of the face. She was natural, no makeup, just lipstick. She dropped down next to him on the couch, a body width between them. 'I'm sorry,' she said, 'would you like a coffee?'

The kitchen was downstairs, the same level as the pool and backyard. Dark wood veneers, marble benches, lots of kit.

'Entertain a lot?' he asked, taking a seat on one of the stools at the island.

She was fiddling with something on the coffee maker. She laughed. 'My husband likes to cook,' she said. 'All this is for him.'

'What's he do?'

She looked away from the coffee machine back to Tanner, a brief puzzled expression. 'He's a Mad Man. Has his own company. Bennett & Cavanagh.'

'Oh,' Tanner said. 'That Bennett.'

She smiled, rolled her eyes playfully, turned back to the machine.

'No milk?' She sat on the stool next to him, bringing two long blacks.

He shook his head. 'Kids at school?'

'Only one's still at school. My daughter. John is twenty. Maria's fifteen.'

'Started young?'

'Thanks, but not really.'

'Where'd you meet – Mr Bennett?'

She picked up her coffee cup, smiled at him over the rim as she sipped. 'Simon. The university bar.'

'And you studied?'

'Interior architecture,' she said. 'Kind of followed Tina, I guess.'

'You're close?'

'She's charged with murder and living with my family. What does that tell you?'

'How's Simon with that?'

'He might never speak to me again.'

'You don't appear upset by that.'

She raised an eyebrow, said nothing.

He took a sip of coffee. It was strong, almost Greek.

'I've seen you on TV,' she said. 'Last year.'

He nodded. 'Did I have my trial face on?'

'What face is that?'

'The face that says it's an outrage my client was charged, and a crime against humanity that they're having to stand trial.'

'Is it?'

'Is it what?'

'Usually a crime against humanity that your client is on trial?'

'Christ, no,' he said.

She shook her head, but still held a wry smile. 'I have no idea how you guys do that.'

'Do what?'

'Defend guilty people.'

'You sound like my fourteen-year-old son. Am I defending a guilty person now, acting for Tina?'

She was leaning towards him, both hands on her cup. She put it down, straightened. 'To the chase, huh?'

'I'm in no rush today,' he said, 'but seeing as you raised it.'

She nodded. 'There's no way my sister is a killer, Peter.'

'You seem certain. Tina doesn't hold grudges? Even against someone whose lies she says ruined her business?'

She shook her head, picked her cup up again. Her face hardened. 'That man did more than ruin her business.'

'I'd better hear this.'

She looked down, and he thought she was considering how much to tell him. Then she said, 'I lied to the police.'

'Don't look at me for disapproval. About what, exactly?'

'When they interviewed me – us – after Tina was arrested, they asked us what Tina thought about Oliver Randall.'

'I've read your statement.'

'She still didn't have him killed.'

'I'm not the police, Taz.'

'He took her dreams,' she said. 'Randall, his bank. That bastard from Lovro Constructions.' She paused, almost lost control of her emotions. 'Sorry. It ripped her apart. She lost her house. Her boys – Alex and Chris – they went with their father. That nearly destroyed her.'

'You're doing a good job of establishing motive, Taz. If Randall wasn't dead, I'd want to kill him.'

'You know what I did when I heard he'd been shot?'

He shook his head.

'I laughed. I laughed and cried. Then I found out Tina –' She stopped, had to compose herself.

'Tina's ex-husband,' Tanner said. 'Would he talk to me?'

'Adrian? Help Tina?' she said, a mocking tone. 'Not a chance.'

'I'd only need him to tell me Randall lied.'

'Would that help Tina? Won't they say that's why she had him killed?'

Tanner shrugged. 'Depends on how the prosecutor plays it. I don't know yet. I'm looking for all the truth I can get. When I have the pieces, I'll start on the puzzle.'

Taz took a sip of coffee, then a deep breath. 'Adrian was told to get his own lawyer,' she said, the heat out of her voice. 'I can't blame him for that.'

'You don't blame him for not giving evidence for Tina? For the company?'

She looked at him, snorted. 'Oh, I blame him. Tina was left with nothing. Not one cent. Do you know what that bank let him have from the sale of their home?'

He nodded.

'Do you know what his defence was, when the bank sued? He said he didn't understand the documents he'd signed. Didn't know he'd guaranteed the company's loans for Limani.'

'I assume he can read and write?'

'Adrian's not a man. He's a weasel.'

'You said you didn't blame him a moment ago?'

She took another deep breath and sighed, calming herself. 'He was able to put a roof over the boys' heads. He at least could do that. Tina couldn't.'

'How did Tina feel about that?'

Her eyes flashed like her sister's. 'She didn't want her children in the gutter with her. How do you think she felt? Could she have killed Oliver Randall at that moment? With her bare hands. I could have too.'

'Don't necessarily expect a summons to give evidence for the defence, Taz.'

She tried to smile. He noticed a few grey roots where her hair was parted. She put her hand up almost instinctively. 'I'm going to my colourist tomorrow. I forgot when we agreed on today. Imagine me after a shower, and with no grey hair.' He smiled. 'Look, Peter, that trial was years ago. She moved on. She didn't have him killed. Listen to her. It was the people who stole Limani from her. They're the ones who wanted Randall shut up. He knew what they'd done.'

'The way SEBC let Tina's ex off the hook . . . that sounds like a bribe. How would he react if I suggested that to him?'

'He won't talk to you.'

'He may have no choice. I can make him come to court, ask him about the bribe there.'

'Tina won't let you do that.'

'Won't let me?'

'He's her sons' father. She won't let you humiliate him. For their sakes.'

'I can see Tina's used to being in charge. Not in this case she's not.'

'She won't let you.'

Tanner finished his coffee, and they sat in silence for a few moments.

'None of this would have happened but for SEBC buying out Tina's old bank. They would have let her finish the project. Nipori would have backed her.'

'Are banks known for that kind of reasonable behaviour?'

'She rang me after her meeting with Randall, Peter. She was under pressure, we talked all the time. She told me he'd agreed to extend her loans, it was all going to be fine. Then they stabbed her in the back. Then he –' She shook her head in disgust, couldn't finish the sentence.

'I haven't asked Tina,' he said. 'How is her relationship – she's still seeing her children?'

Her eyes moistened. 'Alex was about to start his final year exams when his mother was charged with murder. Christos is in year 10. How do you think things are going? Alex is barely talking to her. It's – it is what it is.'

'I'd like them to sit in court during the trial. At least the older boy. Any chance?'

She let out a harsh laugh. 'There is no way Tina would put either of them through that. And there's no way Adrian would allow it.'

'Alex – how old is he?'

'Nineteen.'

'Then he gets to make up his own mind.'

'Don't go there, Peter,' she said firmly. 'You'll just upset Tina.'

He nodded, made a mental note to raise it later with Tina, no matter how much it might upset her. 'Can you tell me anything about Mick Bitar?'

She looked down, almost embarrassed when he said the name. 'Very little,' she said, almost under her breath. 'I never worked for my father, so – I don't know much.' She sighed, forced a smile. 'You want a glass of wine?'

He looked at his watch. 'It's twenty past eleven,' he said. 'I've promised not to drink that early until they make me a judge.'

'It doesn't feel too early to me,' she said softly.

'Something about Mick Bitar makes you need a drink?'

She stood, picked up the coffee cups and put them in the dishwasher. In a nearby room he heard a vacuum being turned on. She opened the fridge, took out a bottle of white wine, poured them each a glass.

'Mick has skills I'm told are useful in the building industry.'

'What kind of skills?'

She glared at him. 'What kind do you think?'

'Tina says he was a thug for hire. He's got a reputation that provides some support for that opinion.'

She shrugged, sipped her wine. 'He deals with subbies. Union officials. Debtors. Creditors. Local Councillors. Planning officials. Politicians.'

'That's a lot of people to have skills with.'

She lifted her gaze from her wine. 'Yes.'

'And Bitar's skills were useful for your father and your brothers?'

Her eyebrows headed for the high moral ground, her chin tilted up too. 'My father started with nothing. He built a great company from nothing.'

'I'm a criminal lawyer, Taz, not a diplomat. Did you socialise with Bitar? Was he a guest at your father's house? Your brothers'?'

'Does that matter?'

He smiled. 'This guy says Tina asked him to kill Randall. It matters enough for me to ask.'

She had more wine, a bigger sip this time. 'A few times,' she said. 'My father liked to entertain. Big barbecues. Lamb and goat on spits, dozens of people. Bitar was sometimes there. I rarely spoke to him. He gave me the creeps.'

'Can you describe him in any way? I'm going to have to cross-examine him and call him a liar. Anything you tell me might help.'

'He's – god, he's a man of Middle Eastern appearance. Is that okay to say?'

'Probably not,' he said. 'I'm familiar with the term, though. The police have a Middle Eastern Crime Squad. I have a cabinet in my chambers labelled "men of Middle Eastern appearance". It's actually labelled MMEA though, to prevent any of my solicitors who are of Middle Eastern appearance from thinking I'm a racist. I also now have a cabinet labelled "racists", who are starting to become a source of work. I have a "white collar businessman" cabinet, a "drug lord" cabinet, and a "sociopath" cabinet. That rounds out my practice.'

She smiled, nearly laughed. 'I'd have thought you'd categorise by the crime committed?'

'I prefer to see my clients as people first, and as violent maniacs second.'

This time she laughed.

'Tell me a bit about your family. Tina says she upset your father before he died. Your brothers too?'

She took some time to consider her answer. 'Daddy was furious at Tina when she left the company to start on her own. He – he never really forgave her. He was so hurt. Theo and Jim pretended to be just as angry, but – I think they were pleased she was out of the way.'

'Why did Tina leave the family business?'

She narrowed her eyes. 'Shouldn't you ask her?'

'Sure. What's your perspective though?'

She nodded. 'Dad was – he – look, he was never going to let her have a third of the say in it. His boys were going to run it when he let go. Christ, he changed the name to Ioannidis & Sons. You know when he did that? The week Tina started to work there. He was – he loved Tina, knew she was the brightest, but –' She paused, searched for the right words. 'He had it in his head, I think, that he was building something for his sons. They came first. They were boys. He never – Tina's ambition caught him by surprise.'

'How do you get on with your brothers?'

She smiled a sad kind of smile. 'They're arseholes. But they're my family. Their kids are my nephews and nieces. They're nicer to me than they were to Tina. I didn't want in.' She looked at her watch for a second time.

'Is my time up? I'm making you late for lunch?'

'Tennis.'

He looked at her empty glass of wine, smiled, stood to leave. 'If I think of something else to ask you, can I give you a call?'

'Come around any time,' she said. 'It's nice to have company in the middle of the day.'

18

Tanner met Kit Gallagher and Jenny Singh in the foyer of the modern tower that was home to the global law firm known as Lattimer & Jones.

Mrs Simone Hargreaves, the former Simone Randall, was unwilling to meet with anyone from the defence team without her lawyers present. That was fair enough – Tanner was surprised she'd agreed to meet the lawyers for the alleged killer of her ex-husband at all. The logistics of the conference had taken over a week to negotiate. Only one time was suitable, and only one place. Two lawyers from Lattimers would be present, one of whom happened to be the former Mrs Randall's second husband, Grant Hargreaves. Counsel had also been retained. No question would be answered without his approval. A list of topics for questions had to be supplied first, and agreed upon. The defence had to meet all of the estimated costs of Mrs Hargreaves' lawyers, which was to be paid up front into Lattimer's trust account.

'What kind of law does the husband do?' Tanner asked as they rode the lift up to Lattimer's reception.

'Tax,' Gallagher said. 'Overseas-based corporates.'

'Interesting choices in husbands,' Tanner said. 'Drug pusher to tax lawyer. She going up or down in the world, do you think?'

First impressions are important. Lattimer & Jones reception informed you that you were at the big end of town. Dark walnut, lighter shades of wood for warmth. Concrete and steel for modernity, strength. Smoke and mirrors. The huge front desk had been assembled from long slats of oak, angled slightly upward from left to right, secured by poles of brass. Above and to the rear of the desk was the firm logo, the letters LJ in backlit swirls of wood. To the right of the desk, over by the floor-to-ceiling windows, were clusters of red and white chairs with curved backs that overlooked the city, the harbour, the world.

They took the window seats the receptionist allocated, and were offered coffee or tea, which they declined. Tanner flicked through a newspaper lying on the low table in front of them. Singh checked her notes. Gallagher fidgeted in her seat.

'These surroundings make you uncomfortable, Kit?' Tanner said, his eyes still on the paper.

'When did the legal profession decide it had to dress itself up like this?' she said, shaking her head.

'Since these guys decided to become part of the bureaucracy.'

'What do you mean?'

'The bureaucracy of the corporates, Kit,' Tanner said. 'The masters these guys serve. The people who run the world. The banks, the big industrials. These guys are their public service.'

Gallagher looked around the space, which was the size of a train station. 'A bit upmarket for the bureaucracy.'

A young woman walked over, asked them to follow her.

'People look down on us criminal lawyers,' Tanner said as he got up, 'including the people who work here. We're what's left of the law as a real profession.'

They were shown into a meeting room big enough to be a boardroom, long table down its spine, ten chairs on either side. Four people were already seated near the middle of the table, their backs to the windows. The former Mrs Simone Randall, and three others. One was introduced as Grant Hargreaves, her current husband. He offered his hand to them, but said nothing. He probably only spoke if $1,500 an hour was already in trust. Once it was, words about minimisation and Panamanian shell companies no doubt flowed freely.

Hargreaves sat three chairs away from his wife. Next to her on her left was someone called Stanovic, a litigation partner in the firm. He was well fed, well dressed. On the other side of the former Mrs Randall was someone called Brent Cooney, a member of the bar with a law degree from Oxford, but a jawline that hadn't developed as fully as his brain, and a faint lisp that would never be suited to addressing twelve members of the community in a criminal trial, who would constantly be second-guessing what the chinless wonder for the accused was saying.

Mrs Simone Hargreaves was in a brilliant white suit, exaggerated lapels on the jacket, which was fastened with a white bow that was tied just above one hip. No shirt, deep tan. Hard to place her age, mid-forties was the logical assumption. Her teeth were as brilliant as the suit. If he had to guess, in no particular order, she'd been buffed, peeled, dermabrased, thermaged, filled, gelled, toxed, and probably enhanced. It sounded like a lot to have done when Tanner ran it through his head, but it was likely no more or less than standard protocol for the ex-wife of a senior banker who's moved on to a leading tax lawyer. There remained, Tanner could see, the remnants of a beautiful woman. Remnants was unfair. It was all there, but in the quest for perpetual youth she was risking altering it in a way that the mere passage of time wouldn't, and probably not for the better.

'I think it's worth going over the ground rules first,' the litigation partner Stanovic said.

'We're aware of the rules,' Tanner said.

Stanovic paused. 'Even so, we want to be clear that Simone won't be answering any personal questions about her marriage to Oliver Randall, about her daughter, or any other question any of us object to.'

'Who's playing judge?'

'I'm sorry?'

'Who's playing judge?' Tanner repeated.

Stanovic smiled faintly. 'We're judge, jury and executioner I'm afraid, Peter.'

'Executioner is a strong word,' Tanner said.

'A figure of speech.'

'I wish a few of my clients hadn't been made to answer some of the questions I'd objected to. They mightn't be sharing studio accommodation with one bathroom if that was the case.'

'We're not in court, Peter,' Stanovic said.

'No,' Tanner said, looking at each of the men briefly. 'This seems like a much friendlier place.'

'We're very grateful for your time, Mrs Hargreaves,' Kit Gallagher butted in. 'We know it's an unusual request.'

'Call me Simone,' she said. Her voice was warm.

'Thank you,' Gallagher said.

'It's not that unusual a request, Kit,' Tanner said. 'Our client says she didn't have Oliver Randall killed. If she's telling the truth, it's worth talking to people who might possibly have an idea of who did.'

'You think I did, Mr Tanner?' Simone said. Vague amusement in the voice. She looked straight at him, head tilted coquettishly. He sensed that she thought she might be raising an eyebrow at him.

'Did you?' Tanner said. 'It would save my client a lot of bother if you say "yes".'

'No,' she said.

Tanner looked at the barrister on her left. 'Just a tip – sorry, I'm no good with names.'

'Brent.'

'Not sure how much criminal work you've done, Brent, but the question I just asked concerning whether your client had her ex-husband bumped off was probably one of the ones you wanted to object to.'

'I didn't view it as a serious question.'

'I was deadly serious. I disguised it by smiling. Did you see your ex-husband when he was in prison, Simone?'

'No,' she said, matter of fact. 'My only contact with him was to have divorce papers served on him.'

'I bet that boosted his morale.'

'I wasn't interested in his morale, Mr Tanner. I was more worried about mine, and my daughter's.'

'Of course. Did you see him after his release?'

'No,' she said, 'I wasn't waiting for him at the prison gates either, and I didn't hold a homecoming party for him.'

'Did he try to see you?'

'Me? No. He tried to see my daughter.'

'His daughter?'

She smiled, put her hand around the glass of water in front of her, turned the glass but didn't pick it up. Her ring finger had the sort of rock on it that only a billionaire or his tax lawyer could buy. 'She was his daughter biologically. That was it. Hannah was very angry at him.'

'Are you – were you still angry at him, when he was released?'

The wan smile again. She'd had a rough time in her life for a while, a shock. She hadn't broken. She'd come out of it knowing what she wanted. 'You do think I had him killed, Mr Tanner, don't you?'

Tanner looked at the barrister Cooney and at Stanovic. 'Can I object to answering that?' he said.

'He tried to ruin my life,' Simone Hargreaves continued. 'He did a better job of ruining our daughter's life. She was a thirteen-year-old schoolgirl when he was convicted. Imagine starting high school with headlines that your father is a drug dealer.'

'Well, to be honest,' Tanner said, 'that's happened to the children of a few of my clients, and some of Kit's. Still, I think they had more of an inkling it was coming than you did.' Tanner picked up his water glass, took a sip. 'Was he, by the way?'

'Was he what?'

'A drug dealer?'

'I don't think that's a relevant question for Mrs Hargreaves,' Brent Cooney said.

'Really?' Tanner said. 'I was just wondering if Simone knew.'

'If I'd known, Mr Tanner,' she said, close to sounding amused, 'I would have been complicit, wouldn't I?'

'You can tell me. I won't tell the police.'

'My late ex-husband was found with six kilograms of cocaine in his study at our home,' she said. 'He tested positive for quite a lot of coke after his arrest. That sounds like a drug dealer to me.'

'And you didn't know about any of that?'

'That's an incredibly offensive question,' Stanovic said, while Cooney and Hargreaves made their own sounds of outrage, and Gallagher muttered something under her breath. The only person who didn't look bothered was the ex-Mrs Randall.

'I'm just fact finding,' Tanner said. 'I'm not making accusations.'

'It sounded like one,' Grant Hargreaves said.

'You tax lawyers obviously have much more sensitive ears than us criminal guys,' Tanner said.

'May I ask you a question, Mrs Hargreaves?' Jenny Singh said. She sounded as cool as the person to whom the question was directed. Tanner looked at Singh in her black pantsuit, then back to Simone. They were like two giant chess pieces. The opposing queens.

'Of course,' Simone Hargreaves said.

'Before his arrest, did your ex-husband strike you as the sort of person who would have six kilos of coke in his study?'

Simone Hargreaves smiled almost pleasantly at Singh. 'He struck me as someone who was a compulsive adulterer, and a pathological liar, and I knew he did more – when he entertained for the bank, I suspected he did more than drink. The police finding a seven-figure sum of cocaine in our house, though – no, that was a surprise.'

'Were you aware he had coke in the house before the morning of his arrest?'

'Again, Mrs Hargreaves is not going to –'

'Not enough for a rock concert, Mr Tanner,' Simone Hargreaves said.

'Were you ever invited to any of the bank's – what's the word? Parties?'

The corners of her mouth turned down a little. 'None that I think Oliver enjoyed.'

'I'm sure you like giving ambiguous answers, Simone,' Tanner said. 'How should I interpret that?'

'That's a very nice watch,' she said, looking at Tanner's wrist.

'It was my father's,' Tanner said.

'Very elegant. Simple. I like the leather band. He gave it to you before he died?'

'He's still going strong. He gave it to me before he went to prison.'

Tanner noticed Mr Hargreaves glaring at his wife over the top of his glasses. Dark clouds were beginning to form on his brow.

'That sounds like an interesting story. What did he do?'

'Cleaned up his partner's mess. Got left with dirty hands.'

There was a long pause before Grant Hargreaves filled the void. 'Are we straying from what's relevant? You're paying for this, Mr Tanner.'

'This is absolutely relevant, Grant,' Tanner said. 'Your wife wants to know if she can trust me. I'm reassuring her by letting her know my father was a fraudster who gave me a 1947 Jaeger-LeCoultre watch that my grandfather gave him. And please, Grant, don't be concerned that I'm paying for anything. Ms Leonard, the accused, is paying for all of this. I'm like you – I'm only in this game for money.'

Hargreaves had only a moment to look offended before his wife said, 'What kind of fraudster?'

'The worst kind if he'd been my client,' Tanner said. 'The largely innocent sort.'

She nodded, and he saw something kind in her face. 'How long did he go to prison?'

'Seven years.'

'How old were you?'

'For god's sake, Simone,' Grant Hargreaves said.

'Fifteen when he was charged. Sixteen when he went away.'

'That's awful.'

'It's not as long as my client is looking at regarding your ex-husband. You were talking about SEBC's client entertainment policies?'

She smiled softly, realised the game part was over. She had big eyes, he noticed, a kind of pool blue. They'd flirted with being green, decided against it. The eyes were all nature's work, he assumed. 'I wasn't invited to the more – the more intimate gatherings.'

'Who was?'

'Oliver's clients. The bank's clients.'

'Who were they?'

'People who borrowed lots of money.'

'Where did these intimate gatherings take place?'

She shrugged. 'The casino here. In Melbourne. If they were big clients, then Vegas, Macau, Atlantic City once. Then there were the sporting junkets – rugby, cricket, soccer, the AFL grand final, tennis in Melbourne. He took a group to a golf tournament once.'

'Did he ever come home with a programme from *King Lear* after one of these events?'

A measured pause, but a smile too. 'No, he didn't.'

'Strange,' Tanner said. '*King Lear* is very bank CEO as a character. What happened on these trips?'

'I didn't ask.'

'Did your husband ever talk to you about SEBC's case against Tina Leonard? He had to give evidence. Tina accused him of lying about an undertaking he'd given concerning a loan.'

'No, he didn't talk to me about it. It wouldn't surprise me though.'

'What wouldn't?'

'Oliver lying.'

'Did he lie to other clients that you knew about?'

'Oliver's whole life turned out to be a lie.'

'Is this getting anywhere?' Stanovic interrupted. 'What's this got to do with the allegations against your client?'

'Do you recall Oliver having to go to court? I mean, before his arrest. For SEBC. Did he say anything about Tina, about the Limani Views development?'

She shrugged. 'We weren't communicating the way a married couple should at that time. I have a vague recollection of Oliver describing it as a pity.'

'What was a pity?'

'Your client's – what's the right word? Downfall. I think he was sorry. Tough world for a woman, he said. Property development, I think he meant.'

'There aren't many women tax attorneys either,' Tanner said.

'I can't think why.'

'Is that all you remember?' he said.

She nodded.

'Could you think about it for me, see if something comes back?'

'Sure,' she said.

Tanner looked at Hargreaves and Stanovic. 'I assume we won't get charged for Simone just thinking about me. I mean – about her late ex-husband?'

Stanovic raised his eyebrows, and was considering an answer when Simone said, 'No, you won't.'

Tanner smiled. 'Can I finish for now by asking – did Oliver ever talk to you about SEBC's buyout of Nipori Bank? Just after the GFC?'

'How could that – ?'

'I only vaguely remember that,' Simone Hargreaves said.

'I know it was a while ago,' Tanner said.

'Oliver and I – I was scared for a while during that period. Oliver – we had a lot of friends in finance at other places who were worried about their jobs.'

'But not Oliver?'

She shook her head. 'SEBC seemed to sail through it.'

'What about Lovro Constructions, Simone? They bought my client's land from SEBC. I'm told at quite a discount. Did Oliver ever say anything about what happened there? There was a tender process. Did he say anything about it?'

'How would Simone know anything about that?' Grant Hargreaves said, doing his best to sound exasperated. The kind of voice he'd put on if the Australian Tax Office ever required one of his foreign-owned clients to pay more than one cent in the dollar.

'Oh, I don't know, Grant,' Tanner said, 'surely you and Simone must have some candlelit dinners or at least pillow talk where the intricacies of our tax code come up?'

Simone Hargreaves stifled a laugh. 'I'll think about it,' she said.

Her husband stood. 'I think we're finished now.'

'You know how to reach me if you remember anything that might help? Like who really killed your husband?' Tanner said.

Against all odds, the eyebrow moved. 'I do,' she said.

'What did we learn from that exercise?' Kit Gallagher asked.

They were in a café in the food court that was in the basement of the tower where Lattimer & Jones had its office.

'I learnt to age gracefully,' Jenny Singh said.

'That's a mean comment,' Tanner said. 'We can't all have your skin.'

'You like that look, Pete?'

'What look?'

'Botox. Surgically modified. Stunt boobs.'

'The nearest Westfield to me is Bondi Junction. Everyone looks like that there.'

'Did she tell us everything she knows?' Gallagher asked.

Tanner shook his head. 'I don't think so. I need a meeting with her when Grant isn't around.'

Gallagher looked at Singh, then back at Tanner and smiled. 'I don't think Mr Hargreaves is going to let you interview his wife on your own, Pete.'

'There's something more she wants to tell me,' Tanner said. 'I can sense it.'

'Sense it only in your head, Pete?' Singh said. There was nothing wrong with her eyebrow movement. The right one moved north by northwest in dramatic fashion.

'What have I done to give you the impression I'm comfortable with you speaking so rudely to me, Jen?'

'Everything,' she said. 'Anything else you sense, Pete? Does she want to elope with you, or just talk?'

'I sense it's unlikely Oliver Randall really had six kilos of coke in his house when he was arrested.'

'Because of what she said?'

'Simone doesn't strike me as the sort of person who would allow six kilos of coke to be in her home with her thirteen-year-old daughter.'

'Maybe she just didn't know?'

'She also strikes me as someone who'd know about it.'

'Why would she know?' Gallagher said.

'Because she was suspicious of everything he was doing. Adulterer. Party boy. That marriage had hit the rocks. She was on to him.'

'How does it help Tina for us to prove Randall wasn't a drug dealer?' Gallagher said.

'It doesn't. But it helps me believe our client when she tells us that Randall told her he was set up. And I want to know exactly what's happened, and why.'

'Since when have you cared about believing the client or not?' Singh asked.

That wasn't a bad question, he thought. Since when?

19

Kit Gallagher called him at about quarter past ten. He was lying on the couch, glass in one hand, tome-like book on his chest. It was raining outside, the sound so loud on the roof that he barely heard the phone. The first downpour he could recall in months, an end of summer release.

'Tina's coming into the office Friday morning.'

'That's nice.'

'Are you okay?'

'I'm fine.'

Gallagher seemed to measure the pause, maybe thought of saying something else, but asked instead, 'Did you have company tonight?'

'Just left,' Tanner said. 'Joe was here with his wife and kids earlier. He cooked dinner for us. Chinese feast. Something he picked up in prison there.'

'How big is the glass you're holding, Pete?'

Tanner paused for an appropriate time to examine his glass. 'You could bathe a jumps jockey in it.'

'That's what I thought.'

'I'm okay.'

'You're sure?'

'Thanks for thinking of me.'

'Right. Well, don't – don't give yourself too much of a hangover.'

'The party here is winding down. I'll see you soon.'

The danger for criminal lawyers is gradually starting to resemble your clients. Kit Gallagher had avoided that. Her heart was still fully intact.

As the call ended, the dog appeared next to his feet. A longing look, then she jumped on the couch, stood and looked at him, slumped down, rested her head on his thigh. Lifted her eyes up, looked at him again. Looked at him like she loved him. He wondered if that was possible. What other word would you give it, if not that?

The dog was one year old when Karen had died. Dan was six. Some people and things keep you going in life. Tanner's parents had been his first foundation. That got busted up. His mother drank herself to death, even if it was called cancer in the end. His father was in prison at the time. Karen was his pillar after that. He'd needed her to be. He focused on his work, relied on her to make the good decisions for their lives. Then she was gone. He needed other people to pull him from the rubble.

He'd had time to think about her death. His world wasn't torn apart in one sentence. He was able to watch it crumble, as she wasted to nothing. The grief still punched him in the face. Eight years later – to the very night – a lot of it was a blur. And some of it was cut into him, like a scar that never fades. Her last hours, when she could only breathe. Seeing her jewellery and clothes in the house. Putting her phone in a drawer. Telling Dan she was not coming home.

Kathleen Gallagher had picked him up. Linda Greig grabbed him too. He could grieve in her room. The space felt enormous to him, the size of a football field. He could cry and shout and swear at all the rotten gods and mortals in that room. She listened to the name of every bastard he could remember.

There were others with special kindnesses. And then there was Daniel. He was Samson. He had the strength he had to pull him from the wreckage.

Tanner looked back down at the dog, contemplated her role in his survival, then heard his phone buzzing again next to the bottle of wine. He picked it up.

'Don't old men need extra sleep, Karl?'

'Sleep is difficult for me now. I've told you. How are you, Peter?'

'Fine.'

'I know this is a difficult day.' His father had always been direct. Not humourless, but something had to be very funny to make him laugh. Not much qualified.

'I'm fine. Joe and Melissa were here earlier.'

'You're slurring, Peter. Have you drunk too much?'

'No, Karl. Have you? You sound a little fresh tonight.'

'I've been to dinner.'

'Who with?'

'My girlfriend.'

Tanner almost cringed. The word 'girlfriend' coming from his father's mouth seemed – there was no English word. Perhaps there was one in Swedish. His fourteen-year-old son had a girlfriend. So did his seventy-five-year-old father. He, however, did not. That possibly explained the half litre of wine in his glass.

'How is she?'

'Well.'

'Where'd you go?'

'A Vietnamese restaurant. Near her house.'

'Are you calling me from her house?'

'I am.'

'Don't let me keep you from her, Karl. I know you septuagenarians do incredible things on modern medicines. How's the Pilates going?'

'You've been in the paper again,' Karl said.

'Have I?'

'Some comment you made about one of these racists you were acting for.'

'I don't have a full book of racists, Karl. It was a one-off.'

'I agreed with you.' His father's voice was deep and rusty. He was a tall and thin man with a heavy voice. When he said he agreed with him, he made Tanner feel like he must be right.

'Good.'

'How is Dan?'

'Moody. Resentful. Ungrateful. Argumentative. Contrary. Magnificent. He has a girlfriend who to me exists as the sound an incoming text makes.'

'You were the same.'

'Prison must have been a relief.'

There was a long pause before Karl Tanner spoke again. 'Are you busy otherwise?'

'Another murder trial in a few weeks.'

'Who does that involved?'

'My client killed her banker. We're lobbying the Queen directly for a pardon.'

'Is she guilty?'

'Possibly. Possibly not.'

'What's your feeling?'

'She has motive, and witnesses say that she organised the killing. I'm not expecting her to confess, though.'

'Shouldn't she confess? If she's guilty?'

'No. And in my experience the only people who confess when they shouldn't are Swedish expats.'

Another pause. 'I suggest you go to bed now, Peter. I'll say goodnight. I'll drop in and see Daniel on the weekend.'

Tanner put his wine glass on the coffee table and went back to the novel. When he read the same paragraph twice again, he decided to go back to it on a night when he'd used a smaller glass. He picked up a copy of a magazine that was on the coffee table next to his wine glass. *The New Yorker.*

Karen had been the one to subscribe to it. After she died it continued to arrive at their home with her name on it. They piled up unopened on the table where he put his keys and wallet when he got home. Maybe three or four months after she died he noticed it began arriving with his name on the packaging, not hers. His father had seen to that.

The following afternoon, Tanner picked Dan up from school. Usually he caught the bus home, but Tanner needed his assistance. They drove to Richmond on the fringe of the city, made it back into town just before six. Tanner parked the old Jag in a no standing zone, but as near as he could get to the offices of *The Daily Informant*. They were on the top floor of a three-storey Art Deco office building in Surry Hills just off Goulburn, walking distance from the south end of Hyde Park.

He walked across the street, Dan carrying their parcel, pushed the buzzer, waited. A woman's voice, friendly, clearly been laughing at something just before she answered, giggled the words 'Daily Informant' into the intercom. He said he had a delivery for Rachel Roth. He was asked who he was. There followed a very impertinent delay between the time he announced himself, and when the 'click' sounded near the door to indicate he was being allowed in.

She was standing at the glass door of their offices when the lift opened. She didn't look pleased to see him. One hand on hip, the other on the door handle. She pulled the door open when he stepped forward.

'I didn't think we arranged another meeting,' she said.

'This is a spur-of-the-moment kind of thing.'

She scratched her head, kept looking at him. Her hair was up, fastened somehow, streaks of titian among the brown. She turned and looked back into the office. It was open plan, a few people in cubicles typing away in front of screens, two women standing in a kitchenette, drinking coffee or tea, looking over at them. There was a boardroom, glass panes and door separating it from the rest of the space, two men in there, casually dressed, discussing something, one of them pointing to a document on the table.

'So this drop in – what is that?'

'My son, Daniel. Dan, this is Rachel.'

Dan put his hand out tentatively. Roth shook it, but looked at Tanner. 'I meant, what is that?' She pointed to the basket Dan was holding in his left hand.

'It's for you,' he said.

Tanner carefully took the puppy from the basket, held it up for her to view. 'Cute, isn't she?'

'You're kidding.'

'No.'

She looked at the dog. He could see she wanted to take it from him; she wanted to push him away. 'Where did you get it from?'

'A breeder. I have the pedigree certificate. Her sire is called Mark of Zorro. I haven't made that up. Feisty bastard. He tried to hump Dan's leg about an hour ago. The dam is Summer Breeze. It sounds very yearling sales, I know, but that's what the certificate says. She cost my client a pretty penny, I can tell you.'

'Your client?'

'I'm not forking out fifteen hundred dollars for you, Rachel. We've only just met. This is a gift from Tina Leonard.'

She was looking at the puppy, then back at him. Two members of staff were now standing behind her, smiling at the dog.

'Does she know – ?'

'Not exactly,' Tanner said. 'She'll find it recorded in the next tax invoice she receives from Gallagher Criminal Lawyers. They'll itemise it simply as "disbursements". For my own bill to Kit Gallagher to get my money back, though, I'm going to record it formally as "Dog – Mark of Zorro out of Summer Breeze". I'm a details kind of lawyer.'

'This is crazy. I'm not taking –'

Tanner handed her the dog. Instinct overcame her. 'It's registered under your name. The breeders were calling her "Bonnie". I'd prefer you to change that. We have our own Bonnie at home. Another brindle, like this.'

'What the fuck are you doing?'

Roth glanced sideways at Dan, like she'd just realised she'd said something truly awful. 'I'm on a retainer to a bikie gang, Rachel. The leadership group occasionally dines at my house. Dan's been familiar with that word since he was the same age as this dog.'

'What are you doing?'

'I'm being nice.'

'Nice?'

'You told me the other day your dog died, and that it was a terrier of some sort. So is this. This is the queen of terriers. I know your other dog – I know it's soon, but when this dog is sitting next to you on your couch late at night, you'll think of me as a prince.'

'I'll think of you as a lunatic.'

'They're nearly the exact words a High Court justice said to me when I asked him to examine his conscience in a recent appeal.'

'This is insane,' she said, perhaps involuntarily stroking the puppy.

'Think of it as a bribe.'

'A bribe?' The colour was up in her cheeks. So were her freckles. Several had emerged since they started talking. Tiny chocolate all-sorts.

'A bribe for information. And one that will piss all over your floor for a while.'

There were four staff members behind her now, three women and one of the men from the boardroom. The women took turns to stroke the pup. The man said, 'Is everything okay here?'

Tanner told Dan to hand him the basket the dog had been in, and gave him some papers he'd been carrying. 'Make sure she reads up on this. She's had her six-week C5 shot. She needs another in four weeks when she turns three months. The feeding instructions are in the papers. There's a leash in the basket. Batteries weren't included, and there's no warranty.'

'This is crazy,' Rachel Roth said again, but he felt she was fighting off a smile.

Tanner turned and walked back to the lift, pushed the down button. 'When you've worked out how to operate that thing,' he said, 'give me a call.'

Tanner looked at Dan when the lift doors closed. He was flushed. He gave him a friendly tap on the upper arm. 'Given your girlfriend a present yet?'

Dan glared at him. 'That lady's your girlfriend now?'

'If someone gave me a dog like that, I'd marry them that day. But no, it's a professional relationship.'

'That was weird,' Dan said. He smiled. 'She's right. You're crazy.'

'Two hours, tops.'

'Two hours what?'

'Two hours before she's in love with that dog.'

The lift doors opened. 'Then what?'

'I have no idea,' Tanner said, putting his arm around the boy's shoulders, 'but I'm certain we've at least found a good home for another of the progeny of Mark of Zorro.'

20

'You ordered?' Tanner asked when he sat down opposite Tom Cable. They were in a café called Tucker in Randwick, near Tanner's home.

'Just tea.'

Cable was in T-shirt, jeans. The T-shirt was still brilliant white, looked new. He was small, nearing sixty, but made up entirely of lean meat and sinew. His skin was tight around his jaw and throat, an athlete's veins running down his neck and arms. He'd done time, but didn't reek of it. You'd have to have been part of the professional thief milieu to have known that.

When the waitress came, Cable ordered more tea, an egg-white omelette, gluten-free toast. Tanner smiled, ordered fried eggs, bacon, all the other sides, black coffee.

'How long you been asking them to hold the wheat?'

'Better for you,' Cable said.

Tanner nodded, complained about two men in spandex at an outside table.

'I ride a road bike,' Cable said.

Tanner frowned. 'Since when?'

'For years.'

'How much did it cost? Or did you steal it?'

Cable glared, didn't answer directly. 'What's wrong with riding a bike?'

Tanner shook his head. 'Nothing. Climate-friendly device. I'm all for them.'

'How are you keeping fit?' Cable asked.

'Same as usual. Red wine, watching football on TV.'

'You're getting away with it now. Wait till you're fifty.'

'Wait for what?'

'Spare tyre around your gut.'

'Not in my genes. Karl hasn't put on a kilo in my lifetime. Besides, my job has too much stress.'

'There are no fat barristers?'

'Not in crime. We're a lean and hungry lot. You can't afford to eat on legal-aid rates.'

Cable raised an eyebrow over the top of the tea cup he'd just put to his lips. 'Not a problem for you these days,' he said.

'I did nothing but legal aid for years. Better money being a paralegal.'

'You had a –' Cable stopped himself. Tanner knew he was about to remind him that he'd had a wife back then who was a doctor earning respectable money. Cable had a pathological fear of raising anything to do with Karen since she'd died.

'For Christ's sake, Tom.'

'Sorry.'

Tanner shook his head, leant back so the waitress could put his coffee in front of him. 'Tell me what we have,' he said when she left.

Cable spoke just loud enough for Tanner to hear. He had a raspy voice, like it was always only an hour after his footy team had won a close game. 'Crawford's where you told me he would be. Leaves the same time most days.'

'What else?'

'Lucky family, the Ioannidises,' he said.

'The eldest daughter of the patriarch is on bail for murder. Not all them are lucky.'

'Big Al was lucky.'

'Go on.'

'Died three years ago. Eighty-two. Migrated out here in the late fifties. Well, jumped off a boat. Started as a brickie. Ended up worth nine figures.'

'Bloody illegal migrants. Bleed the country dry.'

'Started his own building company in the late sixties. Southwest and Western Suburbs. Ended up doing big residential flat developments. Your client's brothers still do.'

'Sounds like hard work so far, not luck.'

'My mail is he got a few surprising development approvals over the years. He also had a habit of buying rural land out west just before it was zoned for industrial or residential.'

'You've just described most developers, Tom. If you tell me that any bribes to local politicians happened, I won't believe it.'

'Big Al was friendly with more than just local councillors. State and federal pollies too. Big donor to both parties.'

'Did you say lucky? That's how you do business in this country.'

Cable shrugged. 'Most of the stories are from the seventies through to the nineties. He'd made a pile by then.'

'Who'd you speak to?'

'Couple of whistle-blowers came out of the woodwork when the corruption commission kick-started. Some independents on a few local councils. One had a story about a few blocks of flats that weren't built entirely in accordance with the approval granted. One bedroom units built and sold as two bedroom, that kind of thing. It got looked into but nothing came of it. Most of this is just historical records plus rumour. I spoke to a council inspector – Phil Roberts is his name, happy to talk to you if you think you need to – who's still pretty worked up about a few developments, but most of this is ancient history. No one's interested now.'

'I'm not going to win this case by establishing my client's father was your typical upstanding property developer, Tom. Anything on the witnesses I need to deal with?'

Cable opened the small notebook he'd placed on the table, flicked over a few pages. 'Bitar was employed from time to time by Ioannidis & Sons — Ioannidis Builders it was called before that. By "employed", I mean he was a "consultant". Hard to know for sure what he did except when it ended up in court. There was one nasty incident with a union official called Steven May I found out about. Worked for the CFMEU, or whatever it was called back then. Construction union.'

'What's a "nasty incident" in your language? For me, it usually involves a murder.'

'Severely bashed. Most facial bones broken or rearranged. In an induced coma for a couple of weeks.'

'And this was done by Bitar?'

'Personally? Maybe, but he was never charged. There was a threatened strike at one of Achilles's sites. Some underpayment issue. This is early nineties. Bitar was only a young pup then, making a name for himself. So to speak.'

'You were a young pup yourself then, Tom. Were you still breaking into residences then, or had you moved to office premises?'

'I don't need the money you pay me, Pete.'

'You'd die of boredom without me.'

'Bitar was charged with GBH on an organiser about ten years later. This was apparently done for Theo Ioannidis — the eldest son. He was under time pressure at some project at Strathfield. Block of apartments near the station. Safety corners were being cut. The union called Safe Work to complain. Did it more than once.'

'And for that you deserve to be nearly beaten to death?'

'Guess it depends on how much money is involved.'

Tanner shook his head. 'Doesn't make sense. Beating up a union official wouldn't make the union back off, would it?'

Cable gently tucked a napkin into the collar of his T-shirt as his omelette was put in front of him, then placed another in his lap. He'd been a meticulous thief. 'I expect violence is the last resort, or one of many arrows in their quiver.' He picked up the salt, liberally covered his egg-white omelette with it. Put on enough to preserve it as a meal for three centuries.

'Had your blood pressure checked lately, Tom?'

'Had yours? The third rap Bitar got off was beating up some local councillor. A guy called Jack Manning. For a while he was the mayor of a council out in the Western Suburbs. His casting vote was holding up a development consent.'

'For Big Al or the brothers?'

Cable shook his head slowly. 'For Leonard Developments. Your girl.'

Tanner picked up the salt, monstered his own eggs with it, tomatoes, spinach, then did the same with pepper. 'Who told you this? When was it?'

Cable took a bite of omelette, wiped his mouth carefully with a third napkin before speaking. 'Cops I know. A couple of blokes who worked on the site when it got approved. Other sources. Hundred-and-twenty–unit development. One of Tina's first big jobs. About twelve years ago.'

'Cops?'

'I'm on the same side as them now. The security business.' Cable's wife, sons and brother-in-law ran an alarm installation and security company. Tom was a silent partner, given his three-and-a-half-year stint for a string of B&Es.

'Other sources?'

'Horse's mouth.'

'The victim?'

Cable nodded, washed down food with tea. 'He's pretty sure who it was, or who was behind it. Cops couldn't prove it.' They ate for a few moments, not talking. 'Bashing someone's not that far off having someone killed. Is that why you're quiet, Pete?'

Tanner signalled for another coffee. Cable passed on more tea. 'I'll ask her about it. I expect it's just standard operating procedure in her industry.'

Cable nodded.

'Anything we don't already know on Jayden Webb?'

Jayden Webb's record sheet in the police brief showed a few assaults, two possessions of meth, but small quantities. That record would be disclosed to the jury.

'Not much. Worked on a few building sites – including for the brothers. Apprentice shopfitter for a while, didn't finish.'

'On any of Tina's sites?'

Cable nodded. 'Once. Mainly for the brothers, though.'

'That's it?'

'I'm not sure there's much else. I can try to find out more about his family if you like?'

'Just doesn't sound like the CV of a hitman. Webb's a guy who's admitted to putting a bullet in each of Randall's knees, then one between the eyes.'

'My CV started with robbing milk bars,' Cable said. 'You gotta start somewhere.'

21

Tina Leonard already looked older, Tanner thought, as she walked into his chambers with Kit Gallagher. Still poised, light grey suit, black trimmings, black shirt buttoned to the top, black heels to stretch her short stature. Rings under her eyes like faint bruises. Waiting for your murder trial wasn't ideal for sleep patterns.

'Everything okay at home?' Tanner said as Leonard took her seat.

'I'm sure it's better than prison,' she said. 'I can understand Simon not wanting me living in his house.'

'Are you eating?'

'I'm finding my predicament to be an appetite suppressant.'

'I could cook you something if you want. I'm pretty good. I could get it delivered?'

She smiled faintly. 'I think I want you more for your court skills.'

'I'm in the three-star section of the Michelin guide for criminal defence lawyers.'

She smiled, looked down at the desk.

'How are you filling in your time?'

'Talking with my sister. Walking her dog. Enjoying this early autumn weather. Some reading.'

'Readers of fiction are much less likely to commit violent

crimes than non-readers,' Tanner said. 'There's verified research on that – *Harvard Law Journal*. Less likely to go into politics too.'

'I didn't commit a violent crime,' Leonard said.

'I know that, Tina,' Tanner said. He paused, then said, 'I'm only asking because my client's mental state is important before a trial. Especially if you're going to give evidence. Have you seen your children lately?'

She sighed, sat back. 'I have,' she said. 'Taz – Taz helped arrange it with Alex. He's my eldest. He's been – well, his mother being charged with murder . . .' She shook her head. 'On top of everything else.'

'This process isn't easy for –'

'I'm not making him sit in court for me, Peter. Neither of the boys will be there. I'm not putting them through a circus like that.'

'The optics of that, Tina. A jury – let me think on it.'

'I'm not negotiating.'

He decided to leave it alone. 'We spoke to Randall's ex-wife.'

Leonard paused. 'About what?' she asked.

'She doesn't think her husband was a drug dealer. Not on the six-kilo scale, anyway. We asked her about some of the things you say Randall told you just before he was killed. She said she didn't know anything about that, but there were a lot of people in the room. I'll try to get one on one. Won't be easy. She's got a husband I'm very prepared to assume is an arsehole.'

'I know the feeling,' Leonard said, no hint of humour in her voice.

'I spoke to Taz about your ex – about the deal he was able to make with SEBC.'

'The bribe, you mean?'

'I think the bank would call it a settlement.'

'They bought him off.'

'Taz said you were relieved your children were left with a home.'

'I wasn't relieved it was his home.'

'She also says there's no chance Adrian will talk to me – is that right? What's your relationship?'

Leonard picked up her glass of water, took a sip, looked at the ceiling as though the words she wanted were up there. 'Cordial. For the sake of – mainly for Chris. He's still at school. Cordial might be too cheerful a description. I pretend not to hear some of what Adrian has to say. It's less painful that way.'

'He's remarried?'

She nodded. 'They have a small child together. A daughter. She's – I don't know – eighteen months.'

'And he won't talk to me?'

'You don't honestly think he'll confirm he was bribed, do you?'

'I'd like to hear him back up your story – that Randall lied in court. That would help me throw mud at the bank and at Lovro in your trial.'

She shook her head. 'Adrian wouldn't back up my story six years ago. He's not going to do that now.'

'That doesn't seem very nice, Tina. You are the mother of his children. What did you do to this guy?'

She smiled, half bitter, half sad. 'I forgot that my only role in our marriage was to make him feel important. I didn't realise I wasn't allowed to be a success.'

'We're a long way past that.'

'He can't talk to you anyway. His settlement was confidential.'

'Not worth the paper it's written on in a courtroom.'

'Peter – I know Adrian. He's never going to admit he didn't give evidence to help me because the bank bought him off.'

'He swore an affidavit saying Randall agreed on the bank's behalf to restructure your loans and give your company another two years. Was he lying then?'

'He said he'd recant that. He said he would tell the court he was lying in the affidavit to protect me. That was the deal SEBC signed him up to. That was what he had to do if he wanted to walk away with money.'

Tanner let it go. He still wanted to talk with Adrian Leonard, but it would have to be without his ex-wife's assistance.

'Pete saw your former lawyer too,' Kit Gallagher said. 'Faulkner.'

'He believed you, for what it's worth,' Tanner said. 'About the conversation with Randall.'

'The judge didn't,' Leonard said.

'Do you know someone called Jack Manning?' Tanner asked. The sudden change of subject was deliberate.

Leonard looked down at her hands, then back at Tanner. 'I don't believe so.'

'Don't waste my time being coy, Tina,' Tanner said, 'What can you tell me about him?'

'You already know then. I asked Mick Bitar to talk to him. That was it.'

'From what I'm told the conversation turned nasty.'

'I didn't tell Mick to hurt him.'

'Do you usually have trouble giving clear instructions, Tina?'

She glared at him. 'No.'

'What did you want Bitar to talk to this man about?'

Leonard said nothing for a few seconds. Tanner waited. 'You said not to waste time, Peter,' she said eventually. 'That's what you're doing. You know the answers to your questions, or you think you do.'

'I'm looking for clarity.'

She took a breath, leant forward. 'That man,' she said, 'spent most of his time on council taking bribes. He was holding up a development of mine to get another one. I sent Mick around to find out how much it would cost me. You mightn't approve of that, Peter, but that's the hand I was dealt. I didn't invent the world. It's how this town operates. I needed a vote to get my development project approved. It should have been approved. It deserved to be. A cost of business in this city is bribing people. I think that's unfortunate, but everyone does it. I sent Mick around to find out this man's price. That's what Mick's good at. He finds out people's price, then he cuts it in half, and makes a deal. This man wouldn't negotiate. Mick took offence. I didn't tell him to hurt anyone. I just wanted to make a deal.'

'Is this what your father taught you about property development, Tina? Or did you learn that from your brothers?'

Black fire in her eyes. 'My father never tried to bribe anyone, Peter. The Australians running things told him he had to pay them. That's how it worked. He had to feed the convicts to get ahead. They called him a wog, but they took his money. Then he got his approvals, and built his buildings. They still called him wog, but he made a great big pile of money he could bury them all in. Are you clear about that?'

'I am, Tina. I'm sure it's the truth. And try to remember the tone you just used with me, and not use it in court. The jury won't like you.'

'Can we return to what this case is really about now? My defence.'

Tanner smiled. 'Tina, this is your defence. I need to know these things. Mick Bitar is giving evidence for the state against you. He says you asked him to kill Randall for you. There are witnesses who saw you and Bitar having lunch at a restaurant just days before Randall's murder. Your money was found in Jayden Webb's flat, that –'

'That money was for a meeting with –'

'What if they ask Bitar about Jack Manning? What if the prosecutor says, if you tell us Tina Leonard paid you to bash him, we'll give you an immunity? What then? It might be unlikely, and I'd complain bitterly if it happened so close to trial. But I need to know everything. Every parking ticket you've had, Tina. Everything.'

'Everything, Peter?' she said softly. 'I didn't ask Mick to hurt that man. Oliver Randall did lie to me. In front of Adrian, in front of my CFO. When he'd done his bit to help his bank steal my land off me, Oliver got greedy. He asked for bigger bonuses, a higher salary. He threatened them with exposure. He was wild on coke when he did that. The bank taught him a five-and-a-half-year lesson about who has the power. That bank sold my land to Lovro Constructions – one of its clients – for a quarter of its worth. That was fraud. Oliver told me that when he got out of prison. They had him killed. When the fool who killed him got caught, they set me up to take the rap. That's everything.'

Tanner waited for a moment, made sure she was done. 'It's sometimes hard to distinguish bullshit from the truth in my game. Luckily half the job is making sure a jury can't either.'

'Everything I just told you is the truth. Including Jack Manning.'

He nodded. 'Okay then. Just make sure I have the whole truth, not what you choose to tell me.'

'That was a long time ago. A lifetime ago.'

'If it involves Mick Bitar, Tina, it's relevant. You're not charged with shoplifting. For murder, I need to know everything. My mentors were insistent about that as an approach to conducting a defence.'

'Luka Ravic and Lovro Constructions stole my land. His bankers helped him. Oliver Randall was going to expose that. That's why they had him killed. That's why they've set me up. That's our defence.'

22

Tanner met Kit Gallagher in the foyer of the building where the firm Kent Marberry kept several floors of lawyers. It was a hot, mid-March day, and she had a single trail of sweat gliding down the makeup on the side of her face.

'You walked?' he said.

'Mistake in this heat.' She was in her big firm attire: dark charcoal skirt and matching jacket, thin ruby stripe. 'It was cool yesterday. It's supposed to be autumn.'

'I like your suit,' he said. 'Are you sure you don't want to join a firm like this, Kit? You look the part.'

'They don't defend crims.'

'I thought that's all they do.'

'Let's go. I don't want to be late.'

They walked to the lifts, then rode up, cocooned in her scent. He glanced at her, smiled.

'Chanel Mademoiselle,' she said, reading his mind. He nodded. 'Too young for me?'

'Of course not. You look great.'

'Are you flirting, Pete?'

'Respectfully. You know you're not old enough for us to have a serious relationship. And you don't have tattoos.'

The lift doors opened. She looked at him. 'How do you know?' she said, walking out.

Greg Stockman had been a partner at Kent Marberry for more than ten years. Corporate practice. He'd also acted for Oliver Randall as his solicitor in his drugs case seven years before. An odd choice. He'd initially said no to talking to Tanner. Eventually Gallagher swayed him. Maybe she'd threatened, maybe she'd negotiated. If it was the latter, Kent Marberry had come out on top. The firm was to be paid for Stockman's time, at his top charge-out rate of a thousand an hour. The firm's general counsel was also to be present, at the reduced rate of seven-fifty per hour.

Not long after taking a seat in the foyer they were ushered by a PA into a conference room. Small table, only four chairs. Joinery against one wall with a few cupboards and drawers, a pewter jug sitting on the top, condensation glistening on the surface, four glasses next to it. Two small artworks on the walls.

'This is the room for the least important clients,' Tanner said, 'or where you're told you've been retrenched.'

The door opened as he spoke. Greg Stockman was tall, dark and handsome in a dreary kind of way. Black suit, white shirt, black and white patterned tie. It was ten am. He looked like he was due his next shave. He shook Tanner's and Gallagher's hands like they were privileged to meet him. He looked Gallagher up and down, rejected her as the wrong side of something. Tanner could have told him that he wasn't her type, almost did, checked himself.

The general counsel, Martin Moore, came in second, carrying a Kent Marberry pad. He was older, balding, sky blue tie, otherwise dressed like Stockman. He gave a hesitant, slightly pained smile when he shook hands. The handshake bordered on what Tanner would describe as 'fey', and only at the end attempted to make a sortie over that line towards something of substance. Tanner sensed nervousness. He suspected Moore would panic easily if pressured. That's what in house GCs are trained to do. Panic easily. Frequently say no. It was usually the safest answer.

Stockman left it to Moore to lay out the ground rules. Grant only had an hour. They'd both already spent time on 'the matter'. A file had been opened. Charge-out rates confirmed at a thousand and seven-fifty an hour.

'You're not as highly valued as Greg, Martin?' Tanner said. A blank look, hint of panic in the lower lip. 'Your charge-out rate is two-fifty less.'

Relief, then a weak smile. 'It's a notional figure for me.'

'Not for our client. Or are you going to notionally charge us?'

'How can I help you?' Stockman said. 'As I told Kathleen when she called the first time, this file has been closed a long time.'

'We want to explore your memory about acting for Oliver Randall on his drug matter.'

'Not much memory left, I'm afraid,' Stockman said, a forcibly weary tone. 'And I know you've both heard of privilege.'

'Your client's dead, Greg.'

'Your client killed him, apparently.'

'With all due respect, you can't possibly know that.' Kit Gallagher's tone was polite, but firm.

Stockman smiled, didn't hide his contempt for the criminal lawyers dirtying his day. 'What do you want?'

Tanner appreciated the directness. 'Was he guilty?'

Stockman narrowed his eyes, looked puzzled, mildly amused. 'He pleaded guilty.'

'Different things. Was he?'

Stockman paused before answering. 'Obviously he was.'

'Why'd he come to you?' Tanner asked quickly. 'Why not someone like Kit?'

Stockman looked at Gallagher at the mention of her name. 'I – this firm acted for SEBC. I was involved in the deal where it bought out Nipori Bank. I had a lot to do with Oliver in those deals. He was on the due diligence team. He knew me – I guess he was comfortable with me as his lawyer. He needed someone urgently. I was the first person he called.'

'You didn't think to refer him on to a criminal specialist?'

The muscles in Stockman's face tightened a little, his head

tilted back. 'We retained a very eminent Queen's Counsel and a senior criminal junior on his behalf.'

'You didn't feel any conflict?'

'What do you mean?' A hint of anger in Stockman's voice now.

'A conflict between Randall's interests and SEBC's?'

Stockman took a long breath, shook his head. 'It had nothing to do with SEBC.'

Tanner laughed. 'He was one of their senior executives and he was found with six kilos of coke in his home. A bit embarrassing for them, wasn't it?'

'It certainly attracted the interest of the media. The bank has a big PR department. They didn't need us to help them with that.'

'They were okay with you acting for him, though?'

'What do you mean "okay"?'

'C'mon, Greg,' Tanner said. 'You have this big bank as one of your clients. They're worth a lot to your firm in fees, right?'

'What's your point?'

'Well, did you have to clear it with SEBC to act for Randall?'

Stockman sighed. 'I don't recall, Peter. It was six years ago. Clearly they had no problem with it.'

'Did they encourage it?'

'What does that mean?'

'Just a question,' Tanner said. 'By the way, if we were clients, we would have been offered water by now, and coffee, wouldn't we? Come to think of it, we are clients, given we're paying for this.'

'We didn't expect it to take long,' Moore said softly.

'Are we nearly done?' Stockman said.

'I'll be upfront, Greg,' Tanner said. 'I've already spoken with Alan Murdoch – the barrister you briefed as junior counsel for Randall. He didn't think your client was guilty. I don't think my client is guilty. Which makes them both unusual.'

'Why do you need my opinion then?' Stockman asked.

'I want to know if Randall was set up.'

This time Stockman laughed. 'What does that have to do with your client?'

'Stick to corporate work, Greg,' Tanner said. 'Guys who have six kilos of coke planted in their house during a police raid usually know some people you wouldn't call friends.'

Stockman let out another long sigh, rubbed a hand over his jaw. 'He was adamant the drugs weren't his,' he said. 'When we first spoke. When I first met with Oliver after bail was granted. He was very clear about that.'

'You believed him?'

'Yes,' Stockman said slowly. 'I did. He told me some of what the police found – in his jacket – was for personal use. But the six kilos he'd never seen.'

'You ever go to any SEBC parties?'

'Jesus, Pete,' Gallagher said.

'What do you mean "parties"?'

'Client entertainment events. Lots of coke and girls.'

'No.'

'I don't think that's a very professional or appropriate question,' Moore said. 'In fact, it's downright rude.'

Tanner wanted to laugh, thought better of it, ignored him. 'When did Randall first tell you he wanted to change his plea?'

'I don't recall exactly. Several weeks after his arrest. We retained counsel on the basis we'd be going to trial.'

'Big call, alleging the police planted six kilos of cocaine.'

Stockman shrugged. 'They were his instructions at first,' he said. 'And we weren't necessarily going to say it was the police. It just wasn't his.'

'Presumably you weren't going to go after his wife as a drug boss, Greg? Or his thirteen-year-old daughter?'

'No, we weren't.'

'Do you recall anything significant about the conversation when he told you he wanted to plead guilty?' Kit Gallagher asked. 'Did he explain why?'

Stockman shook his head. 'He was – he wouldn't explain it.'

'Did anyone at SEBC have a chat with him – suggest perhaps that he should plead guilty?' Tanner asked.

'That's ridiculous.'

'Is it? Did you talk to anyone at SEBC about what Oliver was going to do?'

'No. I did not.'

'So, he's innocent one day, and the next day he says, what? That the couple of million bucks' worth of coke in his gym bag was his after all?'

'That's how it was.'

'Where did he get it?'

'He wouldn't say.'

'Who did he buy it from?'

'I've told you –'

'Did he synthesise it from the coca leaves himself, Greg? Did Randall have ancient Peruvian ancestry we don't know about?'

'He said it would be better for his wife and daughter if he pleaded guilty,' Stockman said, raising his voice. 'I recall him saying that.'

'Did you ask him what he meant by that?'

'I don't –' Stockman hesitated, lowered his voice. 'He may have said it would be quicker, less embarrassment in the long run. It was a long time ago.'

'Was he frightened?'

'No, I don't – look, he seemed to think he had to plead guilty.'

'Had to?' Tanner said loudly. 'He said that?'

'No – I . . .' For the first time, Tanner thought, Stockman didn't look like a smug corporate lawyer.

'He said that to you? Why did he have to?'

Stockman, who had been gradually leaning forward, sat upright again, took a deep breath. 'It – it was probably the weight of evidence against him. That's probably what he meant.'

'But you didn't think he meant that at the time?'

'No. I – why do you care so much about Oliver Randall?'

'I don't give a fuck about Oliver Randall,' Tanner said. 'He sold coke to people in the Eastern Suburbs of Sydney. Some of those people would have on sold to teenagers, kids with money. I'm glad someone shot him. My questions arise from necessary professional curiosity.'

Stockman was composed again, almost laughed. 'Don't you defend drug dealers in your – in your line of work?'

'I've been running a long-standing commission of inquiry into my moral fitness, Greg. Let's not worry about me. Let's stick to Randall. Did someone threaten him?'

'I have no –'

'Did SEBC threaten him?'

'Of course not.'

'How do you know?'

'SEBC is a client of ours,' Moore said. 'I think we should wrap this –'

'Threaten him with what?'

'When did you talk to SEBC about Randall's case, Greg? Because I can tell that you did.'

'You've got a nerve saying that.'

'You have no idea about the size of my nerve. I want you to tell me now what had Oliver Randall so worried he'd plead guilty to something he didn't do.'

'I think this meeting is over,' Moore said. 'This is outrageous.'

Tanner looked at Kit Gallagher. 'Anything else?'

She shook her head.

'Can I ask you one last thing?' Tanner said, the four of them standing at once. 'Did Oliver Randall pay your fees?'

'How's that – why are you asking that?'

'Just curious. Did he?'

'No one told me he didn't.'

'Did SEBC pay his bill?'

'That's none of your business.'

'You've heard of a thing called a subpoena, right?'

'This meeting is over.'

'Did you visit him in prison, Greg?'

'What?'

'Did you visit your client in prison?'

'I don't see how that has anything to do with anything,' Moore said.

Tanner shrugged. 'You see, Martin,' he said, 'if he did pay the bill, and Greg didn't visit him in prison, that's what I consider downright rude.'

23

Tanner heard a tap on his open door, looked up and saw Jenny Singh. She had two wine glasses in one hand, a bottle of red in the other. It was the end of her second week at the bar. She'd started this chapter of her professional career with a steady stream of work ahead of her, courtesy of her now ex-employer. It included 'second chair' in the Tina Leonard trial.

'You joining us?' she said.

'Waiting on a call,' he said.

She came into the room, kicked the door closed with the back of a high heel. She put the bottle on his desk, handed him a wine glass, poured, sat down.

'Long day in court?'

'Medical tribunal,' she said. 'I was for a shrink. Three-year affair with a patient that didn't end well.'

'Quite a brief for a novice like you.'

'I was being led.'

'Who by?'

'Bob Lloyd.'

'Did he keep his hands to himself?'

'Our instructing solicitor supervised him closely.'

'What do shrinks do if they get struck off? What else are they qualified for?'

'What would we do?'

It was a good question. What would he do?

He tasted the wine, looked at the bottle. A Malbec from Argentina. Selected by the floor's resident wine expert. One of about fifteen.

'Where are we with Leonard?' Singh asked.

'That's the call I'm waiting for.'

'Who from?'

'My undercover agent.'

'How is Tom?'

He smiled, then filled her in about the conference with Grant Stockman.

'What if you do throw some doubt on Randall's drug conviction? Forgetting for the moment the problem that he pleaded guilty – how do you introduce that into Leonard's defence? How do you make it relevant?'

Tanner smiled. 'That's your responsibility as co-counsel, Jen. I'm only there to confuse the jury.'

She raised an eyebrow. He'd read her CV for the first time now that she was on the chamber's website. She had a PhD in criminology. She was Dr Singh, but had never called herself that so far as he knew.

'Pete?'

'Yeah?'

'What were you thinking?'

He let out a deep breath. 'What I'd do if I wasn't a lawyer.'

'And?'

His mobile phone vibrated in front of him, started ringing. 'I'll get back to you,' he said, picking it up.

It was a fifteen-minute walk from his chambers to the bar in the Barangaroo precinct he'd been told to go to. It was early evening, and he could walk in shadow, some relief from the unusually hot late March weather. He saw Tom Cable standing in the shade outside the front of a building. Tanner was going to cross the street to speak to him, but saw him punching his phone, and then his own phone vibrated. *Inside*, the message said. Tanner looked from his phone to Cable, and nodded. Cable gave a form of salute, then walked away. Tanner looked through a window, the setting sun glinting on the glass. The place was crowded with human shapes. A gust of wind hit him. Westerly, still hot, carrying the thick toxic sweetness of diesel from the boats in Darling Harbour. He headed for the door.

He felt wetness on his skin when he walked into the air-conditioned room. It was noisy, a young crowd, late twenties, thirties, suits, office clothes, voices rising on their second or third post-work drink, clashing with the music coming from overhead speakers. He walked to the back corner, away from the bar, scanned the room. He spotted the man he was looking for in a few moments. He was in the opposite corner, leaning against the bar. Tall, balding at the crown, big shoulders, broad back, the stitching of his jacket earning its keep. He was with two other men, who nodded occasionally while the man talked. Tanner had cross-examined him three times, the last occasion nearly eight years before.

He squeezed between people, lodged himself at the bar, waited his turn to order a beer. He was only a metre from the man, but still facing the other way, and in the din of voices, Tanner couldn't make out what he was saying, only stray words that were louder than others, or that somehow slipped through the wall of noise. He sipped his beer when it was put in front of him, stepped away, nudged the man next to him with his free arm.

'Nice suit, Brian,' he said.

Brian Crawford stopped talking, looked at him, went to speak, stopped himself in the split second it took to recognise Tanner.

'Pay upgrade from the force?'

Crawford sipped his beer, which was nearly done. 'Long time since I've seen you,' he said.

Tanner smiled. 'You're not arresting my clients any more.'

Crawford nodded.

'How long have you been at the bank?'

Crawford narrowed his eyes. 'Are you here with anyone, Tanner?'

Tanner shook his head.

'I am. Nice seeing you.'

'I'm curious, Brian,' Tanner said quickly. 'How long have you been at SEBC?'

'How's it your business?'

Tanner didn't have a plan other than to rattle his cage, see what happened. He backed himself to have as good an idea afterwards about Oliver Randall's drug conviction as from any other line of inquiry.

'Are these gents from the bank too? Do they know you once arrested one of their own? Maybe it was your last arrest? Was it?'

Crawford looked confused for a moment.

'Poor bloke's dead now,' Tanner continued. 'Murdered.'

The confusion lifted, was replaced by recognition, a kind of smile, the early stages of anger. 'What are you doing?' Crawford said.

'SEBC still throw good parties, Brian? Oliver Randall used to organise them, I'm told.'

Crawford said nothing, but one of the men he was with, mid-forties, probably a colleague from 'security', stepped forward. 'Everything okay here?' he said, aggression in the back of his voice.

'Just tying up loose ends,' Tanner said.

'Do it somewhere else.'

Seventeen years as a criminal defence lawyer had honed Tanner's sense of danger, who he should be afraid of. It took more than a banker on his first beer to put him off. 'I'm guessing mate you're not a distant relative of Barangaroo. Or a custodian of Gadigal territory? If not, fuck off.' He turned to face Crawford again. 'No one I've spoken to seems to think Oliver Randall really kept six kilos of coke in his house. He was smaller time. Can you help me with that?'

'Go to the Police Integrity Commission, Tanner. I'm not interested.'

Tanner laughed. 'I'm a defence counsel. I *am* the Police Integrity Commission.'

'Check the records. There's film of us finding that haul.'

'That film would've been directed by you. Everyone knows how good you were with special effects when you wanted to be.'

'Fuck off.' A demand rather than a suggestion, violence and menace in both words.

'Do you know anyone who would have wanted Oli Randall dead once he got out of prison?'

Crawford took a step towards Tanner. He was tall, heading into obese territory, late middle-aged gut now in residence, there to stay. 'Don't think I'll let a spiv like you drag me into some bullshit.'

'Spiv?' Tanner said, forcing a smile. 'This is a Tom Ford suit, Brian. Spivs don't wear them. I'm a shyster at worst. Maybe I'm a shyster at best. I'm trying to work it out.'

'Piss off.'

'How'd you get a job at SEBC so quickly after arresting one of their executives?'

'I said, piss off.'

'What skill set does someone from the Drug Squad bring to a global bank? Are you there to keep the young bankers in check, or do you get the drugs for the parties now? You'd know where to go, I guess.'

Crawford took in a long breath, let it out slowly, looked like he was weighing things up. 'What's your plan?' he said. 'Coming here, telling me this. How is this going to help you?'

Good question, Tanner thought. Too good to answer. Cat among the pigeons was the best he had. Still, Crawford had stitched up Oliver Randall. He reeked of that.

'You were told to piss off.' It was another of the men Crawford was with. Like his colleague, all tip and no iceberg when it came to intimidation.

Tanner looked at the man, turned back to Crawford. 'Why'd you plant the drugs on Oliver Randall?'

Crawford glared. Tanner felt the chances of him getting belted were shortening.

'If it wasn't your idea, whose was it? Be better to tell me now than wait for the witness box.'

A smile widened on Crawford's face. Almost friendly. He put a big hand on Tanner's shoulder. It felt like a leg of lamb had landed on it. 'You're a brave cunt, Peter,' Crawford said. 'Good luck.' He swung his other hand to his own face, finished his beer, pushed Tanner aside with his gut, shoved a path to the bar.

24

Rachel Roth was waiting for him outside his chambers at seven the next morning.

He put the takeaway coffee cups in the holders when he got in her car. 'Espresso okay?' he said as he did up his seatbelt.

She nodded, sped off from the kerb.

He looked at her. No expression he could discern. Hair down, no makeup, blue jeans, white linen shirt, rolled at the cuffs.

It took ten minutes to reach the Limani Views site. As they drove around looking for a park, Tanner could see construction was in full swing. The main tower of the development was almost all the way up, big cranes with the name 'Lovro Constructions' lining each arm were lugging steel on either side of it. Surrounding the tower, most villas looked near completion, at least for external works. Through the windows of some Tanner could see tradesmen of various kinds involved in the process of internal fit out. They were being built near the water's edge, then up the hill in a formation that meant each had a view of the harbour and parts of the city to the east. On the west side of the tower, running from the foreshore to the top of the hill, was a cleared, vacant area of land.

There was no street parking in the construction zone other than for workers and trucks, so Roth had to drive several streets away to find a place to stop. When she did she cut the engine, grabbed her coffee, got out of the car without saying a word. Tanner followed. Looking at the Limani View development site had been her idea.

They walked as close as they could to the construction zone before coming to an 'authorised personnel only' area, then backtracked to the first street open on the west side of the site, and walked down the hill to the water's edge. Tanner asked her questions about *The Daily Informant*, the current controversies in politics, but her responses were short. She'd invited him on business. She was going to tell him something. She'd expect something in return.

At the bottom of the road was a small public park that bordered the foreshore. There was a faint breeze, but it was already warm.

They watched a ferry head its passengers towards the city, a Rivercat glide the other way, disappearing up the Parramatta, making a soft wake for two rowing boats that slid past it.

'Are you looking for something?' Tanner asked.

She smiled vaguely, turned to face him, her oversized sunnies glinting in the morning sun. 'You can't see what I'm looking for.'

'Is that a cryptic clue?'

She shook her head. 'There used to be warehouses here,' she said.

For some reason he looked down. 'Where we're standing?'

She nodded. 'Where they're building too.'

'You're telling me this because it's significant,' Tanner said. 'What kind of warehouses?'

'Wool in the main. A few other textiles. Wheat. Coal storage – there was a coal mine in Balmain once.'

'Should I assume our environmental laws weren't quite as rigorous then as they are now?'

Roth took her sunglasses off, ran her hand up to her head to tuck some stray strands of hair behind an ear. 'The rigour of our environmental laws varies with how much money you have, and how you share it. But you mightn't be catching my drift yet.' She smiled for the first time.

'What am I missing?'

'What do you know about the history of Sydney Harbour, and the river here?'

'White history, or the true owners?'

'The industrial history.'

'I wouldn't eat a fish I caught here, if that's what you mean?'

She looked out at the water, towards where a marina was being built in front of the main tower of Limani. 'You'd probably be okay if you did. At least here. I wouldn't eat it every day, but you'd live.'

Tanner nodded. 'SEBC released a report before it put this place out for sale by tender. It said this spot was highly polluted. Do you know something we don't?'

'Union Carbide had a factory at Homebush. Did you know that?'

He shook his head.

'They made herbicides there, among other things. Defoliant. Agent Orange.'

'I'm sure they paid the government a lot of rent.'

'The sediments of the river near it are full of dioxins. You wouldn't eat a fish you caught there.'

'I'm a red meat guy. Especially in the lead up to a trial.'

'There was a gas works at Barangaroo,' she said. 'The place is full of benzene. Even cyanide.'

'I know more about cyanide than you'd think.'

'Strange thing is, that report that your client's bank put out, you'd have thought there were once factories here like that. Not warehouses.'

'Who have you spoken to, Rachel? What do you know?'

She laughed. 'Not so fast. You don't get my sources.' She considered him. 'Have you looked at Lovro Constructions' website? Their current projects?'

He shook his head.

'Not very thorough of you.'

'I've been occupied with other things.'

'I wouldn't necessarily need to have a source, Peter. You can read the contamination reports for this place on their website. This site is a lot cleaner than the bank thought.'

'Are they credible? The current reports?'

'Do you mean is Lovro lying now, or was the bank lying then?'

'I like the way you put things. You'd make it at the criminal bar.'

'My money is on the latter. Your client got screwed.'

He looked over at the tower, to the half-complete marina. 'Could the original report have – could it have been a mistake?'

'Have you read it?'

'It's in my brief. Tina Leonard gave me a copy. It was part of her legal papers for her case.'

'They didn't pretend to do thorough testing. Just a few spot sites on the land here, a couple of sediment samples from the river. You can get positives for pollutants that are isolated if you don't do more thorough testing – that can make the site look worse than it is. If it was a mistake, though, it was in the highly to grossly negligent category.'

He nodded. 'At least we don't need Hazmat suits.'

'Convenient for Lovro, don't you think? They buy a development site that other bidders think might come with a big clean-up bill. Once they purchase it for a song and take possession, things are sweeter than they appeared. The remediation cost is cut in half.'

He finished the coffee he'd carried from the car, threw the cup in a nearby bin. 'Is there something more you can help me with. Help my client?'

She smiled, mouth closed. 'I'm just trying to point you in the right direction. I'm a journalist, not part of your legal team.'

'I don't feel you've been much help yet. I'm sure you can do better.'

'I'm sorry you feel that way.'

'Preventing innocent people from being convicted of serious crimes is important work.'

'I don't know if she is innocent, Peter. I'm only giving you some local history of her site.'

'How's the puppy?'

She looked at him for a moment, finished her own coffee. 'She's fine.'

'Does she have a name?'

'Zoe.'

'Zoe? That's Greek. Is there a subliminal message in that?'

She shook her head.

'My client is Greek-Australian. You must want to help?'

Roth walked over to the fence at the western boundary of the Limani site. Against it was a map of the local area. She pointed out the boundaries of the original planning approval, what the site covered now.

'This is a state government project now, not local council,' she said. 'They made it a state significant development when your client's company went belly up. Can't risk prime land like this getting into the wrong hands or having the opportunity squandered by local councillors. The scale of the project's nearly doubled since Tina Leonard had it. Lovro bought more locals out, got granted a bigger approval.'

'Did I miss the headline about doubling the size?'

'They bought people out slowly. They're on about their fifth development consent. It's gotten bigger bit by bit, not in one hit. Most of the land, though, was owned by your client. It's just that all of the land wasn't part of the project. Lovro's managed to get an approval for a project that covers nearly the whole site. And that tower is twenty storeys higher than Tina's, and it's now part five-star hotel, not residential only.'

He stood there listening to her, then looking at the map.

'You look unhappy,' she said. 'What are you thinking?'

'That my client might be innocent.'

She smiled. 'Is that a problem?'

'It is if she's convicted.'

Roth shielded her eyes from the sun to look at him more closely. 'You know SEBC didn't make a loss selling this place to Lovro. Even though they took a bath on your client's loans.'

He nodded. 'Something to do with the deal they reached with Nipori when they bought it. Tina told me.'

THE BURDEN OF LIES

'Nipori's liquidators. Do you know how it worked?'

'Probably not as well as you do.'

'Don't blame yourself. I've seen the contract.'

He paused. 'Can I?'

She shook her head. 'No. The deal's not secret though.' She looked at her watch. 'I don't have long. I suppose I can walk you through it quickly.'

He glanced to the east. 'That sun is going to burn you soon,' he said. 'You'll be fried by the time I understand.'

She drove them back to her carpark in the rear lane behind the terrace in Surry Hills where *The DI* had its office space. There were four spaces reserved for staff. She parked next to a brand-new Tesla.

'This is your copyeditor's, I assume?' he said when they got out of her car.

'I've never pretended my father isn't wealthy.'

They ordered coffee in a café a few doors down the road. The staff knew her well. She got a hello from a waitress, the barista, another woman behind the counter. There were half-a-dozen customers. Between them all, perhaps fifteen to twenty visible tattoos.

'So?' she said as soon as they took a seat.

'Explain this deal to me. The Nipori liquidator actually pays SEBC if it makes a loss on loans it took over from Nipori like the ones Leonard Development had?'

'That's the deal SEBC cut with the liquidator when they bought it. The security they had for buying a collapsing bank.'

'Sounds like a shit deal if you're a creditor of Nipori. How exactly did it work?'

She shrugged. 'Forget figures for a moment. SEBC bought most of Nipori's Asian assets – which included their Australian and New Zealand banks. They bought them from Nipori's parent company, which survived the GFC by offloading assets in this part of the world. It was a complex deal – cash, share and debt swaps. Nipori's parent is registered in Belize. It gets very messy if you try to unpick all the transactions from scratch. Anyway, Nipori in ANZ, and in a lot of other places, was in a pretty distressed state. The deal SEBC negotiated was that it agreed to pay a fixed amount for the ANZ business, but if certain loans Nipori made resulted in a loss because they were under-secured, that money retrospectively came off the purchase price. They had part of the purchase price they'd paid left in some trust or escrow account so that part of the deal could more easily play itself out. The formula is complex, and some panel of independent banking experts was agreed on to make rulings.'

'Nice deal,' he said.

'The quid pro quo was that a small percentage of profits from good loans also got added to the price. There's a complex formula about that, too.'

'So how did this play out with Leonard Developments and Limani?'

'Pretty straightforward from what I know. Let's talk in round numbers. Your client's company owed SEBC about two hundred and thirty million. They sold Limani for a hundred. Other projects then had the pin pulled on them, were sold off, and in rough terms covered the debts, with some left over to be used to reduce what was owing on Limani. The shortfall was still over eighty million. That sum ultimately came out of the Nipori escrow account, refunding SEBC so they effectively lost nothing from Leonard going under.'

'So did SEBC deliberately sell Limani at an undervalue, or just not care because it wouldn't matter to them?'

'I'm sure the agreement they had with Nipori's administrators would require them to sell assets in good faith in a bona fide sale – which would be the same obligation they'd have to your client. But – I don't know. Lovro Constructions is a pretty important client for SEBC. Here and globally.'

They sat silently for a few moments.

'What's your story about, Rachel?' he asked when the coffee came. 'The whole banking industry? The lack of pollution at the site we were at today? How SEBC got hold of it, who it sold it to? Why the government has approved what it has? What is it?'

'We're not discussing that.'

'Why tell me anything?'

'I felt guilty after our drink last week. If your client gets convicted, I don't want the burden of passing on nothing.'

'You sound pessimistic about Tina's chances.'

'I said if she was convicted.'

'I'm pretty good. If you're ever in serious legal trouble I'd be one of the people you should call.'

'I'll keep that in mind.'

'You look like someone who might need somebody like me one day.'

She raised an eyebrow. 'How so?'

'Hard to put into words. I sense it.'

'Should I be offended?'

'Flattered. My impression is the crime you'll commit will be for a worthy cause.'

'Really?'

'Which would put you into my favourite class of client.'

'What class are they?'

'Robin Hood types. Whistle-blowers. Women who kill violent men – particularly with axes or long screwdrivers. Conscientious objectors. My specialty is accused witches.'

'How many rapists and child molesters have you defended, Peter?'

'You just killed the mood.'

'There was a mood?'

'I was heading towards one. That vacant block of land next to Limani,' he said, 'what's happening there?'

She picked up her espresso, sipped on it like she hadn't heard him. 'Sixty-four-billion-dollar question,' she said.

'Billion? What's the development consent say?'

'Nothing.'

'Nothing?'

'Undesignated – currently open space.'

'What are the options?'

'The options will be limited to what makes the most money.'

'And what would that be?'

'I'll keep my suspicions to myself. They might only confuse you.'

'I'm hard to confuse. What if I gave you something in return for hearing your suspicions? And to find out what they're based on.'

'Gave me something? Beyond a dog, you mean?'

'Access.'

'Access to what?'

'My client. Exclusive access. Inside the defence team.'

She leant back, smiled. 'Our publication doesn't do PR for murderers.'

'She's . . .'

'Or even accused murderers.'

'I wasn't talking "PR".'

She shook her head, finished her coffee. 'I've shared with you what I can. Now I have a clear conscience. And I've got to get to work.'

He smiled at her. The big smile, with the good set of teeth and the glint in the eye.

'What?' she said.

'I saw something when you told me that. A tell.'

'A tell?'

'I've had a lot of conversations over the years with people who weren't telling me the truth, or at least not all of it. You just joined the club.'

She stood. 'You're pretty rude, you know that?'

'I've been called much worse. Usually by clients. Sometimes by judges. In and out of court.'

'I'm not surprised.'

'An ex-policeman called me the C-word last night.'

'I wouldn't go that far.'

'This is the best date I've had in a while, then.'

A roll of the green eyes. 'Thanks for the coffee,' she said.

'Thanks for the tour. I'll call you in a day or two with my follow-up questions.'

He watched her walk out of the café and down the street for as far as he could until she disappeared.

25

'I went to the Limani Views site yesterday,' Tanner told Kit Gallagher the next morning. He was seated at the table in her conference room. Gallagher was standing on the other side of the table, sipping a takeaway coffee.

'To prepare for today?'

'Partly. That journo called me. Roth, from *The Daily Informant*. She wanted to tell me a few things.'

'Like?'

'I'll tell you after.'

'I thought she didn't want to talk to you?'

'I bought her a dog. Well, Tina did.'

A substantial pause. 'A dog?'

'When I met her, she told me her dog had died.'

'And so you –'

'I'll itemise it in my next bill.'

Gallagher put her coffee cup on the table and a hand on a hip. 'How much?'

'Fifteen hundred. Plus my travel time.'

'You're not serious?'

'The progeny of Mark of Zorro don't come cheap, Kit.'

'I am not billing my client for a –'

'It's an investment.'

'In what?'

'Possibly in useful information.'

'You can't –' she paused, put her other hand on a hip. 'Pretty girl.'

'Zoe? Adorable. I've put in an order for another from the mother's next litter.'

Gallagher shook her head. 'Rachel Roth. I met her at some charity do once. Very pretty.'

Tanner nodded. 'Less experienced version of you, Kit.'

'Scrawnier than me,' she said absently, glancing at her watch. She let out a deep sigh. 'These people are late.'

They were waiting for Ronald Small and Garry Worner. Small and Worner were professional valuers, both partners in valuation firms. They'd been retained by Tina Leonard for her counterclaim against SEBC, where she alleged they'd sold out Limani Views from under her at such a low price it amounted to bad faith – effectively fraud.

At ten past eleven Jenny Singh opened the conference room door and led them in. Small and Worner were bookends of their calling. Small was off the rack, Worner was Asian tailor. Both had mid-fifties-style combed back hair. Worner's was blow dried with a soft curl. He'd had his teeth whitened. Small hadn't. His were a shade of botrytis, and suited to a Dickens character. He was a pack-a-day man, and he hit the hard spirits every night. Tanner wanted to offer Worner a dry sherry, Small a glass of methylated spirits. Kit Gallagher rang for coffee.

'Were you surprised you lost?' Tanner asked once the introductions were done.

Small looked at Worner for reassurance. Worner turned to Tanner, tilted his head slightly before answering. 'Not really,' he said, a smile on his face that seemed to be an indication of discomfort.

'Not really?'

Worner shook his head. 'Proving a bad faith sale isn't easy. I'm sure you've read the judgement.'

Tanner nodded. Tina Leonard's Limani Views development site had been sold through an expression of interest tender.

The winning bid was $100 million. Worner valued the site at $430 million, and Small had a range up to $400 million. SEBC's valuer's range was $95–$110 million.

'Are you guys usually so far apart in cases?'

Worner glanced at Small, smiled tightly. 'It's not unheard of.'

'Is that because none of you can be relied on?'

Small shrugged. His bottom lip appeared permanently stained from red wine.

'How hard can it be?' Tanner continued. 'You look at a few comparable sales, you fix a price per square metre, you add or minus a few per cent depending on location and size. How do you end up three hundred million apart on land that's about four hundred metres by two hundred metres?'

Worner looked more offended. 'It's not that simple,' he said. 'There were opportunity issues to consider here. Risk percentages. The market was still arguably depressed, most of the comparable sales were from a pre-GFC market, and there were very few true comparables anyway. There was the uncertain issue of contamination.'

'You sound like the bank's valuer, not Tina Leonard's.'

Worner snorted. 'You asked me if I was surprised Tina lost. I'm explaining why I wasn't.'

There was a lull when the coffee was brought in and distributed, and when Tanner was about to ask his next question, Jenny Singh got in first.

'Did you see the winning tender documents?'

There was another silence. The valuers looked at each other. 'It's been a long while since we did our reports,' Worner said. 'I don't even have my file any more, just the copy of the expert report I did that you sent me. Do you, Ron?'

Small shook his head, and mercifully kept his mouth shut.

'What about the under bidders? Did you see their documents?'

Worner shrugged again.

'There's an area about a hundred metres by a hundred metres that's not being built on at the moment – do you know what that's for?' Tanner asked.

Worner looked up, to the right, then back at Tanner. 'Now, or then?'

'Well – start with then.'

'Open space,' Small said. 'A public park.'

'And now?'

Worner smiled. 'Who knows?' he said. 'I'm sure the concept plan still has it as a park. I'm sure also the developer would like it rezoned for residential and resort uses. Preferably both.'

Tanner glared at him. 'You know something we don't, Garry?'

Worner shook his head. 'Just stating the obvious.'

'Can we go back to the beginning?' Kit Gallagher asked. Everyone looked at her. 'I'm still stuck on the difference between your four hundred and thirty million valuation, and SEBC's valuer at one hundred and ten. How can there possibly be that much difference?'

Worner took responsibility for the answer. 'This is eighty-odd thousand square metres of land. When they analysed their comparable sales, they put bigger discount factors in than we did – or at least, didn't put the increases in we did. They wrote it down because there weren't many players in the market for such a big site. I think what they were really doing in their expert report was justifying the valuation SEBC had put on the land before it agreed to accept the bid they received.'

'Why were you so optimistic about value?' Tanner asked.

Worner shrugged, as though the answer was obvious. 'This is a huge waterfront site on the western side of the harbour, close to the CBD. One of the last opportunities of this kind. I thought that was worth a substantial premium. The judge disagreed. He had the luxury of being able to say so did the market. I had to argue the price was so low it shouldn't have been accepted.'

'Was Lovro Constructions issued with a subpoena for the documents showing how they came up with their bid price?'

Neither Small nor Worner answered for a moment. 'I don't know,' Worner said eventually.

'Might've shown if they thought they were trying to make a steal?'

There was an awkward pause, and Tanner took a sip of his coffee, prompting others to follow. 'You think your competition would talk to us?' he asked.

'Who?' Worner said, looking confused.

Tanner checked his notes. 'JVB – the firm who acted for SEBC. Glenn Johnstone, the valuer they used in the case. Do you think he'd talk to us? Do you know him? Valuation's a small world, isn't it?'

Worner looked more confused. 'Of course I know Glenn. What would you talk to him about? To tell him that he was wrong?'

'Not necessarily wrong. More about whether SEBC bribed him to deliberately value this land low.'

There was a long pause as Small and Worner looked at each other again. 'Why would they do that?' Small asked. 'The people at SEBC – they wouldn't want to make a loss from the sale, would they?'

'Wouldn't they?'

Neither valuer answered Tanner's question, which was rhetorical anyway.

'Depends if they got compensated by other means. Depends on how much they like Lovro Constructions. Depends on what they think they can get away with.'

Worner looked more confused. 'How does that make sense?'

Tanner shook his head. 'I don't know how it makes sense. But either you two are the most incompetent valuers in the country, or Tina Leonard and Leonard Developments got well and truly screwed.'

'You think that's why she's supposed to have killed the banker?' Small said.

No one spoke for several seconds, and Tanner assessed if he should punch the cretin in front of him. 'Our job is to argue that she didn't have Mr Randall killed, Ron,' he said instead.

Small's face froze, and then a light went on. Low wattage. 'Right,' he said.

26

She was wearing a black dress, held together by a large bow tied at the back of her neck. He stood to kiss her on the cheek as she reached the table. She was nearly as tall as he was in the heels.

'Thanks for coming over to the east,' he said as she sat. She looked around the dark subterranean bar, thick wooden beams above her head.

She'd had her hair cut into a blonde bob, fringe at the front. Peach lipstick. When she smiled, her faced seemed in better working order than the last time they'd met at her husband's law firm.

'Nice dress,' he said. Nice was the wrong word. He nearly winced. She smiled, thanked him, picked up the wine menu. There was a pink gem on the ring finger of her right hand she wasn't wearing last time, or that he hadn't noticed.

Simone Hargreaves – the ex-Mrs Oliver Randall – had contacted him; a text saying she had something to tell him. She hadn't wanted to talk on the phone. She'd insisted on his side of town.

'You haven't brought a partner from Lattimer Jones, have you?' Tanner asked. 'Do I have to run my questions by counsel?'

Simone Hargreaves shook her head. 'You'll have to put up with just me.'

'You seem taller than last time I met you.'

'I was sitting at that desk the whole time.'

'That explains it. Did your husband stand up? Is he tall?' Sometimes questions came out of Tanner's mouth without thought. Fortunately, that rarely happened in court.

She looked at him for a moment. 'About your height,' she said. 'Similar build.'

'Really. The impression I got was that he was getting chubby.'

'He's got a personal trainer. A guy called "The Chief", who he sees five times a week. He's very fit.'

'The Chief? Is he Native American?'

'Lebanese, I think. Nice bloke. I found him for Grant. He had a female trainer before, but he started sleeping with her, so . . .' She gave a shrug, like it didn't really matter.

Tanner took a breath, a touch stirred by the frankness, recovered his stride, put in an order for drinks with the waiter who had just appeared. She wanted a gin martini. Not what he expected. He ordered two. That was unexpected too. Arguably reckless. Time would tell.

'A tax lawyer, huh?' Tanner said. 'In between workouts?'

'Global corporations. He goes to Bermuda a lot. He had a tax trial on Jersey last year. He thinks he's very – international.'

'Full of terrible people, global corporations. At least the part of them that arranges tax affairs.'

'Grant doesn't like you, Peter,' she said. She said it nicely though. 'He wouldn't like us meeting like this.'

'Do you need his permission to talk to me?'

'I didn't seek it.'

'Why doesn't he like me?'

'You're a criminal lawyer.'

'That's his reason?'

'Perhaps you can give him a better one.'

'Stick to the first one. What's wrong with criminal lawyers?'

'I think he – it's hard to put it politely.'

'It's hard to offend me.'

'Let's just say he doesn't think highly of criminal lawyers. It might not be personal to you.'

Tanner smiled. 'I'm pretty sure I've defended a vampire once, Simone. And the Anti-Christ. I'd take them over an international tax attorney. No offence.'

She smiled vaguely. 'Are his clients really as bad as yours?'

'My clients pay their dues, one way or another. Where is Grant tonight, by the way?'

'He has client engagements most nights. Less than half involve me. Many involve him taking one of the young lawyers that work for him to a hotel. Not just for sex, though. I think they also spend some time snorting something that possibly originated with one of your clients.'

Tanner was taken aback again. She was cool, collected, but part of it was show. 'Hard to read the Tax Act unless you're high. As for the rest – what a cliché. Does he know you know?'

'I found a text from her a year ago, and his response. Graphic, and detailed. I took a photo of it with my own phone. His replies were more – economical.'

'Economical?'

She took in a deep breath. 'He was more to the point. The testosterone and urgent desire for her kept him brief.'

He paused. He wasn't often stuck for words. 'They say the adjective is the killer of good prose,' he finally said. 'I leave them out of all my written submissions. Even when I'm begging for mercy.'

'When I confronted him, he denied it. I texted him the photos of her messages. He said it was over. I'm pretty sure it's not.'

'Criminal lawyers are usually very faithful. It's because we uphold the Golden Thread. A tax lawyer's already doing things that should morally bother them. One step leads to another.'

The blue eyes sparkled, or at least he thought they had. Maybe it was the way she'd moved in the light. 'Perhaps you can do something that might bother him.'

Tanner stilled himself for a moment, tried to stay cool. It was already a bit like waiting for a jury, in some deeply important case. 'I feel obliged to pay my tax, Simone.'

'Something else.'

'I haven't even had a martini yet.'

She leant forward. Floral, citrus, a smell more than the sum of its parts. 'Let's have several.'

'If we have several, Grant's main concern should be that you'll have to carry me out of here.'

She sat back quickly. 'I don't want to talk about Grant.'

'We're here to talk about one of your husbands, though, right? The first?'

Simone nodded slowly, as the waiter put her martini in front of her. She picked up her glass, clinked his. 'Let's get to it,' she said. 'I don't want to be talking about Oliver or Grant by the time we're on our third.'

She'd nearly rung him only minutes after she'd left her husband's office on the morning he'd first talked to her, she told him. Then she'd hesitated, tried to put it out of her mind for a day or two, realised she'd never be able too. She wouldn't be able to live with the guilt if she didn't.

'I don't know if your client really did kill Oliver,' she said after a sip of her drink. She picked up the olive from the glass between a thumb and a long, carnation-coloured nail, pushed it between her lips, looked up at him.

'Can you tell me who did? I'll buy you dinner upstairs if you can.'

'I can make an educated guess. I can possibly do better than that.'

'An educated guess mightn't help. I like the sound of doing better.'

'I spoke to Oliver before he was killed,' she said. 'Not long after his release.'

'That isn't something you told us at the conference we had at your husband's law firm.'

She looked down, then up. 'Grant wouldn't have understood. And he wouldn't have wanted me telling you about it.'

'You didn't seem too fond of Oliver last time we spoke. That was show for Grant, was it?'

'Not really. He – I got a letter from him about six months

before he was released. A mea culpa. Three letters actually. There were details of his failings as a husband and father. "Sins" he called them. More detail than I wanted, frankly.' She paused to take another long sip of her martini. 'They were heartfelt letters, though. Almost an outpouring of grief when it came to Hannah – our daughter. He begged for a chance to make some kind of reparation for what he'd done to her. I – I ended up showing the letters to Han. She wasn't interested. Do you blame her?'

'I've spoken to a lot of kids whose fathers – usually it's the father – have gone to prison. I consider it – Jesus, it's part of the service. I had a mentor – Max – he's . . . Anyway. He always spoke to his clients' kids. Helped them when he could. No, I don't blame your daughter. You though – you agreed to meet with Oliver?'

'Not at first,' she said. 'I didn't reply to the letters. There was a lot of religious stuff in them. Quotes from the Bible. Oli had found religion – God – in prison.'

'A more likely spot than a commercial bank. Or the office of a tax lawyer.'

'It was genuine. He wanted to be a social worker when he was released. A lay minister – helping people on the streets.' She smiled. 'It was some transformation.'

'Did he try to convert you?'

She laughed. 'No, Peter, he didn't. You're not religious at all?'

'I'm very religious. I believe in evil. I've seen what the devil can do.'

She took another sip, emptied the glass. He felt it polite to follow, signalled for two more. They arrived with alarming speed for a busy bar.

'So, anyway,' she said, 'Oliver rang me when he was released.'

'Asking to meet?'

'That. And telling me why.'

'Which was?'

'He said he wanted to come clean about every terrible thing he'd done during our marriage.'

'Long meeting?'

'Not as long as Grant's will be, if you can believe it.'

This time he laughed. 'Hadn't he apologised in the letters?'

'He meant things outside of our marriage as well as within it.'

'His life's worth of sins. I don't envy you. One crime at a time is often too much for me to hear. Where did you meet?'

'Just for coffee at a place I'd never go. Near where he was living – in Redfern somewhere. A secret meeting, I suppose. A bit like tonight.'

'I've got too many sins to confess in one night, Simone. What were his?'

'He told me – he told me first the six kilos of coke really weren't his. He told me all about selling small amounts though, even who to. And how he bought it – with the bank's money.' She paused and shook her head. 'They even approved of it – can you believe it?'

'Very easily.'

'Anyway, he said the six kilos of coke wasn't his. He begged me to believe him. He wanted me to tell Hannah.' She looked into the martini glass like the meaning of life was in there. 'I was sure it was the truth, Peter. I hadn't – at the time I didn't. I didn't for the next six years. But – I'm sure he was telling the truth. I can't say why. I just know it.'

Tanner nodded. 'Which means at least one of the police planted it, or knew it'd been planted.'

'I asked him why someone would do that to him.'

'He have any theories?'

'He said the bank had done it to him.'

'They told him that?'

She shook her head.

'Don't tell me God told him. I'm with him at the moment.'

'He told me he'd done something stupid. More than stupid.'

'More stupid than supplying coke to his employer's clients and then pocketing and selling what was left?'

'He told me he'd done things for them that had made them – helped them with things that had made clients very happy. He'd asked for more money. A lot of money. Then he threatened them when he was high. I mean – he was being paid a lot, but he asked for something – well, he was stupid. Next thing, he ends up in prison.'

'He might have got off lightly at the time.'

'He was told to shut his mouth, or worse would happen. That's why he pleaded guilty.'

'Did he mention my client – any specifics? Because she says he confessed a lot more to her.'

She shook her head. 'I didn't give him long. I said he could have half an hour. Some of this is in one of the letters he sent me and Hannah. I sent him a text after I left. I – was going to talk to Hannah about her meeting with him. He seemed so . . . different. So contrite.'

Tanner nodded, finished his second martini.

'So he – what? Almost tried to blackmail his employer? For committing some kind of crimes for them that he didn't specify to you? And he wonders why they got upset?'

She shook her head. 'Oli was fried a lot of the time back then. Taking coke at work. Behaving erratically. Telling them to pay him vast sums. Selling their coke. He thought in the end they saw him as an unnecessary risk.'

'Who did, though, Simone?'

'The senior executives at SEBC.'

'They're all in on this?'

She looked at the ceiling like she was saying a quick prayer. 'The very senior people. He thought they saw him as a security risk. They dealt with it.'

'Non-lethal force the first time. Not so the second.'

She ordered the third martinis, then closed her eyes, and when she opened them a tear nearly leaked from each. 'He didn't say this,' she said. 'I – I didn't give him the chance. I've been thinking it, though. I think he pleaded guilty to protect us. To protect Hannah.'

Tanner looked down at his empty glass, wondered for a few moments how much sense that made. When Simone had composed herself, he said, 'Do you know if Oliver had spoken to anyone else about this? Anyone other than you? Someone in prison?'

She shook her head. 'He wasn't on a crusade against SEBC, Peter. He knew their power. He wanted to make personal amends, get on with his life.'

'Before my client had him killed, if you believe the prosecution. Make personal amends how?'

'Confess his sins. To me. To my daughter. Not to the world.' She leant back as their next round of drinks arrived, picked the olive straight out. 'He did tell me someone was chasing him. They had even — he was still in prison when they first wrote to him.'

'Chasing him? Who?'

'A journalist who wanted to talk to him about SEBC. Banks generally, I think he said. He didn't want to talk to them.'

'What journalist?'

She shook her head. 'He said it in passing. He was going to meet them to get rid of them I think. That was all he said.'

'Male or female journalist?'

'He didn't say. Is this important?'

'I'm not sure. It could be.' He took a long sip of this third martini. 'The senior people at SEBC when Oliver was arrested — there's someone called Phil Carter. He was CEO then?'

Simone took a deep breath and exhaled slowly before answering. 'Phillip P Carter, Peter. He was the CEO. I think he's on the board. Oli's immediate boss was a guy called Jack Rodriguez. He's the CEO now. A real prick.'

'And — if everything Oliver told you was true — they knew about it?'

Simone picked up her glass, took a healthy swig. 'Oh yeah.'

'The letter Oliver sent to you, the one to your daughter. You've kept copies?'

She nodded.

'And you'll give them to me?'

'I knew you'd ask.'

'They'd help my client. I'd rather they contained his confession of his sins against her, but I'll take what I can get.'

'How can I say no?'

'What about giving evidence?'

She smiled like she was in pain. 'That, I'm not so sure. I can't really say much beyond what Oli said in the letters.'

'The right live witness is better than a document.'

She paused. 'I need to speak to Hannah first. I'm not sure she thinks her late father's sins are the best publicity for her.'

'What about Grant?'

'Fuck Grant.'

'Terrible way to talk about your husband.'

She smiled a kind of sad smile, picked up her phone from the table, pushed a button on it. 'Shall I read this to you?'

'Sure.'

'I'll be late. I have keys. Grant.'

'At least there's no unnecessary adjectives.'

'Romantic, isn't he?'

'Marriage has its ups and downs.'

She tilted her head, paused for a provocative moment. 'I'd like to finish this drink,' she said, 'and then go home with you.'

Part of him wanted to laugh. Part of him didn't. 'Is that wise?'

'Why not?'

'I usually don't sleep with potential witnesses. Witnesses and judges. Everyone else is fair game.'

'I think you should bend the rules.'

'You're being very direct. I tend to flirt around this issue.'

'You don't approve of me, Peter? I'm not your idea of a North Shore housewife?'

'Well, you might be my fantasy of a North Shore housewife. I don't disapprove though. Good criminal lawyers are like Nick Carraway. We reserve all judgements.'

She said nothing for ten seconds. Then, 'Gatsby.'

He was probably going to sleep with her now.

There were still ethical issues to be debated. Simone Hargreaves was the ex-wife of the man his client was charged with having organised to kill. That sat a little – awkwardly. It was also within the realms of possibility that Simone could end up a witness at the trial, or at the very least be the source of a letter he would tender.

Simone was married.

She looked at him, smiled.

Fuck Grant.

Tanner put Simone Hargreaves into an Uber Black just before four am. He wondered if she'd beat Grant home.

To the extent he might need her help for his client, he had to make sure that whatever happened between them didn't turn into a mess. That was a professional obligation. He wondered if defending the accused while having an affair with the ex-wife of her alleged victim was some kind of first. He imagined it happened all the time in Europe. Still, it was a first for him.

When the Uber drove off, he checked his phone. Two texts. Both were from Rachel Roth. The second was sent just before one am. *Can you please call me.* The first had been sent at 11.47 pm. He'd heard it in the background as he was undoing the bow of Simone Hargreaves' dress – not easy after five martinis. A similar message.

He returned Rachel Roth's call at seven, got voicemail. He'd try again after his meeting.

27

Ioannidis & Sons had their office space in Double Bay. They had half the top floor of a newly renovated four-level commercial building off New South Head Road. Jenny Singh was waiting in reception when he arrived. Theo and Jim Ioannidis had finally agreed to speak to their sister's lawyers, as long as they had their own.

Their lawyer's name was Steven Haddid. 'Theo and Jim will see you now,' he said to Tanner, ignoring Jenny Singh. 'We're going to have to get some things straight before you ask any questions though, and they only have forty-five minutes.'

Theo and Jim Ioannidis were sitting at one end of a ten-seat board table, closest to the wall that held an enormous television. Theo, the elder son, had taken the seat at the head of the table. He had on a tradie's T-shirt, and there were flecks of paint on one forearm like he was still on the tools. Jim, the younger brother, was thinner than Theo, and in a smart suit, no tie. Theo was almost all silver now, Jim still dark with flecks of grey. Neither stood when introductions were made, and handshakes were cursory. Theo glared out the window as Haddid started to read out the ground rules.

'What are you doing here, Steve?' Tanner interrupted.

'I'm sorry?'

Tanner looked at the Ioannidi. 'Why do either of you think you need a lawyer to talk to your sister's defence counsel?'

'I don't think that's –'

'Our sister has caused us to see a lot of lawyers,' Jim Ioannidis said, cutting Haddid off.

'You mean because she wanted a small share of your father's estate?'

Jim Ioannidis smiled a kind of smug smile, and Theo turned his gaze from the window to glare at Tanner.

'One of the rules is that we aren't discussing that,' Haddid said. 'We've recently discovered Tina may have perjured herself in an affidavit in that case. There's a chance I might be instructed to seek to re-open the settlement.'

'Good luck with that, Steve. Nothing like kicking someone while they're down. Re-opening a settlement is marginally more difficult than winning an acquittal in China. Trust me, I know these things. And you can stick your rules.'

There was a chance the conference might end more quickly than desirable, but Tanner's instinct was that the Ioannidis brothers weren't going to say much anyway, and getting on the front foot was as good an approach as any.

'What do you want from us, Mr Tanner?' Jim Ioannidis asked.

'Your opinion.'

'Our opinion?'

'Did your sister have Oliver Randall killed?'

Jim Ioannidis laughed out loud. Theo shifted in his seat, muttered, 'For fuck's sake.'

'That's a "no", Theo?' Tanner asked.

'How would we know?' Jim said.

Tanner shrugged as though the answer was obvious. 'She's your sister, Jim. You've known her all your life. Is she a killer?'

'That's a ridiculous question,' Haddid said.

Tanner looked at Haddid, considered an unnecessary insult, said instead, 'It's the most pertinent question anyone can ask in a murder case.'

'What I meant was . . .'

'Oliver Randall was your banker too, wasn't he?' Tanner asked.

'SEBC is one of our lenders,' Jim said.

'Yeah, but you knew Randall too, right? Tina's told me that.'

'Our main funder was Nipori. Randall took over when SEBC bought them.'

'Randall liked to throw big parties, I understand. SEBC did anyway. Did you go to any?'

'Ask Tina if she went with Randall to any of his parties,' Jim said.

'They seem to me to be the kind of affairs only male clients were invited to, Jim. Banking and the financial markets seem like a bit of a boys' club. And I'm asking you if you went?'

Jim Ioannidis looked at Haddid, who took his cue. 'How is this relevant?'

'I don't understand your question, Steve. Relevant to what?'

'Exactly.'

'You're not making sense. What did you have in mind when you said "relevant"?'

'Relevant to why you're here.'

'Why do you think I'm here?'

'Look, are you going to play games or – ?'

'Your clients, Steve – these model brothers – both signed committal statements for the Director of Public Prosecutions saying how big a grudge their sister had against Oliver Randall after her court case with SEBC. Why do you think we're here now?'

'Our statements didn't say that,' Jim cut in, 'and we had no choice. The police put direct questions to us about it. We had to cooperate. We're running a large business.'

'You gave them motive, Jim,' Tanner said.

Jim laughed. 'They already knew, mate.'

'You're her family, Jim. You endorsed their case theory in blood. Are you going to repeat that at trial? Give evidence against your blood?'

'Fuck you,' Jim said. 'Jayden Webb had already confessed by the time we were spoken to. Mick Bitar had told them Tina tried to go through him. Do you expect us to lie to the police?'

'Sure. If it gets your sister acquitted. I'm big on families sticking together.'

'Your attitude is pretty offensive, Mr Tanner,' Haddid said.

Tanner laughed. 'Our paths haven't crossed, Steve. I'm a long way short of my offensive best. I'll pat you on the head when I get there.' He looked back at Jim Ioannidis. 'He was a drug dealer, Oliver Randall. You knew that, right?'

'When?'

'When he was your banker.'

'No.'

'Really?'

'Really.'

'He did five and a half years in prison for it.'

'What's your point?'

'Tina told you Randall and SEBC screwed her – when they called in her loans? That's in your statement to the police.'

Jim Ioannidis took a deep breath, looked at Tanner like he was considering ending the meeting. 'It is,' he said.

'She told you Randall and the bank ratted on a deal to give her more time to complete her Limani Views project?'

Jim shook his head. 'She didn't tell us that level of detail. We rarely spoke. She'd rung asking for a loan from the family company. The company she left.'

'Which you generously refused.'

'She went out on her own. She was a big girl. We had our own bills to pay.'

'Did you run that decision by your father?'

Jim looked unhappy with that comment. 'They weren't talking. My father was not well. Tina had a lot to do with that. We've grown, but we are still a family-owned business, not a multinational. We didn't have two hundred or so million lying around to bail Tina out. She piled up that debt on her own.'

'She asked you to tide her over for a couple of monthly payments and to sort out some arrears, not pay every dime.'

'Her company, her responsibility,' Jim said.

'Did Adrian Leonard ever tell you how Randall and SEBC screwed Tina?'

Jim shook his head. 'No. He didn't tell a court, either.'

'He had a change of heart about that,' Tanner said. 'It's called a bribe.'

'That's bullshit. Adrian's a good father to my nephews. Tina's fuck-up wasn't his fault.'

Tanner looked at the elder Ioannidis, who'd barely spoken. 'Are you mute, Theo? You can talk, right?'

'That is offensive,' Haddid said.

'Let him tell me.'

'I'm not a mute,' Theo Ioannidis said, his voice low and soft.

'Forgive me,' Tanner said.

Theo lifted his hand, pointed at Jenny Singh. 'Is she?'

Singh looked up from the notes she'd been taking on a pad – usually she typed quickly into a laptop but Tanner had told her the day before that this might put the Ioannidis brothers off – and sat up straight. 'You know,' she said, 'one option you both had with the police, which you didn't explore, was to add a qualification to what you told them. You could have said, "I knew my sister wasn't happy with Oliver Randall after she lost her case years ago with the bank, but I know she'd never kill him". Something like that. Did the police leave that bit out, by any chance?'

Tanner looked at Jim first, then Theo. 'I guess she's not a mute. Can I ring the DPP on your behalf and tell him you'd like to add that to your statements?'

The silence was so sudden it was like the ceiling fell down. Tanner broke it.

'How good a friend is Mick Bitar to you?'

Jim Ioannidis shook his head slowly. 'Business acquaintances, not friends.'

'That's not Tina's view. Or Taz's.'

'They're wrong. Maybe Mick is friends with them.'

Tanner laughed loudly. 'Friends? What kind of enemies does Tina have?' He looked at both brothers but got no verbal response, just a heightening of non-verbal hostility. 'Doesn't Bitar work for you? Doesn't he have some business now where he supplies materials for building projects?'

'He's never been one of our employees. Sometimes we buy stuff from his company.'

'He's done more than that, hasn't he?'

Jim looked sideways at Theo, whose face remained unreadable. 'Little jobs that all builders and developers need done from time to time. He's sometimes been used like a subbie for project management–type roles. Making sure things arrive on site on time. Materials. Contractors. Dealing with other stakeholders.'

'Is "dealing with" a euphemism for bribing or beating up?'

'That's it,' Haddid said, standing up.

'Oliver Randall got dealt with by someone. Was he a stakeholder? Is one means of dealing with a stakeholder to shoot them in the head?'

'You should ask our sister about that,' Theo said. 'She had more than one reason not to like Randall.'

'I'm asking you. You've got a lot of experience with developing land. What do you think of the deal Lovro Construction got buying your sister's site? People tell me it was a bargain.'

'Right place at the right time,' Jim said.

'Do you know Luka Ravic?'

'Vaguely. Lovro's in a bigger league to us at the moment.'

'Does Mick Bitar know Ravic?'

'How would we know that?'

'I'm asking you – does he?'

'Maybe.'

'Do you know the hitman, Jayden Webb? He's worked on your sites?'

Jim frowned, shook his head. 'We've told the police this. No. We have dozens of people on our building sites. We don't personally – you already know this. Why are you asking?'

'Sometimes people tell me things they don't tell the police.'

'Not us.'

Tanner took a deep breath, sighed. 'You know – I haven't raised this, but I will. I think your sister is innocent. I think she's been set up. Mick Bitar is part of that. He'll be going to court soon to tell a lie about her. I know you've hired this guy's services in the past. Probably for things you don't want to talk about publicly. Now would be the time to tell me things I can use against him. I'd like everything, but I'll settle for anything.' He looked at the brothers, but neither spoke. 'You care, right. About your sister? How about your nephews, her children?'

'We've done plenty for those boys,' Theo Ioannidis said slowly.

'Last year, Tina contacted you about wanting to come back into the family business. You remember that, right?'

Theo looked at his brother. Theo started to grin, Jim laughed. 'Do you know our sister very well, Mr Tanner?'

'I'm working on it.'

'She would never want to come back to us,' he said.

'Why?'

Jim Ioannidis shook his head, didn't respond otherwise.

'Time's up,' Haddid said. He'd been standing for a few minutes. This time, though, Jim Ioannidis stood, and so did his brother. Tanner looked at Jenny Singh, and they both got up to leave. Tanner took out his wallet before he did, and slid two of his cards to the brothers. They looked at them like he'd thrown dog turds on the table.

'In case you remember something about Bitar or Webb,' he said. 'Or if you hear from anyone about who really had Oliver Randall killed.'

28

Tanner left work early that afternoon.

Tina Leonard's trial was fast approaching. Running a trial was no different to being away on the road. Lawyers lost marriages to long trials. They lost themselves. They take over, wrap their poisonous roots around you, squeeze you dry.

Daniel wasn't home. There was a short text explaining he was at a friend's house. *Want to go out for pizza?* Tanner texted back. *Maybe* was the response.

When Dan did get home, not long before six, he rolled in with two other boys from his school. They took up residence in a guest room in front of PlayStation. Tanner opened a beer, watched them for a few minutes. FIFA was considered, passed over for a game where the combatants are tougher, handy with weapons. The death count was going to be high.

One of the boys turned and looked at him watching them. 'Do you play this?' he said.

Tanner smiled, shook his head. 'I'm familiar with the milieu. I'm these sorts of guys' lawyer.'

The boy pondered that for a moment, nodded at him with a look that could have indicated respect, then turned back to the game.

Tanner finished his beer, took orders from the boys, and was about to call one of the local pizzerias when his phone started to vibrate, and the name Rachel Roth came up on the screen.

She sounded flat, tired. 'The police were at my apartment last night,' she said. 'They left just before I sent that text. If I woke you –'

'The police?'

'I had a break-in.'

'Christ, I'm sorry. What was taken?'

'My computer. Every piece of paper in the house with my writing on it. The place was turned over – at least my study and my bedroom.'

'Jesus, Rachel. I'm so sorry.'

She didn't reply.

Tanner was looking across at the boys on the couch, one of them stroking the small dog lying between them, her ears pricked, as seemingly transfixed by the game as they were. 'Do you have someone with you?' he said.

'I'm fine. My father has – he's taken care of things.' She didn't sound fine.

'I'm going to be driving some boys home in a couple of hours. Then I'm coming around to say hello. Text me the address.'

Rachel Roth turned quickly after opening the door for him, walking towards the floor-to-ceiling glass like she was walking into the ocean. Her hair was pinned up at the back, and she was wearing long pyjama bottoms, a T-shirt; looked like she hadn't slept for a couple of days.

She disappeared into another room, came out holding a towel for him. He was soaked. The weather had turned from summer to bleak autumn in the space of twenty-four hours. A rain storm had arrived as he was parking his car.

She sat at a round table that overlooked the beach, a bottle of white wine open in front of her. The moment she sat she got back up to get a glass for him, poured it without asking whether he wanted it or not.

He sat opposite her, took a sip of the wine before speaking. 'Are you scared?'

She looked mildly insulted for a moment, let it pass. 'My father has organised a security guard. He's in a car in front of the building. The other residents have never been safer.'

Tanner looked around the open-plan living space and kitchen. The side facing the ocean was all glass, two sliding doors in the centre leading out to a terrace. They were on the fifth floor. The only other entrance was the door he'd come through. She had to do something to make the lift take him up.

'How'd they get in?'

She sipped wine, sighed. 'No idea. Front door, it seems.'

'No idea?'

She shook her head.

'No forced entry?'

'I have an alarm. I know it was on. You can't get up in the lift unless I push a button for you — you need a security pass otherwise. The alarm didn't go off, none of the doors were broken or tampered with, the other window is twenty metres from the ground.'

'Wow,' he said. 'Not amateurs.'

She nodded, smiled bitterly. 'Yeah, not amateurs. It's like I'd let them in.'

'Everything's been fingerprinted, I assume? There must be CCTV in this place or outside, right? What's the — ?'

'The film was blank. I was told it was a software glitch, but who knows? No one saw anything.'

'I hate to say this, I guess the cops would have, but if they've got in once —'

'I've had the alarm changed. The security code for the lift has been changed. Then there's the guard. I told Dad no, but I know he'll be following me everywhere.'

'What have you told him? Your father?'

'He's not stupid. He knows what's happened — this kind of break-in — he knows it's something to do with work. He wanted to know what I'm working on, told me me to drop it.'

'What exactly are you working on? This — I know people who are really good at breaking and entering, Rachel. Most aren't this good. I'm trying to think who might be able to do this, and why. What's your thinking?'

'They weren't here for one thing,' she said. 'They took every piece of paper in the apartment. Even some bills. The computer, my backup –'

'The stuff on your computer – you'd have a backup system at work, right?'

She nodded. 'I don't keep everything – there's still some things. Look, we're not a big media company. Some things I had here aren't also at work. I've lost them for –'

'Who knows about the story you're working on? Who at *The Daily Informant*?'

'No one,' she said. 'No one knows all the details.'

'You don't talk to your colleagues? Your employees, I mean? Surely you discuss what you're looking into?'

She shook her head. 'Not this. Not in detail.'

'I find that hard to believe.'

'Believe what you want. I own the company. I don't have to –'

'What did Oliver Randall tell you when you met him, Rachel? And when were you going to tell me about that?'

She looked at him blankly, then drank some more wine before she said, 'He told me nothing.'

He looked at her for several seconds, then said, 'If he told you something that could help Tina Leonard, you have to tell me. You understand that, right? You should tell the police and the prosecutor if he did that, but I'm willing to pass it on for you.'

'He didn't want to talk to me. We met, he said he didn't – who told you this?'

'Forget who told me. What did he tell you?'

'Nothing that will help your client.'

'Let me decide that. What did you ask him?'

She took a deep breath, let it out slowly. 'What do you think? His thoughts about prison? I asked him about his bank, Peter. I knew about the Limani View case involving your client. They did the same thing to two other developers of big projects – one in Melbourne, one on the Gold Coast. I wanted to ask him about that. He didn't want to say anything. He was scared of them. If he'd told me something that might really help Tina Leonard then –'

'Oliver Randall found God in prison, Rachel. The Father, the Son, and the Holy Ghost. He wanted confessional. He wanted to tell people what a sinner he'd been. He'd been talking to the Lord about SEBC. My experience with people like that is that they like to spread the Word. You and your publication would be a perfect means of doing that.'

'He was scared. Whoever he was confessing to, it wasn't going to be a journalist.' She didn't seem to be lying, but it was hard to tell with her.

'Randall wasn't a commercial-level drug dealer. The drugs that put him in prison weren't his. His employer probably set him up. Did he mention that?'

She shook her head. 'He agreed to meet me. It was only to tell me he wasn't interested in answering my questions. He asked me to stop contacting him. He wanted to get on with his life, he said. Something like that.'

They sat in silence for a few moments, then she said, 'Why would they do that to him? Plant drugs in his house?'

'I was hoping he told you that. He told my client. Your word might carry more weight than hers at her trial.'

'And what does she say?'

He smiled, shook his head. 'When you tell me something useful, Rachel, I'll give you something.'

'I don't get it anyway,' she said. 'Wasn't it bad publicity for them? Having a senior executive caught up in a drug bust? Jailed for trafficking?'

Tanner shrugged. 'Being uncompetitive with rates or having their share price drop is bad publicity for a bank. Not meeting the market's expectations on half-yearly results is bad publicity. An employee dealing coke – nothing new for the big end of town in Sydney. And teaching someone a lesson the way they did is potentially less messy than having them killed. Getting caught having one of your employees murdered – that probably is bad publicity.'

Roth stood and walked to the sink, asked him if he wanted a glass of water, poured one for herself.

'You know,' he said, 'Randall – if he wasn't going to talk to you, he could have told you that over the phone. He didn't have to meet you.'

She downed most of the water in one hit. 'I pressed him to meet. He agreed. He wouldn't talk to me about anything I asked him.'

'C'mon, Rachel,' he said, raising his voice. 'Someone just broke into your house. You're doing a story on SEBC. I'm defending one of its victims. We're on the same side. I don't want your story. I'm a lawyer, not a competitor. He must have said something.'

She glared at him, said nothing.

'Who knew you were meeting him?' Tanner said.

'No one.'

'No one? What time was this meeting?'

'The morning. About eleven.'

'What did you say you were doing when you left? You left from the office?'

'I don't have to get permission to go out, Peter.'

'How did you get there? You drove?'

She nodded.

'In your car, or someone else's?'

'Mine.'

'Where was this meeting?'

She shrugged. 'Some café in Alexandria – nearer Redfern maybe. I forget the name. Near his flat.'

He finished his glass of wine. 'I guess I should get going if you're not going to tell me anything,' he said. 'My son's at home. It's getting late. Are you okay here?'

She nodded, and he stood to leave, then suddenly thought of something.

'The dog? The puppy – Zoe? Was she here when – ?'

'She was downstairs,' Rachel said. 'She's still fretting when I'm out. She's – one of my neighbours is looking after her for now. I'll –'

'Nice neighbour,' he said, and walked to the door.

'Pete?' she said.

He turned.

'I probably – I – my old dog. I should tell you. He didn't just die.'

'What do you mean?'

She took a deep breath, sat back down at the table. 'A few weeks ago, the same thing happened.'

'What happened?'

'People got in here.' She looked up at him, eyes moistening. 'I found him on the bed. His neck was broken. All my stuff was taken then. My computer, papers. Tonight – I don't know why they came back tonight. Send me another message, get my new computer, I don't know. Maybe – maybe they would have killed –'

Tanner had been breathing deeply, trying to stay calm, but his words came out loudly. 'Why didn't you tell me?'

'It wasn't any of your business at the –'

'I've met with you twice, Rachel. At a pub. At Limani fucking Views. If someone is following you, then – fuck you!' He was yelling, feeling for his phone at the same time.

'I hadn't even met you the first time –'

'You lied to me. You said your dog died. You should have told me when you called me, not wait until – I've got a teenage boy at home, not just a dog.'

His call was answered. 'You awake?' he said into the phone.

'What is the matter, Peter?' his father said calmly.

'Can you go to my house? You'll get there before me.'

'What is it this – ?'

'Just go, Karl,' he said, hanging up.

'I'm coming with you,' she said.

He ignored her, pushed three times at the button on the lift. She got in when the lift doors opened. He looked at her and had to close his eyes because he wanted to scream in her face. When he opened them she was staring at him, nearly crying, but defiant at the same time. Barefoot and in her pyjamas.

'I'm coming with you,' she said again.

29

Karl Tanner was in the hallway when they walked in.

'What is it this time, Peter?' he said as his son and Rachel Roth walked in. Karl's thinning white hair was standing at a form of attention. He'd been asleep when Tanner rang.

'False alarm,' Tanner said.

'False alarm about what?'

Tanner shrugged.

Karl shook his head, turned and walked off. 'Daniel's gone to bed,' he said as he did. 'We're in the lounge room.'

The 'we' included a woman, only recently a senior citizen, reddy-brown short hair, lipstick freshly applied but no makeup. Generous mouth, generous proportions all round. 'I'm Lorraine,' she said when Tanner and Roth walked into his lounge room. 'Call me Larry. Your father had most of the bottle of wine. I had to drive.'

Larry was new, as was the wine drinking. Karl had been a beer man since leaving prison. Before that, he drank spirits, but rarely.

Larry and Karl sat next to each other on the three-seater couch. Tanner sat next to Rachel Roth on the couch opposite. 'Can I get anyone a drink?' he asked.

'I'll make coffee,' Larry said, standing up.

Tanner looked at her, got up himself. 'In the fridge, there's – and the plunger –'

She walked past him, rubbed him on the shoulder as she did. 'I'll work it out,' she said.

'There was concern in your voice, Peter,' his father said when Tanner sat down.

'How long have you been with Larry, Karl?'

'Why did you think Daniel might be in danger?'

'I was being careful.'

'Is your life in danger?'

Tanner shook his head, smiled. 'My life is always in danger, Karl. It's an occupational hazard.'

'Can you be serious please,' his father said. 'Why call me?'

'I took some precautions.'

'This is obviously to do with the –'

'It was my fault,' Roth said, cutting Karl off. 'I – I didn't tell Peter something I should have.'

Karl looked at her, then Tanner, chose to leave it as some beyond-Delphic clue. Tanner introduced them more formally, gave an edited version of how he knew Roth.

Five minutes later, Larry came back carrying a tray with a plunger of coffee and four mugs.

'When does your trial start, Peter?' Karl asked. 'For this woman – Leonard?'

'Five weeks.'

'How long will it last?'

'Perhaps four. Maybe less. There's some –'

'My spare room will be made up for Daniel,' Karl said, leaning forward to the coffee table, pouring milk for himself and Larry. 'After tonight.'

Tanner took in a deep breath, exhaled slowly. 'Stay here. Do you mind? There's less disruption for him. There's a queen bed in there.'

'Great,' Larry said, smiling like she meant it.

Tanner looked at his father. Karl stared back, said nothing.

'He's – northern European?' Rachel Roth asked when Tanner returned to the lounge after showing Karl and Larry out.

'Swedish,' Tanner said.

'How did – ?'

'He was out here for a conference in the late-seventies. He liked the climate. Liked sailing in a skiff in the harbour. Packed us up and moved here. Before I could remember anything.'

'You were born there?'

Tanner nodded. 'I'm a refugee from long winters and not enough sun.'

'He seems nice,' she said. 'In a kind of reserved way.'

Tanner smiled. 'My father reserves judgements about people. I can usually tell what he disapproves of. What he approves of is harder to know. He approves of Dan, I think.'

She nodded, looked into her empty mug, put it down on the table.

'Your mother? She must be Swedish too, I imagine?'

'She was.'

'She's dead?'

'My mother drank herself to death because my father was sent to prison.'

Roth said nothing for a few moments. 'That's – gee – it's hard to know where to start with that.'

'Don't. Wait for my memoir. That's its title. Sounds like a bestseller, don't you think? Or maybe it's a country and western song, I don't know.'

'Went to prison for what?'

'Complicated story.' She stared at him until he said, 'Fraud. Not entirely innocent, not the originator of the crime. That was his weasel of a partner. Karl tried to clean things up, which was where he strayed from all means legal. Then he engaged a well-regarded but ineffectual defence lawyer who ensured he got full tote odds. I think the judge read Karl's stoic Scandinavian disposition as a lack of remorse.'

'Is that why – I don't mean to be patronising, but is it over-simplifying to ask if that's why you became a criminal lawyer?'

'It's not why I became a criminal lawyer, Rachel. It is why I still fantasise about beating my father's former partner to death with my bare hands.'

She paused to see how serious he was. Extremely, by the looks of things. 'I'm sorry you're carrying that anger around, Peter.'

'You haven't got any idea about the depth of my anger. Some of it's reserved for you now.'

'I'm sorry,' she said. 'I didn't think –'

'You're taking me to everyone you've spoken to.'

'What?'

'Everyone. For – whatever it is precisely you're working on, you are taking me to everyone you've spoken to. In return, I'll let you speak to my client before anyone else. Win or lose.'

'Everyone?'

He nodded. 'It's in your interests that Tina doesn't talk to one of your competitors. It's possibly in hers. Let's not play chicken, Ray.'

'I'm not sure I can –'

He stood up and picked up the coffee mugs from the table. 'Everyone,' he said. 'When I come back from the kitchen, let's start talking priorities.'

30

Trevor Hendricks' home was set among the bushland of the Bouddi Peninsula, high up on an escarpment, an hour and a half north of the city. At the bottom of the driveway, Tanner pushed a button on the side of the gates. A man's voice said simply, 'Yep.'

Rachel Roth said, 'Hi Trevor,' and with no more discussion the gates swung inwards.

The home had been constructed from the cliffs. Sandstone brickwork, sandstone tiles in the lounge and living area, similar tiles surrounding the infinity pool that looked over the peninsula, the bay, and eventually the ocean. The woman who let them in told them she was 'Margaret, Trev's wife'. She led them into a vast and presently empty lounge room. Leather sofa and chairs in front of a two-metre fireplace, thick exposed timber beams in the ceiling above. There was an Arthur Boyd on the wall. At one end of the lounge room was a glass door, a keypad protecting what looked like a cellar for a few thousand bottles.

There were floor-to-ceiling bi-folding glass doors that led out to the pool, and shortly after Margaret had offered them tea or coffee, a man walked through them, a curious smile on his face. Trevor Hendricks was probably late-sixties, medium height, thin, tanned. Faded pink shorts, a cream-coloured cotton T-shirt, collarless but with buttons down the front to mid chest. Brown Havaianas on his feet, a Rolex on his wrist.

He introduced himself to Tanner, said g'day to Roth, told them to have a seat. There was a touch of Noosa in his accent, some Wategos, Palm Beach, US MBA.

'I told Rachel when she rang me again that I can't see how I can help Tina,' he said when he sat in one of the leather chairs, leaving Tanner and Roth to the couch.

'If you help me with a few things, you might help her,' Tanner said.

Trevor Hendricks shrugged almost imperceptibly, said nothing.

'You've retired, Trevor,' Tanner said. Whenever a potential witness said they didn't see how they could help, the trick was to get them talking about anything but the case. Once people start talking, they sometimes tell you what you want them to, even if they don't.

'Eighteen months on December thirty-first just gone,' he said.

'After Nipori finished up here, what – ?'

Hendricks let out a sharp, short laugh. 'Nipori didn't "finish up". It collapsed.'

'Sure.'

'I went to Japan for twelve months with what was left of the bank. When things settled a bit, they sent me to London. Turned sixty-five there, headed home soon after.'

'And how's retirement?'

Hendricks smiled at Tanner. 'You contemplating it? You look a little young.'

'Criminal defence lawyers never retire, Trevor. We die young, often from liver failure, or stress-induced cancer, or of boredom when the briefs stop. The only other scenario is dementia, which unfortunately sometimes coincides with a judicial appointment. We never retire.'

'You don't like golf?'

'Not enough to let innocent people go to prison just so I can lower my handicap.'

'I golf,' Hendricks declared. 'We sail. We travel. We look after grandkids. I'm pretty happy.'

'Who wouldn't be, living here?'

'Beautiful part of the world.'

'This is some house, too. Owned it long?'

Hendricks shook his head. 'The land, yes. Had the place built while we were in London. We've got an apartment in town.'

'You were underpaid, as a banker, were you?'

Tanner said it in a friendly tone, but Hendricks raised his eyebrows. 'I think you guys do all right, don't you?'

'Most of the criminal bar couldn't afford to rent this place for a night. Still, I can't complain.'

'It'd be a wasted complaint on me.'

'Fair enough. How long have you known Tina?'

Hendricks looked up to the ceiling, rubbed his chin as he thought. 'Gee. How long has it been? Must be the best part of twenty years, I'd say. Near enough. She – I don't know, she was young, not long out from the family business. Came to us for her first big project.'

'What's "big" mean?'

'Twenty-five mil, something like that. Development at St Leonards, from memory.'

'You approved the loan?'

Hendricks laughed again, shook his head. 'I met Tina at some charity dinner. We were one of the major sponsors, and she made a large donation. Nipori was her father's lender. The principal one, anyway. I was in management. She was on my table; she was charming, fun, full of – ideas. I liked her. Not many girls in that game – even now. Anyway, I introduced her to people in our property lending team. She was always grateful, we stayed in touch.'

'You became friends?'

'We socialised a bit. She and Adrian – her ex – asked Marg and me to dinner, to parties they threw. We went skiing together once.'

'I'm not sure I even know who my bank manager is.'

Hendricks stood when his wife came into the room with coffees and a plate of biscuits, which she handed around.

'Did you approve any of Tina's loans for her building projects?' Tanner asked when she'd left.

'I looked at the proposal for the last one,' he said. 'Because of how much was involved. She was stretching herself. She'd borrowed a lot just to get all the land. No income coming in from any of it while she put the concept plan together for the . . . for what became . . . Limani, she called it, right? Anyway, took a long time to get her planning approvals too. Huge outgoings on architects, engineers, all the experts, you name it. All during the GFC and beyond. She had no luck with the timing.'

'Stretching herself, you said? Sounds like the Limani Views project was riskier than her previous ones?'

'Yes and no,' Hendricks said. 'Bigger development, more money, but a fantastic project. Great land, great site, first-class architect, wonderful design. Looked great on paper. Everything she did looked good on paper. Like I said, Tina didn't see the GFC coming. For that matter, those of us in my area didn't invent collateralised debt obligations and sub-prime loans or mortgage-backed securities. Other geniuses did that.'

'Was Limani too big a project for a builder the size of Leonard Developments?'

Hendricks shrugged. 'I only lent to businesses I believed in, through my whole career,' Hendricks said. 'Tina was one of them. After the crash came it looked like she had too many projects on the go, one that was too big, and she was in too much debt. The valuations looked overcooked. Everyone's clever looking in a rear-view mirror. Like I said, it was bad timing. Bad luck. That's what brought her down.'

Tanner didn't ask Hendricks much about the collapse of Nipori, nor the sale of its Asian business to SEBC. They briefly touched on the deal SEBC reached with the liquidators of Nipori's assets, but Hendricks clearly didn't see much unusual about the deal itself. When SEBC sued Leonard and her company, Hendricks had sworn an affidavit that a few weeks after the deal was concluded, Tina Leonard had rung him to tell him that Oliver Randall and SEBC had agreed to extend her loans. He gave the same evidence at the trial, via video-link from London. In his judgement, Justice Kerr accepted that the call had been made, but thought it was a case of Tina Leonard passing on her own misunderstanding – or worse – of what had been said to her by Randall about her loans and what SEBC was going to do.

'Peter tells me Tina is still maintaining that Randall lied to her, and she was stitched up by SEBC,' Rachel Roth said. 'You told me something similar when we met. You were pretty sure about it, Trevor. I assume you still think that?'

Hendricks paused before answering, perhaps because he didn't like having words put into his mouth. Especially by a journalist. 'Can't see how that helps with Tina's current predicament, in fact I see it as the reverse, but yeah, I think that's probably right.'

'Do you think the woman you described as fun and charming and who you liked is the kind of person who arranges for someone to be killed?' Tanner asked.

This time the pause was longer. It was just as well they weren't in court. 'Mate, of course I don't. But is someone going to take my word for it? In the circumstances?'

'What circumstances?'

'Well, she lost a lot, didn't she? I don't – she was angry at SEBC. And Oliver Randall. She called me about it. In between the tears . . . Between you and me, she wanted something bad to happen to him.'

Tanner shrugged. 'There's transient anger, and there's having someone killed,' he said. 'The latter almost never follows the former. Do you think an execution-style slaying nearly six years later is Tina's MO?'

'You'd know more about what people can do than me. But I don't see that as her, no. Of course I don't.'

'You told me when we met that Leonard wasn't the only victim of SEBC's practices,' Roth said. 'You mentioned a development in Melbourne, one on the Gold Coast?'

'Blind Freddy could see what they were doing,' Hendricks said. 'All within their contractual rights though. And it makes a lot of business sense. You've got a big borrower, showing signs of stress as far as meeting loan commitments goes, but they've got a nice asset that's secured to you. If the bank has other customers or potential customers who are in the market to buy that asset should they get their hands on it . . . Well. Happy days.'

'Meaning?'

'Meaning it's a win–win for them. A big loan originally belonging to Nipori goes into technical default, SEBC call it in, seize the security, sell it. If they make a loss because the security asset has dropped in value, they claw the money back from the deal with Nipori's liquidators, and get a problematic loan off their books. They can't lose.'

'Predatory behaviour, isn't it?'

Hendricks smiled a tight smile. 'It's called banking.'

'What's it called when you also make sure that the land you've repossessed with its huge development potential is bought by one of your best customers – Lovro Constructions in this case.'

'Well –' Hendricks searched for the right phrase. 'Long bow to draw there, to say – if you're headed where I think you are, bit of a stretch to imply it wasn't above board. I don't know, anyway.'

'Bit of a stretch describes ninety per cent of my clients' defences, Trevor,' Tanner said. 'How closely did you examine the Limani Views proposal yourself?'

'Pretty closely. I had to when more than seventy-five mil was being sought.'

'Any thoughts on whether the land might have contamination issues?'

Hendricks smiled again, looked at Roth, shook his head. 'Rachel asked me that when we met. Look, Tina's experts said some contamination, relatively normal for that area. I know SEBC said it was worse before the forced sale. I hear Lovro fortuitously found out things mightn't be so bad. That sort of scenario – it's not impossible.'

'Hardly seems normal.'

'The bank might have had someone do a quick due diligence. Test in the wrong spot, it makes the whole place look problematic. It was a big site.'

'Yeah. It could also have been a big con between SEBC and Lovro. Those sorts of things ever happen in banking, Trevor?'

Somewhere on the green escarpment below the horizon-edged pool a kookaburra laughed.

Hendricks waited for the bird to finish. Tanner was about to speak when Hendricks said, 'Are – is Tina going to say Randall was killed by – who? Someone at the bank? Lovro Constructions?'

Tanner shrugged. 'She's not going to plead guilty, Trevor. And Oliver Randall is still dead. Two people are going to say that's because of her, including the man who did the actual killing. We're going to have to throw up some other candidates.'

Hendricks' expression went from confusion to something approaching contempt, after it flirted with disgust. Not all the way there, but getting close. 'How well do you know Tina, Peter?'

'You told us before she was fun and charming. Don't tell me you've changed your mind to homicidal maniac?'

'Tina had a lot of luck seeking development consents over the years,' he said. 'And with fortuitous rezonings that facilitated them. The sort of luck that seemed to run in the family.'

'How did she manage that?'

Hendricks shrugged. 'Perhaps ask her. I wouldn't do it in court, though.'

'Are you trying to tell me how the building industry works?'

'Maybe I'm explaining how the world works.'

'I'm only just past forty, Trevor. I'm not ready for that. Are you saying Tina bribed people?'

Hendricks laughed. 'No first-hand knowledge, mate. Just educated guesses. And what one person might call a bribe, a developer might call lobbying.'

'I'm a very naïve person, Trevor. Can you explain that?'

Hendricks shook his head. 'You want me to explain state and local government to you as well? Do you want me to explain what makes this place tick?'

'I've developed a niche practice over the years of acting for misunderstood politicians and public officials of one kind or another. I think I know how Sydney works. I'm probably one of the few nearly honest people still alive who does.'

'Fair enough,' Hendricks said. 'Anyway, I suppose Tina's not the first or last developer who's had to grease a few wheels to get a project up.'

'What's your point? Greasing wheels seems a long way from hiring hitmen to me.'

'I wouldn't know. I just – your defence seems pretty far-fetched, that's all. I agree I don't think Tina would – anyway, I'm just surprised by your angle.'

'You're not up for jury duty any time soon, are you?'

'No.'

'Good.'

'I was asking you about the land that wasn't part of the residential masterplan when we spoke last,' Rachel Roth said. 'We ran out of time.'

Hendricks nodded, said nothing.

'Do you know anything about that spot? It's still vacant land. The rest of the development and villas are being built around it. The main tower is behind it, and to the left looking up from the harbour.'

'Public space land, isn't it?'

'That's what the approval says. It's meant to be public recreation/garden. Some kind of harbourside park. No landscaping's been done yet. Not even a blade of grass.'

'Maybe you should ask Lovro about it.'

The way Hendricks said it caught Tanner's attention. 'What would they tell us?' Tanner asked.

'Have you looked at any of their developments?'

'Would they be part of the hideous and ugly residential flat towers that are spread around our capital cities?'

'Well – I'm no expert on architecture. They're into more than that though. Resorts. Hotels. Big infrastructure. Casinos.'

'Are you telling me you know something about the area we're talking about, Trevor?'

'No, I'm not.'

'Lovro's going to build another hotel in that spot? A casino? Both?'

Hendricks shook his head, chuckled. 'In Luka Ravic's dreams, maybe. Getting an approval for a resort-style hotel in that spot would be a long shot. A casino? Boy, that would take serious lobbying.'

'Do you know something I don't about this, Trevor?'

'I told you. No, I don't.'

'Have you heard a rumour?'

'You can hear rumours about Elvis and UFO sightings. Which might be just as likely as a third casino approval.'

'No one will lobby anyone in government for a UFO sighting, though, will they?'

'Good point.'

'Where do Lovro have casinos?'

'The Seychelles. Belize. India's where they're looking at now. Big time. Growing middle class, like a punt.'

'These – recreational projects. Who finances them?'

'Shouldn't be hard for you to find that out. I wouldn't get too excited, though.'

'Why?'

'Well – I – Tina got her development approval for Limani against the odds. There was a hell of a lot of local opposition, a court challenge. Then Lovro faced the same thing when they expanded the project. State government had to step in – if it was a viable seat for the main parties, maybe the whole place would be a park, I don't know. Getting an approval for another tower? Another gambling facility? That'd be a big call.'

'But not cost you the seat? Or government?'

'I imagine that would be something that might be polled. It might depend on what things looked like. Lovro might bring in a joint venture partner that people like. It could depend on the type of hotel, the kinds of other facilities, who it's open to, how much money was in it for the government and hence the tax coffers, the type of – whatever. The locals will hate it. Sydney's full of very pro-development people unless that development inconveniences them for five minutes. The rest of the punters across the city? Who knows. You can sell anything with the right pitch.'

'Is there anyone in particular that Lovro might do a joint venture with?'

'Who knows. Have a look at India.'

'What will that tell me?'

He smiled. 'Gamblers aren't the only people who like casinos, Peter. There a nice place to wash money if – well, if you are a well-connected type of organisation.'

'Are you talking drug cartels or terrorists, Trevor? Or just the triads and mafia?'

Hendricks laughed. 'I didn't say any of that.'

'Where could I find out Lovro's JV partners for its casino projects?'

Hendricks shook his head. 'How long until your trial?'

'About a month.'

He laughed softly again. 'With all the resources in the world you aren't going to find out their true partners in probably two years of digging. It will look like a standard company, owned by a shelf company set up on a tax haven, etcetera, etcetera. Some trust will hold shares for another trust. These things are done by side deals, codicils, secret contracts that never leave some lawyer's safe in Bermuda, Belize, Panama, Jersey, Moscow – hell, Liberia. You will never find out the UBOs.'

'UBOs?'

'Ultimate beneficial owners, Peter. Your word would be crooks.'

Tanner took a deep breath. 'The term I'd probably end up using is clients.'

'Isn't there – I thought there was a two-casino limit for Sydney?' Roth said.

Hendricks laughed. 'There was meant to be a zero-casino limit. Then after Star got approved, there wasn't meant to be Crown. Once you open the door and roll out the red carpet to a couple, you get yourself in an awkward position for saying no. Can you play favourites in government? Maybe you can, but you can't play favourites among the favourites.'

'Where have you heard all this, Trevor? It doesn't sound like idle gossip or some boys' club rumour.'

Hendricks laughed, stood, picked up the coffee mugs from the floor. 'That's exactly what it is, Peter. There's gossip about deals and projects all the time in banking.'

'What's your source?'

Hendricks looked at his watch. 'If you think I know the source of every rumour I've ever heard, you're –' He didn't need to finish the sentence. He looked at his watch again as though an hour may have passed in a few seconds, explained he was late for lunch with friends.

Tanner stood to shake his hand. 'This doesn't happen that often, Trevor,' he said, 'but you've not only confused me, you've kind of scared me as well.'

'Big construction and big banking are scary worlds. You don't think global banks only do business with nice people or charities, do you?'

Tanner shook his head. 'Do you mind if we subpoena you for Tina's trial?'

Hendricks looked peeved. 'What for?'

'To tell the jury about international-level criminals.'

'What do they have to do with whether Tina had Randall killed?'

Tanner glanced at Roth. 'Relax, Trevor. I'll probably at most get you to confirm the call Tina made to you saying that Randall offered her a loan extension. I may not even do that. Like you said, that kind of gives her motive. It depends on what else I think I can prove.'

'Now you're confusing me,' Hendricks said.

'Well then, if we don't subpoena you, now I would like you on the jury.'

31

'Your tan's faded,' Tanner said.

Gabriella Campbell nodded. 'Less time on the beach the last few months.'

He'd last seen her in Sicily. He'd tried to convince her to come back and tell a story about a mining company. Then he'd realised that to get what he wanted it was better that she kept her mouth shut. By then he'd put her in danger. That danger had passed, and now he'd convinced her to meet him for a coffee in a café in Newcastle, a couple of hours north of Sydney, where she was working.

The woman next to her was Kate McDonald. Like Campbell, she was an environmental scientist. She specialised in soils and water contamination. Eight months ago, Tanner had sent Tom Cable to Newcastle to break into her house. She didn't know that, and he wasn't going to tell her.

'Thanks for agreeing to meet me,' he said. 'Both of you.'

'The last time I had anything to do with you I got a phone call from Lisa Ilves telling me to drop everything and run.'

'She was being dramatic.'

Campbell shook her head. 'Citadel still has its gold mine. What happened?'

'Perspective.'

'What are you talking about?'

'I'm a criminal defence lawyer. The environment is your problem. I had to save a client. Two of them.'

'That's a very narrow world view.'

Tanner laughed. 'Ever driven someone's wife or children home after the father just got ten years? I have. That's perspective.'

'I think some honesty upfront was what was missing with what you did to Lisa.'

'Say hello for me next time you speak to her. Tell her what I did wasn't as planned as she thinks. It came together at the last moment.'

Gabby Campbell said nothing.

'How long have you been back working here?' Tanner asked.

'Two months. Why are you interested?'

'I've got a job for your company. Maybe more in Kate's territory than yours.'

'What are you talking about?'

'You'll be paid. It's a proper job. You won't be breaking any law. Scientific peer review. Your life won't be in danger.'

'That sounds so reassuring. Who's the client?'

'A woman called Tina Leonard.'

Campbell paused, looked at Kate McDonald. 'Why does that name sound familiar?'

'She was a very successful property developer – now she's accused of arranging a man's murder.'

Campbell nodded, opened her mouth and made a noise indicating she'd read about the case somewhere, or had seen something on television.

'How – what would we be doing?' McDonald asked. 'Did you say peer review? Of what?'

'Have you heard of Lovro Constructions?'

They nodded simultaneously. 'I've got a friend who owns a flat in one of their residential towers,' McDonald said. 'You can hear it when someone drops a pin in the apartment next door.'

'Lovro stole a big residential and commercial project off my client.'

'Stole it?'

'Don't worry. That's not part of your brief.'

'So how do we help in a murder trial?'

Tanner stood up to go to the counter. 'It'll take me another coffee to explain that,' he said.

On the drive back to Sydney, Tanner called Alejandro Alvares from his car. There was no answer the first time, but as he turned off the freeway and back into the Northern Suburbs, his phone lit up with the words *Drug Lord*.

'Alejandro,' he said. 'How are you?'

'I'm well, Peter. And you?' Tanner always felt it would be hard to describe how long Alvares lingered over words, or to precisely locate where his accent was from. Up front it was from the Palermo district of Buenos Aires. Each word was dressed in a linen suit. At the back was Sinaloa in Mexico, the tone of a cartel boss ordering another beheading.

'Did you make any progress about that matter we discussed when I last saw you at your home?'

A long pause. 'We're on the phone, Peter.'

'I asked you to try to find out whether a senior New South Wales police officer had planted drugs in someone's house. If an agency of law enforcement is listening to us, they're probably about to hang up.'

'This seems like it will be a short conversation.'

'I take it the answer is no?'

'I have business to attend to. Is there anything else?'

'I may need to borrow your boat. Would you mind?'

A slight pause. 'I'm rigid with anticipation as to why you are asking me, Peter.'

'I want to have a conference on it. I'll pay the petrol bill. My client will anyway.'

There was a snort. 'Why would I agree to that?'

'Alejandro, let's keep this simple. We are on the phone, after all. You know you will always want me on retainer. Just in case.

Bad things happen even to good people. A short spin around the harbour, that's all. You don't even have to cater.'

'I don't have to cater?'

'BYO event.'

32

Tom Cable waited in a soft leather chair in the foyer of the tower where SEBC had its Sydney HQ. He was wearing a suit and tie.

After fifteen minutes, a security guard came over and asked him what he was doing.

'I'm waiting for someone.'

'For someone who works here?'

'Yes.'

'Can I ask who?'

Cable was about to tell the guard that he could ask, but wouldn't be answered, when he stood up from his seat. 'A crooked ex-cop,' he said, walking away.

The person he was referring to walked out of one of the lifts with another man and strode through the lobby. Cable trotted over to cut him off before he got out of the building.

Because of the speed Cable was walking at, and the general purpose behind it, the man he was seeking sensed him as much as saw him, and stopped just before the rotating doors at the front of the building. Cable's fingers slipped a document out from the envelope he was carrying.

'Brian Crawford?' he said loudly. There was a slight wobble in his voice when he said the surname.

The man said nothing.

Cable's eyes dropped from the man's face to his belt. Hanging down from his waist, just under the roll of fat, was a security card. A photo. *Crawford, Brian*, typed underneath.

Cable held out the document, but Crawford didn't take it, kept glaring at him. Cable shrugged, bent down, placed the subpoena at Crawford's feet. 'You're served,' he said.

Crawford's eyes narrowed, and his jawline tightened, but it was his companion who spoke. 'What the fuck is this?' he said, stepping between Cable and Crawford, looking at the subpoena on the ground, then back to Cable.

'Legal service of a subpoena to attend and appear at the trial of Tina Leonard,' Cable said. The aggression from the smaller man stiffened Cable up. He felt his spine slip back into place. He looked at Crawford. 'Pete Tanner says you can call him, or you can come to court on the first day and sit around for three weeks until he's ready for you. Up to you.'

'You can tell him to get fucked,' the smaller man said.

Cable smiled. 'You want a subpoena too, mate? Or how about an indictment — it should be a crime to wear a shitty suit like that.' Involuntarily, one of Cable's hands moved to the front of this jacket, felt the fine Italian fabric. The smaller man stepped forward as though an act of violence was imminent, but Crawford grabbed him by the arm, drew him back with a jerk.

Cable mock saluted both men, and left the building.

'You didn't tell me he was that big,' Cable said when Tanner answered the phone. He'd called a few minutes after he'd served Crawford, when he was a few hundred metres from the building.

'Did he say anything?'

'No.'

'Didn't threaten you?'

'No. The guy he was leaving work with wanted a piece. But no.'

'Didn't think he would.'

'He looks like he can take care of himself.'

'He's not stupid enough to have the cops all over him by belting you in the foyer of his employer's offices. Is your man following him?' The man Tanner was referring to was an employee of the process serving and investigations business run by Cable's wife.

'He should be. He was waiting across the road the whole time.'

'Keep me posted.'

'Pete, can I just ask – are you going to be able to use this guy at the trial? What's he going to say that will help?'

'Just being thorough.'

'What do you want him to say?'

'That before he left the police he planted six kilos of coke in Oliver Randall's house because SEBC paid him to do that, then gave him a job. And that my client didn't have Randall killed.'

'Is he likely to say that?'

'I only need to get him in a position to admissibly ask the question. How he answers won't matter.'

'You know what you're doing.'

'Some of the time. Speaking of that, Kit should have scanned over those other subpoenas. Do you – ?'

'I got them this morning. You want us to serve these simultaneously? Tomorrow morning?'

'Is simultaneous service a problem? Once one of them is served, they'll call the other. I don't want anyone heading out of town.'

'Just means I've got to get some people out of bed as early as I do.'

'No other problem?'

'Ravic's trainer takes him for a run down to Bondi Beach on Friday morning. We can get him there. Carter will either be heading to his golf club for an hour's practice, or into the office. I'll deal with him. Tim can get Rodriguez at the bank. He's got the most security around him, but the least flexibility for getting away.'

'Send me a text when it's done.'

'What about the other witness I asked you to find – Willett? You've got an address?'

'Lives in Byron Bay. I'll text the address now.'

'How'd you get it? Rachel couldn't find him.'

'Who's Rachel?'

'The journo I told you about. The online daily thing.'

'Not hard. House's in the wife's name. They're both on the electoral role. He's not hiding. He's just retired. Seachanged.'

'Thanks. I'll speak to you later.'

'Pete?'

'Yeah.'

'Rachel – does she have any tattoos?'

'Jesus, Tom. None I've seen.'

'Keep me posted.'

Later that day, just before six, Tanner met Detective Sergeant Mark Woods in the same North Cronulla sports bar he'd met him in a few weeks back. They sat at the same bench facing the window with a couple of beers in front of them, the South Pacific beyond that. It was a cool evening, the breeze was up, and with it the swell. That had tempted out a dozen or more surfers still searching for waves in the fading blue light.

'Wouldn't catch me out there at dusk,' Woods said. 'Feeding time.'

'Isn't there a shark net?'

Woods took his first long sip of beer, shook his head. 'Half the sharks get caught up on the beach side of the mesh.'

'Thought you'd like the surf, living in the far southern suburbs.'

'Living here is what we can afford.'

'Seems like a nice spot to me. It's not that tough being an honest cop, is it?'

'We're almost all honest now. You know that.'

'I didn't mean to offend you, Mark,' Tanner said. 'Cops, nurses and school teachers. Grossly underpaid.'

Woods glanced at Tanner as he picked his beer up again, checked if he was serious, saw that he was. 'Will you write to your local member of parliament about that?' he said.

'Never been one to waste my time.'

'Why do you care? You make plenty.'

Tanner smiled. 'Do you really think I only care about my own pay packet?'

Woods shrugged, drained his beer. He was a big guy, with big hands, a rugby player's neck. Tanner almost admired how quickly he could demolish a beer.

'Not many of us make that much money, you know that right?'

'Lawyers?'

'Criminal lawyers. Government lawyers. Lawyers in community centres, smaller firms. None earn big money.'

'I'm shattered.'

'Do you know what legal-aid rates are for crime?'

'I'm so sorry for you. Can I lend you fifty bucks?'

Tanner got off the stool to go buy two more beers. When he returned, Woods said, 'Why all the talk about money?'

'Root of all evil, detective. You must know that.'

'That's something you couldn't tell me on the phone?'

'Lots of people listening in on my calls, mate. You know that. You're probably one. And the Feds. I've started to talk in riddles now when I'm not on the phone.'

'What riddle do I have to listen to now?'

'The riddle of who had Oliver Randall killed.'

Woods shook his head, looked out at the surfers. The day had been overcast, cold, the sky was dark grey, he had to focus hard to see them. 'Are there any clues?'

'You don't need any. I have to solve that riddle, not you.'

'I just have to listen to you?'

Tanner shook his head. 'You can help me with the first clue. One you already know about. It's why I've been talking money.'

'What?'

'Go and pay your old colleague Brian Crawford a visit for me. In that nice house near Clovelly Beach you told me about.

Ask him how he saved for it. If he tells you it was an inheritance, ask him who died, and how they got the money. Ask him how he ended up at SEBC, and what they pay him. Then ask him where he got the six kilos of coke he had planted in Oliver Randall's study, and what he earned out of that bust.'

Woods glared at Tanner, then drank a third of his beer in one hit. He looked back out the window. A few of the surfers had now come in, were walking up the beach. 'You're fucking crazy,' he said.

'I mightn't get the chance to ask him any of this in court. The judge mightn't let me. I'd like to hear what he has to say. Or if I do, I can treat your questioning as a trial run. A deposition.'

'He still has friends in the force, Tanner. I'm not sure if you're crazy enough to think I'd –'

'How'd he get the job at SEBC? How'd he get his house, his car? I bet he's got other investments. I know he has.'

'You know?'

Tanner nodded. 'I think you should open an investigation into Randall's arrest. Go to your Integrity Commission.'

'Do I look suicidal?'

'You'll look like a genius if you get in ahead of the press.'

'That's always been the way to get ahead in the police force: call out another cop as corrupt. What do you really want me to do?'

Tanner drank some beer, slapped Woods on the back. 'Why do the police do what you're doing, Mark?'

Woods eyed his shoulder near where Tanner had slapped him. The gesture had not been appreciated. 'Do what?'

'Make it the job of some of us at the criminal defence bar to police the police. Shouldn't that be part of your job too?'

'I nearly came unstuck last time you –'

'You haven't faced a tough enough situation to be corrupted yet, Mark,' Tanner said, standing up, pushing the rest of his beer away. 'You're still honest. Crawford wasn't. He can't do a fucking thing to you now. And if he's still got friends where you work, they can't either. Tell them I won't let them. Look into the

Randall arrest. Look into Crawford. Find out everything you can about him. Do it in your spare time if you have to. Send me a bill for it later.'

'Send you a bill? That's like offering me a bribe. I should arrest you.'

'I'm putting you on the payroll, not offering you a bribe. You want to live closer to the city, don't you?'

33

The flight to Ballina in the far north of the state took just under an hour. They landed at eleven. They hired a car at the airport, then Tanner and Roth drove another half-hour north to Byron Bay. Peak season was now over, but the streets in the main part of town were busy enough. Holiday makers with school-aged children had made way for those with younger kids looking for a beachside holiday while the weather was still warm in this part of the world. They drove through town, heading in the direction of the lighthouse. The place they were looking for was located halfway between the town centre and Wategos Beach.

The property was owned by Kevin Willett. Willett had been the head of the state planning department at the time Limani Views was first approved, and through several modifications of the project. He'd retired six months ago, and Rachel Roth had tried to speak to him then, but he'd refused, citing some deed he'd signed, and also the general requirement of former senior public servants to keep their mouths shut about government business. When Roth had tried again, to get him to help with some background matters rather than directly breaching any real aspects of confidentiality, she hadn't been able to locate him.

Willett's house was surrounded by a six-foot wooden fence. The door to the double garage was up, and one car was in it. There was an intercom by the gate, but no answer when Tanner tried it. He tried once more, then lifted himself up and jumped the fence.

'What the hell are you doing?' Roth whispered loudly. The Willetts' home was in a street where the houses were tightly packed together, halfway up a hill which gave those at the Willetts' level just enough height for views out to the ocean. Behind them, on the other side of the back lane, houses higher up the hill looked down on them. Tanner could hear people talking nearby, music coming from one yard. A car drove by.

'Just checking,' he said. He walked to the front door of the house, knocked twice, no answer, a third time, still nothing. He pushed on the door. Locked. He headed towards the back of the property down the side of the house. There was an outdoor shower, a beach towel hanging on a hook next to it. He felt the towel. It was damp, remnants of sand in it. The backyard had a modest-sized lawn, no weeds, tropic green, recently cut. The garden was full of native plants, two jacarandas, a couple of small palms.

There were double glass doors at the back, and he could see into two bedrooms. One bedroom had two singles, the other a queen, all beds made up. Next to the back door were two more hooks, a beach towel on one. It was damp too.

At one end of the veranda was a set of wooden stairs leading to a terrace above him. He went up. The terrace was high enough to give a view of the water. The wind was starting to gust, white caps on the waves. The sliding doors to the inside of the house were open. Kitchen and living space, rustically decorated, beach theme, an old wooden surfboard bracketed on a wall as art. Tanner walked in, looked around.

'Do you often break into people's homes?' Roth said when Tanner came back over the fence.

'Not often,' he said. 'I get Tom Cable to do it.'

'There are people around – neighbours.'

'Trespassing at worst,' he said. 'Not breaking and entering. They're here. Just not home at the moment.'

'What were you doing?'

'Getting a feel for the place. Getting a feel for Kevin Willett.'
'A feel for him?'
Tanner nodded.
'And?'
'I don't – this isn't the house of a crook. That's my feeling. We'll come back this afternoon.'
'How do you . . . What time's our flight this afternoon?'
'Been pushed back till tomorrow,' he said, walking away.

When he'd started the engine, she asked, 'What do we do now?'
'Hungry?'
She shook her head.
'Bring something you can swim in?'
She shook her head again, frowned.

Tanner booked motel rooms, bought trunks, sunscreen, beach towels, hired a body-board, headed to the beach. It was mid-twenties, sunny, scattered white clouds. The water was warmer than in Sydney too. He caught waves, pushed back out, rehearsed cross-examinations in his head, tried to settle on one case theory as his Plan A, repeated the process. Roth sat on the sand watching from under a hat that she'd allowed him to buy her.

He was in the water close to an hour, the first half with the board, the second body surfing. When he was done, he lay next to her on his towel, heart pumping, ears full of water, sun on his back.

'Is this usually how you prepare for a case?' she asked after a few minutes.

'No,' he said. 'But I am preparing.'
'Are you serious?'
'Yes.'
'How?'
'Running questions through my mind, possible answers. Trying different methods of attack, thinking about what might happen.'

'How often do you do this when – when you're away from your desk?'

He turned his head, looked up at her out of one eye. 'You'd be surprised, this close to a trial. Every waking moment. Taking notes in the plane up. Thinking about it when I'm driving, having a shower, eating breakfast. Even when I'm talking to you.'

'There's something I've been tossing up whether to tell you,' Roth then said.

Tanner was lying on his stomach, eyes closed. He sat up, leant on an elbow. 'Something to do with Tina Leonard?' She looked at him, nodded. 'You can't stop now then,' he said.

'Robert Temple,' she said. 'You know who he is?'

Tanner sat up fully. 'Was he the – ?'

'He was Tina's CFO. The CFO of Leonard Developments.'

'He and Tina's ex-husband left her high and dry when SEBC sued her. What about him?'

'Do you know where he is now?' He shook his head. 'Have you heard of a company called Mid-World Constructions?'

'No. Tell me about it.'

She shook her head, looked out at the ocean, smiled vaguely. 'Look it up,' she said.

'Who are they, Rachel?' he said loudly. 'What's he have to do with them?'

She looked back at him. 'Mid-World Constructions, Peter. Look them up. I've just shared something with you that was the fruit of my own labour. You can take it from here.'

He let out a long breath. 'I'm guessing you've just helped my client somehow, just by telling me this?' She nodded. 'Thanks.'

Ray Roth lifted her bottle of water, took a sip. 'There's something I want to make clear,' she said. She paused for a moment, looked straight at him. He couldn't see her eyes, only the sun reflected in her shades. 'I'm not sleeping with you.'

Tanner wondered if he'd heard correctly. 'Rachel, so far I've tried to find our witness, booked separate hotel rooms, bought you a hat and had a swim. What you just said is a – a really strange thing to say.'

'Why is it?'

'Are you kidding?'

'Why is it a strange thing to say?'

'Why did you feel the need to say it?'

'I'm just making it clear.'

'Do I seem like someone who needs that kind of – I don't know, proclamation?'

'Yes,' she said.

He sat up straight. 'Really?'

She nodded. 'You look at me like you're expecting it to happen.'

He thought about asking her how she could be so sure, but thought better of it. 'What do you mean "I'm expecting it to happen"?'

She started laughing.

'What?'

'You think you're in control of things, don't you?'

'Are you being serious about the way I look at you?'

She nodded. 'You've got a look I've seen before. You're expecting sex, aren't you?'

Tanner sat back. Was he *expecting* that? Shit. 'I'll exercise my right to silence,' he said. 'But you can't draw any adverse inferences from that. And no one has ever said that to me before.'

Roth turned her water bottle in her fingers, smiled while she did it. 'Are you enjoying trying to save her?'

'What?'

'She's been a bad girl, hasn't she, Tina Leonard? Maybe a murderer. Maybe not. You want to save her?'

'What are you getting at, Rachel? Do you think I want to sleep with my client too?'

Roth swirled the water around in her bottle like it was a potion, smiled again, drank.

'Do you, Pete? And please, no need to answer me. You can have your right to silence.'

34

They drove back to Willett's house around five, after they'd showered and changed in their rooms. The garage door was still up, but this time two cars filled it. The gate to the property was open. Before he knocked on the front door, Tanner heard people talking out the back, looked at Roth, led the way.

The voices were coming from the upstairs terrace. A man's low voice. A short laugh from a woman. Tanner began walking up the stairs. He smiled when the woman saw him, gave her a short wave. She was drinking from a mug, and looked vaguely alarmed until she saw Roth emerge from behind Tanner. The man was on the couch opposite, a newspaper in his hands, a beer in front of him. Stone & Wood, one of the local brews. He too looked alarmed at first, frowned. Then he saw Roth.

'No,' he said calmly, putting the paper down, starting to get up. 'I told you before. Not in a million years.'

'Pete Tanner. I think you've met Rachel.' Tanner looked at the beer. 'I'd kill for one of those right now.'

'You – I'd like you both to leave. Immediately.' Willett had his voice under control, the agitation was in his body language. Not sure what to do with his hands, whether to take a step towards the younger man.

'Not very hospitable of you, Mr Willett,' Tanner said. 'We've come all the way from Sydney. We don't want much of your time.'

'You've wasted your time coming here.'

'Not really,' Tanner said. 'I had a surf. The water's still warm.' No one spoke for a moment, so Tanner added, 'Nice beach house. You had it long?'

Willett took a step forward, as if he was going to usher Tanner and Roth out, but his wife's voice stopped him in his tracks.

'About five years,' she said.

Tanner nodded, smiled. She almost smiled back. Willett looked at her like he might ask for a divorce on the spot.

'I told Rachel before: I can't say anything.'

'Of course you can, Kevin,' Tanner said, moving to first names now. 'You'd have to in court.'

Willett bristled. 'You're threatening me with a subpoena? To say what?'

'Calm down, Kevin,' Tanner said. 'No, I'm not. That almost never works. Most people threatened with a subpoena just call your bluff.'

'I don't know a thing about – about her current predicament.'

'I'm impressed you know who she is. Even better that you obviously know me. And delicately put. She's charged with murder.'

'I don't know a thing about why.'

'Jesus, Kevin,' Tanner said, 'neither do we. The only guy who knows for sure got a bullet in each knee and one in the forehead. Maybe even he wouldn't have known. I don't want to talk to you about any of that.'

'If it's about the development I simply can't talk. I explained that to Rachel.'

'There's got to be some way I can make you talk, Kevin. There almost always is.'

Willett looked at Tanner and then Roth. 'What does that mean?' he said.

'It means that most decent people are willing to help someone when the stakes are high. Even if they think they can't do or say anything. We want to ask you some questions about things that are mainly on the public record. None of it might help Tina

Leonard. I don't know. In case it might, though, I'm asking for half an hour of your time. And one of those beers. Two, if Ray's keen.'

Willett shrank into himself a bit, didn't reply.

'I'm okay without a beer,' Roth said.

'How about a cup of tea then?' Mrs Willett said. Kevin Willett was about to talk to them, because his wife was going to make him.

'Thanks. That would be nice.'

Mrs Willett stood up, held out her hand to Tanner. 'Angela,' she said. They shook hands, she did the same to Roth. 'Our youngest daughter is doing final year law,' she said, looking at Tanner. 'Back in Sydney.'

So many kids doing law these days, just as the entire profession was about to be replaced by artificial intelligence. Apart from the criminal lawyers.

'Does she know what area of law she wants to practise in?'

'She had a summer clerkship at some firm – what was it, Kevin?'

Kevin answered meekly.

'Not easy to get a job these days, I'm told. I think she'd almost take anything at first.'

'Has she thought of crime?'

Angela nodded. 'She's thought about the DPP. I think she did some work experience there.'

'That's disappointing,' Tanner said. 'Tell her to give me a call. She can follow me around for a week in her holidays, see if she likes keeping people out of prison.'

Angela Willett smiled. 'I'll do that,' she said. She turned, walked into the house.

'Some of it was going to be affordable housing,' Willett said, after Tanner had passed on what he knew about Limani Views. 'That's how she got the approval from the council in the first place.'

'What's that mean?'

'Have a look at the approval history. The original DA was aimed at partly high-end, partly more modest housing. Give middle-income earners the chance at owning property in the inner city near the water. That's how she pitched it. Not as a development only for the wealthy. She was pitching it as a community project – a kind of village.'

'And the council bought that?'

Willett shook his head. 'The majority were dead against it, along with a lot of locals. Not because of the village idea, because of its sheer size. Big impacts on the nearby residents' amenity during the construction phase, then noise and traffic impacts when complete. Some people were going to lose water views, that kind of thing. She won a case claiming personal bias against a couple of councillors when she was knocked back the first time. The state government ended up insisting it get referred to an independent planning panel to decide. They gave the original development the green light. Pretty close-run thing.'

'That's what they said?'

'Not a unanimous vote, which is uncommon. The council appealed, lost in court. It's really what happened from there though that made people even more angry.'

'Which was?'

'A couple of months after her DA, Tina lodged a modification application for the big tower. Thirty levels – all residential, with some retail space at the bottom. She also proposed changes to the configuration of the rest of the apartment buildings, the villas, the internals. All high-end stuff now. Bigger floor areas, bigger units and villas. Then Lovro buys the site, and bang – now they want a tower that's close to fifty levels, half residential and half five-star hotel. Now it's a tourism development in part, which is why the state government took it over after Tina lost it to Lovro. Hence it ended up on my desk. They changed the approval so a different part of the Planning Act applied. Now the minister had the decision. Or I should say, ministers. Lovro's five modification applications to make the development bigger each time straddled four planning ministers and two governments.'

'What's wrong with the development as it's approved for now?' Ray Roth asked.

'You said this would take half an hour,' Willett said. 'It'd take me an hour to detail some of the things that are wrong with it.'

'Name a few.'

'Too much bulk. The tower was way above the local height limits. Farcically so. Inappropriate development in an area outside the CBD. Too many units. Inappropriate impacts on the visual amenity and privacy of surrounding residential neighbourhood. Huge traffic impacts – you can build a big development anywhere you can find the land, but if the surrounding streets aren't big enough, chaos. Not that that's stopped high-density development in Sydney. Poor planning is compulsory. Anyway, the whole bloody thing is wrong on every level.'

'And yet you recommended approval, didn't you? Your department? To the minister?' Roth asked.

'I was always against it,' Willett said.

'But you –'

'I was always against it,' Willett said more firmly. He picked up his beer, took a long sip, sat back like he was done.

'Do you know anything about site contamination? The land it's built on? In the harbour in front of it?'

Willett shook his head slowly. 'Mate, I just read the reports. I make sure they're done. I don't prepare them myself. Tina's historical reports indicated some clean up and remediation was necessary, but it's not like Barangaroo, or further west up the river. Lovro's reports said the same, pretty much. I know the bank in the brief period it had the site put out some contrary report, but that seems to have fallen by the wayside as overstating any problem.'

'Why did each minister approve it?' Tanner asked. 'The local residents kicked up a stink, didn't they? I think I can remember some press about it at the time.'

Willett put his beer down, leant forward again. He smiled, looking at the beer at first, then up at Tanner. 'Have you met Luka Ravic?'

'Not yet,' Tanner said. 'I know he's the chairman and biggest shareholder in Lovro Constructions.'

'Well, he –' Willett said, 'he's a very – a very charismatic man.'

'Does charismatic mean rich and criminally inclined?'

'Well – no,' Willett said slowly. 'He's actually quite cultured. He knows a lot about the world of art, sponsors opera –'

'A man of the people.'

'He's on the board of a rugby league club, Peter. A Renaissance man is probably the phrase I'm looking for.'

'How many people has this polymath bribed over the years, Kevin? To get what he wants?'

'I don't know anything about that.'

'Is it your gut feeling?'

'I don't know anything about it.'

'Why were each of the ministers and the government keen on this development? Didn't they take heat for approving it?'

Willett held up his hands. 'The state seat's out of both major parties' hands. It doesn't play out federally. The only people who care are the local residents, and the Greens. If it doesn't affect anyone else, the heat fades away. Tina, then Lovro, and then the government sold it as a classy development adding value to the neighbourhood and giving Sydney another much needed high-end hotel to boost tourism. Some of the villas are timeshares. High-end places for rich tourists and their families, or execs out here for limited-term stays.'

'Would another casino boost tourism?' Roth said.

Willett smiled, raised his eyebrows. 'The owners of the current casinos would say two's enough.'

'There's a spare block of land still at Limani,' Tanner said. 'I hear Lovro's building casinos. One's going up in India at the moment, in Goa. A few more nearly complete. You said Renaissance man. Were the Medicis gamblers? Would Ravic like to build another gambling palace on the harbour?'

Willett shook his head. 'Such an idea never officially landed on my desk.'

'What about unofficially?'

'Wrong department. It never officially landed on my desk. Ask the head of gaming, or the Gaming Minister.'

'We're running out of time and I can guess the response we'll get,' Tanner said. 'Did you ever hear a rumour to that effect?'

'You hear all sorts of rumours in government,' Willett said. 'Some of them even turn out not to be true.'

'Do you know anything about it, Kevin?' Tanner persisted.

Willett sighed. 'You can do anything you want in our state, Peter. Probably the whole country. You just have to pay the right price. If you contact the right people, pay the piper, the doors open. The main planning issues are how much you have to pay, and who you have to pay it to. That's the law that never gets repealed.'

'You're depressing me, Kevin,' Tanner said. 'I might need another one of those beers.'

'Your own client, I think, may have played the game that every big developer plays,' Willett said. 'Not that I'm implying she had someone killed.'

'What do you think of Lovro's other projects? The residential developments in Sydney?'

'Well . . .' Willett smiled, paused for a moment. 'I'm just an old urban planner, Peter. I'm not an expert in the aesthetics of buildings.'

'Not very Renaissance to me, Lovro's buildings. But I'm just a not-so-old criminal lawyer. That may be why, when I think of Luka Ravic, I'm visualising Bugsy Siegel, not Michelangelo.'

Willett shrugged. 'I think you need to meet him.'

'How old are you, Kevin?' Roth asked.

'Strange question to ask,' he said. 'Sixty-three.'

'Did you retire, or were you asked to?'

Willett bristled again, fractionally. 'You asked me that last time,' he said. 'I retired. Why wouldn't I?' He pointed to the bay, the green hills and hinterland in the distance.

'Will anyone get to build a fifty-level resort hotel tower here, do you think?' Tanner asked. 'If they pay the right price to the right people?'

Willett let out his first big laugh. He stood, picked up the empty beer bottles. 'I'd need your business card if that were to happen, Peter.'

'Really? Why?'

'Because it would be over my dead body,' he said, 'or someone else's.'

35

Tanner sat on the new couch in Linda Greig's consulting room. She was in her chair opposite him. She tilted her head a fraction, waited for him to start.

'Am I honest?' Tanner asked her. 'An honest person?'

'With yourself?'

He nodded.

'Inconsistently.'

'Sleazy?'

'Why do you ask that?'

'Yesterday a woman announced she wouldn't sleep with me. I hadn't broached the subject, but she said I was looking at her like I was expecting her to have sex with me.'

'Do you want to have sex with her?'

'I assume you're seeking an unfiltered and completely honest answer?'

'This is your haven for unfiltered and honest answers.'

'Yes.'

'Then you probably are looking at her that way. Cut it out.'

'Why haven't I remarried?'

Greig shook her head. 'I'm glad you're straight to the point today. Are you pressed for time? And that's a different topic, Pete.'

'Is it?'

'Very much so. Why do you think?'

'I'm over the pain. The worst of it.'

'I can tell.'

'The anger still – it catches me when I'm not looking.'

'I can see that too. It might always sometimes. You have to consciously let it go more than you do.'

'Doesn't feel like I'm cheating any more.'

Greig nodded. 'I'm not always convinced you know precisely what you're feeling.'

'What's that mean?'

'Pete – do you ever observe yourself?'

'What?'

Greig shifted in her seat. 'You told me once you rehearsed cross-examinations in your head.'

'I'm doing it now.'

A more exasperated look. 'I take it your imaginary witness answers you? You then ask another question, I presume?'

'They're not imaginary.'

'Whatever. You take in the scene in your head. See how it looks. How it plays with the jury, that kind of thing?'

'In my head I always get to "not guilty".'

'Stop joking for a moment,' she said sharply. 'Do the same in the rest of your life.'

'What?'

'Take a bird's-eye view next time you're with a woman. Observe how you're looking at her. What's happening to your heart rate? Consider exactly how you're feeling. Be conscious of it. What expressions are you pulling? Watch yourself.'

'Why?'

'See if you're being fair, for one thing.'

'Fair?'

'No one's good enough for you, Pete?'

'It's not that.'

'Isn't it? No one good enough for Dan?'

He paused, poured himself a glass of water from the jug she had on the coffee table. 'He's got a girlfriend now. My father reckons he'll be married before me. So will my father, by the look of things.'

'When's the last time you felt love for a woman, Pete? I don't mean lust. I don't mean like, or respect, or warmth. I mean love.'

He shook his head, sipped at the water like it was blood.

'Pete?'

'Do you want me to tell someone I love them when I don't?'

Greig shook her head like he was an idiot. 'You know I don't. I want you to feel love. Let yourself. Stop judging everyone. Love them instead. Stop transporting your wife next to them and holding up a ten for her and some miserable score for them. That's what you do, isn't it? Effectively.'

'It's not quite like that. And I only ever gave Karen a nine. She could be prickly.'

Greig laughed. 'Are you dating anyone?'

'Do you want to know something funny?'

'Not particularly,' Greig said. 'I'd like you to answer my question.'

Tanner took in a breath, blew it out. 'The murder trial I've got coming up. I dated the prosecutor for a while.'

'You –' Linda Greig let out a sharp laugh that had been coated in exasperation before its release. 'You've slept with the prosecutor?'

Tanner paused. 'That's a bit blunt, Linda. It's not uncommon, professional colleagues dating. Lots of lawyers marry lawyers. It's a hazard for both sexes.'

'Who is she?'

'Isabella Gallo of Senior Counsel. Izzy Gallo.'

'Do you know her well?'

Tanner shrugged. 'We dated for a while.'

'When did this happen?'

'Three or four years ago.' Tanner picked up his glass of water, took a sip. 'It probably wasn't – I don't know.'

'I don't recall you telling me this at the time. In fact I'm certain you didn't.'

'I was scarred, as you know. So was she.'

'What happened?'

'She was divorced. She's very nice. Smart. Decent. I liked the way she looked. She can be funny when she's not being a prosecutor. I couldn't fall in love with her. She took that personally, which was awkward for a while. We've been okay since. It was all just – I don't know. Bad timing, I guess.'

'Bad timing?'

Tanner shrugged. 'Maybe it would be different now. If I'd just met her.'

'You'd fall in love with her now?'

'I might.'

'During this trial?'

'That would be bad timing.'

Greig nodded. 'It would, Pete. I'm pleased to hear you think you can fall in love again, but I don't recommend trying to rekindle the flame with the prosecutor during this trial. That would be – that would be more than awkward.'

'Yeah, it would.'

'You still haven't answered my question,' Greig said. 'Are you dating anyone now?'

'No.'

'But the woman who said she's not going to have sex with you is someone you like?'

'Yes. But I'm sleeping with someone else. Well, I had sex with her. I'm seeing her again tomorrow night.'

Greig paused, took in a long breath. 'Is this someone you might fall in love with?'

'I hope not.'

'Why?'

'She's the victim's ex-wife in my murder trial.'

A substantial pause. 'Are you making that up?'

'No.'

A long, long pause. Then, 'For God's sake. Is that an ethical problem? You'd be better off with the prosecutor, wouldn't you?'

'No. It's not even a moral one. She's married, but to a tax attorney. She deserves all the pleasure I can bring her.'

Linda Greig shook her head. 'Does she love you?'

'I doubt it. When I see her tomorrow night I might serve her with a subpoena to give evidence. I thought I should do it personally, in the circumstances. That possibly is getting ethically murky, but the Bar Association has never sanctioned anyone I'm aware of because of a consenting sexual liaison with the wife or ex-wife of the stiff. I doubt they'd ever agree on what their position should be on that one.'

'Christ, Pete. Do you even like her?'

'Sure. She reminds me of someone.'

'Who?'

'I don't know. She's very naughty, but kind as well. She made a lot of favourable comparisons between me and her husband. I think I'm attracted to people who breach the rules.'

'Jesus, Pete.'

'My client is an interesting woman, too. So is her sister. The sister's married to an advertising executive. Probably one of those guys who makes all the misogynist commercials we have to watch.'

Greig looked up from her notepad. 'You're attracted to your client, and to her sister?'

'I try not think about it.'

'And when you do?'

Tanner took another deep breath. There were times in court when he felt like he ruled the world. In here he could see he was still part child, part something else he didn't understand. He shrugged, didn't answer, didn't have to.

'When does your trial start?'

'Not long now. A few weeks.'

'Is she guilty? I suppose you think not, right?'

'Why? And yeah, I don't think she is. I think she's been set up. By a whole bunch of corrupt and nasty men. I'm – yeah, I'm pretty sure of it. Proving it will be harder.'

'I didn't think the defence had to prove anything. Isn't that what you've told me before?'

'You haven't listened. In a lot of cases the defence has to prove something if it's not going down.'

'So you're attracted to this innocent woman, and sleeping with – what? The ex-wife of the man she's meant to have had killed?'

'Superficial analysis, Linda.'

'Perfect client for you, isn't she?'

'She's got a lot of money for her defence, if that's what you're getting at.'

'I wasn't. Attractive woman. Appears guilty, maybe isn't. A damsel in distress? Someone who needs a legal white knight. Along you come. Commitment for the defence, but nothing beyond that.'

'She came to me.'

'And you know what else? The moment she's acquitted you'll lose all interest in her, won't you?'

36

'This place is a long way from home,' Tanner said. 'Why here?'

Simone Hargreaves shrugged. 'It's one of Grant's favourites. He loves restaurants near water.'

Tanner smiled, looking to his right. Some flood lights lit up Bondi Beach. It was windy, cold, the swell was up, frothing seas below them. What had Linda Greig told him to do? Examine himself? Act like an observer in his own life for a while. 'Are we here to punish Grant?'

'Don't psychoanalyse me, Peter.'

The waiter handed them menus and the wine list, and described the specials. When he left she said, 'Why did you ask me to dinner, Pete? Are you in love with me?'

Tanner smiled, nearly said simply, 'No', held on to the word for a moment, caught the sommelier's eye, thought about what she'd asked while he ordered wine.

'Is your marriage worth saving, Simone?' he said.

'That's no answer to my question.'

'It's a side road.'

'Attempting to save a marriage to an arsehole doesn't seem very clever to me.'

'Are you waiting for a better time to leave?' he asked.

'Perhaps a better offer.'

'We're not falling in love, are we?'

'That sounds more like a statement than a question.' She shook her head. 'I fancy you. But I'm not sure you're my type.'

He nodded, let her taste the wine when it came, watched her take the glass to her bronze lips. She had on a silver silk dress, one that she could wear to a cocktail party.

'What type do you like?' he asked.

'Based on my first two husbands? Compulsive liars who break your heart. Cheats. Narcissists.'

'I have a few clients in prison like that who are nearing parole. I could introduce you. I'll probably end up best man. What type am I?'

'You're looking for someone to save,' she said. 'That's its own form of narcissism. It's just a nicer one than either of my husbands.'

'Do you know my shrink, Simone?'

'I know your type.'

'I'm disappointed. You were so quick to see through me.'

'I still want to have sex with you later.'

Good grief. *How does that make me feel?* Tanner asked himself. It makes me feel that dinner is now superfluous. 'You'll need to warm me up with a few adjectives first.'

After main course, before the bill came, he took out a folded two-page document from his jacket pocket, slid it across the table to her.

'What's this?'

'I wanted to do this in person. Having a process server seemed –'

She looked at it, read the first page, looked up at him. It was a subpoena to attend the trial, and to produce documents.

'You think I need one of these to turn up at your client's trial? After I gave you Oli's letters?'

He shrugged. 'I never take chances.'

'What am I supposed to say? That Oli told me he was such a bad boy someone else probably killed him and not your client?'

'The prosecutor might object before you finish that sentence, but try to get it in anyway.'

'Anything else?'

'You could say Oliver told you his bank made him conduct a giant fraud on Tina Leonard on behalf of it and Lovro Constructions.'

'I'd gladly say that, Peter. But he didn't tell me that.'

'Perhaps you've forgotten?'

She leant forward. 'Can I ask you something? What is your defence for Tina Leonard?'

He smiled. 'Smoke and mirrors, Simone. I have smoke and mirrors.'

'Can I ask what that means?'

He shook his head. 'Confidential and privileged. No offence.'

She picked up her wine glass, swirled, gave him a smile he wasn't sure he should like.

'What are you thinking?'

'I'm wondering if I'm ever going to tell my husband about you, before I leave him.'

'You want me to send you a naughty text?'

'If you like.'

'I can try. I prefer to talk dirty in person. Are you telling him about me specifically, Simone, or about someone like me?'

'You specifically.'

'Why would you do that?'

'He's talked about you a few times. Some case you did last year that made headlines. The doctor's son? He says you've acted for some very unsavoury people. Killers, bikies. Drug people.'

'They're the nice ones. So?'

'I think he's scared of you. I might get all his money when we split if I play you as one of my cards.'

'I don't approve of being used for money. I'm not that kind of boy. And I don't have time to save you. I'm flat out saving my client.'

She moved her leg forward, rubbed her foot along the inside of his calf with what felt like both a deft and experienced touch. 'Tina Leonard and I have a lot in common, don't you think?'

'What's that mean?'

'We're both victims of Oliver Randall and his mates, aren't we? You can save both us girls from them, can't you, Pete?'

37

The following morning at nine am, Rick Lees and Colin Martin took a seat in the main lounge of Alejandro Alvares's seventy-two-foot cruiser. It wasn't the finest day for a tour of the harbour. Overcast, muscular steel clouds, a determined southerly chopping up the waves. They'd been shown aboard by Tom Cable, who greeted them out the front of the Cruising Yacht Club in Rose Bay, and led them to where the boat was moored. Alvares had agreed to lend them the yacht until lunch time. He told Tanner that he assumed he knew him well enough to ensure he wouldn't be so stupid as to allow anything to happen that could possibly blow back on him.

Tanner was already aboard, waiting in a below-deck media room. He didn't come to the main lounge until the boat was past Rose Bay, and had headed west beyond the city and the bridge, to what Cable had told them was its ultimate destination up the river. He said he had some land he was thinking of developing that he wanted Lees and Martin to look at from the water, somewhere near Drummoyne. His plan was to build a restaurant/club, with maybe a few mooring spots out the front and a jetty for diners who came by boat. None of this was true, but if it had been, Rick Lees and Col Martin of SBW Environmental Consulting would be the kind of people you'd go to in order to get the land checked to see what contaminates it contained. When Tanner joined the others on the main deck, Cable introduced him as 'Pete', his junior partner on the possible development and part of his legal team. He left out last names in case either recognised Tanner's.

'Three old homes on the site when I bought it,' Cable told the men as the boat passed the quay. 'I think they just put the slabs on top of the pile of – whatever.'

If Lees and Martin thought it was unusual to do a site visit from the water, they didn't say anything. Pastries had been set out for them, filtered coffee, and the ride was sweet despite the bleak weather.

'How long have you had this?' Martin asked Cable, running a hand along the top of the white leather lounge he was sitting on.

'The boat?'

Martin nodded.

'Not long,' Cable said, which was close to the first true thing he'd said to them since he'd made the call to organise the meeting.'What do you expect to find?' were the first words Tanner said.

Lees and Martin looked at each other like they were conjoined.

'Well, it depends,' Lees began. 'What's the site history?'

'A few warehouses,' Tanner said. 'Stored clothing or clothing fabrics, I think. Nothing toxic.'

'You're thinking of seeking approval for a small marina, is that right?'

'If we can.'

'Any factories near the site that you know of?'

'Now?'

'No – historically.'

'Not that we're aware of.'

The men looked at each other, shrugged simultaneously. 'Shouldn't be too bad then. Nothing out of the ordinary.'

Minutes later, Tanner pointed south, to the land that Limani Views sat on, its main tower near complete, the large area of vacant land surrounded by new development waiting – waiting for what?

Lees looked at Martin, turned back to Tanner. 'What about it?' he said.

'Why is it that you found this place to be so fouled up?' Tanner said.

Martin looked confused, Lees like he was wising up to something. 'Who are you?' he asked.

'Just answer my question. What brief were you given when you did the contamination report for this land by SEBC?'

'Who are you?'

'Mr Lees, you're being paid for your time today. We've engaged you properly, for your professional views. Why did you find this land was so polluted? And how did you get it so wrong? We just want to know it was an aberration if we're going to trust you.'

Lees looked at Cable. 'And who are you?'

Tom Cable frowned, shook his head. 'Answer the man's questions,' he said.

'We want to get off the boat,' Martin said.

Tanner laughed. 'We'll let you off when we're ready, mate. Answer my questions first.'

'This is – who the fuck are you?'

Tanner told them who he was, that his client was Tina Leonard.

'You've brought us out here on false pretences,' Lees said to Cable first. Then he looked at Tanner. 'You can't do that.'

Tanner laughed, then said, 'Why did your report for this place have much higher levels of pollutants than people tell me could've been expected for a site with its history?'

'I'm not –'

'Did someone at SEBC pay you to dodgy your report up?'

'We don't – let us off this boat. Now.'

'Did someone else pay you?'

'Let us off the boat.'

'Lovro Constructions. You guys do work for them, don't you?'

'You must have a screw loose, mate.'

'Why did you say that if a marina is put in here, a poison soup will get stirred up in the process?'

Lees stood up, walked to the corner of the lounge area. 'Do you know anything about water pollution in this harbour?' he asked, looking at Tanner.

'My speciality is river pollution. What do you want to tell me about the harbour?'

'This whole fucking place is loaded with poisons, mate. Dioxins. Heavy metals. We weren't wrong about that. The government has a website warning people not to eat any fish caught west of the Harbour Bridge. Shit, I wouldn't eat a fish I caught on the Manly ferry. Our report on the sediments wasn't that far out.'

'But you were about the land.'

'So what? And no, we were in the ballpark. Just the high end. Now let us off this boat.'

'Were you paid by someone to get it so wrong?'

As conferences with potential witnesses go, this was unconventional. Martin and Lees, though, were never going to agree to a meeting. At least this way Tanner got their spontaneous reaction to what he wanted to know without calling them cold in a trial. He mightn't even be able to even get that far. It would depend on how broad a view the judge took of relevance.

'No,' Lees said. 'And fuck you for asking.'

'You're welcome, but I wouldn't advise you to answer me like that in court.'

Martin looked at Cable again. 'Whose boat is this, anyway?'

Tanner laughed. 'You don't want to know that, Mr Martin. And trust me, when we do let you off, you won't want to go complaining to anyone. This boat is owned by an important client of mine. He's not someone you want to upset. It isn't possible for me to emphasise that more clearly. You could find yourself permanently joining the contaminated sediments at the bottom of this harbour if you do. He will not expect the name of his boat to appear in any police report, or complaint to a professional association. Trust me on that.'

'You're threatening us now?'

'I'm giving you advice. And a subpoena. Tom?'

Cable stood and took some documents from a drawer that formed part of the mahogany joinery in the boat's lounge area. He handed one to Martin, one to Lees.

'What the fuck is this?' Martin said.

'I'm calling you to give evidence for the defence in the trial of Tina Leonard.'

Martin glared at the document, ripped it in half, screwed up what was left in his hands, threw it on the floor.

'At least he didn't throw it in the harbour,' Tanner said to Cable.

'I don't know much about water and land pollution,' Cable said to Martin, 'but I'm an expert on service of court processes. You can eat that if you want. You're still served.'

'What – what's the point of this?' Lees said.

Tanner shrugged. 'Not sure yet.'

Lees shook his head, nearly laughed. 'You're not fucking sure?'

Tanner walked up to Lees, got inside his personal space. 'My job's a lot harder than yours, mate. I have to conduct a test on a toxic legacy of greed in this town, not just the harbour sediments. What I'm doing is part anthropology, part magic. When I get out my saw, you're going in the box. Who knows if I'll cut you in half or not.'

38

'Have you made your mind up yet about Tina?' Kit Gallagher asked Tanner. 'Is she going to give evidence?'

Tanner shrugged. 'I think she probably has to. We don't need to make that call until near the end though, and we won't be telling anyone before we have to.'

They were in Gallagher's conference room. The meeting had been arranged ahead of the final pre-trial conferences with Tina Leonard – the first of those being to discuss strategy, the prosecution and defence witnesses, details about the judge and prosecutor, and the second to deal in detail with Leonard's evidence if they decided to call her.

Over the last two weeks, Tanner had worked solely on the Leonard trial. He'd filled Gallagher in on the meetings he'd had with Trevor Hendricks and Kevin Willett, and had given an edited version of his 'conference' with Lees and Martin. A subpoena to appear had been served on all of them.

'Tina might be the only defence witness,' Gallagher said. She opened a manila folder she had in front of her and slid some documents across the table.

The documents were a series of motions that sought to have various subpoenas to appear set aside. On top of the pile were motions filed on behalf of Phillip P Carter, the current Chairman of SEBC, and its CEO at the time the bank wound up Leonard

Developments, and Jack Rodriguez, its current CEO. There was a similar motion concerning the subpoena served on Brian Crawford. Below that was an application on behalf of Luka Ravic, the CEO and majority shareholder of Lovro Constructions.

'There's another one there,' Kit said, 'filed on behalf of Simone Hargreaves.'

'I'm disappointed with Simone,' Tanner said. 'She's gone out of her way to give me the impression she's on my side. Besides, she's already given me copies of the documents we're seeking in this subpoena.'

'Her application is from her husband's firm. They're also acting for Carter and Rodriguez.'

'These motions came with affidavits, I assume?'

Gallagher nodded. 'Bottom of the pile. All the affidavits are from instructing solicitors. Giving evidence on information and belief from their clients.'

'I might have fun testing Simone Hargreaves' solicitor out on whether his instructions are really coming from her, or Grant Hargreaves instead. When are they listed for hearing?'

'What was going to be the first day of the trial. Today week. The judge has pushed jury empanelment and openings back to the Tuesday.'

'What are these based on?'

'They're all saying no forensic purpose for the service of the subpoena.'

'How would they know?'

Gallagher put on her glasses, and held up a letter from Lattimers that was served with the motions and supporting affidavits. 'They're saying that there's no evidence they could give that could be of any relevance to the charge against Tina, and that you seem to be seeking to rerun SEBC's civil case against Tina and Leonard Developments, rather than any kind of defence to a murder charge.'

'So what?' Tanner said.

'Pete,' Kit Gallagher said softly, putting down the letter, 'what are you going to ask them? I understand a defence case that's based on attacking the credibility of Webb and Bitar. But the kind of conspiracy theory you want to run – it could really backfire unless you land a few blows.'

Tanner shrugged. 'I'm still working out some things. If we hadn't served these, though, if something does come up –'

'Working out things one week before trial isn't the kind of thing that fills me with confidence. And what are you going to tell the judge about the motions?' Gallagher said.

'Enough to buy some time.'

'Enough of what?'

'We've got until next Monday to finalise that. You've served the valuation evidence now?'

She nodded, opened a second folder she had with her. 'Oh, yes,' she said, 'which brings me to this application. This is from the prosecutor seeking to have that evidence ruled out on the grounds of relevance. That's for Monday too.'

'I hate procedural fights that I don't instigate,' Tanner said.

'My reputation is on the line here, Pete,' Gallagher said. 'You're keeping that in mind, right?'

Tanner laughed. 'Kit, your reputation has been built on acquittals, or going down fighting like hell. This is part of fighting like hell.'

Gallagher frowned, nodded, put her glasses back on, opened a third manila folder. She slid a letter across the conference table to Tanner. It was from lawyers acting for the pollution experts Lees and Martin. He read the first paragraph, screwed the letter up into a ball, threw it at a bin in the corner of the room.

'I haven't heard from the Bar Association yet,' Tanner said.

'I've heard from the Law Society,' Gallagher said.

'You knew nothing.'

'Great defence. They're saying they were held against their will. What were you doing on the boat? Whose was it?'

'Alejandro Alvares's.'

'Jesus Christ.'

Tanner nodded. 'Alejandro will be really pissed off if he gets a phone call from the police over these guys.'

'You should have thought of that.'

'Hope they've all got life insurance.'

'This isn't funny, Pete. It's stupid. What the hell did you do it for? A stunt like that?'

'Because these spivs wouldn't talk to us no matter how nicely we asked them. I put them in a spot where I could read if they were telling the truth or not.'

'Oh, really? Are they?'

'Not sure.'

Kit Gallagher shook her head. 'I'm not going to ask –' She chose not to finish her sentence, seemed on the verge of some more critical remark, which then disappeared from her lips before it had formed.

'Kit?' Tanner said, standing.

She glared at him. 'Yes?'

'Write back to the law firms. Every solicitor who's sworn an affidavit is required for cross-examination. All of them.'

Tina Leonard glided through the door to Tanner's chambers. Her legs, her entire body moved slowly. Her sister followed her into the room a few strides later, with the same unrushed, elegant movement of limbs.

Leonard was in an ivory suit. Her hair was pushed back dramatically into a voluminous, shining black bun. Topaz lipstick, matching eyeshadow, dark, sculptured brows and lashes. Taz was the lady in waiting. Beige suit, but instead of a jacket, she had on a long, ankle-length coat of fine wool. Her hair was down, same black shine, same makeup.

Tanner had acted for many men who were monumentally unattractive. He'd made them have haircuts, shave, put on suits. The wheel turns. Now he was defending a particular kind of beauty. Strong, imperious looking. This was going to present its own difficulties. That fabulous white suit was fit for a party on a billionaire's yacht, but not for a jury. He'd delegate Kit Gallagher to deal with that. He needed Tina Leonard to exude less power, weep vulnerability instead.

'You don't look nervous, Tina,' Tanner said when all of them had taken their seats. Gallagher next to Leonard, Jenny Singh to Tanner's right, by the side of his desk. Perhaps because she was there only for moral support, Taz had dropped her handbag on Tanner's three-seater on the other side of the room, before gracefully reclining into one end of the couch like she was attending pre-supper drinks in the salon.

'Should I be?' Tina said. That smooth, rich voice, without being deep. Each word was beautifully dressed. Not a voice that belonged behind bars.

'It's one week until your murder trial starts. Most clients are edgy at this stage. Even the veterans.'

'Are you nervous?'

Tanner smiled. 'I am, although nervous no longer fully defines my state before a trial.'

'What's the right word then?'

'Volatile, but composed. Wired, but focused. It's a very complex state that only other good criminal lawyers would understand.'

'Are you confident?'

'In my abilities, or in your defence?'

'How about both?'

'You're only paying for my abilities. Confidence in the outcome is extra.'

'I just saw your last bill, Peter. I think I'm paying for both.'

Tanner and Kit Gallagher took Tina Leonard through the subpoenas they'd issued, and why. Then they explained the motions they'd received which sought orders from the court excusing the proposed witnesses from giving evidence.

Leonard seemed to take it in like a deep breath. 'You'll have to be nervous about all of this for me, Peter,' she said. 'Maybe if you look nervous enough the prosecutor will feel sorry for you.'

Tanner laughed. 'You don't know the prosecutor.'

'Kit told me it was a woman,' Leonard said. 'What's her name?'

'Isabella Gallo. Izzy for short.'

Leonard nodded, lifted her big eyes towards the ceiling like they were heavy stones, seemed to ponder whether she knew the name. 'Gallo. That's Italian, is it?'

'Is that a problem?'

'I'm sure it isn't. Is she good?'

'Very.'

'Perhaps that's a problem?'

'I haven't come across many stupid prosecutors running murder cases, Tina. The stupid ones end up in other areas of the law. Defamation is a good area for the less able, so I'm told.'

'Does she like women?'

'I haven't thought about it. I'm sure she does. Just not ones charged with murder whom she's prosecuting.'

'I meant would – will she be more – difficult?'

'She won't like you, Tina. She has two witnesses who say you ordered a murder.'

'They're liars.'

'She won't like them either, but that doesn't mean they're liars in her world. She has them, and she has a motive. She has you giving one of them a large quantity of cash. She has your heated argument with Randall in a coffee shop.'

'That argument was because I was upset Randall lied in the beginning. When he ruined me. I was angry he hadn't come forward earlier. I was angry at his new-found religious beliefs. I was angry about having to wait until – until *Jesus* told him to come clean.'

'He'd have been better off if Jesus told him not to answer the door to Jayden Webb.'

'Can't you talk to this woman?' It was Taz Leonard, uncrossing her legs, sitting up, her voice more agitated than the accused's. 'The police haven't even investigated the people you have. Can't you make her see what's happened?'

Tanner shook his head. 'Izzy Gallo's not going to back down with what she's got. Her boss wouldn't let her, anyway.'

Taz shook her head in disgust, reclined again into her corner of the couch.

'Am I to give evidence?' Leonard asked.

'Maybe,' Tanner said. 'We don't make that call until the very last moment.'

'I want to. I've told you that. I believe I should.'

'I believe what you've told me, Tina,' Tanner said. 'It doesn't matter to the case or to me that I do, but for what it's worth. The thing is, though, I could have my best case ever, I could raise a million doubts in the juror's minds, the whole thing might go our way. But if I then call you, and the jury doesn't like you, if they don't believe you – then you're going to go to prison for a very long time.'

'I want to say I didn't do it. I want to look them in the eye, and say that.'

'You might have to make do with telling us. I'm not promising anything more than that. We'll have you ready to give evidence if I think you should.'

'I don't understand how anyone can be found innocent if they don't say that they are.'

'We're aiming for not guilty. I have to prove there's sufficient doubt it was you. I'm not clearing your name, Tina. I'm throwing mud.'

'That's it?' Tina Leonard said, her voice composed again. 'You're throwing mud?'

'Some other dude did it. That's our case.'

She glared, but more through him than at him. 'Will we win these hearings about the subpoenas?' she asked. 'Whatever they're trying to do to stop having to face the court?'

Tanner nodded. 'I think so. The harder part might be having them as witnesses. I'll be calling them, so unless the judge lets me, I have to lead evidence from them, not cross-examine. That can be tricky.'

'Might the judge let you? Another woman, so I'm told.'

'Women are lawyers, Tina. I know there's not many female property developers, perhaps because the art of the bribe is more often found on the male chromosome, but in law we've had to let you in.'

'That's not what I meant.'

'I may not need much. Just enough to confuse the jury, to make them think there's more to it than revenge.'

'There is more. I'm innocent. And I don't like my fate resting on – god, confusing the jury. I want them to know who did this.'

Tanner shook his head, smiled. 'Then we are not on the same page.'

She paused again. 'How is that?'

'Because I want them to not know who did it.'

39

One week later, early on the morning of the hearing of the motions to set aside subpoenas, Tanner reviewed the notes he'd made over the previous weeks. He then re-read the key documents he thought he'd need, before returning them to their binder. It was a familiar process. Be prepared. Know the material. Work out what had to be argued, what had to be asked, what evidence was required to prove each point. Free your brain for that last-minute flash.

Among the documents he'd put in his folder that morning were copies of the letters Simone Hargreaves had given him that Oliver Randall had written. As he packed his papers into his bag, he thought of the letters he'd written in his life. A few to Karen before they were married while he was travelling, or when she was away studying. Three or four a year to his father when he was in prison. Two letters to his politician brother, complaining about him not visiting Karl. And, when he was still a teenager, one letter to his father's ex-business partner and co-felon, telling him that while Karl Tanner held no grudges, his son did. That letter had resulted in a warning from the police.

That was about it. Who wrote letters any more in the age of email, text, Snapchat, Instagram, Facebook? And while he mused on these few old handwritten documents while he drove into work, Tanner remembered he'd kept a copy of them all.

Each letter he'd sent, he'd photocopied first, as though he was already preserving his records. He wasn't sure why. In case they were lost, not received? Vanity? Whatever it was, it occurred to him that this practice was probably not unique.

At a red light, he sent a text to Simone Hargreaves. *Can I call you? Not about the subpoena.*

She rang him moments later.

'I thought we were friends,' he said when he answered.

'My husband did it. Don't worry, I've taken care of it. I'll be in court if you need me.'

'It's okay,' he said. 'Those letters you gave me that Oliver wrote to you and your daughter – would he be the sort to make a copy before he sent them?'

'I'm not sure about handwritten letters like those. Other correspondence – that was typed – sure, he kept copies saved in the computer, or –'

'Where would all that be now? Oliver's private papers, that kind of stuff?'

'Um, I'd say –'

'Did he have a will?'

'Yes. Everything was left to Hannah.'

'His papers?'

'No – I don't think so. He left some money that he had after prison, his superannuation. That was it. There was no property – no house at least. Some family heirlooms, which we sold. I can't remember any papers or anything like –'

'Who was the executor of the will?'

'A solicitor friend of Oli's. Of ours, when we were married.'

'What's his name?'

'Harry. Harry Hartfield.'

'What firm is he at?'

'He's – he's got his own firm. He's just a small-time kind of guy. His office is in Edgecliff.'

'Can you call him for me? Tell him I'm going to give him a ring?'

'About what?'

'About Oliver's papers. If – look, he may have nothing, there may be nothing useful, or there could be copies of what he sent you. I want to call him and ask him.'

'Sure. Okay.'

'Thanks.'

'Good luck today, Pete.'

'Is your husband home?'

'Getting dressed. Why?'

'Maybe you should put him on. I could explain to him the penalties for filing a motion without the client's authority.'

She paused. He could tell she was smiling. 'Why don't you surprise him in court with that?'

The trial was listed in the Darlinghurst Criminal Courts. It was a big sandstone building, Greek Revival style, where the guilty or unlucky had been sentenced to death or prison for close to two hundred years. The driveway and green public space out the front of the courthouse left plenty of room for the media, and three TV vans were in place by the time the defence team and their client arrived. The victim was an ex-high-flying banker who did nearly six years for coke distribution. He was not long out of prison when someone had fragmented his kneecaps to bits of bloody gravel and then removed the back of his head with a close-range shot. The accused was an attractive and once successful businesswoman in a man's game who'd been ruined by the dead guy and the financial leviathan he'd once worked for. There was a young hitman, and another crown witness with a criminal record and overtones of the underworld. There was nothing the press didn't like about *R v Athina Leonard*.

Tanner was polite to journalists, but never said much. It rarely helped. Journos had an annoying habit of reporting more of the prosecution case than the defence. Even when he'd won newsworthy cases, he didn't give post-verdict press conferences or make statements to the media. His old mentor Max Rourke QC hated lawyers who grandstanded afterwards. 'If you win a trial,' he'd told Tanner years ago, 'the triumph belongs to justice, not to you.' Tanner had laughed at the time, a reaction Max didn't appreciate. When he won a case, Max drank for Justice, but never stole her glory.

There were a couple of journalists standing on the left of the portico at the front of the court who usually made a showing at a big trial like Tina Leonard's. One was checking email or sending a tweet, the other was talking on her phone. There were some familiar newshounds on the crime beat of the two dailies, then the TV and radio reporters on the far right, ready to pounce with their cameramen and microphones. And, through the throng of people, Tanner saw Rachel Roth sitting on what looked like a park bench on the right side of the entrance doors. She was leaning forward, typing a message on her phone with her thumb, but looked up as he saw her. For the help she'd given him to get Trevor Hendricks and Kevin Willett to speak to him, he'd promised to talk to her briefly at the end of each court day to discuss whatever she wanted, on the proviso that nothing sensitive to the defence was published until after the jury verdict, or any appeals had been exhausted. He'd also promised her exclusive access to Tina Leonard at the end of the trial, win or lose.

Isabella Gallo SC, the head prosecutor, was already at the bar table when Tanner walked in, talking to a member of her team. He wasn't surprised she was there first. They were the same age, and she'd spent her first few years as a barrister at his chambers. Never be late for court was one of the first things Max Rourke QC had told them both. He'd said it to them during a long lunch, where Max's incessant drinking had only been broken by his intermittent trips to the gents to relieve an alcohol-shrunken bladder. But he'd said it with a deep, echoing voice, and with the kind of gravitas you acquire after many years of gaining acquittals or winning appeals. To both of them it seemed like a Commandment, the 11th or 12th, maybe even a lower number. Tanner had always liked Izzy Gallo, and if he hadn't been married at the time and obeying at least the 7th Commandment, well. After Karen died, and they'd spent a few months together, he was sorry it hadn't worked. He'd expected it would, was almost surprised to find he was not going to fall in love with her. Looking at her in the courtroom, talking earnestly to her junior counsel, organised, ready for battle, turning, smiling knowingly at him – he still didn't know why he hadn't.

'You're not supporting these attempts to pervert the course of justice, are you, Izzy?' Tanner said when he took his seat on the defence side of the bar table. She feigned not hearing him. He glared at her. 'Izzy?'

'How are you, Pete?'

'Are you going to oppose the motions with me?'

She laughed. 'You're on your own.'

'Surely the Director of Public Prosecutions doesn't want to see an accused deprived of their right to conduct a legitimate defence? Has this country swung that far to the right?'

'They're your witnesses, your problem.'

'You should be calling them.'

She shook her head, poured herself a glass of water. Women barristers, no matter how senior, usually poured their own water. The male silks waited for their juniors to do it. 'Why would I call any of them, Pete?'

'Because in a case like this you can't rely on the police to get the right person.'

'I'm running a murder trial, not trying to clean up Sydney for you.'

Tanner shook his head. He picked up the jug, poured himself and Jenny Singh a glass of water. 'Very unambitious of you.'

Gallo turned away from him and said something to her junior. Tanner turned himself, looked around at the excited souls in the courtroom, then saw the rest of his opponents enter the court. 'Here they come,' he said loudly.

Jack Rodriguez, the CEO of SEBC, and Phillip P Carter, its chairman and ex-CEO, were being represented by Tom Burton QC. Burton was also appearing for their employee and head of security, Brian Crawford. Tanner didn't know Burton personally, and had only been told that he was colloquially known as 'Richard', not on account of having a baritone voice, but because he had an acne-scarred face and four wives. Luka Ravic, the chairman and majority shareholder of Lovro Constructions, was being represented by a barrister called Robert Russell SC. Tanner didn't know him either.

Russell pushed his way past Burton to get to the bar table, and thumped his brief folder down on the lectern. Tanner estimated his height at five-four, maybe five-two without the uppers. He thought about asking Russell if he needed a box to stand on, but then remembered another piece of advice Max Rourke QC had given him.

Hold the insults for when the audience was listening.

40

At precisely ten am, Justice Caitlin Francis entered the court and took her seat on the bench. She took appearances immediately, and had clearly read the motions, the affidavits, and the written submissions that had been filed in support. Before the motions were formally read, though, Tom Burton QC was on his feet. He wanted the court closed, and the arguments suppressed.

'Why?' the judge said curtly.

'To prevent unnecessary embarrassment to my clients and the other witnesses who are seeking to have their subpoenas set aside, your Honour.'

'Embarrassment from what?' Tanner said from his seat.

The judge glared at him over the top of her glasses. 'I'll run this part of the hearing, Mr Tanner,' she said.

Tanner nodded an apology.

'Your Honour, my clients Mr Rodriguez and Mr Carter – and this application I'm making now is supported by all the counsel representing the various witnesses here today – have absolutely no connection to the accused, or to the facts, matters and circumstances outlined in the indictment and contained in the prosecution witness statements that were tendered on committal. My clients' names weren't mentioned at the committal. Nothing to do with them was mentioned at the committal.

We don't know what Mr Tanner is going to say today because he hasn't filed any written submissions despite your Honour's order for that when these motions were listed, but we're confident that what he will say will be first, irrelevant, but secondly, embarrassing, and perhaps even scandalous.'

The judge looked at Tanner. 'Why haven't you filed written submissions, Mr Tanner?'

'These motions are so ill-conceived, your Honour, that I didn't think it was necessary. And I don't intend to become unnecessarily scandalous. I'm happy to stick to the facts. If they turn out to be scandalous, they turn out to be scandalous.'

Tanner sensed the judge was going to comment more about his failure to file submissions, but then thought better of it. 'Do you have a view about this application?'

'Open justice is best, your Honour,' he said. 'The average person rarely gets a suppression order. It's always the rich and powerful who want justice behind closed doors. They're usually the people with the most to hide.'

'Leaving that irrelevant and inaccurate observation aside, do you yourself have any submission you want to make of a specific kind about Mr Burton's application, other than reminding me of the principle of open justice?'

'Nothing further, your Honour, but I suspect Ms Crown will be outraged by the thought that the court might be closed for these motions.'

Justice Francis sighed, then looked at Izzy Gallo. 'Are you outraged, Ms Crown?'

Gallo stood, shook her head. 'Unaffected, your Honour.'

The judge looked mildly surprised by the prosecutor's reaction. 'You have no position?'

'In order to be consistent, no, your Honour. The applicants involved are witnesses the defence intends to call, not the Crown. We don't take any position on the motions, so we take none on any related application about them.'

The judge didn't look entirely convinced, and so Gallo decided to further clarify. 'I should add, your Honour, it seems to us that Mr Tanner is seeking to somehow rerun a civil case the accused was involved in many years ago with a particular bank. That seems an odd defence to the charge. If that's what he attempts to do, or if the evidence he seeks to lead from these witnesses is otherwise irrelevant to this trial, I'll be objecting to him doing that when the time comes.'

The judge nodded, then heard brief arguments in support from the other barristers, then decided to close the court and grant a temporary suppression order on any evidence. When the court cleared and they were ready to resume, the judge turned to Tanner first.

'Why have you served these people with subpoenas, Mr Tanner? Can you clear that up?'

'No, your Honour, we can't.'

Justice Francis took off her glasses and put the tip of one arm into her mouth. 'We can't?'

'No.' A long pause. 'But I'm not meaning any disrespect in saying that, your Honour.'

'You're not?'

'I don't have to tell the prosecutor why I'm calling these witnesses. So I don't see why I have to tell anyone else. I have to give the prosecutor notice of an alibi, and copies of any expert reports I want to rely on. I've done the latter. An alibi isn't relevant to this case. I don't have to announce my case theory yet. I can if I choose to, or I can wait until opening, or I can waive that and wait until closing. But it's my forensic choice with respect, your Honour, not the court's.'

'Thank you for the one-oh-one, Mr Tanner.'

'It wasn't for your Honour's benefit. It was for Mr Burton's and Mr Russell's.'

'I object to that,' Russell said, in an angry tone Tanner suspected he probably said his first word with. Tanner felt the urge to be rude, resisted for a moment, gave up the next.

'In case your Honour's wondering if Mr Russell is being disrespectful,' Tanner said, leaning on the lectern, 'I can confirm my learned friend is standing.'

There was a further outburst from Russell and a long, admonishing look from Justice Francis, before she said, 'You know, Mr Tanner, given the motions that have been brought, you may have to say something about why you're calling people to convince me not to make the orders the applicants seek.'

'I don't know Mr Burton and Mr Russell, your Honour, but I'll assume they're competent lawyers. So they already know you won't be making any of the orders they seek, because they know your Honour won't deprive my client of a fair trial, and the right to run a defence inconsistent with the prosecution case theory. What they're trying to do by this is to get a heads-up on what I might ask their clients about before they end up in the witness box.'

Burton and Russell simultaneously stood to protest, but the judge intervened.

'So I get nothing from you for now, Mr Tanner? Not even something to assist me?'

'What I think would assist your Honour most, with respect, is if my friends withdrew their motions. If they don't want to do that, then, with respect, let's get on with the argument.'

'What if I'm trying to help you, Mr Tanner?'

'Help me?'

'What if my preliminary view is that these applications are premature? That we should proceed with the prosecution case, and even part of the defence case, before I rule on them?'

'Is that what your Honour's thinking?'

'It's one of a number of things I'm thinking, Mr Tanner. Do you want to assist me?'

Tanner hadn't wanted to say anything at all if he could get away with it, but the judge's message seemed to be that he'd be better off playing ball. 'Your Honour has undoubtedly guessed, even if my friends may have overlooked this, but my client's not guilty plea is as a matter of logic linked to an instruction that she didn't order the killing of Oliver Randall.'

'I had guessed that, Mr Tanner. Thank you for the courtesy of making that assumption.'

'Mr Randall was killed by Mr Webb. It seems unlikely that a low-level criminal like Mr Webb would come up with the idea of murdering Mr Randall without cause or instructions. As a matter of logic, our case theory extends to Mr Webb being told to kill Mr Randall by someone other than my client. Logic points to Mr Bitar, a man with a criminal record and much longer criminal history.' Tanner was tempted to say a criminal history much longer than Mr Russell's legs, but restrained himself. It was a murder trial, not petty larceny. 'Then there's Mr Webb himself. A killer, on my instructions a liar as well, and a man who for some reason has the benefit of a deal with the DPP about the length of his sentence.'

The judge raised an eyebrow at Tanner that appeared to want to get straight to the point. 'Does your case theory extend to nominating who it was that ordered Mr Randall to be killed beyond Mr Bitar, or is he top of the tree?'

Tanner smiled. 'Nominations aren't closed yet, your Honour. When I settle on a pick from a crowded field, you and the jury will find out.'

The judge closed her eyes for a moment, and shook her head. 'I look forward to that. Anything else?'

'Mr Randall was a convicted drug dealer, your Honour. He did nearly six years for that. Mr Webb was found with coke and meth in his car, and meth in his system when arrested. Mr Randall worked for a bank called South-East Banking Corporation. It sold Tina Leonard's development site to their client Lovro Constructions at what the expert evidence suggests was a huge undervalue. The witnesses I've had subpoenas served on are from SEBC and Lovro or have links to them somehow. I'm sure if I start asking irrelevant questions when I call them, Ms Crown will object and your Honour will make any rulings you think appropriate. I can't be shut out now though.'

'Thank you for that, Mr Tanner. Do you want to say anything more?'

'Your Honour can take what I've just said as both my opening and closing submissions on these motions.'

Justice Francis smiled. 'I might hold you to that.'

After the motions were formally read, along with the supporting affidavits, Tanner applied to cross-examine the first deponent, a lawyer called Sean Rosser, a 'dispute resolution specialist' partner of a large commercial law firm called Billingtons that were acting for Ravic, presumably because they did work for Lovro Constructions. Robert Russell objected to cross-examination on the basis that the motion was an interlocutory hearing, but given the stakes involved in the trial, the judge ruled in Tanner's favour. 'Keep it relevant,' she said.

'You've sworn this affidavit based on, among other things, what your client Mr Ravic has told you, correct?'

'Among other things.'

'Am I correct?'

'Yes, but –'

'And he told you –'

'My client hadn't finished his answer, your Honour,' Russell objected.

'Actually he had, your Honour,' Tanner said. '"Am I correct?" only requires yes or no. And, Mr Rosser, he told you he'd never heard of or met Mr Webb or Mr Bitar, right?'

'Yes.'

'Have you?'

'Me?'

'Yeah. Do you know them?'

'No. Of course not.'

'Why "of course not", Mr Rosser? Your firm doesn't act for informants with histories of violence, is that what you're saying?'

'Mr Tanner,' the judge said sharply.

'You don't know them personally?'

'No.'

'So, you personally weren't there when Mr Webb shot Mr Randall?'

'I object, your honour,' Russell said. 'That's a ridiculous question.'

'I'm inclined to agree, Mr Tanner. I said be relevant.'

'It is relevant, your Honour. Mr Rosser, were you with Mr Webb when someone instructed him to kill Mr Randall?'

'C'mon, Mr Tanner.'

'Was your client there when that message was conveyed to Mr Webb?'

'I'm sorry?'

'I object –'

'How is that relevant, Mr Tanner?' the judge snapped.

'How is it not, your Honour?'

'I beg your pardon?'

'I want an answer, your Honour. If the question isn't ruled out, I'd like an answer.'

The judge shook her head, raised her eyes to the ceiling, but let it go. 'Just answer, Mr Rosser. It might be quicker.'

'My instructions are –'

'I couldn't care less about your instructions, Mr Rosser. What do you know, is what I'm asking. Do you know where your client was at the precise moment someone told Mr Webb to kill Mr Randall?'

'Of course not.'

'And do you know, to your own knowledge, leaving aside what your client has instructed you, that Mr Ravic has never spoken to Mr Bitar?'

'Are you seriously intending to put that to him in the trial?'

Tanner glared at Rosser. 'What I intend to ask a witness is none of your business. Neither is what I'll be allowed to ask. What I want to find out is what you actually know, not what your client has instructed you about. Is the answer to my question about your personal knowledge "no"?'

'I believe my client.'

'And I believe mine, Mr Rosser. Perhaps I should swear an affidavit and hand it to the jury and tell them I'm instructed she's not guilty, and ask for a verdict accordingly? How do you reckon I'd go?'

'Are you done, Mr Tanner?'

'Pretty much, your Honour, but that's my point. These affidavits are absurd. A bunch of lawyers giving evidence that amounts to "my client tells me and I believe". How probative is that? This is a criminal court. Witnesses shouldn't get to hide behind lawyers' coat-tails here. These motions, and the spineless so-called evidence filed in support of them, are a waste of the court's time.'

'Speaking of which,' Justice Francis said, 'is there anything you just got from this witness you couldn't have made a submission about?'

'You never know, your Honour.'

The judge shook her head, started to say something, then paused, like she'd thought better of putting whatever it was on a transcript. 'I'll see all Counsel in chambers,' she then said.

Tanner stood against the bookcase that was built into the wall on the right of the desk in the judge's chambers, and let the others fuss over the seats. Justice Francis looked older up close, smoky streaks mixed in with the light brown hair that was under the wig. A sturdy physique filled her chair. Lots of late nights in chambers over the last twenty-five or so years, Tanner thought. Not much play.

'I'm not sure I can do much about this,' the judge began. 'I can't stop a defendant from running a defence. I do want to say this though –' She stopped, scanned the room like she'd lost something, then noticed Tanner on her right. 'Mr Tanner, I won't let you embark on an exercise that's no more than court-protected defamation, or a series of unsubstantiated slurs against any witness who –'

'My slurs are always substantiated, judge.'

'Let me finish, please. I'm giving you this warning with the courtesy of not putting it on the record for now. You know what I mean. You're calling these witnesses. You'll have to ask them questions of relevance. I won't allow some circus.'

'Does that mean your Honour's dismissing these motions?'

'I'll hear submission from the others on that. I'm saying I'm heading that way, but letting you know what it means for the way you conduct yourself.'

'Juries don't like stunts or having their time wasted, judge. That's not my aim.'

'Judges don't like stunts or having their time wasted either, Mr Tanner.'

'Which is why your Honour should make personal costs orders against Mr Russell and Mr Burton when you dismiss their clients' motions.'

Russell started yapping, but the judge shut him down. 'Let's go back and finish this,' she said.

When they returned to court and the other lawyers had their say, the judge refused to grant the orders to release anyone from their subpoena. She'd rule on relevance objections if the prosecution made them, and if nothing proper was asked of a particular witness, she'd put a stop to further questions from Tanner, and excuse that witness herself.

'Are you going to tell me which of these people you're actually really going to call, Pete?' Izzy Gallo said to Tanner when the judge had left the bench.

'All of them.'

'All of them?'

He nodded.

'Care to tell me what order you're going to call them in?'

Tanner smiled. 'In an ascending order of guilt,' he said.

She smiled back. 'So we finish with your client, do we?'

41

The office was in Edgecliff, down the hill from the shopping precinct of Bondi Junction. From the outside it looked like any other renovated terrace, but for the brass plate out the front that announced, 'Harry Hartfield, Solicitors'.

Despite the plural, Hartfield ran a one-man show. Tanner assumed there was a receptionist, but by the time he arrived after court at about a quarter to six, she'd gone. The front door was locked, but when he pushed the intercom button a male voice answered, told him to come in when he heard a click, take a seat and he'd be down soon.

When Tanner walked into the reception area, Simone Hargreaves was seated in a red leather chair. He kissed her hello. A longer kiss than he usually received from a witness.

'Nice room,' he said as he looked around. The décor was modern. A trapezoid-shaped coffee table in the middle, sitting on a cow-hide carpet, *Architectural Digest* magazines fanned out on top. The guy didn't do crime, Tanner thought. On the wall behind him was a canvas by an Aboriginal artist, shades of pink from carnation to magenta, grey and white dots.

'Harry's wife's a designer,' Simone said.

Tanner nodded. 'Thanks for doing this.'

She looked at him, took a deep breath, slowly let it out. 'Sorry about the motion to have my subpoena set aside. I assume they didn't go ahead with it. I rang the partner at Lattimers – I made it clear that I wouldn't play along. I could kill Grant.'

'Perhaps you should ask my client who to hire?'

'It's a nice thought, Peter. Do you think I could get away with it?'

'If I was defending you.'

'Would you?'

'For the right fee.'

'Would people get suspicious? Two dead husbands?'

Tanner shrugged. 'If they knew either of them you could probably plead and get a small fine.'

She laughed, a little too happily for his liking.

They sat in silence for a moment, listening to footsteps in a room above them, before Tanner said, 'Did you tell your husband you were coming here?'

She narrowed her eyes. 'He doesn't get to tell me what to do.'

'I've figured that. Especially on the last two nights we've spent together. I'd be flabbergasted if he was telling you what to do.'

'He's at work. He won't miss me.'

'Tough gig, our profession. Working for an hourly rate.'

'You should charge a success fee.'

Tanner smiled. 'Some grateful people have slung me the odd victory bonus over the years.'

'Really? Have you declared them as income?'

'Was I meant to? Shall we ask Grant? Let's call him later from my bedroom.'

She laughed again, like a wicked girl. She was all right for the wife of a lawyer whose career involved cheating the Australian public out of its money, he thought.

'How well do you know this guy, Hartfield?' Tanner asked.

She shrugged. 'Oli knew him from school. I met him at university.'

'Law school?'

She shook her head. 'Arts,' she said. 'Sociology majors, both of us.'

'Really?'

'You look surprised.'

'No.'

'I told you I had an arts degree? You think I'm only a bored North Shore housewife?'

'You're not bored all the time now, are you?'

There was a long pause, then a smile. 'Not all the time,' she said.

'I've just had a thought. Are you attracted to me, or is it really the thrill of a murder case that's got you – interested?'

'I guess I'm a living cliché.'

'Your first husband did five years' jail for coke distribution, and then got whacked. I don't know if that's a cliché. Maybe it depends on what suburb you live in.'

'Maybe it does.'

When Harry Hartfield descended the stairs and materialised in the doorway of his reception room, he was wearing a three-piece glen-check suit, white shirt, navy tie, linen kerchief in the lapel pocket. Tanner checked the shoes. Probably Artioli. Two-hundred-dollar haircut. Was the role of M up again? Self-assured smile, a gesture with both hands. *Follow me.*

'How did you know Oliver?' Tanner asked after they'd been through formalities, sitting in what had once been a bedroom, now a small conference room. Glass table, chairs of Danish origin, more Indigenous work on the walls.

'From school,' Hartfield said, voice as crisp as his cotton shirt.

'Which one?' Tanner asked. Hartfield told him. 'Unusual number of high-end felons seem to come from there.'

Hartfield shrugged, smiled. 'The competitor schools don't produce boys with enough imagination for what I assume you mean by "high end". Dodgy stockbrokers and realtors at best.'

'I wouldn't know. Spoken like a blue blood, by the way.'

'I'm just a butcher's son made good,' Hartfield said.

Tanner looked at his kerchief, his perfectly knotted tie. 'How'd you end up at that school?'

Hartfield smiled. 'A very successful butcher's son.'

There was a stainless-steel water pitcher in the middle of the table, four tumblers surrounding it. Ergonomic handle to prevent the clientele getting RSI in long meetings. Tanner poured himself a cup. 'Simone has explained why I'm here?' he asked.

'To discuss Oli's will, she told me.' Hartfield looked at Simone, forced a smile. If there'd been love, it had been lost.

'You have his personal papers, I'm told?'

Hartfield didn't respond for a moment, just looked at Tanner. 'How do they interest you, Peter?' he said.

'I'd like to check.'

'You think I should help the woman who had my friend killed?'

'You do much crime, Harry?' Tanner asked.

'None.'

'Didn't think so. If you had some of my clients they'd have boosted most of your artworks in a couple of weeks. Even this jug would go. God knows what they'd use it for. Presumption of innocence, you know that one?'

'I have a very vague recollection from law school. How often are your clients innocent?'

'How often are yours?'

Hartfield narrowed his eyes. 'What does that mean?'

'She didn't do it, Harry.'

'You know that for a fact?'

'I don't think she did it. I don't always feel that way, if you're interested. Usually I don't.'

'Who did it then? Who had Oli killed?'

'A dipshit junky called Jayden Webb killed him, Harry. A thug-for-hire called Bitar probably told him to, for someone else. Beyond that, I can't give you the chain of command. I can only tell you I don't think Tina Leonard's on it.'

Hartfield shifted in his seat, poured himself a glass of water, didn't offer Simone one.

'Simone's told you I want to look at any correspondence or copies of correspondence you have of Oliver's. The fact that you haven't told us you don't have anything of relevance yet tells me you think you might. Can I read what you have?'

'Oli's papers were left to me,' Hartfield said quickly, 'to deal with as per my discretion as his executor.'

'Can I see them?'

'I don't litigate, Peter,' Hartfield said slowly, 'but wouldn't a subpoena be best? More conventional?'

'I'd rather not do it that way.'

'Why not?'

'Because then the prosecutor will know. I'd like to surprise her.'

Hartfield smiled. 'You think I have something that proves your client is innocent?'

Tanner shook his head quickly. 'I like giving myself a forensic advantage if I can.'

Hartfield sipped from his tumbler.

'Harry, you know what Oli did to us. What he did to Hannah and me?' Simone Hargreaves said. A decidedly unsympathetic look from Hartfield. 'He changed in prison. All that – he found God. He found, I don't know, truth.'

'I know, Simone,' Hartfield said. 'I visited him. Unlike you. Unlike Hannah.'

Simone paused, shook her head. 'I was angry. I had good cause. I had to sell our house because of him. I didn't stop Hannah visiting him. She didn't want to. I had to take her out of her school. I didn't think I should make her.'

'Nearly six years without seeing his child.'

'We're getting side-tracked,' Tanner said.

'He wrote me that apology, Harry,' Simone said over him. 'He said those drugs weren't his, but that he'd done other bad things. If he – if you help in this Leonard case, it might clear his name for the drugs. He was set up. I believe that now. I don't know why, but I do.'

'You kept something, right?' Tanner asked. 'Copies of his letters from prison. Stuff he wrote after God spoke to him? You have that?'

Hartfield sighed, closed his eyes. 'I'd be more comfortable if I had a subpoena.'

'Just let me look first. After that, then I promise – we'll do the paperwork then.'

A few minutes after leaving, Hartfield returned to the room, placed a bundle of documents in front of Tanner. Three clumps, each several inches thick, pink legal tape holding them together.

'I've got a few boxes of papers and documents in my storage room,' Hartfield said, 'but I've got a feeling you're after these.' He left the room again.

Tanner looked at Simone. She got the message, left him to it.

He found photocopies of the letters he already had that Randall had written to Simone and Hannah, two before his release, one after. There were several copies of separate letters to Hannah. He read the first couple he came across, but they were expressions of love, of sorrow, pleas for forgiveness, hopes for his future, hopes for hers. There were letters to his parents, apologies again, reports of how he was doing, what his plans were. He was going to make some things right that he could.

It was towards the back of the second pile he looked through that he found a copy of a letter he thought he should have seen before. It was to Tina Leonard, written after his release, dated a week before his death. Oliver Randall was sorry for the hurt that he'd caused Leonard. Sorry for what his bank had done. He'd tried to stop it, but couldn't. Not quite going on to admit fraud, but something to work with. Tanner already had a letter like that from Leonard. What he didn't have was:

> *You know I loved you. I tried to leave Simone. I did more than once. You know how hard it was for me with Hannah only just starting senior school. I just didn't think I could forgive myself if I put her through what I knew would be a horrible divorce. And it was not a good time – you of all people know that, Tina. The coke had a grip on me. I was not thinking straight at home, or at work. I was a mess. I loved you, but I could not simply walk out. I am so sorry I wasn't honest then. I'm so sorry about what I was made to do. Your trial nearly killed me. I hope you know that. It nearly killed me. But what is the point now? What is the point of threatening me the way you did yesterday? The whole thing nearly killed me.*

Maybe it did, Oliver?

Tanner folded the letter in half, then over again. He felt its weight. The weight of more motive. The weight of lies, Tina Leonard's lies. Lies that could get her convicted. He put it inside the leather satchel he'd brought with him, locked it up, left the room.

When he walked back to the reception area, Simone was waiting for him, flicking through one of the magazines that were on the coffee table.

She looked up at him. 'Anything?'

He shook his head. 'Copies of what you gave me. Letters to Hannah. A few to his parents. Nothing else of relevance. Harry here?'

'Up in his office, I think.'

Tanner walked up the stairs, turned on the landing behind them, walked to the end of a corridor. The door was open, Hartfield was in the room. It would once have been the master bedroom. French doors, the wood painted white, led out to the balcony. Hartfield was looking at his iMac. He had a beer next to his pens. A Corona. Christ, it's got a lime in it, Tanner thought.

'Anything of use?' Hartfield asked. He saw Tanner looking at his beer. 'Can I get you one? Something stronger?'

Tanner assumed Hartfield had read the letters. It was likely that he knew Leonard and Randall had been lovers, not just, for a relatively short time, borrower and banker. Maybe Hartfield had kept quiet about that for the sake of what was left of his murdered friend's reputation. Maybe there was some other reason, and maybe he assumed people knew. Simone didn't know, Tanner was sure. Tina and Randall must have been discreet. He wondered whether Harry Hartfield had drawn the same conclusion that Izzy Gallo would if she knew about the affair. That revenge for pulling the pin on her loans and sinking her business wasn't the only reason Tina Leonard wanted Oliver Randall dead. She'd been jilted too, by the same guy who bankrupted her. Worse still, she'd made some kind of threat. There was no way Tanner wanted Gallo to get hold of that letter.

Tanner patted the satchel he had slung over his shoulder. 'I've put a couple of documents in here,' he said. 'I'd like to read them at home.'

'What?'

'You'll get them back.'

Hartfield stood up. 'Hang on a second. What documents? I didn't say you could take anything.'

'Are you going to stop me?'

'What does that mean?'

'I'm asking you, Harry — are you going to physically try to stop me?'

'Are you — are you threatening me? Are you crazy?'

'No. I'm just seeking clarity. Are you going to try to stop me? Will you call the police?'

'The police? Look —'

'I'm taking what I need, Harry, and you're going to forget that I have. The letters to Simone you've got? The copies of the originals she gave me? Oliver says he was set up. If you use your imagination, read between the lines, use your common sense — he more or less says SEBC was a criminal outfit. That's how I read it. You don't want to get messed up in this. I just didn't want to give you a shock in case you thought something was missing when I left. Forget it, Harry. Don't make a fuss. Your friend Oliver Randall had six kilos of coke that wasn't his found in his study by a crooked cop because that's what SEBC wanted to happen. I'm calling the cop who did that to him in Tina Leonard's murder trial. I'm calling another crook who's made a pile of money bigger than you and I will ever see in ten lifetimes out of Limani Views. Let me get messed up in it. Stick to the kind of law you do, whatever that is. I know it's not my kind of law. My kind of law involves people who would rearrange this nice office and rearrange you in the process. Forget I was here.'

Tanner waited for an acknowledgement, but Hartfield kept glaring at him. 'Harry?'

'Yes.'

'Finish your beer. Shut down your computer. Go home.'

42

The jury ended up eight to four. Females in the majority, one as their leader, both alternates male. Tanner used two challenges on women, one on a man. No science involved. When all you had was how someone looked, you're left with prejudice. They 'looked' the most ready to convict.

Justice Caitlin Francis addressed the jury slowly, from notes she'd prepared. The indictment was murder, the accused was Athina Leonard, the plea was not guilty. She introduced Gallo and Tanner, told the jurors they'd been around the track a few times, told them to listen carefully when they spoke, said the same for each witness called. Tina Leonard sat motionless in the dock as the judge spoke, but couldn't help but be the star of the show. She was in her ivory suit, white silk shirt, makeup fractionally on the sedate side of the Ptolemaic dynasty. She looked like she was sitting on a throne, not in a dock.

'My main job in this trial,' the judge continued, 'is to decide what evidence is ruled in or out in the event of a dispute. I don't decide who to believe, or what to accept. That's now your duty.'

She gave the usual warnings about media reports, told them not to read what was in the papers about the case, not to watch TV, to leave social media alone until they'd done their service. Until it was not guilty, or it was guilty beyond any reasonable doubt.

Beyond reasonable doubt. She said she'd come back to that crucial concept in her summing up. For now, though, she told them to remember one last thing: the prosecutor has to prove guilt. The defence has to prove nothing.

Tanner looked down at the folder of notes and documents he had in front of him when the judge said that. It had his witness list inside it. He was going to a whole lot of trouble if the defence had to prove nothing.

'The accused ordered the murder of Oliver Randall,' Izzy Gallo SC began her opening statement to the jury. 'By order I mean "bought". She paid to have him shot once in each knee before he was fatally shot in the head.'

Gallo paused to let her last words sit with the jury. Then she went straight to motive. 'I guess you may have a question right now about this crime – why? Why did Tina Leonard pay to have Oliver Randall killed?'

Gallo succinctly took the jury through the financial rise of Leonard Developments, its Limani Views project, and its collapse after the GFC. 'So you see, members of the jury,' she said once she'd dealt with the key facts and findings from the trial between Leonard, her company and SEBC, 'Tina Leonard has already once not been believed by a judge of this court. She said she had a deal regarding her company's loans with Mr Randall. He said she didn't. The judge believed him. She never got over that.'

Gallo then cut the case into small chunks, but they were massive blows to Tina Leonard. Her company liquidated, wound up. Bankruptcy. Her assets gone. Her house gone. Custody of her children to her ex-husband. Everything she had, gone.

'And who did Tina Leonard blame for this?' Gallo asked. 'The economy? Her business plan? Her advisors? Herself?' She shook her head. 'No, none of those. She blamed Oliver Randall. She blamed him, and she hated him.'

Gallo had to deal with the sensitive parts of the prosecution case. She told the jury she had to be 'frank' about some matters. Oliver Randall's own fall, his six kilos of coke and five and a half years in prison. She told them the man paid to kill him, Jayden Webb, had a criminal record before the killing, had pleaded guilty, and had received a discounted sentence for his evidence against Leonard. Mick Bitar would tell them Tina Leonard had tried to hire him to make the arrangements to have Randall killed – apart from Bitar's own evidence, the Crown would call the manager of a restaurant who'd seen Bitar and the accused having lunch just days before the murder. Then there was the coffee meeting Leonard had with the victim just over a week before he was killed. She'd yelled at him. The café owner would give evidence about that. Bitar too had a criminal record. He'd only agreed to talk on his terms. He'd been given an immunity from any charge.

'Mick Bitar wasn't a stranger to Tina Leonard,' Gallo told the jury. 'They were old friends. And she knew of Jayden Webb. He'd worked on her father's and brothers' building sites, once on hers. She knew he had a reputation for violence. And when Oliver Randall was released from prison, and Tina Leonard's wait for revenge was over, she wanted violence. She paid for it. Fifty thousand dollars up front, another fifty later. I'll lead evidence of that, members of the jury. I'll prove payment of the first tranche. It was found in Jayden Webb's flat. It can be traced from cash withdrawals from the accused's bank account. It was payment delivered with a message: "I want him dead. I want him gone."'

Tanner saw at least four of the jurors making a note on the pads they'd been given. He knew what they were writing down. *Fifty thousand dollars.*

'Some people let go of anger, members of the jury,' Gallo then said. 'Some slights, some wrongs are forgiven, some forgotten. Others are always remembered, but the heat, even the fury, gradually fades. Not for Tina Leonard. Oliver Randall, in her mind, had destroyed her. Destroyed the business she'd spent years building in a man's world. He crushed her dreams, wrecked her family. He'd stolen her children, not just her wealth. Her anger didn't fade. It burnt. Burnt into rage. So she had him killed.

This man she had grown to hate. Once she got hold of some of her late father's money, she paid to have him killed. Her revenge was to have him executed. Now your job is to seek the community's redress for that crime.'

When Gallo sat down, the judge looked at Tanner. He had three choices. He could open the defence case now, not at all, or wait until the prosecution case was over. Before he called his own witnesses, he was going to have to say something to the jury about what he was doing. He'd been uncertain at the start of the trial, but now he was sure. Something was needed for Leonard immediately. The headline was already written: A hundred thousand to buy an execution, fifty up front in cash. He didn't want to leave the jury only with that.

When he told Justice Francis he'd be giving a short opening, she gave the jury a break and adjourned for fifteen minutes. Tanner stayed in the courtroom, highlighting some notes he'd already made, discussing with Gallagher and Singh what he would say. When the fifteen minutes were up, the judge's associate approached the bar table and asked if counsel were ready. 'Two minutes, please,' Tanner said.

'So you know,' he said to Tina Leonard when he reached her in the dock, 'I'm not about to provide a response to all she just said. That's for later.'

She looked at him, big black eyes, nodded just enough.

'This will be short. I want them thinking about something other than your fifty thousand.'

'She's very good,' Leonard said calmly. 'Her voice – it's seductive.'

'I can't control the prosecutor's competence, Tina.'

She smiled. He wanted to tell her to look more anxious, more betrayed, more wronged by her predicament. 'You're good friends, I see.'

Tanner examined her face. An aura of certainty. For a moment he wanted to ask her about Oliver Randall. Why hadn't she told him they'd been lovers? He could have asked her that morning, the night before, but something stopped him. It was one part of what became the mess of her life that she didn't want to revisit. He needed her composed for the start of the trial. He'd pick his moment.

'She's a colleague, Tina. Mutual respect. I'm only rude to prosecutors who are rude to me.'

'She's been in love with you.'

'What?'

Tina Leonard's lips formed a vague smile. 'I was young and beautiful once, Peter. I know about love. Did it last long? Did you end it?'

'Tina,' Tanner said, searching for a response. 'I'm – I'm going to do everything to try to win this case. I've *been* doing everything to try to win this case. We all are.'

'I know you are,' she said slowly. 'I'm making an observation, not an accusation.'

'You know, Tina, I have to confess, I've already made one big error in this case.'

'Already?'

'If you're so good at reading people,' he said, 'I should have had you pick the jury.'

'My client, Tina Leonard,' Tanner began, 'is forty-nine years old. I don't want to embarrass her, but I mention that because she may look younger than that to you. And I mention it at all because in those forty-nine years, she's not been convicted of a single crime. Not one. We couldn't even find a traffic offence.' He paused, looked briefly at Izzy Gallo, back at the jury. 'And I mention that, members of the jury, because if I started to talk to you about the crimes committed by the main prosecution witnesses you're going to hear from, I'd be up here talking to you for a very long time.' He said the last three words slowly, a noticeable gap between each.

'Mr Webb has a criminal record. He's a violent young man. I know my friend mentioned it, but she had to do that. It's worth more than mentioning. It's going to be worth thinking about. It's also worth thinking about the fact that he shot a man in the head. There's an executioner in this case, all right. The prosecutor will call him. She'll ask you to believe him. Be very careful about that.

'And Mr Bitar? He's got a more colourful history than Mr Webb. I guess he would have. He's older, he's had more time.' Tanner had to be careful with Bitar. He'd need to make what he could of his record, his reputation. But he'd done work for Leonard and her family. There was no way out of that.

'And Mr Randall, the deceased? What happened to him was truly awful. I suspect my friend will want to show you photos. I can tell you now, the aftermath of gun violence is always shocking. Still, maybe Mr Webb can tell us about it. And he can tell us about the drug habit he has, and about the methylamphetamine – 'ice' as you may had heard it referred to – that the police found in his car, along with some cocaine. The sort of drug Mr Randall used to sell. I know my friend mentioned that as well. Again, she has to. Ever heard of a drug dealer being killed? I have. I'm sure you have too. It's not uncommon. I think we might find that Mr Randall – well, it's a terrible crime, what happened to him. I mean that. But we might find that he took some secrets to the grave with him.'

He had to be deliberately vague. There was no way of knowing yet what evidence he'd get in, what leeway the judge would permit, what rabbits he'd be allowed to set running. He couldn't afford to set a hurdle he wouldn't be able to jump. Drug dealer. Secrets to the grave. That would have to do for now.

'Revenge is a dish best served cold. You'd have all heard that expression, members of the jury? Boy, the prosecutor hangs a lot on that, doesn't she? Nearly six years in prison – that's how long Oliver Randall was there. Imagine if someone lied about something to do with you in a court case that harmed you, but *they* got six years' jail after that. Would you still want revenge? Wouldn't you think the gods or luck or chance or fate or whatever you believe in had given it to you? Tina Leonard did. She didn't pay to have Oliver Randall harmed. She didn't want him dead. There may have been people who did. There must have been. Believe me, though, members of the jury, Tina Leonard wasn't one of them.'

43

There's a question that every lawyer should ask long before they start a trial: What do I have to prove to win? There are few short cuts to proof in a murder trial. Cause of death. When. Where. Who. Motive. None can be skimmed over.

Izzy Gallo led Detective Senior Sergeant Gavin Walters through the essentials of her case. He didn't need much help from her. He knew his way around a courtroom.

Video of the crime scene was tendered first. A narrow hallway in shadow, a brightly lit room at its end, a body crumpled in front of a small kitchen table in a one-bedroom flat. Blood on the lino floor. Didn't die on his knees, Oliver Randall. They'd been blown apart. One from a few feet, the other close range, like the shot to the head. 'Executed' was a fair enough term.

Next came the details of Jayden Webb's arrest. He'd driven straight into a police random breath test station set up in Ravier Street, Alexandria. He pulled a U-turn over the median strip to avoid it, sideswiped a car when he did. Then he drove up a dead-end street. That made the pursuit simpler than it might otherwise have been. He still had the gun in the car. The police smelt it before they dragged it out from under the seat. When they searched his person, they found a few grams of ice in the pocket of his jeans, a hit of coke in the other. Just to round out things, he was driving unlicensed. Criminal record for violence, larceny, drug possession. Jayden Webb may as well have shot Randall, then walked straight to the nearest police station and confessed.

Video of his police interviews was next. He said nothing at first. Five days later, once he'd changed lawyers, once a deal was on the table, he told them about Tina Leonard.

Then a short video of Tina Leonard's one police interview. 'I've been set up,' she said. She didn't talk further until they'd told her Webb said it was her. 'If this man has told you I paid him to kill Randall,' she said, 'then you need to arrest Mick Bitar.' Then she shut up for good.

Tanner began his cross-examination. 'How many times did Jayden Webb mention my client's name during his first police interview, detective?'

'He didn't, Mr Tanner. I've already said that. You've seen the video.'

Tanner smiled. 'The jury's not as familiar with all this material as we are, detective. You want them to fully understand the evidence, don't you?'

Walters didn't answer for a few moments, realised he should when Gallo let the question go with a roll of her eyes. 'Of course,' he said.

'Do you?'

Another pause, this time confusion. 'Do I what?'

'Do you want to understand the evidence? Does the New South Wales police? The DPP? Do they want to understand what's happened here?'

'I think you might need to clarify that question, Mr Tanner,' the judge said as Gallo was rising to her feet.

'I'll come back to it at some stage, your Honour. In exactly the same terms. Mr Mick Bitar, detective. You knew him before he was interviewed?'

'Knew him?'

'Yes.'

'No. I knew of him. I was told –'

'You knew of his criminal record?'

'I was shown it.'

'Not exactly a law-abiding citizen, is he?'

'I'm sure you'll take him through the mistakes he's made.'

'Mistakes?' Tanner said loudly. 'Breaking someone's jaw with a punch. That's a mistake, is it?'

'If what – the conviction you're referring to I believe followed a fight. I don't know if there was intent to cause a particular injury.'

'You swing a punch now, and the police no longer think you're intending to cause injury? It's just a mistake if that happens, is it detective?'

'That's not how I meant it, Mr Tanner, and you know it.'

'Do I? It was your word, detective.'

'Then I made a mistake in using it.'

'Perhaps we can move on, Mr Tanner?' the judge intervened. Izzy Gallo once would have been objecting herself, when she was a more junior prosecutor. She had restraint now. She got up when she had to, when it really mattered.

'Mr Bitar's also been charged with a few other crimes too, hasn't he?'

'Well – charged. I know you know about the presumption of innocence, Mr Tanner.'

'Mr Randall, the deceased. You knew about his criminal record, right?'

'I was informed.'

'He pleaded guilty to the supply of a large commercial quantity of cocaine, correct?'

'As I said before, yes.'

'Nearly six years in prison, right? Six kilos of cocaine found in his house?'

'That's right.'

'Hell of a lot, you'd agree?'

'I would.'

'Couple of million bucks' worth in street value, correct? Maybe a bit more?'

'You'd know more, I suspect, Mr Tanner.'

'Very funny, detective. I don't intend to call some of my ex-clients to prove that. Ballpark, right?'

'Sure.'

'Probably not all his coke, correct? Not that amount?'

'I wouldn't know.'

'Really? If it wasn't his, or he owed money on it, whoever did own it would be a bit upset at him losing it to the police, wouldn't they?'

'I've never thought about it. I don't think that's something Mr Randall told anyone in the Drug Squad.'

'Did he name his suppliers?'

'He didn't.'

'Could have got a lighter sentence, couldn't he? If he'd named his supplier? People further up the chain?'

'I imagine so.'

'Why didn't he, detective?'

'I don't know why for sure, Mr Tanner. I've read the file, though, as you know. He told the police and the court he was afraid to.'

'Why was he afraid?'

'Well – we can't ask him, can we?'

'We don't need to, do we, detective? Use your imagination. How about afraid they might hurt him; would that seem like the most likely reason?'

'Perhaps. At the time.'

'At the time? You don't think drug importers can wait for retribution. Only my client?'

'I don't know what drug importers might do, Mr Tanner. They didn't harm Mr Randall, as far as I know.'

'He's afraid to name his suppliers because he thinks they might harm him even though he could have done at least two years less in prison, and when he's released, he's harmed. Fatally. That doesn't sound much like a coincidence to me, detective.'

'Mr Webb and Mr Bitar told us a different story. Your client gave Mr Webb fifty thousand dollars in cash.'

Tanner didn't like that he'd given Walters the chance to

mention the money again. He'd asked a question that could have been a submission, and Walters had slipped in one of the Crown's strongest points.

'We'll be giving an explanation for that money in due course, detective. You know that.'

'Not from your client I don't.'

Tanner paused, looked at the judge for a moment, then back to Walters. 'Mr Randall, in addition to being a drug trafficker, was a banker, correct? Before his conviction?'

'Yes.'

'He was a witness for his employer, South-East Banking Corporation, in a trial involving my client.'

'I believe so.'

'And you're familiar with the Limani Views development in the western harbour?'

'I wouldn't say I'm familiar with it. I know of it.'

'You looked into the claims and counterclaims over my client's development of that land, though, in the SEBC trial, correct?'

'I read the judgement, if that's what you mean.'

'You know who owns it, don't you? Now?'

'The judgement says Lovro Constructions bought it.'

'At a massive discount for what it was worth.'

'I object,' Gallo said. 'The trial judge didn't find that.'

'I'll rephrase,' Tanner said. 'At what my client claimed was a fraction of its true market value. Did you look into that?'

Walters looked at Gallo, then the judge, as though they should intervene. Then he said, 'No.'

'Why not?'

'Because we were investigating a paid murder, not the history of an old court case.'

'But that's your motive, isn't it, detective? That old history?'

'We read the judgement. We had what the witnesses and informants told us.'

'Lovro Constructions is a client of SEBC, you know that, don't you?'

'It might well be.'

'Did you talk to anyone at SEBC about what my client alleged it did to her?'

This time Izzy Gallo did object. 'What does that even mean, your Honour? "Did" to her? Did what? When? How could it be relevant, whatever it is?'

Justice Francis looked at Tanner.

'Did you investigate whether Oliver Randall had lied in that court case over how long my client had to pay her loans, and had decided to come clean about that upon his release from prison?' he said.

Walters smiled, shook his head. 'No.'

'No? Did you talk to anyone at SEBC or Lovro Constructions to ascertain how Lovro was able to get my client's land so cheaply?'

Gallo stood again. 'Putting aside for the moment how that could be relevant once again your Honour, it hasn't been established that they did get it cheaply. My friend has some valuations he wants to try to tender, which I'll object to at the right time, but the foundation for the question isn't there.'

'If the executives at this bank, and at Lovro Constructions, if they were convicted, violent criminals like Mr Webb and Mr Bitar, would you have spoken to them then, detective? Would that make them more reliable to form part of your investigation?'

'I object,' Gallo said loudly.

'Withdrawn, your Honour. Thank you, detective.'

What was left of the day belonged to the doctor who'd performed the post-mortem. The defence had admitted the cause of death, and the injuries and damage caused by the three bullets, but Gallo wanted the theatre for the jury. She'd called it an execution. She wanted images to go with the word. Tanner sat and listened for a short while, then opened a folder of documents and started reading as though nothing being said was of any relevance.

And it wasn't. The case wasn't about a Smith & Wesson handgun, or three 10 mm bullets. It wasn't about the speed and energy of metal on bone, or tissue, or vessels and brain. It was not about the physics or the physiology of death.

It was about the desire for causing it.

How much Tina Leonard craved it, how much he could prove someone else might have.

44

'She had an affair with Randall,' Tanner said.

He was in his chambers after the day in court, sitting behind his desk. It was just after six, and Kit Gallagher was about to leave.

Gallagher looked at Singh, who indicated this was news to her, looked back at Tanner.

'She told you this?'

He shook his head. 'I found out,' he said. 'And I have it in writing.'

He told them about his visit with Simone Hargreaves to the office of Harry Hartfield solicitors and attorneys in Edgecliff, the bundle of letters Randall had copied, then left to his executor's discretion.

'You just took this letter?' Singh asked.

'Why didn't you tell me you were doing this?' Gallagher said. 'I should have gone with you to this – this fellow's firm.'

'Didn't need the company, Kit,' he said. 'And I didn't take the letter. I borrowed it. Possibly permanently.'

'Have you asked her about it?'

Tanner shook his head. 'Not yet.'

'Why?'

'Because I wanted to get the trial going. The first morning didn't seem like the right time.'

'We're not under any obligation to tell Gallo about this, right?' Singh said.

'No. We aren't.'

'Do you think it could come out somehow?' she asked.

Tanner opened the folder of documents he had on his desk. In it were his most important notes, the key documents for his part of the case. 'We're going to tender these two letters in here from Oliver Randall to his ex-wife and daughter confessing largely unspecified sins. We're also going to tender one of his other letters to Tina.'

'And?'

'And I'll have to say where I got them.'

'Which is from the ex-wife and from Tina, right?'

'It is.'

'Where does it go pear-shaped?'

Tanner shook his head, stood up. He turned and looked out of his window. The street lights were on, it was dark, starting to rain. You had to think in parallel lines about cases, Max Rourke had told him when he'd started at the bar. What is the list of things that can win me a case? What are the things that can lose it? The list of things that could make you a winner was usually linear. Things got tangential with the other list. What might go wrong was a never-ending story of twists and turns, snakes and ladders. He turned back to the others.

'It goes pear-shaped if Gallo thinks like me,' he said.

'Thinks like you?'

'She'll ask herself who else he may have written to. Did he keep copies? Where might they be if they exist? She's thorough. It's not that far-fetched that Hartfield ends up with a subpoena. And there's a bigger risk than that, too.'

'Which is?'

'Hartfield just rings the DPP, and tells them what I did.'

Gallagher closed her eyes, shook her head. 'How likely is that, Pete?'

'Twenty-five to thirty per cent chance. Not a scientific guess.'

'And if she gets the letter you – that you took,' Singh said, 'what's the worst-case scenario?'

'She'll say it's a lot more motive. Jilted lover, that kind of thing. Evidence of a threat. She's already running some kind of crime of passion case that was years in the making. A broken heart and a threat goes nicely with that. And a jury might think so too.'

'And what do you think, Pete?' Singh said. 'Do you think – it is some evidence of extra motive, isn't it?'

'What do I think? I think I'm pissed off because she lied to me. Not telling me about that is as good as lying. Does it mean she had him killed? No. Despite how a prosecutor like Gallo could make it look, my view is: so what if they had an affair. This guy lied and destroyed her company. Maybe he jilted her too. Maybe it was much worse for her because she loved him. In the end though, he got six years in prison. I'd call that plenty of jilted lover's revenge, wouldn't you? Tina may have never forgiven this guy, but she's not going to have him killed after six years in the can.'

'What are the options, then?' Gallagher asked. 'Disclose this letter to Gallo – try to play it down?'

'That's one option.'

'There are others?'

Tanner took a deep breath. There was only one other. 'I have to talk to Tina first,' he said.

'In the morning?'

He shook his head. 'I have to cross Webb and Bitar first. We can deal with it Friday or on the weekend.'

'Do you want me to talk to her?' Gallagher asked.

Tanner shook his head. 'I created the issue, Kit. I'll fix it.'

Just on eleven, when Tanner was turning the lights off in his room, about to head home, his direct line rang. It was Woods, from the Drug Squad.

'Mark, how are you?'

A pause. 'I'm fine.'

'You sound – something wrong?'

'No. You used my Christian name. You usually don't.'
'My apologies, detective.'
'I did you that favour.'
'Brian Crawford?'
'Sort of.'
'What's that mean? I'm not paying you anything unless you beat a confession out of him. He killed Randall, right? Who paid him to – the bank or Lovro?'
'Save the craziness for the jury, Tanner.'
'It's late. Is there anything useful you can tell me?'
'Not about Crawford.'
'Well, that's not a good start.'
'His son.'
'His son?'
'Crawford has a son, two daughters. The son is the eldest, about thirty or so. I'm told he's already a big fat fuck like him.'
'I have a mental image. What about him?'
'Just thought you'd like to know where he works.'
'I'm listening.'
'He worked as a real estate agent after school, until about five years ago.'
'He's not at SEBC too, is he?'
'Uh-uh,' Woods said. 'Lovro. Well, one of its subsidiaries. Lovro Resorts. He's based in India at the moment.'
Tanner let out a short laugh. 'What a fucking town this is.'
'Yeah.'
'What's he do?'
'Middle management. I asked someone here I can trust. Manages sites. Rentals of time shares. Sales of places at resorts, that kind of thing.'
'"Manages" is a broad word.'
'I don't have a detailed job description. He's in India at the moment. Based there selling condos near the casino they're building.'
'That's it?'
'You're welcome.'

'Nothing on Crawford?'

'Mate, he works as security at that bank. Ordinary security, whatever that involves. Not cyber stuff. He goes to work, he goes drinking, he goes to a classy brothel occasionally, has done for years.'

'The son. What's his name?'

'Ted. Edward.'

'Little Ted gets a subpoena tomorrow.'

'You can bring him back from India?'

'No, but we try to. My client's defence is about perception and innuendo, not proof.'

'What would you ask him if you could get him back from India?'

'How he got a job at Lovro Resorts might be a good start. And, if I really wanted to piss the judge off, I'd ask him if he's ever gone to the same brothel as the old man.'

'Want me to find out?'

'Is that a serious offer?'

'No. Seriously, though. I'm curious now. What would you ask him?'

'Oliver Randall goes away for six kilos of coke that wasn't his on the back of Brian Crawford's arrest. Crawford ends up working at Randall's bank. That bank screws Tina Leonard out of her biggest ever project, and sells it for a pittance to Lovro, and then – fuck, Crawford's son ends up working at Lovro.'

'What's that all mean?'

'I don't know, detective, but I'll find a way of amusing myself with it.'

There was a pause before Woods spoke again. 'Should you win?'

'She didn't do it, Mark. I'm sure. She has been screwed by some really bad people. And Oliver Randall was a loose cannon who might have – I don't know. He lied in that case against Tina. The bank did. I'm certain of that.'

There was another long pause, then Woods said, 'He gave me twenty grand once.'

'What?'

'Crawford. When I first joined the squad. I took it. I bought a fucking car.'

Now Tanner paused. 'I'm not an agony aunt, Mark. And I'm not your priest. If you're going to keep talking I'd better start being your lawyer. Especially as I've long suspected the federal police illegally listen to all my phone calls.'

'We busted a crime ring that had brought in two tonnes of ecstasy tablets in, fuck, cans of tomatoes. Raided the ringleader's house, four-point-four million there in cash. Lots of smaller notes too. Do you know how big that pile of cash looks?'

'Mark, maybe you should . . .'

'Crawf skimmed a couple of hundred K off the top before the Feds got there. Late calling in the raid to them. Made some shit up about it. Gave me twenty. Said we were paid chicken shit for what we did, this was the only way of getting ahead. He told me to keep it for a deposit.'

'Probably sound advice. That car would have dropped in value as soon as you drove it from the showroom. Sydney property prices, though –'

'It's the only time. I swear. He put it in my hands. I didn't see how I could – he just put it in my hands. Then he told me to put it under the spare tyre in the cop car. Fuck.'

'I believe you.'

'Even a fucking crook's brief like you wouldn't have done anything like that, I bet.'

'I wouldn't count on it.'

'You've stolen twenty grand?'

Tanner laughed. 'I've been paid in cash. When I started. I can't seem to remember if I rendered bills all the time. Or for the full amount.'

'You ripped off the tax man?'

'My wife was in medical training. I was new to the bar. I didn't view it as ripping off the tax man.'

'What was it then?'

'I've paid a lot of tax since. Representing the people I do in court is a form of public service. You've arrested a lot of bad people since. I've forgiven myself for the few guilty pleas I did for a few grand each fifteen years ago that I forgot to declare on my tax. You should forgive yourself too. You didn't steal from anyone who was going to miss that money.'

'I've got to go. It's late. My wife is calling –'

'I think that's a good idea. I think you should go to bed. I think we should forget about this call. You're clearly delusional. I'll email you my fee retainer agreement in the morning.'

'I drove past Crawford's house the other day. Nice house. For some reason I kept going, ended up driving past Ravic's spread. Buggered if I know why. Must've been something you said. Very, very big house in Point Piper. Not much change out of forty or fifty mil I'd say.'

'There's always been big money to be made building shitboxes for the punters in this town, detective.'

'Yeah.'

'Listen, Mark. Thanks. And apart from Ted Crawford, I've forgotten about this call.'

'Sure. Just don't ask for any more favours.'

'Mark?'

'Yeah.'

'You don't still own that car, do you?'

'Fuck off.'

'Welcome back. Good night.'

45

The suit Izzy Gallo must have arranged for Jayden Webb was too big. Nothing would look right on his tall and thin frame.

He'd been in prison for over six months now, and had acquired what was probably a permanent look of dejection. He had the emaciated body of an addict. Hollowed-out cheeks. Bloodless, tight lips. Hairline giving consideration to thinning out at the front. Pale skin, a red blotch just below his right eye that was either in the process of healing, or of worsening. Thirty-one years old. Grooves of a much older man running down from the sides of his nose.

Two crimes of violence. Three drug counts, just below commercial quantities. One stretch of twelve months, another of fourteen. AVO from an ex-girlfriend. Stolen cars.

Jayden Webb had killed a man in cold blood for pay. Shot a man in the knees, then blew his brains out.

He took his oath on the Bible.

Looking at him in the witness box, face like a skull, pathetic but insolent, pitiful but unremorseful, and then looking at the imperial Tina Leonard – it was hard to believe they could have any connection at all. Tanner knew Gallo was not going to try to rehabilitate his character in the box.

She took him through the parts of his life she had to. His father was gone before he could remember. Mum unemployed;

on drugs. She had violent boyfriends. He left school at fourteen, not exactly top of the class before that, ended up labouring on building sites. He'd been addicted to ice for long stretches. A fight over money had ended with a broken jaw, a long wound, his first stint in prison. He never finished a trade – an ageing Boy Friday on building sites.

Once she'd covered this, Gallo took him step by step through the events leading up to the death of Oliver Randall.

Jayden Webb knew who Tina Leonard was. He'd worked on a few of her father's projects, some of her brothers', at least one, maybe two sites of hers. He'd been given a message to visit her at her flat. She asked what it might cost to hurt a man who had wronged her. He'd told her he wasn't muscle, suggested someone else. Then she made it clear. This was a task that required a gun.

He'd hurt his back a few months before, needed money, couldn't work. He could barely get out of bed. When he did, he knew he was done for hard physical work.

She told him this guy had done something terrible to her. He was why her business went south. He thought: what the fuck. Why the fuck not?

A hundred thousand was the first figure that came into his head. She didn't argue, just said fifty up front, fifty once it was done. He came back a week later to collect the cash. He told her the second tranche had to be fifty, plus what he'd paid for the gun.

That's when she'd told him, he said, that she wanted it done a particular way. 'Don't let him beg,' she'd said. She spelt out what that meant. Knees first, head second. He was an ex-banker. How hard could it be?

Everything was fine. It all went fine. His hand was steady. Then he drove straight into the RBT.

Telling the cops about Leonard didn't feel right. It didn't feel right for nearly a week. But getting out at forty-five, or getting out at sixty-five. They were his choices. Sixty-five? He couldn't do that. Didn't have a real choice.

The jury didn't have to like him. They could despise him. About his most appalling sin, they just had to believe him.

'Do you remember your first interview with police, Mr Webb?'

A slight pause let Tanner jump in again.

'Not for your other crimes. For killing Mr Randall. Do you remember that?'

'At the station?'

'Yes. With the detectives and the video camera. The first interview. Do you recall it? You admitted shooting Mr Randall in the head, so I'm going to assume you remember.'

'I remember.' A hint of offence in his voice that Tanner liked.

'Do you know how many times you mentioned the name Tina Leonard in that interview?'

'That's because –'

'I'm not asking you why, Mr Webb. Listen to me. You didn't mention my client's name once, did you?'

'That's because I wasn't sure if I should.'

Tanner could have persisted with telling Webb to answer his question directly, but jurors get bored if you overdo that. Sometimes, you go with the flow. 'I see. You don't hesitate to shoot a man in the face, but you do hesitate to name a name? Is that it?'

'It didn't seem right at first.'

Tanner wanted to laugh, settled on a kind of smile instead. 'But it did later? After Mr Bitar's lawyer had seen you?'

Gallo objected to the reference to Bitar's lawyer. Tanner didn't push it yet.

'It felt right after you'd seen a new lawyer?'

'I explained that. Fifteen to twenty years, versus thirty. That's what my lawyer told me.'

'Tina Leonard's name was mentioned to you by someone in between the first interview you had with police, and your second, correct?'

'No.'

'Mr Bitar got you a message telling you to say the job was for Tina Leonard, didn't he?'

'No.'

'You've known Mr Bitar for a long time, haven't you?'

'Well – since I started work. I guess, yeah.'

'You've not only worked at building sites where he was working, you've done things for him? Run errands, that kind of thing?'

'Sometimes.'

'And you share the same criminal lawyer?'

'I wouldn't know.'

'You told the prosecutor you shot Mr Randall in the knees because that's what Tina Leonard wanted done?'

'Yeah. That's what she told me.'

'You didn't tell police that when they interviewed you first. You told them you didn't know why you did that, didn't you?'

'Yeah, but –'

'So that part was a lie, right?'

'I didn't know if I should name her first. I had nothing against her. I agreed to do a job for her, and I was the one that stuffed it up in the end, not her.'

'You had nothing against her. I see. What did you have against Oliver Randall, Mr Webb?'

'I object to that,' Gallo said.

'I press it, your Honour. The jury's entitled to know what kind of man Mr Webb is.'

'It's a stunt question, your Honour. It's not probative.'

'Of his character it is.'

Justice Francis held up her hand. She looked at Webb. 'Did you personally have any reason to harm Mr Randall? The evidence was you didn't know him.'

'No, your Honour.'

'So you had nothing against him, Mr Webb?' Tanner asked again.

'I guess not.'

'Can you understand how he and his family might have a different view, after you shot him in the knees and then the head?'

'I object.'

'Don't answer that, Mr Webb,' the judge said.

'Nothing against Oliver Randall, nothing against Tina Leonard, nothing against your ex-girlfriend who got the

AVO – you hurt a lot of people one way or another you've got nothing against, don't you?'

'I object.'

'And you're out to harm Tina Leonard who you've got nothing against too because Mick Bitar got a message to you to do that?'

'No.'

'Was a hundred thousand about the right sum, do you think, Mr Webb? To take a life? Put a bullet in each of Mr Randall's legs, one in his head. Did you think that sum was fair?'

Gallo got up to object but Webb answered as the words left her mouth. 'I needed the money. I explained that. I'm an addict. I hurt me back. I couldn't – I explained it. I'm not proud.'

'Not proud? That's good to hear, Mr Webb. Rehabilitated already after six months in prison.'

'I object.'

'Are you proud of not ratting on Tina Leonard until after a lawyer who acted for Mr Bitar saw you?'

'I didn't name her at first. Not till the deal.'

'No. You lasted five and a half days. How did Tina Leonard get in contact with you again?'

'I already said. Someone told me she wanted to see me. I don't know the guy's name, never seen him before. I was at the pub. I knew her, he gives me the address. I went to see her, she told me what she wanted done, how much she'd pay. I went back for the fifty thousand cash a few days later. That's it.'

'She asked you to kill Mr Randall, right there and then?'

'I said that.'

'How many times had you met her before?'

'Only a couple. I done work for her father, and a couple of times for her on her sites.'

'And a few days after asking you to kill for her, she hands you fifty thousand in cash?'

'Yeah.'

'Do you think it was your trustworthy face, Mr Webb? Is that why she thought she could so quickly hand you fifty thousand dollars and a licence to kill someone? What do you think?'

'I object.'

'I don't know.'

'The meth found in your car, Mr Webb. The ice. Did you buy that off Mr Randall?'

'No.'

'What about the hit of cocaine? Did you steal that off him before shooting him?'

'No.'

'Who then?'

'I told the police. I don't know. Some guy.'

'Now, now, Mr Webb. Don't stop squealing on people on my behalf. Would you tell us if Ms Gallo asked?'

'I object.'

'Was it the same guy who told you Tina Leonard wanted Mr Randall shot? The mystery man?'

'No. A different man.'

'Oh, so there are two mystery men?'

'Yeah.'

'You got a reward for mentioning my client's name, didn't you, Mr Webb?'

'I got a – I've still got at least fifteen years.'

'How harsh. And to think all you did was kill someone for money. You'll do anything for a gift, won't you, Mr Webb? Lie about my client, shoot a man in the face . . .'

'I object.'

'Not many more questions, your Honour. Mr Webb, when you were in Mr Randall's house – You remember that, of course?'

'Yeah.'

'Did he beg for his life?'

'What?'

'I object.'

'Did he beg for mercy, Mr Webb?'

'Fuck you.'

'When you held the gun to his head, did he plead for his life?'

46

'Who made your suit?'

Tanner's first question to Michael 'Mick' Bitar took the witness by surprise, before prompting mild amusement. Bitar smiled, looked on the inside of his jacket as Izzy Gallo shook her head for the judge's benefit, who said, 'How can that be a relevant question, Mr Tanner?'

'Just wondering, your Honour,' Tanner said, as he signalled to the court officer he wanted something shown to the witness. He handed a plastic sleeve of blown-up photographs to Izzy Gallo, gave a bundle to the court officer for the jury, the witness, the judge.

Gallo had already examined Bitar about the restaurant meeting with Tina Leonard during which he alleged she told him she wanted him to help her kill Oliver Randall. He'd ungenerously declined. He told the court that he'd known Jayden Webb as a young kid on construction sites, befriended him, gave him work from time to time, tried to get him off drugs – they'd stayed in touch. In his interview with police, when they'd asked him if he'd been involved in Oliver Randall's death, he'd told them that Leonard was making up some fantasy to save herself. He felt sorry for her. No family, no friends, no money but what her father had left her.

Gallo had also been through his work history, the jobs he did for Ioannidis & Sons, setting up his own businesses, and his one prior criminal conviction for assault. Tanner wanted to show he was lucky.

'The first photo, Mr Bitar,' Tanner said. 'You're not wearing a suit in that one, are you?'

The photograph was about ten years old. Bitar was topless. He appeared to have much the same physique as now: all muscle, thick neck, high-protein diet, lots of dumbbell and bench-press action. Beer in hand, arm around another topless man. Perhaps at a barbecue, someone's backyard, a very casual get-together. Bitar's tattoos on his chest could be clearly read. 'Such is life' ran across the top of his chest in an arc, a comma after the last word. Further down the chest, in an arc bringing symmetry to the first, were the words 'so fuck the pigs'.

The magic of Facebook.

Bitar didn't answer the question, just looked at the photo, then back at Tanner with a mean grin.

'Not wearing a suit, Mr Bitar?'

'Obviously not.'

'Who are "the pigs"?'

'I was very young when I had that done. Very stupid.'

'Have you had it removed?'

'I've been thinking about it. It's not easy. Writing that large.'

'Want to show us?'

The grin slid away from Bitar's face.

'Mr Tanner,' the judge said sharply.

'It's okay, Mr Bitar,' Tanner said. 'Keep your shirt on.'

Tanner looked down at his document folder to his own copy of the photo, held it up. 'The man you're with, Mr Bitar. He looks familiar to me. Would I know him?'

Bitar shook his head, like Tanner was playing a game he should be red carded in. 'How would I know?'

'It's not Jimmy Hawkins, is it?'

'I guess you know it is.'

'Where's Jimmy now, do you know?'

'I guess he'd be in prison.'

'What for, do you know?'

'You know what for.'

'This is just time-wasting, your Honour,' Gallo said.

'Why is he in prison, Mr Bitar?' Tanner said loudly, ignoring Gallo. The judge looked at Bitar for an answer.

'He got done for murder.'

Tanner smiled. 'By "done" you mean he killed someone, was charged with murder, convicted by a jury, and is currently five years into a twenty-eight-year sentence?'

'You obviously know the details more than me.'

'Turn to the next photo, Mr Bitar.'

A table of people, a busy restaurant. Bitar and another man, arms around each other, beer bottles and wine glasses in front of them, plates smeared with the remnants of dinner.

'Who's that?'

'Gassim Azzi.'

'Catchy name,' Tanner said. 'Gaz Az, right?'

'Yeah.'

'Where's Gaz?'

'You know where. In prison.'

'Did he give you any coke the night this photo was taken, Mr Bitar?'

'I object,' Gallo said.

'Don't answer,' Tanner said. 'He's got a drug conviction, right? Ecstasy tablets and coke, correct?'

'Yes.'

'But he's in jail for something else?'

'He said she lied.'

Tanner hated Mick Bitar, but wanted to kiss him then. 'The woman he raped, you mean?'

'She was his girlfriend, de facto. Whatever.'

'That was his defence?'

Tanner looked at Gallo. She was staring ahead, but she couldn't help the colour in her face.

'I didn't mean that –' Bitar said, realising his mistake, stopping himself.

'No, no, Mr Bitar. Please continue,' Tanner said.

'They were splitting up. Custody of their kid, financials –'

'Made it up, did she? The rape?'

'I wasn't there.'

'Neither was the jury, Mr Bitar. They obviously believed her, given he's in prison for rape.'

'Just saying what he – what he said at the time,' Bitar said.

'Good friend of yours, Mr Bitar? This drug-trafficking rapist? And what about Mr Hawkins, who killed his wife's brother over an argument over – what was it? The appropriate share of the proceeds of stolen goods? Bashed his head against a brick wall, didn't he? Is he one of your good mates, too?'

'I object to this,' Gallo said.

'The photos are all on Facebook, your Honour,' Tanner said. 'The prosecutor should be blaming Mark Zuckerberg, not me. I'm not the one calling this witness saying he should be believed. The jury is entitled to see him in all his glory.'

'How much longer, Mr Tanner?' Justice Francis asked.

'For what, your Honour?'

'With the photos and what you're doing.'

'When I've made my point, your Honour, with respect. My client is charged with murder, and this man, so I'm instructed, is lying. I'm allowed to do what I'm doing.'

'As efficiently as you can, please,' she said.

The third photo was Bitar and three other men outside a sports ground. At least five years ago from the healthier look of Jayden Webb.

'We know who the man in the navy T-shirt is, don't we?' Tanner said.

'Jayden.'

'Another killer. Do you know anyone who isn't a murderer, a drug addict, a trafficker or a rapist, Mr Bitar?'

'I object.'

'Mr Tanner,' the judge said.

'It's a fair enough question based on the searches my investigator did of Facebook, your Honour.'

'Make it good, or withdraw it, Mr Tanner.'

'Last photo, Mr Bitar. Can you look at that one please?'

A recent photo. An upmarket affair. Bitar and another man standing on the harbour foreshore at night. Casino in the background. Bitar is holding a bottle of beer, the other man a glass of sparkling water. Both in suits and ties.

'Is that the suit you've got on today, Mr Bitar?'

'Possibly.'

'And who's the other well-dressed man? He looks familiar to me too.'

'Luka Ravic.'

'Luka Ravic?'

'Yeah.'

'The CEO and owner of Lovro Constructions?'

'Yeah.'

'When was this photo taken?'

'I don't know. A year or so ago.'

'Out for a flutter?'

'Industry night. A dinner. Construction industry.'

'Anyone at this dinner not a criminal?'

'I object.'

'Withdrawn. Mr Ravic, is he a criminal?'

'Your Honour,' Gallo almost yelled, but Bitar answered with an equally loud, 'No.'

'I reject that question. Mr Tanner, that is enough,' Justice Francis said.

Tanner looked at her. He'd pushed it as far as he could, he figured. She said they were taking a fifteen-minute adjournment. The associate was at the bar table only moments after the judge left the court.

'Her Honour would like to see you both in chambers,' he said.

'Should I bring these photos?' he said, holding them up.

The associate smiled. 'Probably not.'

'I made it clear before we started I wouldn't stand for that, Mr Tanner,' Justice Francis said as soon as Tanner and Gallo walked into her chambers.

'The last question I went too far for now. I apologise.'

'Too far?' Gallo said. 'You implied one of your own witnesses is a criminal. A well-known business person with no criminal record.'

'He's in the construction industry, Izzy. But you're right, I shouldn't have added that flourish. Just like you shouldn't be relying on the word of a man who thinks spouse rape isn't a crime.'

Gallo glared at him a long time. 'I really resent you saying that, Peter,' she said.

'I didn't mean it as personally as it sounded.'

He knew she wanted to tell him to go fuck himself. But for the judge, she would have.

'Enough,' the judge said. She stood, indicating she was nearly done. 'No more unsubstantiated allegations dressed as questions, Mr Tanner,' she said. 'Not one more.'

When they returned to court, Tanner quickly reviewed his notes for his cross of Bitar. The Facebook search had been Singh's idea, and she'd spent a late night on it with Tom Cable, who was big on social media now he had grandkids to show off. It'd worked better than Tanner had hoped. He could move more quickly, take fewer risks.

'Just to finish with the photos, Mr Bitar. We know Mr Hawkins, the convicted murderer, is a friend of yours. And –'

'He's an acquaintance.'

'Suit yourself. An acquaintance. We know Mr Azzi, the drug-dealing rapist, is – what? An acquaintance of yours also. Then we have Mr Webb, the hitman, another acquaintance. Or is he more . . . protégé, would that be the word?'

'Is there a question coming?' Gallo asked.

'Just adding to the progression of this country's living treasures, your Honour. Mr Bitar, how close are you to Mr Ravic, the head of Lovro Constructions?'

'Your Honour, that is an outrageous way of framing a –'

'Withdrawn. How well do you know Mr Ravic, Mr Bitar? You must be close to him, based on that photo?'

'I barely know him. I went up to him at that event and asked for his photo. I think I'd met him once before. We're not even acquaintances – he didn't know who I was. I introduced myself. My company does a small amount of business with Lovro. They're a minor customer. Nothing we do gets anywhere near his level.'

'Do you remember being interviewed by police about an assault on Sam Diab?'

Bitar shook his head. 'I was interviewed. That's it.'

'He was a local councillor, right? Five Dock Council?'

'I don't remember.'

'Voted against a DA submitted by Ioannidis & Sons, a development and construction company you're very familiar with.'

'I have no idea.'

'No idea how he got a broken jaw, fractured eye sockets?'

'Is my friend running a prosecution on Mr Bitar?' Izzy Gallo said.

'Okay,' Tanner said. 'Let's stick to your official record. My learned friend took you to a conviction you have for assault causing actual bodily harm. Mr Doug Lott. He owns a small building company. Well, smaller than Ioannidis & Sons, anyway.'

'That was a fight in a pub. It was self-defence. I was provoked. I've already said that –'

'They're separate concepts, Mr Bitar. You pleaded guilty?'

'Like I told the prosecutor. On legal advice. The prosecutor and the judge accepted it was just a fight. I got a good behaviour bond.'

'Self-defence? And you pleaded guilty? You should have come to me.'

'No, thanks.'

'You could afford me, based on the look of your suit.'

'Mr Tanner!'

Tanner handed another photo to the witness, and provided copies for the judge and jury. Doug Lott after the fight in the pub. Black swollen eyes. Stitches across the right cheekbone, just to the left of the bridge of the nose; a jagged gash from his right nostril to the top of his lip on the left side.

'Mr Lott was involved in a tender with Ioannidis & Sons at the time of this act of self-defence by you, wasn't he? To build an office and retail complex?'

'I wouldn't know.'

'That photo I just showed you. That was your work – defending yourself?'

'He threw the first punch. The judge accepted that.'

'Remind me not to provoke you, Mr Bitar. Why'd he punch you?'

'It – God, it was twelve years ago. Lip about his son, that was it. He went off.'

'You defended yourself thoroughly, would you say?'

'He confirmed it was just a fight. He told the court he threw the first punch. I only got done for losing my rag, going too far.'

'What did you have to pay him to make him say that?'

'I – that's a lie.'

'Did his company drop out of the tender, Mr Bitar?'

'I wouldn't know.'

'The photo I took you to with you and Mr Ravic, from Lovro Constructions. What's his company worth to you again, per annum?'

'I'd have to check the books. Not much – I've told you this.'

'C'mon, Mr Bitar. Just a ballpark.'

'I got someone who does that for me. A financial officer. They're a small customer – big company, but not a big customer of ours. We sometimes supply them with materials for jobs, like I told the prosecutor.'

'Jayden Webb's lawyer is also usually your lawyer, correct?'

'I've told the court that already. I heard he was in trouble, he'd been arrested. I helped him out.'

'And after that he mentions my client's name for the first time. What a coincidence. Does that seem strange to you?'

'Not really. He had to look after himself. I knew what had

happened because Tina had come to me. I knew she knew the kid. I felt sorry for him. She used him. He's vulnerable.'

Tanner laughed bitterly, looked at the jury. 'Mr Webb is vulnerable?' he said slowly, emphasising the last word. 'Would you like to ask Oliver Randall's relatives how vulnerable Jayden Webb is? The vulnerable Mr Webb shot him in the knees and the face. Are your other friends in prison for murder and rape also vulnerable, Mr Bitar? Is that how we should describe them?'

'What I meant was —'

'Were you feeling vulnerable when you nearly bashed the life out of Mr Lott? Are you a vulnerable soul too?'

'I meant because of the drugs. Vulnerable because of that. He'd do anything for a fix.'

'What would you do for Lovro, Mr Bitar? For your good friend Mr Ravic?'

'I explained he's not a friend. That photo was me —'

'Tina Leonard didn't ask you to help her kill Oliver Randall, did she?'

'She did.'

'Since when did you become a snitch, Mr Bitar?'

'What was I supposed to do? The cops came to me. Tina lied about me, I had to tell them.'

'You met with Tina Leonard the week before Mr Randall was killed, didn't you? You had lunch with her?'

'You mean when she asked me to kill him?'

Tanner paused. He glared at Bitar, and smiled. 'Do you think you're clever, Mr Bitar — getting that in?'

'Just telling the truth.'

'She asked you at that lunch to speak to her brothers for her, correct?'

'No.'

'She told you she wanted back into the family firm, and they wouldn't talk to her.'

'Rubbish.'

'And you said you could help, for fifty thousand dollars in cash.'

Bitar laughed. 'I wish I could charge fifty thousand in cash to set up one meeting.'

'And you sent Jayden Webb to her home to collect it.'

'I didn't send Jayden to Tina's home.'

'She told you Oliver Randall had lied for her bankers, didn't she? At this same lunch.'

'She told me that years ago. Not at that lunch.'

'She told you he knew they'd conspired with their client Mr Ravic from Lovro Constructions to virtually steal her land, her Limani Views project, didn't she?'

'Could have, but not that day.'

'She showed you a letter he'd written her in prison, didn't she?'

'No.'

'And you thought that all of that might be a big problem for your friend at Lovro, didn't you?'

'She wanted Randall dead. She was – she was crazy with rage at him for what he did years ago. She never let it go. She lost her business, her house, her kids – I get it.'

'You sound suspiciously like the prosecutor, Mr Bitar. Let's stick to answering my questions. After Tina Leonard told you what she knew, Mr Randall was killed, correct?'

'She had Jayden kill him.'

'He's not very smart, is he? Jayden?'

'Not a rocket scientist.'

'And you told him how to beat a murder rap didn't you? Blame Tina Leonard, cut a deal for the information. Information that was lies. Is that what you had passed on to him?'

'I told him to look out for himself. I told you, I felt sorry for him.'

'Yeah, because he was feeling vulnerable after blowing someone's brains out, right? Just one more question for now, Mr Bitar. Are you listening to me?'

'Whose money bought that nice suit for you? Was it Lovro's?'

47

'My husband isn't happy about this.'

Taz Bennett was leaning against her front door like it was her lover.

'Not happy about what?' Tanner said. It was ten am Saturday, he was there to see Tina Leonard.

'Our home being used for legal conferences with my sister.'

Tanner smiled. 'Is he here?'

She shook her head. 'Riding his bike with his group.'

'Then why does he care?'

'I wouldn't know.'

'Does he wax his legs?'

She smiled. 'I'm late for my trainer. Tina's in the kitchen making coffee.'

She brushed by him as she left the house. He looked at her as she walked away from him. Mr Bennett could have spent the morning with his wife, Tanner thought. He was on a bike instead, his arse in padded lycra, glutes aching.

Fuckwit.

Once the evidence of Webb and Bitar was done, the prosecution case had been nuts and bolts on Friday. Izzy Gallo had called some bank witnesses to establish Tina Leonard's withdrawal of fifty thousand over a series of days from various branches, which had ended up with Jayden Webb. The owner of a café was called to say that Leonard had a loud and raucous shouting match with a man who looked like Oliver Randall only days before he was shot. A restaurant manager from a Leichhardt trattoria had confirmed the lunch between Leonard and Mick Bitar a few days later.

Now the defence case would begin.

'I've just made this,' she said when he walked in the kitchen. She was holding up a plunger of coffee.

'Black, thanks,' he said.

They went to a lounge room with their coffee, the one overlooking the pool and the harbour in the distance. A cruise ship was gliding its way through the heads.

'I never know how they stay afloat,' she said.

Tanner sat in a chair opposite the couch she chose. 'I sometimes think that about cases I'm running.'

She lifted her chin slightly. She was barefoot, in jeans, a white shirt. It was the first time he'd seen her without makeup. Her skin wasn't perfect. A red blotch on one cheek, slightly less on the other. She still had the imperial air. She looked like she'd lived a previous life, had been an important person in some ancient dynasty.

'You seemed pleased yesterday afternoon. With how the week went? Has something happened?'

'Were you planning on telling me about your affair with Oliver Randall during your evidence-in-chief?'

There was a barely perceptible change in her face. A moment of uncertainty. A deep breath, then, 'I didn't have him killed, Peter.'

'I didn't ask you that.'

She paused for a second, then said, 'How do you know?'

He told her about the visit to Harry Hartfield, and the stash of documents Randall had left with his friend and executor. 'Where's the original?'

'I threw it out.'

'But kept the letter that didn't mention your affair or that you'd threatened him.'

'I didn't – that was threatened to sue. Not hurt. When I lost my temper in that coffee shop, that was – he was reluctant to help me. I've told you that. I said something silly about taking him to court with the others.'

'The letter I've read doesn't indicate much enthusiasm for helping you that way. Just the opposite.'

'He was going to change his mind, Peter. I could tell. Why else confess to me?'

'It's one thing to confess and apologise. It's another to take on SEBC and Lovro.'

She shook her head. 'He met with that journalist,' she said. 'You know that. They must have panicked at that, or Bitar tipped them off after I'd had lunch with Mick and told him about what Oliver had told me. We've been over this.'

'The journalist chased him. He agreed to meet her. He told her nothing.'

'What, you don't believe me now? I'm guilty?'

'I don't care, Tina.'

She let out a snort, something like disgust, then they were both silent for a moment.

'Does she have it?'

'Izzy? No, she'd have to disclose it to us if she was going to use it. And trust me, if she had it, she'd use it.'

'But we don't have to –' She didn't finish the sentence.

'It depends. Who else knows?'

'About Oliver and me? No one.'

'No one?'

'He was married, Peter. We didn't – we were careful.'

'I've heard that before. So has the Family Court. Why didn't you tell me, Tina? Why lie?'

'It didn't seem . . .' She stopped. 'I don't know –'

'Don't say the word "relevant",' he said. 'Just answer – why didn't you tell me?'

'I didn't think you needed to know,' she said, her voice rising. 'It has nothing to do with anything.'

Tanner laughed. 'You had an affair with the man you're accused of having killed, Tina. He ruined you, he dumped you.'

'He didn't dump me. He was married. He –'

'Then he gets out of jail, you threaten him, he ends up shot in the head. Run that "nothing to do with anything" thing by me again.'

She shook her head, but said nothing.

'How long did it last?' he said.

'Six months. A bit longer.'

'How did it happen?'

She looked offended, then said, 'Trevor Hendricks introduced us. When Nipori was being taken over by SEBC. We discussed my plans, my projects – he seemed interested.' She stopped, and Tanner waited for her to continue. 'I was getting divorced. Adrian was like a minor business partner, not a husband. We'd agreed on sharing the kids, we were otherwise living separate lives. I didn't have anyone to talk to about – I had my staff, my advisors. He seemed – he was more than a lender. He told me he wanted to help me grow. We had lunch. It just happened.'

'Was it love, or just an affair?'

She smiled. 'It might have been both. It's hard to remember.'

'Most women I've met remember love, Tina.'

'I was –' She shook her head.

Tanner nodded. She would be giving evidence soon. There was a limit to how much he could afford to upset her. 'What did he have that I don't?' he said.

She laughed, stopped herself. An eyebrow flickered up. 'He wasn't charging me as much as you are.'

'You've been untruthful to me, Tina. Don't do it again with my next few questions, okay? Were you doing coke with him? If the answer was yes, did anyone else know?'

A flash of anger that she just contained. 'I was running a business. I wasn't doing coke. Oli had his demons. He was – I don't know.'

'Okay. You told me your affair was discreet. No one else knew?'

'Yes.'

'You're on bail for murder, and living in your little sister's house against her husband's wishes. I'll ask again, did anyone else know you were having an affair with Randall?'

She paused. 'I swear only Taz.'

'Could she have told someone?'

'She wouldn't.'

'I'll have to ask her myself. You can forewarn her if you like. Just make sure she doesn't lie.'

She nodded.

'Back to Oliver. He loved you, then lied to harm you, and ruined you. That must've hurt?'

She closed her eyes, composed herself. 'It did hurt, Peter. It hurt a lot. But I didn't have him killed.'

He put his mug down on the table to his left, then stood. 'If you give evidence, and this comes up, you can't lie. I won't let you. You will have to answer the way you just did.'

'Will it come up?'

'Not from me – unless Taz has told someone. Then a thousand people know. Then we might have to get out in front of it so as to not look like we've been caught trying to hide something if Gallo were to cross you about it.'

'This lawyer. The executor. Could he – ?'

Tanner shrugged. 'He could. I don't think he will. I had a blunt exchange with him. But he could.'

'Can we – can we do something about that?'

Tanner glared at her. 'Like what?'

'I meant talk to him. That's all.'

'You mean, like send someone like Mick Bitar around to have a chat with him?'

He eyes darkened. 'No, Peter. I meant me tell him the truth. Convince him not to – whatever.'

He shook his head. 'Best not. I'll let myself out. We'll talk Monday morning.'

She stood. 'You still believe me, don't you? I didn't do this.'

'I've explained the rules of the game. That doesn't matter.'

'It matters to me.'

He smiled, but the look on her face told him that wouldn't cut it. 'I do, Tina,' he said. 'I still believe you.'

48

Tanner spent Sunday afternoon in his chambers, part of the time with Jenny Singh discussing the evidence he'd try to call from the remaining witnesses, part working on that task alone. It was close to nine when he decided to leave for home. He'd still have time to say hello to Dan before he went to bed, and grab something to eat before it became too late.

The foyer of the building was dark when he walked out of the lift, then lit up suddenly as his presence activated a sensor. It was cold outside, a strong breeze from the south blowing up Elizabeth Street, dry autumn leaves scattering in the gutter, not much traffic. He rubbed his hands, then turned left to head to a taxi rank outside a hotel a short distance away. As he did a deep voice said to him, 'Thought I'd catch you here.'

A large figure walked out of the shadows from one side of the entrance of the building. Hands in the pockets of a bomber jacket, cheeks a little flushed. 'Can we go inside?' Brian Crawford said. 'Fucking cold out here.'

Tanner paused for a moment, felt an immediate jump in his heart rate. 'I only see people who've made an appointment, Brian. You done something wrong again?'

'Nothing I need your help for.'

'Pity,' Tanner said. 'I'm guessing you could afford me these days.'

'Let's go inside. We need to talk.' Crawford took a couple of steps towards the glass entrance doors of the building Tanner had just walked out of. Tanner knew the time, looked at his watch anyway. 'It's late, Brian. I'm due home.'

'I said, we need to talk.'

'Do you think that's what Jayden Webb said when Oliver Randall opened the doors to him?'

Crawford shook his head. 'Wouldn't know.'

'There are closed circuit cameras around here somewhere. One in the foyer right there.'

Crawford laughed. 'I'd really like to beat the shit out of you, Tanner. I still might. Someone will. They might go further. But that's not what I'm being paid for now.'

'What are you being paid for?'

'To be your client's witness. You served me with a subpoena. Why else would I see you? I'm here for a conference. I got a letter from the dyke that's briefing you, inviting me to give a statement. So if you do end up with the shit beaten out of you soon, or if you just fall off the planet, and I'm on some video with you – big fucking deal. We need to talk.'

Tanner took in a breath. He didn't want Crawford in his room. He started walking. 'This way,' he said.

The Sheraton on the Park was only a few hundred metres up the road. There were only a handful of patrons in the Conservatory Bar. Tanner walked to its far end, sat in a white leather chair at a table for two, next to the windows overlooking Hyde Park. As he looked out the branches of its huge figs were startled by the wind.

'Celebrate getting crooks off here?' Crawford asked, sitting down in his chair.

'I don't celebrate after trials, Brian. Justice wins. It's not about me.'

Crawford snorted. 'You're a stupid prick, you know that?'

Tanner glared at him. 'The last person who said that to me and still has his teeth is the Chief Justice. And he can count himself lucky.'

A waitress joined them to take their orders. Crawford looked her up and down, then up again, and said he'd have a whisky. A Glenffidich, twenty-one years in a rum cask.

'I always pictured you as a fruit daiquiri kind of guy,' Tanner said. He ordered a mineral water.

'Don't drink now?' Crawford said when the waitress left.

'I'm running a trial at the moment. You haven't noticed?'

'It's why I'm here.'

'So you said. We invited you to talk to us when we served the subpoena. So, who paid you to plant those drugs in Oliver Randall's gym bag?'

Crawford leant forward, eyes on the cocktail menu. He looked up at Tanner and said, 'If you say that to me in court, I guarantee – I guarantee you will regret it.'

'Did the bank pay you, Brian? How much did you get? Apart from the job for life, I mean.'

Crawford sat back, squeezed his nose with a thumb and forefinger, like he was extracting a thought. 'A successful guy like you. And a sole parent. I'd have expected you to value your safety more than you do. Why don't you?'

'Do you expect me to answer that?'

'What about the safety of those you love? Small family, but you've got one.'

Tanner felt an artery start to throb on the side of his cheek near his ear. 'Are you threatening my dog, Brian?'

'Fuck your dog.'

Tanner put a hand to his chin to rub it, almost involuntarily. He felt it shaking, put it back down. 'It is a small family. But I have many very violent friends. People who owe me, one way or another. They could become very agitated if something were to happen to my dog. Especially at the hands of an ex-cop.'

Crawford smiled. 'Must be tough, having your wife die so young. That was unfortunate. Stressful job, single dad. Can't have been easy.'

The waitress approached, put the drinks on coasters on the table, asked if she could get them anything else. 'Bring the bill now, please,' Tanner said.

'It might take more than one drink, this chat,' Crawford said. He picked up his whisky, took a sip.

'Do you have children, Brian? I imagine they must be adults?'

'I'm not the subject of this conversation, mate,' Crawford said.

'Are you getting overtime for it? Or do they consider you management?'

Crawford sighed, took another sip. 'The message I have for you is simple. You're not going to want to go into that courtroom and make any foolish allegations about people.'

'You want to deprive me of my entire court-craft, Brian? People will notice.'

'I am deadly serious, mate. This is not a joke.'

'Which people?'

'Use your imagination. Take a conservative approach. Anyone or anything.'

'Your employer?'

'You need to think very carefully about who you call to give evidence. Stick to beating up the prosecution's witnesses.'

'That would be only half the fun.' Tanner picked up his glass, wished he hadn't. His hand was shaking like he had Parkinson's.

Crawford notice, smiled. 'She was fucking him, you know that?'

Tanner looked away quickly, out the window to the shivering figs, the swirling leaves. 'News to me. You got proof?'

'He told people at the bank,' Crawford said. 'It's recorded in a confidential part of his employment file. I guess we really should have given that to the police. Not too late, I suppose.'

Tanner tried to smile. 'SEBC's not going to do that.'

'Why not?'

Tanner shook his head. 'Terrible look. Using a bank executive to give evidence against a customer they've been having an affair with. What sort of headline would that make? And bullshit it's in some confidential part of his employment file. That piece of news would be as cremated as Randall is.'

Crawford shrugged. 'It'd blow over in a week. One of about fifteen hundred your client will do in the women's joint.'

Tanner wanted to pick up his glass again, show that his hand was steady, didn't risk it.

'You can tell Mr Carter that I'll still be calling him to give evidence. And I might call him a killer too, amongst other things. You can tell Ravic the same thing, if you're here for him as well. I hope that news doesn't cost you a bonus, Brian.'

'That would be a very unwise thing to do,' Crawford said slowly.

Tanner risked going for his glass, nearly knocked it over trying to pick it up. Gripped it hard enough to break it when he did. 'Be odd, if something happened to me after I call your employer a criminal, don't you think?'

Crawford laughed. 'Typical. Only thinking of yourself, mate?' He drained the last of his drink, put his glass down on the table. 'Shit happens,' he said. 'Shit happens all the time.'

Tanner's left hand was in the pocket of his coat. He was turning his phone over in his hand. He took it out, not sure why at first. He could hear a thumping of blood in his left ear. 'I need to call someone,' he said. 'Old acquaintance of yours.' He tapped at the screen, found what he was looking for, waited, hoped.

'What are you doing?' Crawford asked.

As he spoke, someone answered Tanner's call. Tanner put his hand over the mic. 'Just a second,' he said to Crawford. 'I'm talking to the police.'

'It's too late to call, Tanner,' Mark Woods said.

'No choice, detective. My apologies.'

'What is it?'

Tanner paused. He hadn't thought out the call. There hadn't been time. He'd acted on instinct. 'Near hostage situation,' he said.

'What the fuck are you talking about?'

'I'm at a bar in the Sheraton Hotel, having a drink.'

'Good for you.'

'I'm with an ex-colleague of yours.'

'What?'

'Former Detective Senior Sergeant Brian Crawford. Remember him?'

'Tanner – what are you talking about?'

'Big house in Clovelly. Ocean views, are there Mark? Works for a bank now. High flyer. Likes aged single malt. Surprised me when I left my chambers tonight. Wanted to buy me a drink, give me some free advice. Are you listening, Mark?'

'I'm listening,' Woods said.

'Brian's advice is that there are some witnesses I shouldn't call in the Tina Leonard trial. He says it would be a very big mistake for me to ask these people certain questions. A mistake by reference to my own safety and that of my family. It may be that I'm being a tad sensitive, but I'm interpreting Brian's advice as not being completely legal in nature. As you can imagine, I'm particularly nervous about our dog. Are you still listening, detective?'

'You fucking idiot,' Crawford said.

'I appreciate how big a favour I'm asking, detective, but I'm wondering – I'm wondering if you'd like to talk to your former colleague. Remind him that he now has to act within the law at all times. Any message you could give him that might convince him to stick to his day job, leave the legal strategy to me?'

It seemed to take Woods a long time to speak, but it was probably only seconds. 'Put him on,' he said softly.

Tanner handed his phone to Crawford, who looked at it like it stunk, but eventually took it, put it to his ear.

Tanner wasn't sure how long Woods spoke for. A minute. Maybe a minute and a half. Crawford said nothing. When Woods must have been done, Crawford put the phone down on the table, got up. 'You stupid prick,' he said to Tanner, before turning to walk out of the bar.

'Something I said, Brian? I thought we were getting on great,' Tanner shouted after him. 'You sure you don't want to get a room?'

Tanner watched Crawford walk away, picked up his phone. 'Mark?'

There was a long pause, then Woods said, 'Don't ever do that to me again. Don't ever do that –'

'What did you say?'

'I mean it, Peter,' Woods said. 'Don't involve me in your – don't involve me in any of your shit again.'

'Mark, what did you say to him? I need to –'

'This is the last time. You've got a kid.' The line went dead.

Tanner stood to leave, extracted a fifty from his wallet, his hand still shaking as he left it on the table.

49

Tanner asked the judge for a break so the jury could read the documents he'd just tendered when opening the defence case. A letter from Randall to Tina Leonard apologising for how he'd hurt her, how the bank had. Asking for a meeting with her upon his imminent release from prison. Tanner couldn't tell the jury what was said at that meeting without committing to calling Tina Leonard. He had to leave them hanging on that one. That was okay, though. No good lawyer reads the whole novel in an opening. You read a poem, make the jury think.

Next, Randall's two letters to Simone Hargreaves, his ex-wife, and to Hannah, his daughter. Confessing his sins as husband and parent. Asking them to believe him about what were and weren't his sins. Sorry for what he did to them. Pleading for a chance to explain.

Kit Gallagher had obtained a handwriting expert to prove the letters were in Randall's hand, but Tanner didn't have to tender it. Izzy Gallo SC conceded for the prosecution the victim had written the letters. They were part of her case theory too. She would say they showed an even greater desire for revenge, more motive for murder.

The first live witness called was the valuer, Garry Worner. His evidence hadn't been rejected by the trial judge in the case between SEBC and Leonard and her company. She'd lost because she hadn't proved a sale in bad faith, not because her valuation evidence was necessarily wrong.

Gallo objected to the evidence and Worner's expert report on the grounds of relevance, but the judge ruled that it could proceed. If it proved of marginal relevance once the defence case was closed, Justice Francis said, she'd make that clear in her address to the jury. If it was of no relevance in the end, she'd have the evidence struck from the record. She had to give the defendant a chance to make whatever defence case they were trying to make out.

'The jury gets to hear it, though, your Honour, even if you rule it out in the end. The damage is done.'

The judge nodded slowly. 'If the damage is done, Ms Crown,' she said, 'then perhaps the evidence is relevant after all.'

Tanner kept Worner's evidence short and succinct. Lovro Constructions had paid one hundred million for the Limani Views site after SEBC sold it at public tender. In Worner's view, its market value was four times that at least.

'When my client's company sued SEBC, the bank's valuer said the site was only worth about a hundred million. Clearly you don't agree. Why?'

'We were well past the GFC,' Worner said. 'The market was – look, some people said the market was flat, but the truth is the market for land like this is pretty small. It's a huge parcel of land in a unique spot. I thought – I still think – the site, given the development approval it had then and has now, was a spectacular opportunity.'

'Anything else worry the bank's valuers?'

'They placed a lot of reliance on the contamination report – SBW Environmental Consulting – which indicated that any developer would have a pretty large bill for remediating the site of dioxins and the like before construction. Including for building the marina.'

'Did that worry you?'

'To a degree, but Leonard Constructions in my view had more thorough reports that pointed to a more benign contamination problem. More what I'd expect from land that was a warehouse, not an old factory where hazardous substances might have been used.'

'Lucky Lovro Constructions, hey?'

'You could say that.'

'They were pretty lucky anyway. One hundred million for this site. You'd describe that how – as an enormous bargain?'

'Does my friend want to get in the witness box himself and give evidence?' Gallo said.

'How would you describe the deal Lovro Constructions got, Mr Worner?'

'Considering every sale I've analysed in my career? The deal of a lifetime.'

"The deal of a lifetime" was where Tanner decided to leave it.

'You've read the judgement of Justice Kerr in the case of *SEBC v Leonard Developments*, I assume?' Izzy Gallo began her cross-examination.

'I have.'

'And his Honour dismissed Leonard Development's cross claim in which it alleged a bad faith sale, correct?'

'He did.'

'Do you recall why?'

'It's very hard to prove a *mala fides* sale,' Worner said.

'Did I ask you that, Mr Worner? The case failed because SEBC put the land up for sale in a perfectly orthodox public tender, is that right?'

'It proceeded on an unusually tight time-frame in my view, but otherwise, yes.'

'And the highest of three bids was from Lovro Constructions, correct?'

'That's correct.'

'For one hundred million?'

'Yes.'

'Being the market value of the land?'

'I disagree.'

'Isn't evidence from the market the best evidence to assess market value?'

'Like I've said in my report, along with other reasons, I think the unusually fast nature of the public tender resulted in a sale that didn't reflect market value. And of course the pre-construction clean-up costs turned out to be a lot less than expected.'

'And Justice Kerr considered that issue of speed of tender in his judgement, and still ruled against Leonard Developments.'

'He did.'

Gallo let the witness go shortly after. She wanted to throw a few punches, but Tanner thought she probably didn't want to make it look like the evidence was more than nuisance value.

Trevor Hendricks, retired banker from the Nipori Bank whose Asian businesses had collapsed and been bought out by SEBC, was the next witness Tanner called. Navy suit, pale blue tie. The sort of serious-looking business type you wanted in front of a jury to help with a wild conspiracy case theory.

'Not thrilled to be here, Mr Hendricks?' Tanner began.

A reserved smile. 'Something has usually gone wrong if bankers end up in a court, Mr Tanner. Even retired bankers.'

'Fair enough. We've met, though. You agreed to meet and talk with me, at your home?'

'I did.'

'And I told you you'd get a subpoena after?'

'Yes. Thanks.'

'You're welcome.'

Tanner then led Hendricks through his business career with Nipori, his role with the bank, what went wrong in the GFC, the purchase of Nipori's assets in Asia by SEBC, the finish of his career in Japan and the UK.

'You known my client reasonably well?'

'I'd say so.'

'You were her banker for several years?'

'Not exactly. People who worked for me were. I kept an eye on her business growth, though.'

'You knew her socially, as well as through lending to her building company?'

'A little bit. My wife and I had dinner a few times with Tina and her husband – her ex-husband – when she started to become a more important client. We had a friendly relationship.'

'You liked her?'

'Yes.'

'Do you think she's a killer, Mr Hendricks?'

'Don't answer that,' the judge said calmly, before the words 'I object' had even left Gallo's mouth.

'Limani Views was Tina's biggest ever project, correct? Her company's biggest project?'

'By far.'

'You provided loans to her company to support that project?'

'We did. Nipori did.'

'You – I'm sorry, your bank presumably had valuations of the land Leonard Developments proposed to purchase for the Limani Views project in the west of the harbour?'

'We did. Valuations from her valuers but also our own. The bank's own.'

'And valuations later when she – when Leonard Developments was given development consent?'

'We keep up-to-date valuations for a project of that size.'

'Do you recall Nipori's valuation? I have a copy here from my client's files, if you need your memory refreshed?'

'No. We valued the land at two hundred million.'

'And once development approval was given?'

'Upwards of four hundred million.'

'You know Lovro Constructions bought it from SEBC for a hundred million?'

'Yes.'

'How's that deal sound to you? Unbelievable or just incredible?'

'I object, your Honour. Apart from the ridiculous leading, Mr Hendricks isn't a valuer.'

'C'mon, your Honour. This is a man who lent money to big builders and construction companies on huge projects for thirty years. Surely he can give a view about a deal?'

'He can,' the judge said, 'but his own view. Mr Hendricks?'

'Based on the valuations I saw, and my experience of this size of project, the great location – Lovro did very, very well. I think it's a bargain. A below-fire-sale price.'

'But SEBC wasn't burnt in the fire sale, was it Mr Hendricks?'

Hendricks shook his head.

'Please tell the court why not.'

Hendricks told the court about the deal the liquidators of Nipori struck with SEBC for the purchase of Nipori's Asian assets.

'Can we explain this through Leonard Developments?' Tanner asked.

'Sure.'

'When its loans were called in, they totalled about two hundred and thirty million over four projects, correct? Limani being the biggest?'

'Sounds about right.'

'Assume after SEBC took possession of all of Leonard Developments' projects and other security, and sold them all, a debt was left of eighty million. That should have been a loss to SEBC, correct?

'It would have been, but for the deal between Nipori and SEBC.'

'So despite the notional big loss from winding up Leonard Developments, in the end there's no loss to SEBC?'

'That's right.'

'Very good deal for SEBC, isn't it?'

'Not completely unheard of – especially in the GFC. And there was some money that goes the other way with profitable loans.'

'Just sticking to Limani Views, though, not only does SEBC make no loss, but in this case they sell a project to one of their biggest customers, Lovro Constructions. Is that what you call a win–win in the business world?'

'I object,' Gallo said.

'Is my friend going to argue Lovro Constructions aren't in bed with SEBC, your Honour?'

'She mightn't agree with the way you just put that question, Mr Tanner,' Justice Francis said. 'And nor do I.'

'I'll withdraw it then, your Honour,' Tanner said. 'I'll save it for closing.'

50

Kevin Willett was even less happy about his subpoena than Trevor Hendricks. Gallagher told Tanner he'd arrived just after the judge adjourned the court for lunch, but he was in no mood to talk. He sat in the lobby of the courthouse and wouldn't take up the offer of using one of the witness rooms allocated to the defence. Tanner tried talking to him but got glared down, and only a consoling shake of the head from Willett's wife, who'd made the trip down from Byron Bay with him.

'My apologies for interrupting your retirement,' Tanner said, after Willett was sworn in to give evidence as soon as the trial resumed after lunch.

Willett looked at Tanner, then turned to the judge. 'Do I have to answer that, your Honour?'

The judge smiled. 'I'm not sure it was a question, Mr Willett. You have some questions I assume, Mr Tanner?'

Tanner took Willett quickly through his work history as a planner in private practice before reaching the top of the state government planning department. Then he had Willett take the jury through the approvals process for Limani Views. Leonard Developments eventually gained approval for high end residential development, but Lovro Constructions wanted more once it owned the site.

'Lovro Constructions – it's a very big company. You were familiar with it?'

'All planners are familiar with the big developers.'

'It constructs tourist-style resorts around the world, is that right, not just residential developments?'

'Yes.'

'And it ultimately won approval for a resort-style hotel on the Limani Views site?'

'Yes.'

'It won that approval from the state government?'

'I wouldn't call it "won". It was granted approval.'

'Against your department's advice?'

'That's not completely correct. My department recommended a smaller scale tower, if one was going to be approved.'

'You weren't as sold on the tourism benefits of a so-called six-star hotel on the site as the government was?'

'I thought a building with less bulk and scale was more desirable for the area. The minister didn't.'

'Lovro is a big donor to state and federal governments, correct?'

'I wouldn't – I'm not sure that's strictly accurate, Mr Tanner. I doubt any large company considers that it makes donations to a government. I think they disclose donations that they make to political parties. And I think you'll find it donates to all the main political parties, though, if you check.'

'I have, Mr Willett. And you're right. Even your semantic distinction between government and political party is technically accurate. But Lovro is more generous to parties that are in government, would you believe?'

'I'll take your word for it.'

'Lovro has started to get in the business of developing hotels that have casinos or gambling facilities, am I right?'

'I think that might be right.'

'You think?'

'Yes. They have.'

'Four. One in the Caribbean, one in the Seychelles, two in India. Ring a bell?'

'Yes.'

'Before you retired, did you go to a meeting where Lovro made inquiries about the possibility of being granted a gaming licence for a proposed new building on the Limani Views site? A new tower?'

'No.'

'Did you hear a rumour to that effect?'

'I object, your Honour,' Gallo said. 'Rumour? Really? That's twice in a few questions. The defence is going to be based on rumours? And as I've asked before, what's the relevance of all this?'

'It all has a link to Mr Randall, your Honour,' Tanner said. 'I'll make that good.'

'Not with rumours you won't, Mr Tanner.'

'And at some point I'll remind the jury that the prosecution case is based on the word of a killer, and another man whose Facebook friends are murderers and rapists, but I'll move on for now, your Honour. Mr Willett, are you aware that a meeting took place – in secret – between the gaming minister and representatives of Lovro just before you resigned?'

'I was – no, not aware of my own knowledge.'

'Did someone tell you of such a meeting?'

'I object, your Honour – hearsay?'

'It's first hand, your Honour, and the reason that's the best I can do will soon become apparent.'

'Let's get to that bit first,' the judge said.

'Who told you, Mr Willett?'

'A colleague.'

'You're not an investigative journalist, Mr Willett. A name please.'

Willett looked at Tanner with venom. 'Joe Watson.'

'Who is he?'

'He was my equivalent in the Department of Liquor and Gaming.'

'My favourite department. He's still there?'

'You know he's not.'

'The jury don't, Mr Willett. Tell them where he now works?'
'He works in India.'
'Who for, do you know?'
'For a company called Goa Resorts and Gaming, I believe.'
'Who owns that company?'
'I don't know all the owners.'
'Have a guess who the majority shareholder is.'
'It's Lovro Resorts.'
'A subsidiary of Lovro Constructions?'
'I believe so.'
'Really. Wow. Will the Gaming Minister and the Planning Minister be given jobs by Lovro when they've qualified for parliamentary pensions, Mr Willett?'
'I object.'
'So do I, your Honour,' Tanner said. 'What do you think was discussed at this meeting between the head of gaming and Lovro last year?'
'I have no idea. You'd have to ask someone who might know.'

'How do you think we're doing?'
Kit Gallagher was seated at the head of a conference table in the main room allocated to the defence in the court complex, Jenny Singh next to her. Tina Leonard sat opposite, hands clasped together on top of the table, looking calm. Her sister sat next to her, her demeanour like that expected of an accused. Tanner was at the other end.
'We haven't been thrown off course yet.'
Gallagher nodded. She looked at her client. 'Tina – any questions?'
Leonard shook her head slowly, said nothing.
'Ravic is tomorrow?' Taz asked, looking at Tanner.
He nodded.
'And you're going to accuse him of having Randall killed?'

THE BURDEN OF LIES

Tanner smiled. 'I might need to be a bit subtler than that. I'm not ready to take a forced retirement.'

'What, then?'

'We're not going to be able to prove Luka Ravic ordered Oliver Randall to be killed, Taz. I don't do miracles.'

'What do you do?'

He laughed, looked at Gallagher, back to Taz. 'Magic.'

'Magic?'

'Yeah.'

'Tell me the difference between miracles and magic,' Taz asked, smiling in a vague kind of way.

'Magic isn't real. Miracles are meant to be.'

'I'm not following.'

'Hocus pocus, Taz. Sleight of hand. Smoke and mirrors, chicanery and conjuring, illusion and mirage. That's what I'm being paid to do. Red herrings and subterfuge, blinds and bluffs. I don't do miracles. Just magic.'

'I'm confused,' Taz said. 'You – you believe Tina, right? She didn't do it.'

'I do believe it, Taz. But it's unlikely I can prove Ravic had Randall killed. I can't prove Carter or Rodriguez from SEBC had him killed. I can try, though, to show the jury that it is awfully nice for them that Randall's dead. And I don't have to prove the Crown's main witnesses are scumbags. One of them already has that tattooed on his chest. So it's about doubt. Pulling doubt out of the hat, alive and kicking. It's also, in a strange way, contrary to all I just said, about the whole truth. You and Tina should discuss that on the way home.'

'I had an interesting conference with a witness on Sunday night,' Tanner said. 'You can't say anything about it – not yet, anyway.

Tanner was in his chambers after court. It was just after six, and Rachel Roth was sitting on the other side of his desk, cashing in on the fifteen-minute trial update he'd promised her for her assistance with Willett and Hendricks. Half an hour earlier, before he'd sent them away so he could work on his own, Gallagher and Singh had been in his room, listening to him tell them about the drink he'd had with Crawford. He'd told them he thought the threat was only directed at him, not to them, and that he was confident as he could be that it had been defused. They agreed not to take it up with the police – that might make things messy with the trial. And their obligations to Tina Leonard remained the same.

'I thought witness conferences are privileged,' Roth said. 'Should I be flattered you trust me?'

Tanner trusted her enough to think she would honour their agreement to not report or publish anything that might be harmful to Tina Leonard, at least while the trial was running. He didn't trust her enough to tell her his client had lied about an affair with Oliver Randall. That was information restricted to defence team only. Crawford's visit was different. He told her the essence of what had occurred, the threat that had been made, and, without naming him, his call to Mark Woods.

'And you don't know what – this cop you called, what's his name?'

Tanner shook his head. 'No name, Rachel. He wouldn't like it.'

She shrugged, pushed a strand of hair behind an ear. 'And you have no idea what he said?'

'Not precisely.'

'Any educated guesses?'

'He's got dirt on Crawford. Something you're unlikely ever to be able to substantiate or print. Perhaps he has things on Crawford he hasn't told me. Maybe he just threatened him. My contact doesn't like criminal lawyers, but I may be the one he hates the least. He knows I have a teenage son.'

'And how long did they talk for?'

'A minute. A bit longer maybe. Enough time for my heart to do about three hundred beats.'

Roth frowned. 'You're afraid?'

'What of?'

She glared at him for a moment. 'For your safety, Pete. Whether – are you afraid for your son?'

'Are you afraid for me?'

She shook her head. 'Don't do that,' she said softly, slight annoyance in her voice.

He twirled a pen around in his fingers and thought. 'I – I trust the guy I called. He doesn't pull punches. I'm afraid – I think I'm more afraid of losing.'

'Of losing?'

'Just before you got here, I was commiserating with Kit and Jenny,' he said. 'It seems almost certain now we have an innocent client. As a defence lawyer, Tina's the second-worst-case scenario you can have.'

Roth didn't speak for a moment, but a faint smile crept over her face. 'What's the worst?'

'She could be innocent, but have no money for our fees.' Roth stifled a laugh. 'I'm serious,' Tanner said. 'Innocent clients are a pain in the arse.'

'From the perspective of someone who isn't a defence lawyer, you have a very twisted view of your clients and your job.'

Tanner shrugged. 'It's stressful acting for someone who's innocent.'

She nodded. 'When the trial's finished,' she said, 'I can contact this ex-cop Crawford, right? Ask him about threatening you?'

'He's not going to admit that. He'll say he was seeing me because I was calling him as my witness. That's it. No proof of anything else.'

She nodded, looked at her watch. 'My time's up,' she said.

'That flew.'

She stood, looked at him. 'Are you okay, Pete?'

'For a guy who's representing someone who didn't do it – sure.'

'What now then?'

'The duty I owe Tina Leonard would be the same if Crawford hadn't come near me, or if he'd pulled a gun on me. I still have to go after these bastards just as hard.'

She shook her head, but there was something like a smile on her face. 'You're all talk, Peter,' she said. 'I think you live for having an innocent client.'

51

Ravic's father had started with nothing. Land out west, growing his own fruit and veg, not much English. His son, though, had the manner of a highborn. Tall and slim, long, thin face, soft silver hair. When he put his hand on the Bible to swear his oath, Tanner saw how thin his wrists were. Heirloom watch on his right, a south-paw. He was a patron of the arts in his spare time, when he wasn't building slums and casinos.

'You didn't want to come today, Mr Ravic?' Tanner began.

'Does anyone want to come to court?' he said, pleasant tone.

'Your lawyer did – you sent him here before the trial began. To have your subpoena set aside? You recall that, of course?'

'We were unsuccessful.'

'Why did you do that?'

'Well – I suppose I don't see how I can possibly help the court with this case. I took legal advice and –'

'What was the advice?'

'I object,' Gallo said.

'He's your witness now, is he?' Tanner said.

'Your Honour, I'm only –'

'You don't have to reveal your legal advice, Mr Ravic,' Justice Francis said.

'Thank you, your Honour.'

'Of course not,' Tanner said. 'It's only a murder trial. You've got secrets you want to keep from us, Mr Ravic?'

'I don't know what you –'

'I object. And can I remind my friend this is his witness. A whole lot of leading questions so far. The jury hasn't even been told who the witness is.'

'My friend's correct,' Tanner said. 'Rude of me not to introduce Mr Ravic, of Lovro Constructions. That's who you are, Mr Ravic?'

'Well – I own shares in Lovro.'

'Lots.'

'My father started the company. I retain a majority interest, yes.'

'I may need some leniency with leading, your Honour. Not too much. Hopefully my friend can resist objecting to everything and stick to when it's really needed. I doubt it will be.'

Tanner then got Ravic to tell the jury about Lovro Constructions. Its humble beginning, spectacular growth, now global reach. Revenue of nearly three billion. Over seven thousand employees.

'Ted Crawford is one of those employees, isn't he, Mr Ravic?'

Ravic paused, looked mildly amused. 'My father once knew everyone's name by heart. Once you're in the thousands – I'm sorry.'

'He's some kind of manager for Lovro Resorts. Based in India.'

'I have too many managers, Mr Tanner.'

'Would you mind producing an employment file for us? I can get a subpoena drawn up if you insist. Edward Crawford, Lovro Resorts.'

'I suppose, I'm sure we can. If it's really necessary.'

'We'd be grateful. Your company owns the Limani Views project, Mr Ravic. I think I can lead that, it's well known.'

'Yes.'

'Who did you buy it off?'

'Well, we acquired the land, and the development consent that ran with it, at a public tender.'

'Who from though? Who ran the tender?'

'The bank who had taken possession of the site. SEBC.'

'Well, that's funny. You know why?'

'I'm sure you'll tell me.'

'SEBC employs a security expert I've subpoenaed to give evidence following you. His name is Brian Crawford. Do you know him?'

'No, I don't.'

'He used to be in the New South Wales Drug Squad. Does that help refresh your memory?'

The merest sniff at the impertinence of the question. 'No, it doesn't.'

'He once arrested a man called Oliver Randall. You've heard of him? He gets called the victim in this court.'

'I'm aware of who he is.'

'So, Brian Crawford, who once worked for the police, and who put Oliver Randall away for six kilos of cocaine in his study, now works for SEBC. Who sold you Limani Views. And his son, Ted Crawford, works for you.'

'If you say so.'

'Do you think that's a coincidence, Mr Ravic?'

'I'm not sure what you mean. It can be a small world, I suppose.'

'A small world? Okay. What did you pay, by the way? For Limani Views?'

'I think our tender price was a hundred million.'

'And when did you pay that money? Three years ago?'

'Something like that.'

'What's it worth now?'

'Now?' Ravic smiled. 'There are buildings on it now. A tower. We've built condominium-style residences. It's nearing completion. The development consent – we secured some modifications. I don't have all our construction costs handy, or details of sales to date or – You can't –'

'Well, tell me this – how much profit does Lovro expect to make once the project is completed?'

'There is no way of knowing that yet.'

'Humour me, Mr Ravic. The state wants to put my client in prison for life and she's not guilty, so just do me this favour. I'll help you. Let me make it very easy. I can show you your own valuations of just the land with the current development consent if you like. The ones we got from you in a subpoena. C'mon. Between five and six hundred million. Am I close?'

Ravic took in a deep breath, let it out slowly. 'Something like that.'

'Quite a profit on your original one hundred million investment.'

'Our aim is to make money, Mr Tanner.'

'Yes, capitalism. I get it, Mr Ravic. It makes people do all kinds of wicked things. Hell of a bargain you got, wouldn't you agree?'

'Tenders can be funny things.'

'C'mon, Mr Ravic. Talk it up. I bet you do to your financiers and shareholders and the market generally. You got a great deal, didn't you?'

'It was complicated. There was –'

'A contamination report?'

'I object, your Honour. Mr Tanner is not letting his own witness finish his answers, and the leading has gone far enough, in my submission.'

'Mr Ravic is a very well-educated, intelligent and extremely successful man, your Honour. He negotiates with much smarter and tougher people than me every day. I'm not going to be able to lead him where he doesn't want to go. I need some sensible latitude with that, or we'll be here a week with this witness. He won't like it, you won't like it, and the jury won't like it. I'm not putting words in a more challenged person's mouth.'

'Let the witness answer your question before asking the next, Mr Tanner.'

Tanner nodded, smiled. 'You wanted to tell me it was complicated, this great bargain you got?'

Gallo shook her head for the jury, but didn't object.

'The contamination report was a factor. So were limits on the then development approval.'

'The contamination report. Who gave it to you?'

'It was given to all – I mean, it was made public.'

'By whom?'

'The bank.'

'Mr Crawford's employer. Brian Crawford.'

'If you say so.'

'And that report – and I'll paraphrase – suggested the site might need a bigger clean up than the previous owner had given it?'

'It suggested higher levels of contaminates – metals, dioxins, yes.'

'Big cost to do it?'

'A cost, yes.'

'That you didn't have to pay, right?'

'Well – no, I don't agree with you entirely.'

'You got a break, didn't you? It turned out to be a cleaner site than the report indicated.'

'There were differences. It was not as extensive a report as what we conducted ourselves once we took control of the site.'

'Who did that contamination report? The one SEBC felt it had to make public.'

'The firm, you mean?'

'Yeah.'

'I don't recall.'

'You've heard of SBW Environmental Consultants?'

'Yes. It may have been them.'

'Your company, Lovro Constructions, uses SBW for reports? From time to time? For development applications?'

'I'm not involved in that level of detail, but I will take your word for it.'

'And they did this report for SEBC?'

'That's possible. I'll take your word for it.'

'Wow. What was the phrase you used before? Small world?'

'Well, they're aren't an unlimited number of –'

'And you use them despite their report for SEBC on Limani Views being completely wrong and utterly negligent?'

'I object. How can – ?'

'I withdraw that. You use them even though their report for SEBC turned out to be wrong?'

'I don't know it was "wrong", Mr Tanner,' Ravic said. 'It may have contained false positives, and estimates that turned out, upon further testing, not to be borne out.'

'Is that your very long way of agreeing with me that they stuffed things up, possibly including the tender?'

'Mr Tanner!' the judge snapped.

'Who is Jack Rodriguez, Mr Ravic?'

'He's the CEO of SEBC.'

'What about Phillip P Carter, who's he?'

'The chairman of their board.'

'The CEO until recently?'

'I believe so.'

'You believe – you know, don't you?'

'Well – yes, he was the CEO until about two years ago.'

'These men are your friends, aren't they?'

'I object again, your Honour. Relevance for the record again, and leading.'

'Does my friend really want me to ask Mr Ravic something like "what's your relationship with these men"?'

'He is your witness, Mr Tanner.'

'What golf club are you a member of, Mr Ravic?'

'The Anglo.'

'What golf club is Mr Rodriguez a member of?'

'The same.'

'Mr Carter?'

'We play golf together, Mr Tanner. If that's what you want to know. Very occasionally. I work long hours. I'd like to lower my handicap. So would Jack and Phil.'

'You've known Jack and Phil for a long time, Mr Ravic?'

'Please call them by their surnames, Mr Tanner,' Justice Francis said.

'Just adopting what the witness called them, your Honour. If the court pleases though. Mr Rodriguez or Mr Carter – SEBC – it's bankrolled a few of your developments over the years, correct?'

Ravic smiled. 'I don't want to be difficult, Mr Tanner, but –'

'Then don't be, Mr Ravic. Be helpful.'

Ravic paused for a second, looked at the judge, then said, 'I'm not sure "bankrolled" is a term I would adopt. They have provided loan facilities from time to time to my company and some of its subsidiaries.'

'Mr Carter – he doesn't happen to be a member of a yacht club you're a member of, is he, Mr Ravic?'

'He is.'

'Small world. So, SEBC sells my client's land. It's your bank. You play golf and sail to Hobart on Boxing Day with its most senior people, then you buy my client's land from this bank, is that right?'

'I think the process of sale and purchase was far more complicated than that, but the ultimate position is yes.'

'When did you first discuss buying Limani Views from SEBC, Mr Ravic?'

'We didn't buy it from SEBC. They sold it as mortgagee in possession, not owner.'

'Have it your way, Mr Ravic. SEBC put the land up for public tender, we agree on that?'

'Yes.'

'When did you first talk to, say, Mr Phillip P Carter about it?'

'I didn't.'

'Really. Never?'

'Not before the tender, no.'

'Not over a beer or a martini at the golf club or yacht club one long afternoon or early evening. He never said, "Hey, Luka, we've got a site for sale you'd just love"?'

'I'm a teetotaller, Mr Tanner.'

'My condolences. Mr Carter didn't speak to you or someone on your staff about what a huge opportunity might come up for you with Limani Views?'

'No.'

'You're a pretty big customer of theirs, right? They're the main finance for your casinos in India, am I correct?'

'One of them.'

'Someone from SEBC didn't talk to you or one of your minions about the dodgy contamination report they were going to make public, tell you not to worry about it?'

'Absolutely not.'

'You didn't talk to Mr Lees or a Mr Martin from SBW, who told you not to worry about their report, they had an off day when they did it?'

'Of course not.'

'Whose idea, then, was it to steal my client's land, Mr Ravic? Yours or your bank's?'

'I object.'

'Or was it by mutual agreement made on the eighteenth green?'

'Don't answer that, Mr Ravic.'

'You like casinos, Mr Ravic?'

'I'm going to put a stop to this soon, Mr Tanner,' Justice Francis said.

'I'm nearly finished, your Honour. You're fond of casinos, Mr Ravic? You and your company?'

Ravic let out a theatrical sigh. 'We build them, Mr Tanner. We have four licences. Two in India, one in –'

'Like to build one here? In Sydney?'

'That seems highly unlikely.'

'You can buy anything here, Mr Ravic, if you're willing to pay the right people. You know that by now, don't you?'

'Don't answer that, Mr Ravic.'

'Ever talked with anyone about building a casino at Limani Views, Mr Ravic?'

Ravic paused for a moment longer than he might have wished for. 'Not formally, no.'

'Informally?'

'Informally we always consider lots of options.'

'Limani Views isn't fully completed yet, is it? It's a staged development?'

'Correct.'

'And there's an undeveloped part of the site still? In the middle. A few thousand square metres, a bit more than that?'

'Designated as public open space.'

'You haven't talked informally to anyone about building another tower there, sticking in a few pokies and gambling tables, that kind of thing?'

'We – no. This city is very unlikely to move on from its two-casino policy.'

'It was unlikely to get one casino. Then two were unlikely. You and the executives of your company know who to lobby when you want things, don't you, Mr Ravic?'

'Don't answer that question, Mr Ravic.'

'You know who Robert Temple is, Mr Ravic, or is he another person who works for you you've not heard of?'

'He is, I'm afraid, Mr Tanner. I don't believe I know him.'

'He works in Dubai. For a company called Mid-World Construction. I've got his details from Mid-World's website. He's the deputy chief financial officer.'

'I don't know him, I'm sorry.'

'You know Mid-World, right?'

'Of course. It's one of our subsidiaries. Lovro is its parent company.'

'Do you know Mr Temple's work history?'

'No.'

'He used to work for Leonard Constructions. He was its CFO.'

'I'm not aware of that, or of his employment with Mid-World.'

Tanner opened his folder, took out a document. 'In my hand I have an affidavit sworn by Mr Temple, Mr Ravic. It was filed in a case called *SEBC v Leonard Constructions*. Have you seen this affidavit?'

'No.'

'In the affidavit, Mr Temple attested to the fact that Oliver Randall told Tina Leonard and him at a meeting that SEBC had agreed to grant Leonard Developments a twenty-four-month extension on its loan terms for the Limani Views project before the bank would reassess. In less than a week, those loans were called in. You haven't heard that story?'

'I – not really. I was vaguely aware of Leonard Developments' liquidation and collapse, of course. Not the details.'

'Mr Temple swore this affidavit, then didn't turn up for the trial. He disappeared overseas. Does that sound like a decent thing to do?'

'Well –'

'And he ends up in Dubai one day, working for you. Wow, small world, Mr Ravic?'

'I object, your Honour,' Gallo said flatly.

'Don't answer, Mr Ravic.'

'What kind of quality control and due diligence do you and your companies undertake before you employ someone, Mr Ravic? To employ a man who runs away from a court case like that leaving my client high and dry? Does that sound honourable to you?'

'Don't answer, Mr Ravic. Mr Tanner, this needs to –'

'I have no idea who he is, Mr Tanner,' Ravic said over the top of the judge. 'I have no idea who Mid-World employs in such a position.'

'When did Mr Randall tell you he had the deal of the century for you, Mr Ravic? Or was it Mr Carter or Mr Rodriguez who told you first?'

'No one told me anything of the kind.'

'When were you told the contamination report was a fraud to ensure you got the land?'

'That is a fantastic lie.'

'Why would Mr Randall tell my client there was this big

conspiracy between your company and his bank to steal my client's land, Mr Ravic? Can you explain that?'

And there it was. The question that meant Tina Leonard would now have to give evidence. A question like that had to be backed up. If Tina Leonard was going to be acquitted, she'd have to help Tanner earn it for her.

'I object,' Gallo said. 'How can – ?' But Ravic ignored her too.

'If he said such a thing, Mr Tanner – and of course I don't know that – but if he did, he is either sadly mistaken, or frankly unwell.'

'He's actually very unwell, Mr Ravic. Someone shot him in the head. I'd like to know why. You're making – Lovro is making – a big profit out of Limani Views, you'd agree with that?'

'I – yes. We discussed this. After buying land and building on it, we hope to eventually make a profit. That's what we aim to do. It's what we have to do. All companies.'

'But a really big profit?'

'Again – you use the word "big" and I –'

'You're hundreds of millions in front just on land value, Mr Ravic. Can we agree that hundreds of millions of dollars in profit is "big" to any company, in any language, anywhere and anytime, Mr Ravic?'

Ravic paused, looked to the judge for intervention, but none came. 'Yes, Mr Tanner, a substantial profit.'

'And if Oliver Randall was running about town saying you and SEBC fraudulently schemed to steal the project from my client, that wouldn't be a good look for you, right?'

'I have no idea what you're talking about.'

'And it would be even worse if what he was saying were true, you agree?'

'It's not true. None of it.'

'So you buy this land for a hundred million, it's meant to come with a big clean-up bill, but it doesn't, and the project's now worth what, a few billion? Lucky, lucky, lucky, Mr Ravic.'

'I object.'

'And Oliver Randall, who writes to my client apologising for bringing her down, ends up dead. Lucky, lucky, lucky, Mr Ravic.'

'You're a disgrace,' Ravic said loudly as Gallo objected.

'Just one more question, your Honour,' Tanner said equally loudly. 'Jayden Webb, Mr Ravic. And Mick Bitar? They're not up for membership at your golf club, are they?'

52

Brian Jeffrey Crawford had the decency to take his oath by affirmation.

His hair had been damp the other night, thinning but thick with product. He'd blow dried it for today, Tanner thought, taken the ash out, left the smoke. He was wearing a navy suit, sky blue tie, matching kerchief in his breast pocket. That was a new touch. The pocket hanky was a million miles from the Drug Squad, and yet he still looked like a cop. He either had too many miles on the clock in the job, or Tanner couldn't see him any other way.

'You were a police officer for how many years, Mr Crawford?' Tanner began.

'Just over twenty-five.'

'You finished up as a Detective Senior Sergeant in the Drug Squad?'

'I did.'

'You've been in a witness box before today?'

Crawford gave a tight smile. 'I guess that's fair. A few times.'

Tanner shook his head. 'Never guess in the witness box, Mr Crawford. Surely someone once told you that?'

'Sorry. Figure of speech. I agree with you.'

'I've even had the pleasure of your company before in a courtroom.'

Crawford paused before answering. 'I'm not convinced pleasure is the right word, Mr Tanner. No disrespect intended.'

'Occupational hazard for both of us.'

'I guess so.'

'It was nearly seven years ago that you arrested Oliver Randall, correct?'

'I did.'

'You found six kilos of cocaine in his home. In a gym bag, I believe?'

'Another police officer located the drugs. I was on the scene, though.'

'Even for a home in the eastern suburbs of Sydney, that's quite a lot of coke, do you agree?'

Crawford smiled a fraction, shook his head. 'No comment about the location, Mr Tanner. I agree it's a substantial amount of cocaine. So do the statute books.'

'A street value of a couple of million?'

'That sounds about right, from memory. I don't disagree.'

'You interviewed Mr Randall?'

'I did, along with another detective.'

'He denied the cocaine was his?'

Crawford paused, then said, 'He pleaded guilty to possession of a large commercial quantity of a prohibited drug.'

Tanner smiled, mockingly wagged a finger at Crawford. 'C'mon, Mr Crawford, you know how this works. Yes, he pleaded guilty – eventually. Before that, he denied the drugs were his when you interviewed him, didn't he?'

'He did.'

'And when he was charged and applied for bail?'

'Yes.'

'I'm sorry, your Honour,' Izzy Gallo said, 'but are we still in the trial relating to the murder charge against the accused, Ms Leonard?'

The judge nodded, looked at Tanner over the top of her reading glasses. 'I'll get there, your Honour. I am dealing with Mr Randall. It's not as though he's not a central figure in this trial.'

Justice Francis let out a small sigh, but allowed him to continue.

'Only after all that did Mr Randall change his plea, correct?'

'After that, he did.'

'And before he was released from prison, he wrote to his ex-wife and daughter telling them he'd been set up – you've heard that evidence, right?'

Crawford shook his head. 'I'll take your word that's what he told them, Mr Tanner. I only know he pleaded guilty.'

Tanner had to be careful with this. Tina Leonard had instructed him that Oliver Randall had confessed to being part of a conspiracy to steal her land. Tanner had letters Randall had written to her, and to Simone, from which, at a stretch, some support for that could be implied. That was enough for him to go after Ravic and Carter, but it didn't allow him to flat out accuse Crawford of planting six kilos of cocaine in Randall's gym bag, or of knowing the coke had been planted. He had no doubt that was the truth, but the legal basis for directly putting such an allegation was thin at best. Randall was dead, and there was no one else who could back that claim up. He'd pleaded guilty. What he'd told Leonard and his ex-wife might not be enough to point the finger at Crawford. It might be a question the judge would not let go. It might head him into mistrial territory, which he wanted to avoid. Tina Leonard's trial was unlikely to get better for her on a re-run. He had to leave it hanging, jab at another soft spot instead.

'How many more arrests did you make, detective, after Oliver Randall?'

Crawford frowned. 'I never kept count.'

'Not a stats man?'

'Get to the point, Mr Tanner,' Justice Francis said.

'Do you recall any?'

'Off the top of my head – no.'

'That's not surprising, is it? You took some long service leave owing to you after Randall changed his plea to guilty, do you recall that?'

'I did. It was long overdue.'

'And then you resigned from the police force?'

'I got a position at SEBC, Mr Tanner. I think that's what you want to ask me, isn't it?'

'Do you want to ask the questions, Mr Crawford? If you do, can I give the answers? Ask me how those drugs found their way into Oliver Randall's gym bag.'

'Mr Tanner!' the judge said, raising her voice.

Tanner and Crawford glared at each other, the older man wanting to see how far Tanner would go. Almost egging him on, Tanner felt.

'What's your job at SEBC, Mr Crawford?'

'I'm one of the security managers.'

'One of them?'

'Yes.'

'What's your job description?'

'What do you mean?'

'What do you do?'

'Your Honour,' Gallo objected, 'how can this possibly be relevant?'

'The prosecutor's objecting because she knows I'm heading right into relevant territory, your Honour, and she wants you to cut me off.'

Justice Francis motioned to say something, stopped herself, paused. 'You should already be in relevant territory, Mr Tanner. Get there quickly, please.'

'Tell us what you do, Mr Crawford.'

Crawford sighed, like he was being forced to indulge a child who wanted to play some tedious game. 'I help draft and update the bank's guidelines and blueprint for its security practices. I manage some of the people who oversee the details of that, and the practical implementation. By security I am talking broadly. Real property security, the security of staff and management. The security of our customers and their records. Information security. I'm involved in risk assessment reviews. I help coordinate our policies between our offices and branches. They are some of the general parameters of what I do.'

'Boy,' Tanner said. 'You learned all that making drug busts?'

'Don't answer that, Mr Crawford,' the judge said.

'Was this position advertised?'

Crawford waited to see if the judge or Gallo would intervene, but neither did. 'I don't remember.'

'Do you think your employer could produce any advertising for your job just before you were employed, Mr Crawford?'

'I have no idea.'

'I'll let that be a challenge for the Crown to take that up if it wants to. Were you headhunted, Mr Crawford?'

'I don't know.'

'Well – did you approach SEBC for a job, or did they come to a member of the state's Drug Squad for their long term strategic security advice?'

'Don't answer that question, Mr Crawford.'

'I press the question, your Honour.'

'I'm not allowing it, Mr Tanner.'

'My client is accused of having Mr Randall killed, your Honour. She's entitled to explore who else might have wanted him dead. I'm interested in how the man who arrested him for drug possession ends up working for the bank that took my client's land. I press the question. I want a ruling from you as to why you won't allow it.'

The judge glared at Tanner. 'I won't allow that question in that form, Mr Tanner.'

'Did SEBC approach you and ask if you wanted to work for them, Mr Crawford?'

'Yes.'

'Who at SEBC?'

'I don't recall.'

Tanner looked at Crawford, looked down at his notes, then towards the jurors. 'How old are you, Mr Crawford?'

'Fifty-eight.'

'Is your memory failing you these days?'

'I don't recall who made the first call to me, Mr Tanner. My memory is fine.'

'Who interviewed you, then?'

'The ex-head of the Security Division. He's retired.'

'Were there other candidates for the position?'

'I don't know.'

'Did you replace someone who left or was leaving, or was it a new position?'

'I don't know.'

'The ex-head of security. Were you recommended to him by someone? Did a person you arrested who dealt in commercial quantities of prohibited drugs recommend you for a security position at a global bank? Did a drug cartel boss recommend you, Mr Crawford?'

'Mr Tanner!' Justice Francis shouted.

'Did someone recommend you, Mr Crawford?'

'I don't know.'

'Well, why did SEBC approach you? Did this ex-head of security tell you?'

'Not that I recall. I think he – I think he may have heard on the grapevine that I wanted to leave the force and do something else. I'm not sure how that happened.'

'On the grapevine,' Tanner said, raising his voice. 'What grapevine is that, Mr Crawford? What grapevine exists between the Drug Squad and our banks?'

'It was another figure of speech, Mr Tanner,' Crawford said, raising his own voice for the first time.

'Even so, Mr Crawford, help me out here. You made an arrest of a very senior banking executive of SEBC. You found six kilos of cocaine in his gym bag at his home, and spare in the pocket of his jacket. What happens then? You tell the "grapevine" you want out of the force, that you're interested in some un-advertised security position at the bank the perp works for? Is that how it worked?'

'I don't know what happened, Mr Tanner. It's nearly seven years ago.'

'What are you paid, Mr Crawford, out of interest?'

'I object,' Gallo said. 'How can that be relevant, your Honour?'

'Your interest in what Mr Crawford is paid and what's relevant to this case don't seem to line up, Mr Tanner,' Justice Francis said.

'Your Honour, my client was told by Mr Randall, shortly before Mr Webb killed him, that the six kilos of cocaine he did prison time for weren't his, and that he was part of a conspiracy to fraudulently obtain my client's land. This question is tangentially relevant to a theme I'm going to make submissions on. That's enough.'

Justice Francis decided to clear things up with Crawford herself. 'Are you able to tell us your salary, Mr Crawford?' she said, exasperation in her tone.

'About seven hundred thousand, your Honour.'

'Wow,' Tanner said. 'Big pay increase from working in the police force, Mr Crawford.'

'It is.'

'I bet some of your former colleagues are jealous?'

'Don't answer that, Mr Crawford.'

'Hard for a police officer to make that sort of money from their day job, Mr Crawford, isn't it?'

'Mr Tanner, move on,' the judge said, her voice rising.

'You have a grown son, Mr Crawford?'

Crawford took in a deep breath at the change of topic, shook his head slowly like he was suddenly bored again. 'I have two, Mr Tanner.'

'Your Honour, how can that be relevant to – ?'

'I'm nearly done, your Honour,' Tanner said. 'These questions relate directly to a submission I'll be making to the jury at the conclusion of the evidence. You can send the jury out now so I can elaborate, or you can let me finish without that. I only need a few more minutes.'

'I'm going to hold you to that, Mr Tanner,' Justice Francis said.

'Your eldest son, Edward is his name, Mr Crawford?'

'Yes.'

'He's how old? Thirty?'

'Thirty-two.'

'And he works for Lovro Constructions. He's some kind of property manager, is that right?'

'He works for Lovro Resorts.'

'How long has he worked for them?'

'I can't give you an exact time – perhaps four or five years.'

'How did he get that job?'

'I don't know. You'd have to ask him.'

'When's he next back from India, Mr Crawford? We couldn't get a response to our invitation to help my client. Why is that, do you know?'

'Don't answer that, Mr Crawford.'

'Was his job advertised before he got it, do you know?'

'I have no idea.'

'Was he employed via the grapevine, Mr Crawford?'

'Don't answer that, Mr Crawford.'

'You've seriously never discussed with your own son how he came to be employed by the Lovro Group?'

'Not in detail, no. He's always worked in property management and real estate.'

'You must have a different relationship with your son than I have with mine, Mr Crawford?'

'Don't answer that, Mr Crawford.'

'You know I have a son, Mr Crawford, don't you? And a dog?'

'Mr Tanner!'

'Oliver Randall, Mr Crawford, and his six kilos of cocaine. Can we go back to that, please?'

'Quickly, Mr Tanner,' the judge said. 'I thought you were done with that topic.'

'Who did he buy the cocaine from?'

Crawford sighed. 'He wouldn't tell us.'

'I assume, when he changed his plea, you asked him?'

'Yes.'

'And no doubt informed him that if he told you who supplied him with all that coke it could lead to a lesser sentence for him?'

'I don't – look, probably something like that was said.'

'And undoubtedly, had he told you, it would have led to a lesser sentence?'

'It may have.'

'Why didn't he tell you, Mr Crawford?'

'I have no idea.'

'Really? No idea. Could he have been afraid of his supplier, Mr Crawford?'

'I don't know.'

'Had he paid for the drugs?'

'I don't know.'

'Did his banking records provide any evidence that he'd purchased six kilos of cocaine from a person or entity capable of supplying such large quantities?'

'No. There's always the possibility he paid in cash.'

'Cash? Really, Mr Crawford? Raided his daughter's piggy bank, did he? There was no evidence of cash payment either, was there?'

'You mean, apart from him having possession of the drugs, Mr Tanner?'

'Answer the question. Any record or direct evidence of payment?'

'Do you think his bank statements would have an entry for cocaine purchase, Mr Tanner?'

'I'll ask a third time. And a tenth if I must. Any direct evidence of payment?'

'No.'

'In your experience as a former senior member of the Drug Squad, how many drug cartels take kindly to being stiffed out of payment of large sums of money, Mr Crawford?'

'I – Hypothetically? Probably none.'

'Hypothetically suits me, Mr Crawford. Hypothetically then, if what Mr Randall told his ex-wife and daughter was true, and the drugs were planted, who might have done that? Any ideas?'

'Don't answer that, Mr Crawford.'

'Do you remember us having a witness conference recently, Mr Crawford? Just you and me?'

Crawford paused before answering, unable to help his eyes darting towards Gallo and then the judge. 'Yes,' he eventually said. Then he smiled. Smiled at Tanner like they were about to reminisce about one of the great nights of their lives.

'At a bar at the Sheraton Hotel on Sunday night. You recall that?'

'Yes.'

'Strange place for a conference. Why did you pick there again?'

Crawford shook his head. 'That was your idea.'

'Was it? I don't recall it that way. Anyway, do you recall if you gave me any insight during that conference as to who might have hypothetically planted those drugs in Oliver Randall's gym bag?'

Gallo stood, looking a fraction rattled. 'I don't – This is extremely odd, your Honour. To say the least. But – "insight"? That's the first objection. And I'm repeating myself, but what does this have to do with the accused?'

Justice Francis looked at Tanner. There was no apparent anger in her expression. More confusion, or curiosity, or a mix of both. 'The witness can't say what insight you had, Mr Tanner,' she said. 'I reject the question.'

'You left in a hurry, Mr Crawford. Did something come up?'

'Don't answer that, Mr Crawford.'

'And you left me with the bill, didn't you?'

'Mr Tanner!'

'No further questions, your Honour.'

Gallo had a choice to make when Tanner sat down. One way of dealing with Crawford's evidence would be to simply say 'No questions'. While it risked giving it a relevance she wanted to deny, she decided to tidy up the facts of Randall's arrest.

'How many police officers went to Oliver Randall's home on the day he was arrested, Mr Crawford?'

'I don't recall exactly. About eight to ten of us from memory.'

'Who found the six kilos of cocaine?'
'A detective constable, I believe.'
'And the cocaine in Mr Randall's jacket?'
'Another detective.'
'You were carrying out a search warrant?'
'Yes.'
And Mr Randall had sold some cocaine the night before to an undercover police officer in a hotel in Double Bay?'
'Yes.'
'And that followed a tip from an informant?'
'Yes.'
'Your informant?'
'No. The informant of another detective.'
'When the warrant was executed, and the search of Mr Randall's home carried out, that whole process was videotaped, correct?'
'Yes.'
'Including finding the drugs in the gym bag?'
'Yes.'
'Prior to Mr Randall's arrest, had you indicated to your superiors in the police force an intention of retiring?'
'Yes – for a couple of years. As I said earlier, I'd been in the force a very long time. My whole working life.'
'When you were interviewed by SEBC for your current job, was Mr Randall mentioned?'
'Yes.'
'By whom?'
'Me. I disclosed it. I told them I'd arrested one of their executives.'
'Was it discussed further?'
'Not at all.'
'Did you know the accused, Ms Leonard, at the time of Mr Randall's arrest?'
'No.'
'Did you know SEBC had been her company's lender?'
'No.'

'Did you know anything about the Limani Views development?'

'No.'

'Do you know anyone employed by the Lovro Group of companies other than your son?'

Crawford shook his head. 'I've met a couple of Ted's work colleagues socially. Apart from that, no.'

'Thank you, Mr Crawford. Nothing further, your Honour.'

53

Tanner worked in his chambers after court until about seven, went home and had dinner with Dan and Karl, then continued working in his study. He still had Kate McDonald and Phillip P Carter to call, and then a final decision had to be made about Tina Leonard.

Tina wanted to give evidence. She'd said that from the beginning. Unpleasant past experiences had taught him to only call an accused if there is absolutely no alternative. Call the client, and they get caught in a lie, or the jury don't like them, and the show is over. This was one of those cases where the accused had to be called. If the jury were going to be convinced to believe that Oliver Randall had confessed things to her, she had to get in the box and say what those things were. And then there was the issue of the fifty grand she'd given to Webb. It was one thing for Tanner to cross-examine Webb and Bitar about that money, and what it was for. The jury was likely to feel it was something that required an explanation directly from Tina.

Tanner was thinking about packing it in for the night when the front doorbell rang. He looked at the corner of his screen – 10.54 pm.

When he opened the door, he saw that Mick Bitar was in the same suit he'd worn in court. White shirt, no tie, smile on his face.

Tanner's heart started thudding. For a second he thought he might slam the door, call the police. Instead, he found a way of saying, 'Crawford can't be dumb enough to send you around here, can he, Mick?'

Bitar looked confused for a moment, then smiled again and said, 'Nearly as tall as you.' He was looking over Tanner's left shoulder. Dan had opened his bedroom door to see who it was.

Tanner put a hand up to signal it was okay. 'Go back to bed,' he said. He thought he sounded as calm as he wanted to, wondered how well he'd faked it.

'What do you want, Mick?' Tanner said when Dan had closed his door.

'Just to talk.'

'I'm busy. I'm sure you understand.'

'You're going to want to hear what I have to say.'

'Ring my clerk and make an appointment.'

'This can't wait.'

'It's going to have to. Leave.'

Bitar shook his head, smiled. 'If I was here to hurt you, you'd be hurt by now. Do you think I'm that stupid?'

'Trick question, Mick?'

Bitar half frowned, half smiled. 'I'm here to help you. Can I come in? It won't take long.'

Tanner paused, thought about it. 'I'll talk to you out in the street,' he said.

Bitar shook his head. 'Suit yourself,' he said, and turned to walk towards the front gate. Before he went outside, Tanner took a step towards Dan's door to tell him that he'd only be a few minutes. He found himself facing his father, who'd left the lounge room where he was watching TV with Larry.

'Is this a friend, Peter, or a late-night client?'

Tanner shook his head. 'It's okay, Karl,' he said. 'Go back to your show.'

Karl glared at him, shook his head, then walked away.

When he walked out of the front gate to the footpath, Tanner couldn't see Bitar. Then he noticed the orange Lamborghini parked across the road. Of course.

'I assume the intent of this car is so you can get around town unnoticed, Mick?' Tanner said when he shut the passenger's side door.

'Too cold to stand outside,' Bitar said. 'Besides, it's going to rain soon.'

Bitar's profile was lit only by the soft light of a street lamp filtered through the branches of a tree above them. *That's a nose that has been broken*, Tanner thought. He wondered how the other guy looked.

'It's a Brioni, by the way,' Bitar said.

'What is?'

'My suit.'

'That's what you're here to tell me?'

Bitar shook his head. 'Nice house,' turning to look across the road. 'What's a guy like you charge these days?'

'You need a lawyer, Mick?'

'Not a lawyer like you. I'm being sloppy if I do. We can pretend you're my brief, if that makes this easier for you.'

'If what makes it easier?'

'This chat we're about to have.'

Tanner shook his head, took a deep breath. 'Are you the next cab off the rank for Crawford?' he asked. 'Did Luka Ravic send you? Or his bank?'

Bitar ran a hand over his skull like there was still hair to push back. 'I don't know what you're talking about with Crawford,' he said. 'And I don't give a fuck about Luka Ravic.'

'Isn't he a customer?'

'I've got others. Not really my main game anyway, is it? Supplying building materials? I can tell you that, can't I? Part laundry, that business. You know what I mean?'

'I'd rather not know.'

Bitar nodded, put his hand inside his jacket. For a moment Tanner thought he was reaching for a gun. It was a phone. He turned it over in one hand, and the screen lit up, illuminating his face as it did. 'What's your case?' he said, looking at the object in his hand.

'My case?'

'Yeah, your defence,' Bitar said, turning to look at Tanner. 'Tina was screwed by Ravic, right? And that bank. Stole the land off her, didn't they? That big project of hers. The bank gave it to Ravic. Isn't that your angle?'

'Sounds like you know as much as I do, Mick.'

'Then Randall gets out of prison and tells Tina he lied in court. He tells her the bank made him do it. Lovro wanted that land, they delivered. Am I right?'

The light on the phone went off. The inside of the car now seemed darker than before. Tanner said nothing.

'Lovro or someone big at the bank learns Randall's out, spilling his guts, apologising, praying to God, whatever the fuck he's doing – they've got to shut him up, don't they?'

Tanner waited for Bitar to continue, but he sat there, smiling at him, his grin widening until the capped teeth were on show. A near glowing white in the dim light of the car.

'If I was a juror, I'd be thinking about buying it,' he said.

'I think the prosecutor might have you excluded from a jury pool, Mick. No offence.'

None was taken. 'I'd buy it, because some of it's probably true.' He shook his head. 'Fucking banks, eh? Greedy bastards. Pretend to be your friends, but when things get tough?'

'You should run a Royal Commission into them, Mick.'

Bitar laughed. 'What good would that do? Be another white-wash, wouldn't it?'

Tanner waited, but this time Bitar seemed done. He spun the phone around in his hand a few more times, waited for Tanner.

'What's not true, Mick?' Tanner said slowly. 'Are you here to tell me that?'

Bitar stopped smiling. 'Do you really think Ravic would use someone like me to kill Randall?'

'Another trick question, Mick? My intel is you're an expert.'

'Do you think they'd let me use a fuck-up like Jayden Webb?'

'What are you telling me?'

Bitar shook his head, looked at the phone. 'Jayden was my fuck-up. I thought he was clean enough. Simple job.' He looked at Tanner. 'Fucking RBT. Do you believe that? And he's unlicensed. What a prick.'

'Some things you've got to do yourself, I guess.'

'I told him to dump the gun anywhere. No way it could be traced.'

'You live and learn, Mick.'

'Do you?'

'Do I what?'

'Live and learn, mate?'

'Learn about what?'

'If Lovro and that bank arranged for that bloke to be offed, do you think we'd be talking now?'

'We are talking.'

'That's what I mean. He wasn't dismembered, mate. He wasn't vaporised.'

'Are those your preferred methods of dealing with problem people, Mick?'

Bitar stopped playing with the phone, held it up to Tanner. 'Ever had one of these?'

It was a BlackBerry. 'Been a long time. Once.'

Bitar smiled. 'Not like this. Encrypted messages. Untraceable shit. No records.'

'That was exactly the kind I had, Mick. What kind of criminal lawyer do you think I am?'

'You think I'm joking?'

'You vaporise people. I wouldn't describe you as a stand-up comic.'

'What do you think I haven't wiped from this yet?'

Tanner looked at him, felt his heart surge again, his throat tighten. 'Ravic telling you to dismember Randall?'

Bitar shook his head, didn't smile. 'Me and your client. Messages between me and Tina.'

The oxygen was leaving the inside of the car. That's what it felt like. It happened to him in court occasionally. Usually in the old days, when he'd called the client. When he'd made that mistake, and they'd been – well, when a prosecutor had *vaporised* them. Heart beating harder again now, a drum in his ears.

'Don't tell me she's in love with you, Mick. It'd break my heart.'

Bitar started to chuckle, ended with a full laugh. 'You should see your face,' he said, the smile suddenly dropping away. 'You believed her, didn't you?' He laughed again. 'You must want to fuck her bad.'

'What's on the phone?' Tanner's words clung to his throat, barely got out.

'He wouldn't play ball with her, she told me. He took her business, her fucking house. Stuffed things up for her with her fucking kids. Then he tells her he's so fucking sorry. But he's apologising to her and to God, and no one else. Can you believe this prick? After all that, he's going to just say sorry to Tina, and to fucking Jesus. As if Jesus is going to listen to a prick like that.'

'Jesus called for the sinners to follow him, Mick, not the righteous. He was an ancient version of me.'

'I've never seen hatred like that,' Bitar said, shaking his head. 'Her kids ended up with her ex – I guess I get that. Were they fucking, though, do you know, Tina and this Randall? She didn't tell me, but I got the feeling.'

Tanner took a deep breath. Found his voice. 'Are you lying to me?'

Bitar shook his head. Something in the way he did it – sombre, wistful – Tanner knew he was hearing the truth. 'Two hundred grand she'd pay me. That's what we agreed. Jayden on top with his fifty.'

As Bitar finished his sentence, Tanner heard a noise coming towards them. Low at first, gradually louder, like the volume was controlled by a dial being slowly turned up. Then a single, fat rain drop found its way through the branches of the tree, and splattered against the windscreen. Another soon followed. Then ten. Then a thousand. It was like a rain cloud had burst right above them.

'There's no evidence of you being paid.'

'Fuck evidence. You think I'd take that up front? She was good for it. She knows me. We go back. Only Jayden needed his.'

Bitar said nothing for a few seconds, looked at Tanner, almost with concern. 'You okay, mate?'

'What's on the phone?'

Bitar shook his head. 'Between me and her. For now. Or do you want me to show you?' He turned the screen back on as the rain grew even heavier, held it up to Tanner's face.

Tanner glared at him, shut his eyes. 'Put the phone down,' he said. 'I don't want to see.'

'You can still pretend that I'm lying that way, can't ya?'

Tanner kept his eyes shut, but could feel the smirk on Bitar's face.

There was silence again for a moment, then Bitar said, 'She wanted his knees shot off. Can you believe that? You know why?'

Tanner sighed, shook his head.

'All that God shit. When she asked him to come forward – I don't know, help her sue them, to tell his story. She wanted his knees blown off so he couldn't pray for his life when Jayden done him for good.' He gave a short, sharp laugh. 'How fucken angry do you have to be to want that?'

Tanner rubbed his eyes, watched the water streaming down the windscreen. 'What do you want?'

'What's this phone worth to you, would you say?'

'It's worth nothing to me,' Tanner said, raising his voice against the deluge. 'Not a cent.'

Bitar smiled. 'To your client?'

'I don't know. I won't be finding out.'

'That prosecutor would like this phone, I bet. I could get immunity, couldn't I? If I had what would win the case? What do you think? If you were my lawyer?'

'I'd tell you to plead guilty, Mick.'

'And I'd get another lawyer. I want my two hundred grand, mate. And another fifty for the shit I took from you in court. I want it now.'

They glared at each other in the darkness of the car before Bitar started to smile. 'Cheer up, mate,' he said. 'Isn't everyone guilty?'

Bitar followed Tanner's car on the thirty-minute drive through the Harbour Tunnel to Taz Bennett's house at Balmoral Beach. He'd rung before he'd left, said he had to talk to Leonard urgently. It had to be face to face.

He rang the intercom at the side gate to the property when they arrived. The rain had now eased to a steady drizzle. 'Who is it?' Male voice, agitated, angry. Mr Bennett.

'My name's Tanner. I'm her to see Tina.'

'Not tonight. You can see her in the morning.'

'What?'

'I'm not having my house used for this. You can see her in your office in the morning.'

Tanner looked at Mick Bitar, pointed to the locked gate. 'I'm built for speed,' he said.

Bitar lifted a leg, kicked at the gate where the lock was. Pieces of mortar went flying. It was open.

Bennett was at the front door before they reached it. 'I'm calling the police,' he said.

Tanner wanted to laugh. He needed a big laugh. Bottle of red, big laugh. He wanted to smack Bennett in the face.

'Ever seen one of those cold case shows on TV, Mr Bennett? The cops are still looking for a body or a killer twenty years after some poor bastard disappeared? You can be the subject of one of those shows if you like. Or I can talk to my client. Now.'

Bennett didn't look like he had much more to say, or like he was really going to call the police, but his wife would have stopped him anyway.

'What the fuck are you doing?' She held the door open, looked at Tanner, then Bitar, then back to her husband. 'Go to bed,' she said, disgust in her voice.

Taz took them into the lounge room where he'd spoken to

Leonard only a few days before. She was standing when they walked in. Tanner watched her look at Bitar. There was the slightest shiver of her whole body, but no quake. If anything, her face hardened.

'Don't tell me anything, Tina,' Tanner said, his voice flat, dry. 'And don't tell me you had him fucking killed.'

She tilted her head back. Unrepentant. She said nothing.

Instead, Taz said, 'What's going on?'

Tanner turned, looked at her. She didn't know. 'Ask your sister,' he said. 'Not while I'm around.'

'You need to talk to Mick, Tina,' Tanner then said. 'I don't want to know what arrangements you make. I'll see you in court tomorrow.'

'What's going on?' Taz said more urgently, but Tanner was already walking out of the room, heading to the door, back out into the rain towards the busted gate. Back to his study.

54

A light was on in Dan's room when Tanner got home. He knocked, expected to find him on his laptop or phone, but it was the bedside light. He was reading a book. *Lord of the Flies.*

'They're still doing that at school?' Tanner said.

Dan nodded vaguely.

'Not a great endorsement for male leadership.'

'Who was that guy, Dad?'

'Old friend.'

'Dad?'

'Karl's girlfriend's ex. I'm worried for his life.'

'Who was it?' Firmer. Said with something close to a man's voice.

'Not a great human being,' he said. 'A witness in the trial I'm doing. No one we have to worry about. He had some information for me.'

Tanner took a deep breath, sat on the side of Dan's bed, put a hand on the doona where a leg was.

'Looked pretty scary. Seemed friendly enough.'

Tanner wanted to laugh, didn't. 'You sure you don't want to be a criminal lawyer?'

'What information?'

Tanner smiled. 'Legal professional privilege, Dan. We've discussed this.'

'Did she kill that guy?'

'What?' Tanner said, examining his son. 'No. Why would you say that?'

'The way you're looking.'

Tanner stood, reached out and ruffled the boy's hair. Not a gesture that was overly appreciated. 'I look tired, Dan. I'm just tired.'

Tanner took his court notebook from the study, went to the kitchen, opened a bottle of wine. He never drank during a case. Never. Golden rule. About to be broken.

He assumed Karl and Larry had gone to bed. He opened the wine, poured half the contents into a magnificently large glass.

'I thought you didn't –'

Tanner looked up and saw his father in the doorway to the kitchen–lounge area, T-shirt and boxer shorts on, starting his sentence with words, finishing by pointing to the glass.

'I don't.'

The older man nodded, shuffled to a cabinet, took out an identical glass, poured himself some wine.

'Do I look like I want to share?'

'Who was that man, Peter?' Karl said.

'I just told Dan. He's my wine merchant. Brought me this to try. Keen to impress.'

'Are you in some kind of trouble?'

'Not as much as my client.'

Karl nodded. Swirled his wine. Sniffed. Larry had given him oenophilia behind Tanner's back. 'Why is that?' Karl said when he was done.

'She's guilty.'

Karl appeared to contemplate this the way he contemplated the characteristics of the red. 'You know this how?'

'Trust me, Karl. I know.'

'This man told you?'

'Yes.'

'He's reliable? He looked – less than that.'

'He is much less and much more than reliable, Karl. If you wanted someone killed, though, he'd be extremely reliable. He's good at washing money too. And getting large quantities of prohibited drugs into the country.'

Karl put his wine glass down like he'd lost the taste for it. 'A man like that should not be allowed in your home, Peter. Never. You have a son. You –'

Karl Tanner couldn't finish the sentence, but his son could. 'I didn't let him in. And he's done less years in prison than you, Karl. A lot less.' It was a shitty thing to say. He regretted it straightaway.

His father looked at him. Passive. Unmoved.

'Forget I said that. I'm angry.'

Karl nodded. 'What are you angry about, Peter? Specifically.' His didn't talk much, but wasn't a generalist when he did. To the point. To the exact point. Specifically.

'I'm angry at me.'

'Because this woman lied to you?'

'Because –' Fuck, why was he angry? 'Because I thought she was telling the truth. I thought –' He shook his head. 'I don't know.'

A vague smile came over his father's face. 'You know you always tell me, Peter – and I ask you often, I know – you always tell me that doesn't matter. Fascinating to me. Horrifying, I would say. You say it doesn't matter if they're guilty or innocent. You always say you don't care.'

Tanner wanted to laugh, but nothing was funny. He took a long swig of wine instead. 'Maybe I was lying, Karl.'

He sat with his father in silence, sipping wine, thinking about that. Karl let you do that in conversations. Think upon things, didn't rush you. Most times he didn't care. This time . . .

'What will you do?' his father finally said.

'What I'm doing.'

'Defend her?'

'She's paying me, Karl.'

The old man looked carefully at him to see if he was serious. 'That's monstrous.'

Tanner let out a laugh of sorts. 'She hasn't told me herself.'

'But you said you know.'

'She hasn't told me.'

'It can't be right, Peter. It can't be.'

'Lawyers as police informants would not be right, Karl.'

His father shook his head, looked disgusted. 'What kind of system do they have for criminal trials in Sweden, Karl?' Tanner asked.

Karl pushed his glass away, stood. 'Get some sleep, Peter,' he said. 'I don't know how you can, but get some sleep.'

55

'How long have you been here?'

Jenny Singh took her seat in the court the next morning at nine forty-five. Kit Gallagher was behind her, dropping her folders on the desk she occupied. Tanner had been sitting in court for half an hour. Not physically alone – the tipstaff kept coming in and out, a court officer, the gallery quickly filled behind him – but alone in his thoughts.

'A while,' he said.

'Why?'

He smiled. 'Looking for my mojo.'

'Pete?'

'Thinking about the case, Jen. What else would I be thinking about?'

She opened a folder of documents, one eye on him. 'Are you going to tell me what about?'

He shook his head.

'Kit wants to speak to you.'

He heard Gallagher moving from behind her desk, smelt her perfume as she leant down towards his ear. 'We're calling Tina, right?' she whispered.

'Later, Kit.'

'She wants to know.'

'It depends on what she's going to say.'

'What?'

'Ask her what she's going to say.'

Gallagher leant closer now, her lips almost touching his lobe. 'What the hell does that mean, Pete?'

He heard movement behind them, saw Leonard walk in, take her seat in the box. She was in the navy suit today. She held his gaze when he looked at her. Whatever had happened between her and Bitar the night before, she was undaunted.

He'd defended the guilty before. Many times. They hadn't told him – if they did, the game was up – but he knew. Sometimes it was just the mad implausibility of their alibi. Other times, they stank of lies. There were cases the evidence was overwhelming. He'd still go through the motions of a defence. More than the motions. He always fought on if someone insisted 'it wasn't me', 'I didn't do it'.

This felt different.

To put a gap between the witnesses he needed to take a confrontational approach with, Tanner had decided to put Kate McDonald, the soil and water contamination expert, into the witness box before he called Phillip P Carter of SEBC. He wanted to toss another expert to the jury before he got back to conspiracies with the bank.

McDonald had done a peer review of the report of SBW by Lees and Martin that found the land was possibly highly contaminated, and the sediments of the proposed marina even more so. She then reviewed the subsequent Lovro report, and the earlier report prepared by Leonard when it bought the site. The Lees/Martin report was based on rudimentary and inadequate testing and sampling, so it was no surprise it was wrong. That might be something only a similarly qualified expert would pick up on, not a developer looking to buy the land. Particularly not a developer under the time pressure of the Limani Views tender. By the end of McDonald's evidence in chief, Tanner was confident the jury had to be convinced that every tenderer for the Limani Views site was left to bid for it on an incorrect assumption as to the clean-up cost of contamination. At the end of the trial his intent was to tell them it was every tenderer but Lovro.

Izzy Gallo didn't ask McDonald many questions. Her submission and case was that the evidence wasn't relevant – she didn't want to defeat that by spending an hour or more challenging the unchallengeable. She got a concession that there was no evidence the report was anything other than human error, and left it at that.

In the mid-morning break, when the gallery had departed to stretch legs, smoke, make phone calls, and the legal teams had run off to get coffees to go, Tanner found himself alone for a few minutes in the courtroom with Tina Leonard. During the trial she was surrendered to the custody of the court, and usually didn't leave the dock. She rarely moved while court was in session, sat up straight, a kind of nobleness in the way she defied each and every one of the circumstances of being a defendant in a murder trial. If they ever wrote a book on etiquette for accused killers, she should write the foreword.

'What are you looking at on your phone, Tina?' Tanner asked.

She looked up. 'Checking emails, Peter. Texts of support.'

'I hope you're not doing updates on Facebook?'

'No.'

'And leave the tweets to the journos.'

'I'm not on Twitter, Peter.'

'I wonder if Mick Bitar is?'

She said nothing.

He left the bar table, walked the few feet to the dock. 'Not an encrypted BlackBerry, Tina?'

She looked up at him. Teal eyeshadow, professional makeup, black hair down today, shoulder length, blue-black sheen. Cleopatra. Her handbag was on her lap. He wouldn't have been surprised if it had been full of asps. One with his name on it if he asked the wrong question.

'You know how most cases are won and lost?' he said. She glared. 'By themselves.'

She kept looking at him, tilted her head upwards just a fraction.

'Eighty per cent, I'd say. The solicitors put the evidence together, the truth is the truth, the law is the law, and the result turns out the way it was always going to turn out.'

'And the rest?'

'Fifteen per cent are lost by the incompetence of the lawyers.'

'And the rest won by good lawyers?'

'The rest,' Tanner said, 'are won by people like me.'

A vague smile. 'I'm relieved my counsel has faith in his own abilities. I'm looking forward to telling my story through you.'

'What story will that be?'

'You know it, Peter. The truth.'

'What will you say about Oliver Randall's death?'

'I've told you. The truth.'

'I feel like Oliver Randall,' he said.

She paused, narrowed her eyes. 'I have no idea what you mean.'

'I feel that I need to talk to God before I decide to call you.'

She smiled faintly. 'God isn't your client, Peter. I am.'

Tanner glared back at her, then nodded. 'When you give your evidence,' he said, 'I'm not going to be part of the five per cent. You're going to be on your own. Maybe I was ripe for the fooling. I'm sure you can fool the jury.'

She shook her head slowly. 'You have no idea, do you?'

'No idea of what? Of what Mick Bitar told me?'

'No.'

'Of what then?'

'Of what it's like to be me.'

Phillip P Carter swore his oath on the Bible too. Captains of capitalism. All Jesus' men.

After Ravic, Tanner only needed to reinforce a few points. If that went okay, he'd give Jack Rodriguez a pass. Nearly everything about the trial had gone to plan – if only it hadn't been interrupted by finding out his client was the killer.

Carter was sixty-six years old. Originally from Texas, he'd worked for a bank in LA, it got bought by a competitor, then by a bank from San Francisco. That bank ended up being part of what became SEBC. He moved to Asia for a while, Bangkok, Hong Kong, finally Sydney. Tanner had him chart the rise of SEBC from boutique investment bank with a floor on an old building in Sydney's 'Rocks' area, to spreading its wings in Asia and moving into commercial and retail banking, with a focus on larger scale construction projects. After the turn of the millennium, he was made CEO of the Australasian division, made Sydney his home. Stood down two years ago for Rodriguez, was now chairman of the board.

'You're not carrying a gun, are you, Mr Carter?'

'I'm sorry?' Most of the Texan had fused with Australian.

'A gun? You're from Houston. You're not carrying, are you? We don't like that here.'

'Mr Tanner,' Justice Francis said, loudly.

'Just checking, your Honour. Mr Randall was shot with a Smith & Wesson. You never know. How much did you lose on the Limani Views sale, Mr Carter? How much did your bank lose?'

Carter looked at the judge to see if she was done with Tanner. She wasn't, but she was holding it inside. 'A great deal. It hasn't been finally quantified yet.'

Tanner smiled. 'A great deal? Unquantified? Have a go, Mr Carter. Ballpark.'

'There are a lot of internal costs in management and staff time when you –'

'Ah, I see. I meant –'

'Let him finish,' Gallo said.

'I asked for a ballpark figure, not a nine-innings story, your Honour. What did you lose on paper, Mr Carter? On your books?

In the financial records and statements of the bank? What's the figure?'

'Limited to that? Nothing.'

'Nothing? That's funny. Leonard Developments owed your bank nearly two hundred and thirty million when you called in its loans, didn't it?'

'I'd have to check.'

'Take my word for it?'

Carter leant back in the witness chair, a kind of smirk on his face. He angled his head to emphasise the fat in his neck. He liked golf, had the heads of dead animals mounted on the walls in a room of his house. 'I wouldn't ordinarily be inclined to do that, sir,' he said.

'What does that mean, Mr Carter?'

'Well – I'm not sure of your reliability.'

'Meaning?'

'What you're doing in this case, sir.'

'What am I doing?'

'Who knows.'

'You just said, "what you're doing in this case". I'm asking, for the sake of the jury's understanding: what do you mean?'

'I think it would be quicker if you just accepted the assumptions Mr Tanner puts to you, Mr Carter, and he'll have to make them good later.'

'Yes, your Honour.'

Gallo would have interviewed Carter once he'd subpoenaed him, Tanner guessed. *Don't argue with him* would have been her advice.

'Most of the money owing was for Limani Views, correct?'

'Yes.'

'And you sold it for a mere hundred million?'

'I don't agree with "mere". That was the winning tender.'

'And so you should have made a big loss. What happened?'

'I think you know the answer to that. You've already raised the terms of our deal with Nipori when we bought out their business here.'

'You've been following this trial closely, have you, Mr Carter?'
'You've been defaming a lot of people.'
'Have you been sitting in the gallery?'
'Of course not.'
'Have you had a lawyer sitting in the gallery?'
Momentary hesitation. 'That was the advice I got.'
'Is that lawyer in court now?'
He looked up at the gallery. 'Yes.'
'Man or woman?'
'Man.'
'Could be your first mistake. Point them out, Mr Carter.'
'What?'
'Point your lawyer out.'
'Why is that necessary, Mr Tanner?' Justice Francis asked.
'Your lawyer, Mr Carter. What kind are they?'
'What kind?'
'What area do they practice in?'
'Litigation.'
'Crime?'
'Dispute resolution.'
'So not crime?'
'I don't know about crime specifically.'

'You shouldn't bring a knife to a gun fight, Mr Carter. So selling Limani Views at a loss, other than for the time employees spent on the matter, resulted in no loss in the end, because you got the money back from Nipori's liquidators, correct?'

'That was the deal. Not unheard of when buying distressed loan assets.'

'The other bidders in the tender your bank conducted for the Limani Views site – were they customers of your bank?'

'I don't know.'

'Can you assume we've checked and they weren't? Can you make that assumption?'

'Okay, sure. I wish they were.'

'I bet they do too, Mr Carter. Then one of them might've gotten the deal of the century by buying my client's land in a tricked-up fire sale.'

'I object.'

'Withdrawn. But Lovro was a long-standing client of SEBC?'

'Yes.'

'And you've provided finance to them on some big projects. Resorts and casinos in India for example?'

'Yes.'

'Did you personally employ Brian Crawford, Mr Carter?'

'Of course not.'

'You know who he is, though?'

'Yes.'

'And you knew who Oliver Randall was? One of your senior executives? On the Limani Views–Leonard Developments account?'

'Yes.'

'And Brian Crawford arrested him when he found six kilos of cocaine in Mr Randall's study?'

'I'm aware Mr Randall pleaded guilty to drug offences. I had no idea who arrested him.'

'Was the cocaine for the entire executive team of your bank, Mr Carter, or did more junior staff get a look in?'

'Mr Tanner.'

'I press the question.'

'You don't have to answer, Mr Carter. That's enough, Mr Tanner.'

'Mr Crawford was then employed by you in some security position in your bank, right?'

'Yes.'

'To weed out more coke dealers? What skills did he have?'

'I object.'

'I press the question, your Honour. I want to know how and why Mr Crawford ended up at SEBC.'

'Can you answer, Mr Carter?'

'I'm sorry, your Honour,' Carter said. 'Employing people at that level – I was the CEO. I'm aware Mr Crawford is an employee. I know him. He's the head of one section of the bank's Security Division. I had no role in employing him. I met him first after he started work for us.'

'What salary is Mr Crawford on, Mr Carter?'

'I don't have those details.'

'Does seven hundred thousand a year sound about right? That was his evidence.'

'Then why ask me, if you know?'

Tanner smiled. 'Would you like to take over from me, Mr Carter? How would you go, trying to prove my client's innocence?'

'I don't know that she is innocent, Mr Tanner.'

'Oh, she is, Mr Carter. Innocent until proven otherwise. It's almost the same system in Texas, isn't it?'

'Ask a question, Mr Tanner.'

'Are Mr Crawford's employment and salary a reward, Mr Carter, for services rendered regarding Oliver Randall?'

'That's absurd.'

'Let's leave the employment of the Crawford and Sons Inc. to one side as an unknown mystery. Why do you think Oliver Randall told my client that your bank and Lovro Constructions entered into a conspiracy to steal her land?'

'I don't know that he did.'

'Assume he did. Why would he do that, do you think?'

'I don't know, Mr Tanner. Maybe he believed it. It wasn't true, but maybe he went – I don't know what happened to Oliver. A breakdown through drugs? Maybe he went crazy.'

'That's almost exactly what Mr Ravic said. It really is a small world. You know what I think? I think he was telling the truth.'

'I know he wasn't.'

'What's your experience with crazy people, Mr Carter?'

'I beg your pardon?'

'Mr Randall. You said maybe he went crazy. What do you know about mental illness?'

'It's – I meant it as a figure of speech.'

'Was he crazy when you employed him?'

'No.'

'When you made him a senior executive?'

'Of course not.'

'When he gave evidence against my client in the case your bank brought against her and her company for payment of its debts. Was he crazy then?'

'No.'

'When did he become crazy?'

'I explained, it was a figure of speech. If he told your client that – if – then that's crazy. Loans went into default. We took possession of an asset and sold it in a tender. It was a perfectly conventional repossession and sale of a security asset. We then sued for the balance owing on our debt. It was all standard.'

'Standard? Land with a DA on it that makes it worth over five hundred million in the end is sold for a hundred million. That's standard?'

'I don't control the property market or the economy, Mr Tanner.'

'What kind of banker are you, then?'

'Don't answer that, Mr Carter.'

'When did you tell Oliver Randall to make sure Luka Ravic got my client's land, Mr Carter?'

'That didn't happen.'

'When did you and Mr Ravic first decide to defraud my client? At the golf club? At the yacht club?'

'That's the most insulting thing that's ever been said to me.'

'What Mr Randall's told my client is the truth, isn't it, Mr Carter?'

'It is not.'

'Because you're partly right, aren't you? It's either the truth, or he was one of the craziest men on earth, Mr Carter.'

'None of this is remotely true.'

'And someone decided to shoot him in the knees and the head. What's more likely, Mr Carter? He was telling the truth about you and Ravic, or he was just crazy?'

56

You didn't see someone like Tina Leonard charged with murder every day.

She wore a navy suit, cream shirt underneath, buttoned all the way up. A modest strand of white pearls sat below her collar. Hair back, but she had half a fringe today to soften the look. Athina Ireni Ioannidis. Third child of Achilles 'Al' Ioannidis and Fotini Ioannidis. Two big brothers, Theo and Gianni – 'Little Jimmy, we called him,' Leonard said. 'He's six foot four.' Living with younger sister, Anastasia, who had come to her rescue.

'My father started with nothing,' Leonard told the jury. 'Not even tools. He borrowed my uncle's.'

No bank would lend Achilles money at first. He never forgot that. He was called a wog. He never forgot that either. The day came when the big banks clamoured for his business. By then Ioannidis Builders had become Ioannidis & Sons, and had made its name. Residential and retail building projects. Commercial office buildings. 'Nothing overly big when Dad was running things,' she said. 'He was careful with debt.' Now her brothers planned to build sky-scrapers.

She did well at school. Excelled in everything, whereas her brothers had – well, academics weren't their thing, though they were smart enough. No Ioannidis had been to university before, to her father's knowledge. She loved design, great buildings, had an interest in urban planning. She did architecture, then commerce after she started in the family business. Her brothers didn't want her there. 'They thought I was spoilt, a princess.' She did an MBA while working for her father. He thought she was mad.

When her father went to the backseat of the firm, Leonard wanted an equal share with her brothers and Taz. And 'Ioannidis Constructions' sounded better than '& Sons'. Her father was lukewarm about it. Her mother said nothing. Her brothers said over their dead bodies. She told them all to go to hell.

'It was very tough at first,' Leonard responded when Tanner asked her how things were when she went out on her own. 'I'd just started a family, hadn't been married long, and – yeah, my father had been my financial and emotional rock all my life. Suddenly it was gone.'

She grew the business by acting as architect/builder first. People liked her work. She had style, she was quick, she didn't overcharge, projects came in on time and on budget. She was always ambitious, but became bolder. Nipori Bank, who'd been the banker for the family business, got behind her. She moved into bigger projects. Blocks of apartments. Seniors living. A council library. High-density residential. Tourist resorts on the east coast. The projects got bigger and bigger. Then she mortgaged the lot on Limani Views.

Limani hadn't been a one-off purchase. Her father had bought land in the area for years, she told the jury. He'd had some grand plan, but had gotten side-tracked with other projects. Even though they'd stopped talking when she left the family firm, he agreed to sell to her. Perhaps he felt guilty. Maybe one day he'd want her back. She'd kept buying land in the area over a number of years. An old warehouse site came up and she extended herself for that. She bought individual houses, old blocks of flats. Soon she had enough sites dotted around the area to get someone to prepare a masterplan. She bought people out; paid over the odds. When the price of property kept going up, her purchases looked wise.

Consumed with work, building a business, hoping to build something like an empire, her marriage fell apart.

When the GFC hit, it was a sudden jolt. For a while, everyone thought the world was ending. Nipori crashed and burned. Oliver Randall and SEBC came into her life.

He was a supporter at first. He got to know her projects; a huge enthusiast for Limani Views. He could see the potential. Her loan-to-asset ratio started to tighten, but he told her not to panic. They were short on a couple of monthly loan repayments. He said he'd restructure the loans. The worst of the GFC had bypassed the country, things had stabilised. People were keeping their heads, including the powers that be in his bank.

Leonard and her team met with Randall to sort out new loan terms, and enter into a heads of agreement: a twenty-four-month extension of the loans to get most of the construction done. Forgiveness for the few short payments. Her CFO and husband were at the meeting. Within two weeks SEBC had called in her debts, and she had notices of demand for over two hundred and thirty million. When her Limani site was taken from her and sold at tender, it went for a fraction of what it was worth then, a tiny percentage of what it was worth now.

'My CFO disappeared before the trial. You found out where he was working for me. For Lovro. I thought I'd feel shocked,' Leonard said, 'but it made complete sense.'

Her husband was allowed to keep his share of the sale of their matrimonial home by SEBC. She thought he'd been bribed. 'At least my kids had that money,' she said. 'At least he could put a roof over their heads. I couldn't. The Family Court —' She didn't let herself collapse into a fit of tears when she talked about not being able to house her kids. She was silent for a long time, held the tears, held the anger and grief back. That made it more powerful.

She lost the case. She should have won. Randall lied; the bank lied – she was up against something too big to defeat. She was bankrupt, separated, homeless. Stayed with friends. Stayed with her sister from time to time. Gradually dragged herself back to her feet. Got a job in the office of a friend who was an architect. Then she got a letter from Oliver Randall.

She knew he'd been sent to jail. 'I didn't know what to feel when I read about that,' she told Tanner when he asked. 'I – I don't know, whatever happened to him. It didn't get my company back. Or my land. Or the fact that I couldn't provide a home for my children. I'd – I was angry with him at the trial. More than angry. But five years in prison? I – I honestly felt some pity for him. And his family. I knew he had a young daughter. I felt so sorry for her.'

They discussed the letter. The apology for 'wrongs', for the 'lies' he'd told her.

'What were those wrongs, Tina?' Tanner asked when she'd told the jury she agreed to meet Randall for coffee when he was released.

'He told me that he was told to forget about any agreement he'd reached to rearrange my company's loan terms. Then he was told to lie about it.'

'Who by?'

'His superiors.'

'Who were they?'

'His immediate divisional boss was a man called Jack Rodriguez, who's now CEO, but he told me he was personally spoken to by Phil Carter, the then CEO.'

'And what did he say Mr Carter told him to do?'

'Issue me with letters of demand, and serve a winding-up notice on my company. Sue me for possession of all the land the company owned, and all the other security we'd given them, including my family home.'

'And that happened pretty quickly?'

'Barely a week after we'd reached an agreement with Randall.'

'You were technically in default of your loans. I know Ms Gallo for the Crown will put that to you.'

'We reached a deal. My CFO had restructured everything. We would have been fine. I would have paid back those loans. The economy was heading upwards – the GFC was well behind us by then, it was a blip on the radar for property here – especially prime land like the Limani site. It's a dress circle location and they sold it for nothing. To their best client – Lovro.'

Tanner took her through her contamination reports and subsequently Lovro's, and the report SEBC put out before the tender.

'Oliver told me it was a fraud. He wasn't allowed to be involved in the tender. He just had to lie in court. Then they got him.'

'Got him?'

She explained how Randall told her he'd been greedy. He'd lied for the bank, their client had the land, everyone was a big winner but Leonard. Randall got a huge bonus, but wanted more.

'His guess was that they saw him as a liability. He told me Phil Carter told him to pull his head in when he asked for an even bigger bonus. He thought they must have become worried about his drug problem. He said some loose things when high about how much he was worth to them and Lovro over what he'd done to me. He implied it was well worth their while to keep him happy.

'Oliver told me he'd said something really stupid to Carter and Rodriguez,' she said. 'He told me he said to them something like, "I know where the bodies are buried", or some other cliché like that. Next thing he has six kilos of cocaine found in his study he swears wasn't his. He told me he never had anything like that quantity.'

'So he thought the bank and Lovro did what?'

'He told me they got a bent cop to plant the drugs and set him up. Then they had someone tell him that he was putting his family at risk. He pleaded guilty because he was scared for them – his daughter especially.'

The whole time he was asking Leonard questions, Tanner made several glances at the jurors. Not many took notes. They were listening intently.

'Did you ask him to help you? To expose Lovro and SEBC?'

She nodded. 'I did.'

'And?'

'He was still afraid. These people – he thought – well, he ended up dead, didn't he? I was sure he was going to help. I know he was talking to other people. They must have got wind.'

Gallo objected again at that point. She had done each time Leonard had engaged in speculation. The judge noted it, told the jury to treat it as just that, pay it no more regard than guesswork by the accused, not evidence. 'They must have got wind' she struck from the record, but the jury had heard it.

'Do you know Mick Bitar, Tina?' Tanner asked.

She took him through meeting Bitar when they were both very young. Whatever use Ioannidis & Sons put him to, she didn't know for sure. She knew he had a reputation, though, and a record.

'Did you try to hire him to kill Oliver Randall, Tina?'

'No.'

'You weren't full of rage towards Randall? This man destroyed your business, your family. You didn't want to kill him?'

'If you'd asked me at the time of my trial, Mr Tanner, I may have used that term. I would never be able to forgive him. Not even now. He betrayed me. There's no other word I have for it. He –' She took a deep breath, more like she was trying to remember something than compose herself. 'He was so enthusiastic about my company when SEBC took over our loans. He was so – he seemed so behind Limani, what I wanted to do.' She paused, shook her head. 'Yes, I was angry. More than angry. Oliver, his bank – they – it wasn't just his lies. They abandoned my company. They didn't have to do that. It was one rough patch, and we could have ridden it out. I did hate him for that, for a while. I admit it. But I don't have people killed.'

'What about the fifty thousand dollars you gave Jayden Webb? You admit that, don't you?'

'Yes. That money was for Mick. He sent Webb to collect it.'

'For Mick?'

'My brothers wouldn't talk to me. I had a right to be involved in that business – the family business. I wanted back in. I knew they were well acquainted. I spoke to Mick at that restaurant.

He said he would talk to them, set up a meeting. Fifty thousand cash was his fee.'

'Fifty thousand just to set up a meeting? Really? Mr Bitar should be in banking.'

'Do you know Mick, Mr Tanner?'

Tanner smiled. Inside he could barely believe her front. Of all that she'd said so far, what was true, what wasn't, he didn't know. The big part was a lie, he knew that. The rest was background. 'I know him now, Tina, better than I would like,' he said.

'He told me he thought he could talk my brothers around to allowing me back into the family business. At the time they wouldn't even talk to me because of the fight we'd had over my father's estate. It's a lot of money for a meeting, but it didn't seem to me that I had much choice.'

'Last one, Tina. Is Oliver Randall dead because of you?'

She glared at him for what felt like a long time, close to too long, but then said, looking at the jury, 'He's dead because he lied. He's dead because he told me he lied. He's dead because some people couldn't afford to let him speak the truth.'

Izzy Gallo SC went through her cross-examination in the manner of a professional advocate of the Crown. She put to Tina Leonard everything she had to. She started with the pain that Leonard must have suffered when she lost her business, her project, her family, because of Oliver Randall. Revenge was the case theory, but that now ran counter to some of the evidence that Tanner had called. The businessmen who had given evidence – Ravic, Carter – had said that Leonard was the liar. That she'd made up Randall's agreement to extend her loans and not foreclose on her. The prosecution case – at least in part – was that Leonard may have felt betrayed by a man who had promised her one thing, then stabbed her in the back.

Gallo put questions to Leonard about the fifty thousand dollars she admitted to giving Jayden Webb. She asked her all about Mick Bitar. She put to Tina Leonard every possible reason she might have had for wanting to have Oliver Randall killed. And halfway through, Tanner looked at Gallo, and wondered if she believed it any more. Did she still believe Tina Leonard was guilty?

He was no longer sure.

Maybe Tina Leonard had her fooled too.

57

When the others had gone to bed, Tanner moved to the table in the dining area off the kitchen to finish his closing address. It was bigger than his desk in the study, and he had more room to cover it with notes and the documents he'd need. Just after eleven thirty he heard a door open, footsteps in the hallway. Dan walked into the kitchen.

'What are you doing?'

'I'm hungry.'

'It's pretty late to be up now on a school night.'

The boy ignored him, loaded the toaster with bread, grabbed the peanut butter and honey from a cupboard, took the milk out of the fridge.

'What day is it?' he asked.

'Wednesday.'

'I meant the date.'

'How can you not know that? May seventeenth.'

Dan examined the milk bottle, poured a long glass, downed most of it in one hit. He kept one eye on Tanner the whole time. 'You going to win?' he asked when he'd put the glass down.

'Never sure,' Tanner said. 'Not with a jury.'

'Should you?'

Tanner put his pen down, rubbed at his eyes. Should he? 'I haven't worked that out yet.'

Dan looked confused. 'Did she kill him, or not?'

From one perspective, really the only question that mattered. 'I'm not talking about that.'

'What do you think?'

'I said I'm not talking about that. I'm not even thinking about that.'

'What are you thinking about?'

He smiled. 'What you asked me.'

'What was that again?'

'Whether we should win.'

***

'Whenever I have a legal argument, members of the jury,' Tanner began his closing address, 'I want to go first. I've never been much of a fan of listening to other lawyers talk. That's one of the things I find hardest about being a defence barrister – when the evidence is done, I'm always stuck over this side of the courtroom, the furthest away from you, listening to a prosecutor ask you to convict my client. And, I have to say, it's been worse than usual in this case.'

Tanner paused, took a sip of water he didn't need to pace himself. He had no intention of taking long. If they were anywhere near siding with him, the shorter the better. He wanted to swat the prosecution case away, then leave the room.

'Worse, because I'm confused. I don't want to invite my friend to go again, but what exactly is the reason she says my client had for having Oliver Randall killed? It's like she wants a piece of three different cakes. Was Tina Leonard full of hate for Oliver Randall because he just happened to be the banker who called in her company's loans? Was that it? Nearly six years of rage built up over that? Or is there more? Is she angry because she lost her case, and he didn't lie to save her? Is that why all these years later she paid someone to shoot him? Or is the prosecution case theory that Oliver Randall really did lie for SEBC, and that's what made my client mad enough to have him killed? Ms Crown says it's the first slice, but she doesn't mind if you prefer the other two. She says she doesn't have to prove exactly why Tina had Oliver Randall killed. Whatever her precise motive was, it doesn't matter – she still hired Webb to kill him.

'Well, what do you think about that? Don't you think the person asking you to convict should tell you?'

He paused again, turned a page of notes he knew by heart, looked back at the jurors. 'Small world. Remember when Mr Ravic said that? It's a small world. And he's right, isn't he? You already know that. Small groups of people in this world seem to have all the power. A small group has most of the money. They like to keep that world small, don't they? You know about wealthy people, don't you, members of the jury? You know about big companies. And I know you know about banks.' Tanner looked at the jurors, nodded slowly.

'Do corporations, rich men, banks – do they ever lie? Do they ever cheat? What do you think? Do they manipulate the truth, twist the facts? Has that ever happened?

'You know, you don't have to find my client Tina Leonard innocent. That's not our test, that's not her burden. If there's reasonable doubt, you acquit, you find her not guilty. But you know what? I wouldn't blame you if you came back from your deliberations – after you've applied your common sense, what you know about this small world, after you've examined the evidence – and just said one word: innocent. That's our finding. Innocent.

'That was my thinking, members of the jury, not long after I took over this case. It's not only about acquittal – it's about innocence.

'So, why do I think that?

'The prosecutor might say it's because I'm a conspiracy theorist. That's what she called me in her address. Really? In this small world?

'She asked you to only look at the facts that have been proved. Okay, let's do that.

'Lovro Constructions bought my client's land for a pittance – I could take you back to the numbers, the valuation evidence, but I know you know that well enough. No one is denying it. They got the deal of the century. That's a fact.

'Lovro's long-standing banker, SEBC, which funds its casino construction in India, sold the land to it. That's a fact.

'SEBC said the land was polluted before the tender. That was wrong. People want to explain why, but no one suggests it wasn't hopelessly wrong. That's a fact.

'SEBC made no loss on the sale of my client's land. Lovro made a huge profit. A profit that's already stretched to hundreds of millions of dollars. It's a small world when you get to those numbers, isn't it, members of the jury? That's another fact.

'Brian Crawford, who arrested Oliver Randall for drug trafficking, now works at SEBC – the bank where Mr Randall used to work. Small world again.

'Mr Crawford's son works at Lovro Resorts. What a small world.

'Oliver Randall, before he was released from prison, wrote to my client apologising for things he'd done. You have that letter. He wrote to his ex-wife and daughter, apologising for what he described as his sins. You have those letters.

'My client's CFO swore an affidavit saying Mr Randall had agreed to restructure and extend the loans it had granted to Leonard Developments. He disappeared before the civil trial. He now works for a company owned by Lovro Constructions in Dubai. Small world, isn't it?

'My client's ex-husband swore an affidavit to help her and the company in the case against the bank. Then they let him keep nearly five million dollars from the sale of the matrimonial home. And guess what he does? After that, he sides with the bank. What a surprise.

'Mr Ravic and Mr Carter and their friends sit around in golf clubs and yacht clubs. No surprise there, though, we know it's a small world for rich people.

'They said they didn't talk about my client's land when it was put out to tender? Really? What was the term Tina Leonard used to describe this site? Dress circle? Nice spot, don't you think, right on the water there? And they never discussed it once? Sydney Harbour is one of the great harbours of the world. And they don't discuss this site that's up for grabs? Not one word? Not one? Do you believe that? Or does that sound too incredible to believe?

'The prosecution case is built on two witnesses. A drug addict with a criminal record, and a professional thug. What do you think about people like Jayden Webb and Mick Bitar? Would you make a habit of believing what they were telling you?

'Think about Jayden Webb, members of the jury. Picture him in your mind. Think about Mick Bitar. Think about those photos I showed you from Facebook. "Fuck the pigs." Think about his choice of friends. Murderers. Convicted rapists. Think about that photo of him with Luka Ravic. What a small world.

'Then think about Tina Leonard. Not one criminal offence to her name. Think about Webb, think about Bitar, think about Mr Phillip P Carter, think about Mr Ravic in his golf club or on his yacht. Then think about Tina Leonard. Think about what she told you Oliver Randall confessed to her. Did it sound like she was she lying?

'Members of the jury, when the bankers and the property developers get together to talk, what do you think they talk about? Do you think it might be about money? Follow the money – you've heard that term? Ask yourself – who made the money here? The prosecutor mentioned what Tina had lost, over and over again. Let's turn the tables on that. Let's think about closer to Mr Randall's murder. Who had the most money to lose then? And what do you think they start to talk about when they hear Oliver Randall's on parole, and he's out telling the truth?

'This trial involves a very small world, members of the jury.

'Oliver Randall was shot in each knee, then in the head. Look at my client. Do you think she ordered that?

'Reasonable doubt. Can you feel it? Do you have *any* doubt?

'Doubt means you acquit. You stop there, and you acquit.

'But do you have any doubt Tina Leonard is not guilty?

'Do you have any doubt who had Oliver Randall killed? Do I have to name them?

'I don't think I have to. Because, like we all know, it's a small world, and a very small town.'

58

The judge summed up for an hour and forty-five minutes. It was a faultless display of lack of apparent bias. A careful summary of all the evidence, an unemotional analysis of the examinations of Ravic, Carter and Crawford. Of what was proven, and what was merely alleged. A reminder of the evidence of Bitar and Webb, which the jury might find to be 'more important, in the end'. A summing up that leant towards conviction, but not quite so brazenly that Tanner had grounds for immediate complaint. After all, if Webb and Bitar were telling the truth, Tina Leonard had ordered the killing of Oliver Randall. And, after all, that's exactly what she had done.

It took the jury slightly more than an hour to ask their first questions.

The judge read out the note the foreperson had sent to her through the court officer: '1. *Do we have to follow the findings made by the judge in SEBC v Leonard Developments? 2. What weight do we put on those findings if we don't have to accept them?*'

There was a short legal argument about question one, more about the wording of the answer. Whatever the jury were stuck with, they weren't stuck with the findings of Justice Kerr when it came to the murder trial of Tina Leonard.

The answer to the second question proved more controversial. Tanner wanted no weight put on it. Gallo wanted some.

The judge opted for telling the jury once more that they had to decide this case on their own views of the evidence they had heard, not the findings made by a judge nearly six years before.

By six pm no verdict had been reached, and the judge sent the jurors home.

That night, Tanner took Karl, Dan and Larry out for pizza at a restaurant in Bronte, and had a couple of glasses of wine. His work for Tina Leonard was almost done. He doubted there would be any more questions from the jury to deal with. Either his client was going to walk free, or he'd have to go through the motions of a hopeless bail application, pending a possible, perhaps equally hopeless appeal.

Before dinner, he'd convinced his father it was time for him to return to his own home. Whatever danger there'd been he downplayed, told Karl it had now passed. When the meal was over, Karl and Larry went back to Tanner's house, collected their things, and headed back to Karl's flat in a cab.

Tanner had another glass of wine at home, sitting on the couch, dog next to him. He watched some television for the first time in more than a month, flicked off the late-night news when it commenced a report on the trial of Tina Leonard. Win or lose, he felt over it. Before he found anything worth watching, his phone rang.

'Not too late, is it?'

'I'm awake, if that's what you mean. How are you, Rachel?'

'Wondering what will happen tomorrow.'

'Your guess is as good as mine.'

'I doubt that. What's your feeling? You must have developed a sense of when you're going to win or not by this stage of your career.'

'Winning or losing aren't the benchmarks I'd set for this case. And I'm strangely absent feeling at the moment.'

'Why is that?'

'Exhaustion, probably. A depletion of adrenaline.'

There was a slight pause, before she said, 'you sound – you sound very flat. Are you okay?'

'I told you. I'm tired. And I'm on my third glass of wine. It has an exaggerated effect on me when combined with fatigue, and when I use a five hundred mil glass.'

'Do you usually drink during trials?'

'I'm off the clock. The jury's working now, not me.'

'Pete – is there something you can tell me? Something I don't know.'

He laughed. 'Tell you as a journalist, Rachel, or as a friend?'

There was a long pause, then Roth said, 'You choose.'

'There's – there's nothing I can tell you now. Let me – let's wait until this is all done. It's not fair to ask me questions unless my blood alcohol is under point 05.'

'Okay,' she said. 'You were just on the television, by the way. The late news. It's why I –'

'Where are you?'

'Where? Home.'

'Watching TV on your couch?'

'Yes.'

'Is your dog next to you?'

'Why are you asking me that?'

'Just wondering. Is your dog next to you?'

'On the floor. Asleep.'

'Do you think of me when you see your dog?'

She laughed. 'What kind of question is that?'

'I don't know,' he said. 'My forensic skills are impaired for the moment. I was just wondering.'

'Well – sometimes I remember you gave her to me. I can't forget how strange that was.'

'Sounds like we're friends.'

There was another long pause, before Roth said, 'Did Tina have him killed, Peter? Is that what you think? Is that why – is that why you sound like you do?'

This time he hesitated. 'I just told a jury she didn't do it, Rachel,' he eventually said. 'So that must be the truth, mustn't it?'

At five pm the following day, the foreperson had told the judge that a unanimous verdict appeared unlikely. They were told to keep trying, but sent home again an hour later.

At two pm the following day the foreperson told the judge that a unanimous verdict was not going to happen, but a majority verdict — allowed in the state for crime at eleven to one — was a distinct possibility. Tanner didn't like the sound of that. He felt he either had them all, or it was going to go the other way. The judge told the jury they could reach a majority verdict.

When the jury retired again, Tanner sent Kit Gallagher and Jenny Singh back to chambers to work on submissions for bail pending appeal if the verdict went against them. There was no hope for that following a conviction for murder, but they'd have to put on a show.

When he walked into the defence room to wait, Tina Leonard was already there, her sister Taz next to her. There was a third person too, whom he hadn't seen before. Dark hair, dark eyes, lanky and thin. So good looking he was pretty.

Leonard looked at Tanner. 'Peter, this is my son Alex,' she said.

Alex stood and shook Tanner's hand. Alexander the Great. Perhaps a foot and a half taller. The young man had shed a tear or two before Tanner had walked in. Strands from his long dark lashes were clumped together. For Leonard and Taz, there was no disguising recent tears. Smudged mascara, red eyes, tissues piled on the table.

'I told him not to come here,' Leonard said, trying to laugh, nerves and pain in her voice.

Tanner took a seat. Alex was looking at him. A kind of pleading look, wanting to know things will be okay.

'What do you think will happen?' Alex asked.

'I think there's going to be a verdict,' Tanner said.

'I've worked that out.'

'Then you're as up to speed as me. I don't know, Alex. You almost never do. It's a jury. They're – you never really know.'

'It's been three days. Does that mean something? Is that a good sign, or – ?'

'It means one or two jurors are against us, or are for us. It's taken time for that to fall out. There's no other way of knowing until we hear from them.'

'If they'd been quick, would it have been better?'

Tanner shrugged. 'There's a few things for them to think about, and the stakes are pretty high. They were never going to be quick.'

'Why can't they see my mother's been set up?' Alex Leonard said. 'It's – why can't they see?'

'Maybe they will.'

'What happens if they say guilty. I mean, straight after, what will happen?'

'Alex,' Leonard said, 'please don't –'

'We'll apply for bail again,' Tanner said, 'pending an appeal.'

'And will – ?'

'Let's see what happens first,' Tanner said.

Alex Leonard didn't look satisfied with that answer.

'Sorry, Alex. Superstition of mine. Is it okay if we don't discuss bail or an appeal? I don't ever do that with a jury out. It's – let's stay positive.'

Alex Leonard still didn't look satisfied, and Tanner could see something more was quivering inside him. He wanted to shut it down. 'Look, I need to talk to Tina about something,' he said. 'Alex, could you take your aunt out for a moment? Just five minutes, please?'

Alex took in a deep breath, nearly said something, let it go. He and Taz left the room.

'Good-looking boy,' Tanner said.

Tina Leonard smiled for a second, nodded.

'Looks like you.'

'He's got his father's face,' she said. 'A bigger heart.' Leonard blew her nose on a tissue, blew away her tears, shook herself back.

'Have you slept the last few nights?' he asked.

She nodded. 'Taz has plenty of pills.'

'Don't get any ideas, Tina. Make sure you resist feeding them to her husband.'

They sat and looked at each other for a moment, the game almost played out, when Leonard said, 'Your son. Does he look like you?'

'Some people think so,' he said. 'I can only see his mother.'

'How old is he again?'

'Nearly fifteen.'

'Is he like you?' Her voice was soft, but deep. She was calm again. No sadness, no remorse.

'What am I like, Tina?'

She almost smiled, raised one of those black eyebrows. 'You don't know?'

'My life's a slow journey of self-discovery. So is my career.'

This time she did smile, as though he were an old friend. 'You're a type of warrior. You were what I needed.'

He glared at her for a few moments. The smile faded. Eyes black as coal.

'Tell me that Oliver Randall at least lied in that trial. You told the truth about that, right?'

She nodded. 'That was true. He lied. He told me what they did to me – Ravic, the bank. All of that was true. Does that make you feel better?'

'What makes you think I want to feel better?'

'You don't look happy.'

'I'm waiting on a verdict. There's nothing to be happy about.'

'Will you be? If I win?'

'I can't be a hundred per cent certain yet, Tina,' he said. 'But I'm not expecting to be.'

'If we lose? That will make you pleased?'

He shook his head. 'It's a lose–lose kind of case.'

She said nothing.

'Did you love him?' Tanner asked. 'Did you love Oliver, Tina?'

She ran her hand slowly through her hair, like she was trying to remember. 'Do you share your successes with someone?' she said.

'My successes?'

'When you win a case?'

He shrugged. 'Not all my successes are worth sharing. Neither are the losses. I'm very philosophical.'

'Did you share them with your wife?'

'I don't want to discuss that with you, Tina. No offence.'

She smiled. 'My brothers never liked me, Peter. And when my business took off – well. More than didn't like. My father was just confused, I think. He didn't understand why I'd want something of my own. Something I built. And my husband – he was in our marriage for himself.'

'What does that have to do with Oliver Randall?'

'Oliver was different. I thought he wanted to make my company as big and as great as I did. I needed him. Do you know what it's like? There wasn't a single person I had to share what I was doing with. The ups and downs. The struggle. The whole thing. Do you know how lonely that made me feel? Oliver was on my side.'

'So there are good bank managers?'

'Do you really want to talk about this, Peter?'

'This ended with you having him killed. That's quite a journey. I've played my role. I'd like to know exactly what I've done.'

'You need me to make you feel better? We might still lose, Peter. Then you don't have to be bothered.'

'I'll be bothered. I'm invested. I got invested when I thought you were innocent. It's hard to shake off.'

'Shall I tell you how much he deserved it?'

'You're not going to be able to do that,' he said.

She got up from her seat, walked to the corner of the room. 'Oliver saw the figures,' she said to the world, not to him. 'He knew we could ride things out. In the long term we were going to be fine. They just had to be patient. He said he'd make sure –' She stopped. She wasn't sad, he thought. She still sounded angry.

'What happened?' he said.

'You know what happened,' she said quickly. 'Greed happened. The banks. His. Lovro's. That's what happened. Greed paid my husband out, my CFO off. You know what happened.' She turned, looked at him. 'Every word of that is true.'

He took in a deep breath, let it out slowly. 'When did you decide to kill him?'

She laughed, like the question was rude, impertinent. 'When would *you* have decided that, Peter?'

'I don't kill people, Tina.'

She almost sneered. 'Then you're not quite the warrior I thought you were.'

He stood to leave. There was no good in this.

'When he was in the witness box lying, I was in tears. I remember that. I'd shared everything with this man. My work, my dreams, my fears, my plans. I'd shared my body with him. I remember how hot those tears felt. How betrayed – I could have killed him then.' She held up her hands, long nails to the ceiling. 'I could have killed him with these. I could have ripped him to shreds.'

'You spent a long time hanging on to that rage, Tina. Why weren't five years in prison enough for you?'

'That's not when I decided,' she said softly. She paused for a moment, going back in time. 'I had to drop my children at my ex-husband's house. The first week after they took our home.' Her eyes filled with tears and anger all at once. She pointed to the door. 'I had to pack that boy's clothes into a suitcase. I had to pack up his things in a box.' She was nearly yelling now, black mascara running down each cheek. 'I had to deliver him and my other son to a man I hated. Who took a bribe to betray me? Can you imagine how that felt?' She glared at him, eyes wide and wild. He could see that she could kill Oliver Randall all over again. In this room now, he'd be down on his bloody knees.

'You know what loss is like, Peter? Don't you? Imagine feeling like you've just lost your son. Can you do that?'

He looked at her, said nothing. For the first time she seemed more brittle, closer to pain than to rage.

'I had no one. That company was all my hard work. I didn't want to be Ioannidis & Sons. He took it all from me. All of it.'

'I'm not going to tell you it's okay to kill someone, Tina. I can't do that. I won't.'

She took some deep breaths, picked up some tissues, dabbed at her eyes. Then she started to laugh. A strange, almost silent laugh. 'Do you know what he said to me, when we met? When I had to hear his apology? When I asked for his help?'

Tanner shook his head.

'That he was scared of them. Of the bank and of Lovro. Scared of what they might do if he did as I asked.' She could throw off her frailty in moments. Something close to hatred was now in her voice. 'And I thought, why aren't you scared of me, Oliver? Why aren't you afraid of me?'

There was a knock on the door. When he opened it, he was expecting to see Taz and Alex. It was the court officer instead. 'Jury's ready,' he said. Tanner thanked him, closed the door.

She stood up again, as though the judge had just asked her to. 'He told me he only answered to God,' she said. 'And I thought, no. You will answer to me.'

There would be remorse one day, Tanner thought. She was still fighting it. 'Why not Ravic, Tina? Why not Carter? Weren't they worse? Why not kill them?'

Tina Leonard straightened her jacket, looked right at him. 'Give me time,' she said.

59

Taz Bennett cried the whole time. As the jurors entered the courtroom, as the associate read out the charge, as she asked them for their verdict. As the foreperson stood.

She cried harder when the words 'not guilty' were said.

Tina Leonard simply nodded. She mouthed thank you to the jurors from the other side of the room. She thanked the judge when she was told she was free to go.

Tanner leant over towards Izzy Gallo. 'Do you know Carter's lawyer?' he asked her, pointing to where he sat in the gallery.

'No, Pete, I don't,' she said.

'Pity,' he said.

'Why is that?'

He stood to leave. 'Because one of us should tell him to warn his client to watch his back.'

When Tanner arrived in his chambers the following morning, he dictated his final account to Kit Gallagher for the defence of Tina Leonard.

For well-funded clients, he often added something extra for an acquittal.

For Tina Leonard, he worked out what he was owed under his fee agreement, then doubled it. If you do the crime but don't do the time, you should at least pay for it somehow.

When the account was done and emailed to Gallagher, his phone rang. Reception. He felt like going home, but it had to be dealt with.

Rachel Roth was in jeans, sneakers that had been designed to look old, a loose-fitting sweater that had expensive holes. She was holding a takeaway coffee cup in each hand, put one of them on his desk in front of him.

'Been into work yet?' he asked.

She shook her head. 'It was a long night at Taz Bennett's.'

He'd skipped the after-party. 'How's Mr Bennett?' he asked. 'Had his gate fixed yet?'

'What?'

'Doesn't matter.'

'You're going to set up some meetings for me with Tina. Can we do that now?'

'The verdict's still warm. Can we wait a day or two?'

She shook her head. 'Who killed Oliver Randall is the story of the year. I want my exclusive with her.'

'She wasn't in a talkative mood last night?'

'It wasn't the time or place to arrange it.'

'Who invited you there, anyway?'

'Your solicitor. Kit. She's doing a long interview with me tomorrow about the trial. Her own "thank you" for getting Bennett and Willett to talk to you. Do you want to be part of it?'

He shook his head. 'The better members of the criminal bar leave self-promotion to other colleagues. Leaving that aside, I'm happy for Kit to take the glory. She's done plenty for me.'

Roth leant towards him, brows raised. 'Pete? Are you going to help set up that meeting with Tina for me that you promised?'

He nodded. 'I'll talk to her. Be careful what you print, though.'

She sat back. 'I only want the truth.'

He laughed. 'Sorry,' he said. 'Amazing how the best of your profession usually seeks the exact opposite of what I almost invariably need to seek if I'm doing my job properly. I rarely deal in the truth.'

'What do you deal in?'

'Didn't you watch the trial? Anything that can be argued.'

'The truth doesn't matter to you? Only winning?'

He shook his head. 'I'm all for the truth, Ray. But the case is over.'

'Not for me. I've barely begun.'

'Have you already forgotten your house being broken into, Rachel?'

She put her cup on the edge of his desk. 'Do you think they'd risk hurting someone else now?'

'I don't know what they'd risk.'

'Why weren't you at the party last night, Pete?'

'I was tired. Long day. Takes it out of you, winning murder cases. You need the strength of a superhero.'

'How well does Kit know you?'

'Well enough to keep knocking back my proposals of marriage. I'm thinking of trying my luck with her wife next.'

'You know what she said last night? When it was clear you weren't going to show?'

'I deny I was with the judge's associate, Ray. He and I are just good friends.'

'She said you knew she was guilty. She said, "He's knows she did it. Somehow, he knows. That's why he's not here."'

'I had dinner with my son.'

She looked at him like she was trying to burn it out of him. 'Did she do it, Pete?'

'You asked me that the other night.'

'And you told me you'd told the jury the truth. Do you have a different view today?'

He paused before answering. 'There would be worse crimes.'

'What does that mean?' Her voice was more intent, she sat on the edge of her chair.

'My job is due process. It ends there.'

She shook her head, smiled like she couldn't believe it. 'Due process? You went after people for murder. You made a case against them. When did you know?'

'I can't say someone's innocent if they tell me they're not, Rachel. My sub-branch of the legal profession has ethics.'

'When did you know?'

He glared at her. 'I don't answer to you, Rachel.'

'Who do you answer to?'

He smiled. 'To the same thing Oliver Randall answered to.'

'What was that?'

'To the gods, Ray. To Shiva. To Issitoq. To Dike. To Zeus and to Jupiter. Personally, I answer to Iustitia.'

She picked up her empty cup, threw it in the bin. She was still staring at him.

'If you want to say something, Rachel, just say it.'

'Don't you – I don't know what the word is. Don't you feel bad? Christ, "dirty" is the word. Soiled.'

'Why should I?'

Her eyes widened. 'She shot a man in the fucking head, Pete.'

'Webb pulled the trigger.'

'Aren't you – ?'

'Angry. That's how I feel. Not enough to kill someone. But I don't feel dirty.'

'A man was killed.'

'I didn't do it, Rachel.'

'You think he deserved it? What she did to him?'

'I'm not saying she did anything. You ask her. I've told you. I answer to gods. I don't make judgements.'

'You don't make judgements? On a fucking hit?'

'I'll set up that meeting with Tina for you, Ray. My guess is that she'll be sticking with the not guilty version of her life, but if she goes rogue on herself – who knows, maybe you'll hear an interesting perspective.'

Roth stood up, looked at him with what may have been sadness, he wasn't sure. 'Are you in love with her, Pete? Is that it?'

'Sure I am, Ray. And don't leave out her sister. Or the stiff's ex-wife.'

'What?'

'I prefer you. Can we leave it at that? I'm done with the Ioannidis family, believe me.'

Roth turned for the door, but before she got there he said, 'In my second year at the bar, I acted for a serial killer. He scared the shit out of me.' She stopped, looked at him. 'He helped kill seven women. Kill is a euphemism of course. He helped dismember them. From there, I've graduated to child killers, people who –' He stopped, shook his head, his voice starting to shake, surprising him. 'Fuck, Ray. I acted for a guy, some – Jesus, he killed an eighteen-month-old boy with an iron because – because he wouldn't stop crying at night. Do you know what it's like making submissions on behalf of someone that's done that? I had to sit in a legal interview room with him, and the whole time – the whole time I sat there I was wishing I had something with me, something that I could beat his fucking brains out with. And I promise you, Ray, I could have done it. I could have dug his sick brain out of his skull and splattered it against the wall. That's – that's a lot to carry around. I had another piece of work who cut a fellow drug dealer's head off with a knife. But I can top that story. Do you want me to?'

She stood at the door, looking at him, took in a deep breath. 'I didn't – I didn't mean to upset you. I just – is what she did somehow fine? By comparison to some monster? A run-of-the-mill revenge killing?'

He shook his head. 'Murder is not fine, Rachel. And Tina Leonard didn't have Oliver Randall killed. Not on the instructions I had for her trial. But if she did, well – well, he didn't just cut her off in traffic. He broke her. I know something about that feeling.'

60

Linda Greig's last patient for the day looked at Tanner like she knew him. For a moment he thought she was going to say something. Then she dropped her gaze and headed for the door.

'You can't do this again,' Greig said, standing in the doorway of her room.

He stood up. 'Do what?'

'Turn up here at the end of the day without an appointment and expect to see me.'

'Trial's over. It's been three weeks since –'

'Make an appointment, Pete.'

'People commit crimes at very inconvenient times for me, Linda. I still have to deal with it.'

She turned, and he followed her into the room.

'You won. I saw it on the news last night,' she said when he'd taken a seat in a chair in front of the desk. She wasn't going over to the couch with him. 'Congratulations.'

'She did it,' Tanner said.

Greig had started to write something in a book, stopped, looked at him.

'She had a man shot in the knees, then in the head. The cost is two hundred grand, if you're ever interested. Although my client didn't shop around I know people who'd have done it for a fraction of that.'

Linda Greig put her pen down. 'Wow,' she said.

'Obviously doctor–patient confidentiality applies here. Let's not make notes.'

'She told you?'

'Nah. Well, not before. The guy she paid to arrange it told me. It was – well, he wanted his bill paid.'

She sat back in her chair, and rocked back and forth. 'Christ. How do you feel?'

'How should I feel? That's why I'm here.'

'How do you feel, Pete?' she said again.

'Foolish.'

'Foolish?'

'You were right.'

'I was right?'

'She's my perfect client, you said. Damsel in distress.'

She took a deep breath and sighed. 'Tell me you're not in love with her.'

He laughed. 'No.'

'In lust?'

'No.'

'How do you feel?'

He smiled. 'Not enough.'

'What's that mean?'

'I don't feel sorry. I don't feel sorry she was acquitted. Is that wrong?'

'Yes,' she said firmly. 'She killed a man.'

'He'd wronged her badly.'

'Enough for the death penalty, Peter?'

He took his own deep breath. He'd been thinking on that one. What is the beginning and the end point for justified killing? 'She should have told the guy to stop at the knees,' he said. 'Maybe.'

Greig shook her head. She stood up, went over to a built-in closet in the corner behind the desk, took out a bottle of scotch, two glasses. She poured them both a drink.

'What kind of shrink are you?'

'Everyone needs a drink sometimes, Pete. It can't all be about anti-depressants and anti-psychotics.'

'How many patients have you had a drink with?'

'You're the first.'

He smiled.

'Did you at least want her to be innocent, Pete?'

In every legal trial, there is a burden of proof. In civil hearings, it comes down to probability. In criminal, beyond all reasonable doubt. Much of Tanner's life was spent fighting that burden. He'd done the same for Tina Leonard, even though for most of the time he was unaware of what he was really doing. He'd been helping to carry the burden for her. The burden of lies.

He picked up his glass, drained the scotch in one hit. 'Jesus, Linda. What kind of question is that?'

ACKNOWLEDGEMENTS

Thank you to Tara Wynne, my agent at Curtis Brown, for her efforts and enthusiasm for this series. I'm saving her suggested title *Property, Cocaine, Prison* for a memoir.

A big thank you to the whole team at Simon & Schuster – sales, marketing and publicity as well as editorial – for getting behind *The Burden of Lies*. A special mention though to Roberta Ivers at S&S, and to Kylie Mason my editor. Their thoughts, judgment and skill greatly benefited the final drafts.

Thank you to Lewis Csizmazia for the cover design, and the new design for the first book – I think they look great.

Thanks to David Staehli SC for again reading an early draft to spot legal error. In contrast to *Cyanide Games*, almost none were identified. I may take up criminal law as a result.

Anyone who lives in Sydney and enjoys writing novels about crime and corruption is obliged to thank the city itself – it never stops inspiring. Even when you think 'this is bound to be the end of it now', it turns out it isn't.

Finally, thanks to my wife Trish for her support and encouragement with another book, despite it now being clear to me she wishes I was Peter Tanner. So do I.

Richard Beasley

ABOUT THE AUTHOR

Richard Beasley grew up in Adelaide, before moving to Sydney where he has worked as a barrister since 1997. He is the author of four previous novels: *Hell Has Harbour Views* (which was adapted for ABC Television in 2005), *The Ambulance Chaser*, *Me and Rory Macbeath*, and *Cyanide Games*, the first in the series featuring Peter Tanner.

If you liked *The Burden of Lies*, you'll love *Cyanide Games*, the first in Richard Beasley's thrillers featuring Peter Tanner. Read on for the first chapter.

RICHARD BEASLEY

A PETER TANNER THRILLER

CYANIDE GAMES

IF YOU LOVE MICHAEL CONNELLY YOU'LL LOVE RICHARD BEASLEY

'A gutsy legal thriller ... the very best of crime fiction' *THE AGE*

A tough, gritty legal thriller from bestselling Richard Beasley

'Tanner's way with words, his wit and repartee, put him up there with the best of those legal eagles who have triumphed on page and screen . . . A cracking read.'
Sydney Morning Herald

PROLOGUE

She assumed the jet was company owned. Citadel Resources was in the top twenty of the *Fortune* Global 500 list of the world's largest companies; it owned mining and exploration projects in twenty-eight countries. And probably many jets.

Anne Warren knew Citadel's environmental and human rights record mirrored that of its competitors and was murky at best, but she had found ways of letting herself off what she knew was a moral hook – her work helped companies like Citadel at least mitigate their impact. She helped them be as 'green' as they could be.

The document she was given when she boarded the jet was headed *Confidentiality Agreement*. It had her name on it, her work address, and described her as a 'water consultant'. The counterparty was Citadel Resources. She read it quickly. Citadel sought to forbid her from discussing anything to do with the reasons for her travel to Tovosevu Island, or from saying anything about what work she might perform there. She was not allowed to reveal, unless compelled by law, that she'd even been to the island.

According to the next clause, she was to be forbidden from revealing the details of any work she'd performed for the company. It was as though she was to expunge Citadel Resources from her life.

The final section of the document was headed 'Penalties'. Should she breach any of her 'Confidentiality Obligations', she would be liable for liquidated damages of five hundred thousand dollars per breach, even if Citadel was unable to establish such damage in a court. Beyond that she had to indemnify Citadel for *any loss it suffers as a result, directly or indirectly, of any breach of the confidentiality obligations outlined above.*

'Would you mind signing that now?'

Warren's mind was still scrambling when the man standing next to her spoke, his soft voice deadened by the sound of the jet's engines being started. She looked up and saw an Asian man, perhaps late thirties, smiling faintly at her.

'Here,' he said, holding out a pen. She took it instinctively.

'I can't,' she said. She looked at the paper in her hands, then back at him.

The jet started to taxi, and the man placed his hand momentarily on the back of her seat to steady himself. 'Sorry,' he said. 'My name's Joe Cheung. I'm a lawyer for the company. You're . . . ?'

'Anne,' she said quickly. 'There's a problem with this. It has to be changed. I can't –'

'Anne,' he said, 'I'm not sure there's scope for negotiation.'

'You don't understand. I'm nearing the end of my PhD. Some of my research has been at Citadel mines.' She looked up at him, waiting for him to acknowledge he was following. 'Surely it can't be meant to cover –'

'It's okay,' he said, nodding like he understood. 'I'm sure it's only meant to cover what you're about to do, and where we're going now.'

'But that's not what it says. I need to speak to Martin. My boss, from GreenDay? Martin O'Brien? He's sitting at the back.'

The lawyer crouched down. 'Mr O'Brien has already signed one of these. I'm sure it will be okay. It's not my understanding that it's meant to cover what you're talking about.'

'That's not what it says,' she repeated. 'It covers everything.'

'Is there some problem?'

Anne looked at O'Brien as he joined them. 'Martin, this document,' she began, 'it's too wide. It –'

Joe Cheung held up a hand. 'Anne was just explaining about her PhD thesis,' Cheung said. 'I'll talk to Citadel.'

'I have to be able to –'

'Calm down, Anne,' O'Brien said. 'Think about it. If this was enforced strictly, we wouldn't be able to lodge an EIS with the government for Citadel. Don't get so literal with every–'

'I still don't think I should –'

'Anne, this isn't the place for –'

'– be forced to sign a document like this.'

'Anne,' the lawyer said calmly, 'I'm sure for your thesis, Citadel will give you a specific release from the obligations in this agreement.'

'Can't we just cut that clause out, then?'

'I've been told we can't take off unless everyone signs,' O'Brien said.

Cheung laughed slightly, and shook his head. 'That's a bit dramatic, Martin.' He turned back to Anne. 'Look, I'll sit down with one of the guys and talk to them. I'm sure I can sort something out to give you comfort. Hang on to it for now. I'll come back once we've taken off.'

He smiled at her and she nodded. O'Brien sighed, shook his head, and went back to his seat at the rear of the jet.

When he returned thirty minutes after take-off, Cheung said, 'I've spoken to one of the guys. There shouldn't be any problem with what you've done so far on your thesis.'

'Who are "the guys"?' He made them sound like a pop group.

Cheung smiled. 'They might need to check what you intend to cover. This thing though,' he said, pointing to the confidentiality agreement she still held in her hands, 'isn't intended to stop you using the work you've done on their other mines for your thesis. You'll just need permission.' He paused to look at her over the top of his glasses. She nodded slightly. 'Just sign it for now. When your thesis is done, Martin will get the all clear from Citadel. I'm sure there won't be a problem.' He smiled the kind of smile she assumed a lawyer gives when he's expecting a yes.

'So why then – ?'

'When your thesis is done,' Cheung said, 'Martin can call me. I'll liaise with Citadel for you.'

He handed her a card. Black embossed lettering. *Joseph Cheung. Bloomberg Butler Kelly. Partner, Mergers & Acquisitions/ Energy & Resources.* Her instincts still told her not to sign the document.

'If there's not going to be a problem about what I've done other than whatever it is on Tovosevu, can't we just cross out – ?'

'Anne, they aren't going to negotiate with you.'

'And if I don't sign it?'

'They're not anticipating that.'

'But . . . what would happen? Hypothetically?'

Cheung squatted. 'Can I give you the benefit of my experience?' he said softly. 'They're not that well acquainted with people saying no to them. Do you understand?'

She shook her head slowly. 'Actually, I don't.' There was anxiety in her voice, but also defiance.

'You really have to sign this.' His tone was calm, but firm.

She sighed and ran her hand through her short hair. 'I should have my own lawyer look at this.'

'Do you have a lawyer, Anne?'

The wry grin he gave her almost made her smile. 'I guess you guys would be out of my league, price-wise?'

He smiled. 'This is about Tovosevu, Anne. They're just being cautious. Sign it for now, then have Martin call me when your thesis is done.'

She didn't trust Citadel, though she felt she could trust this man, for no particularly rational reason other than he seemed trustworthy. He spoke like he was on her side. She wondered if it was an act, some lawyer's trick. He was, after all, Citadel's lawyer, not hers. But she needed her job. Making an enemy of Citadel wouldn't help her prospects.

She signed the document quickly.

'We'll mail you a copy,' Cheung said.

When they disembarked at the island's airstrip, they were driven to the mine site, and allocated worker's huts. Warren was shown to hers by a man dressed in khaki shorts and work boots, his shirt wet with sweat. 'Someone will get you soon,' he said.

She looked out of the window, and saw a square-shaped area about the size of two football fields, that had been cleared of trees. About two dozen army tents had been set up on the cut native grass. In the background, over the crest of a hill covered in shrubs through which a dirt road had been carved, was the mine she'd seen as they flew in to land. From above, it sat like a giant grey wound on the jungle floor. An enormous open cut pit, and the entrance to the underground workings.

Fifteen minutes later another worker knocked on her door. 'Miss Warren?'

'Anne.'

'I'm Greg,' he replied. An Australian accent, a touch of sunburn on his nose, a waspish blond beard. He looked not much more than twenty. 'Ready?'

'For what?'

'To go.'

'Where?'

He looked confused. 'To the river,' he then said.

There were four others in the jeep. Greg was the driver. In the passenger seat was an older man, in Citadel khaki attire, and a green floppy hat. He said his name was Ivan, and that he was the deputy mine manager. His neck glistened with sweat, and its thick band of fat swelled and rolled like the tide with the movements of his head. O'Brien sat next to her, looking tense, saying nothing. It was humid, thirty-two degrees Celsius. Someone had told her it was always thirty-two degrees on Tovosevu. Sometimes it rained, sometimes it didn't.

As they drove towards the gate of the workers' compound, a truck overtook them on the dirt road, swerving close as it went past. It was carrying twelve men in the back, sitting six a side on two benches, shaded by a canvas tarpaulin. The men had rifles. The truck pulled away from them on the unsealed road, a cloud of dust in its wake.

'Who are they?' Warren asked. No one answered. Ivan had put his window down when the truck went past, and the jeep's diesel engine was loud, so she wondered if she'd been heard.

'Who are – ?'

'Just security,' Ivan said.

'Security for what?'

'For the mine,' he replied.

'What does the mine need protection from?'

Again Ivan was slow to answer. 'Every mine in the world we have has security,' he eventually said.

'Where are they going?'

'Routine patrol.'

Tovosevu Island had five villages, and about three thousand native inhabitants. She knew that from the internet search she'd done. She wondered how dangerous they must be for such security. Citadel had a lease from the PNG government over the whole island. The terms of the lease were effectively a grant of sovereignty. Citadel controlled communications, who arrived and who left. As a condition of its mine approval, it had to fund a school and a medical centre. Almost everyone on the island worked for the company.

'The rifles,' she said. 'They look –'

Ivan laughed. 'They're private security, miss. They wouldn't be security without being armed.'

Because the window was down, she knew what had happened before they stopped. Greg pulled the vehicle as far off the unsealed road as he could. When the engine cut, she could hear the river, somewhere down at the bottom of a ravine to her right.

'We'll go down here,' Ivan said as he opened his door. He and Greg got out of the jeep.

'You can't smell that?' Warren said, looking at O'Brien. He shook his head. 'Anything now?' she said when they got out.

'Jungle,' O'Brien said. She saw him sniff though, and something registered on his face.

'Now?' she asked.

'Something burnt?'

'Something bitter,' she said, correcting him. 'Can you smell almonds?'

He looked down the green ravine. 'Perhaps,' he said.

'It's not almonds,' she said. 'It's cyanide.'

The affinity of gold for cyanide was the kind of chemical paradox that amused Anne Warren – the bond between wealth and death. Down the green slope, at the edge of the riverbank, there was death. Several fish had washed up near them, she saw others floating down stream. The smell was strong near the water; the spill recent. The toxic plume was still spreading down the river from somewhere.

'We had a breach of the main tailings dam,' Ivan said.

'A breach?'

'A wall collapse. Incredible rains the last few months – even into what's meant to be the dry months. No one could have predicted it.'

'What was the capacity?'

'We think maybe two hundred million litres,' he said.

'And the dam has been built near this river?'

'We need water to mine, miss.'

'How much tailing slurry has flowed into it?' she asked.

He shook his head, turned up his palms. 'The wall collapsed at night,' he said. 'Assume most of it.'

'Have any of the villagers been – ?'

'We're taking care of that.'

'They've been warned though, right? The cyanide is lethal. You'll need to truck in water or –'

'We're taking care of that, miss.'

She wanted to tell him to stop calling her 'miss'. 'I'm just saying –'

'There's going to be a thorough clean up,' Ivan said. 'We're doing it right now.'

Whatever part of the river the cyanide plume flowed through, the fish that swam in it would have died within minutes. But cyanide degrades quickly and she knew already what her test kits and lab results would reveal. Arsenic. Cadmium. Copper. Lead. In concentrations lethal to complex life. All much harder to remove than cyanide.

'You need to clean up the dead fish,' she said. 'If anyone or anything eats them –'

'As we understand it,' Ivan said, 'the cyanide will break down in –'

'The cyanide isn't the only problem. I assume you're taking steps to stop any flow into tributaries or aquifers? You're going to need to dredge a lot of the river, especially closest to the dam. Do you – I mean, this is a massive task, and in the meantime none of the villagers who use this river should be –'

'Miss, miss,' Ivan said, smiling. 'We have a lot of people working on all that. You have to focus on your tasks. We've picked out some spots for you to test the water and sediments.'

'I'll decide where I need to test.'

He gave her a crooked smile, and used his index finger to wipe some sweat from his moustache. 'Let's get started, then.'

It was forty hours since the spill. She tested the water, and took samples of the river sediment using a small boat, two hundred metres from where the tailings dam water had first flowed into the river, and at five hundred metre intervals downstream.

Warren knew that three of the island's five villages were on the river, downstream of where the contaminated water had flowed into it. She'd expected to be taken into the affected villages, to test the waters the people used, take samples of the nearby sediments, make sure that warnings were being given. She was told they could not go in.

'I need to test there,' she protested. 'It's crucial that I –'

'Things are sensitive,' Ivan said. 'We're trucking in water.'

'But if you explain we're only helping,' she said. 'I need to know –'

'We cannot go into any village,' Ivan said, closing the subject.